A Most Ambiguous Sunday, and Other Stories

TITLES IN THE LIBRARY OF KOREAN LITERATURE
AVAILABLE FROM DALKEY ARCHIVE PRESS

1. *Stingray*
Kim Joo-young

2. *One Spoon on This Earth*
Hyun Ki Young

3. *When Adam Opens His Eyes*
Jang Jung-il

4. *My Son's Girlfriend*
Jung Mi-kyung

5. *A Most Ambiguous Sunday, and Other Stories*
Jung Young Moon

6. *The House with a Sunken Courtyard*
Kim Won-il

7. *At Least We Can Apologize*
Lee Ki-ho

8. *The Soil*
Yi Kwang-su

9. *Lonesome You*
Park Wan-suh

10. *No One Writes Back*
Jang Eun-jin

LIBRARY OF KOREAN LITERATURE

5

A Most Ambiguous Sunday, and Other Stories

Jung Young Moon

Translated by
Jung Yewon, Inrae You Vinciguerra,
Louis Vinciguerra, and the author

DALKEY ARCHIVE PRESS
CHAMPAIGN / LONDON / DUBLIN

Originally published in Korean as *Moksin ŭi ŏttŏn ohu* by Munhak Tongne, Paju, 2008

Copyright © 2008 by Jung Young Moon
Translation © 2013 by Jung Young Moon, Jung Yewon, Inrae You Vinciguerra, and
Louis Vinciguerra

First edition, 2013
All rights reserved

Library of Congress Cataloging-in-Publication Data

Chong, Yong-mun, 1965- author.
[Moksin ui otton ohu. English]
A Most Ambiguous Sunday, and other stories / Jung Young-moon ; translated by Jung
Young-moon, Yewon Jung, Inrae You Vinciguerra, and Louis Vinciguerra. -- First edition.
pages cm
ISBN 978-1-56478-916-7 (acid-free paper)
1. Short stories, Korean. I. Chong, Yong-mun, 1965- translator. II. Jung, Yewon, translator. III. You, Inrae, translator. IV. Vinciguerra, Louis, translator. V. Title.
PL992.2.Y625M6513 2013
895.7'35--dc23
2013027225

Partially funded by a grant from the Illinois Arts Council, a state agency

Library of Korean Literature
Published in collaboration with the Literature Translation Institute of Korea

www.dalkeyarchive.com

Cover: design and composition by Mikhail Iliatov

Thanks to Wei-Ling Woo of Epigram Books (Singapore)
for helping with the editing of this book.

Printed on permanent/durable acid-free paper

Table of Contents

Mrs. Brown

Mrs. Brown is a woman I've come to know recently. She's from the same part of the world as me and came to America around the same time. She's of average height with charming eyes, and she always has a faint smile on her lips. She's a smoker, and when she talks, she seems to forget about the cigarette lodged between her thin fingers. When we became friends, she told me a fascinating story.

They had long since finished supper. Mr. Brown was watching television in the living room and Mrs. Brown was reading a magazine, when someone knocked on the front door. They looked at each other briefly, as they had not been expecting any visitors. Mr. Brown turned his attention back to the television, and Mrs. Brown got up and went to the front door. He watched her silently. She looked out through a small peephole in the door. It was dark. A man was at the door, holding what looked like a briefcase.

"Who is it?"

"My c-car broke down. Could I use your ph-phone?"

He sounded very young. There was a small forest road in front of their house, which was unused except by those who lived in the few neighboring houses. Once in a while, people who had taken a wrong turn somewhere would show up. She had a funny feeling, but she opened the door without much thought, as she wanted to help a person in trouble. She had never been in a seriously dangerous situation before, and where she lived felt very safe. The visitor was very young and looked to be in his late teens. The boy stared at her but didn't say anything. Instead, he glanced inside the house briefly, then took a gun out of the briefcase he was carrying. The gun was very long, and she had the vague thought that it looked like something from a movie. She thought it might be a type of revolver called a Magnum. But the boy had pulled out the gun, which looked too heavy for him to be carrying around so naturally, like an insurance agent on a house call brandishing documents or a salesperson presenting a new product. As a result, she was not all that surprised. He had taken it out only after rummaging around in the briefcase for a moment.

"You're n-not expecting a-anyone, right?" The boy asked, stepping inside the house. She nodded involuntarily. They weren't expecting anyone at that hour. Guests were rare at their house. She realized immediately that she had made a mistake, but it was too late. The boy had already entered the house, and she followed him inside.

Her husband looked very surprised to see his wife enter the living room with a boy carrying a gun. He looked back and forth between the boy and the television, debating whether or not he should turn it off. But instead he stood up and raised both hands, then lowered them at once, realizing it wasn't necessary. His wife thought he was acting a little silly.

The boy had them sit on the sofa. Mrs. Brown saw that her husband was glaring at her. She realized she had made a huge mistake. The boy went to the window and peeked out between the curtains, not bothering to aim the gun at them properly. She looked at his profile. He didn't look like the kind of person who would hurt someone else. He looked harmless, even naïve. But is there such a thing as a person who looks like they would hurt someone? One couldn't rely on that assumption. A harmless appearance can hide cruelty and viciousness. For all she knew, a nightmarish hostage scene like something out of a movie had just begun. Since he hadn't covered his face, he was probably going to kill them.

He turned his face. He looked no more sinister from the front than from the side. He didn't sit down. He paced around the living room restlessly. Mrs. Brown thought that he might be on drugs. But he didn't look like he was high on anything. Though he stammered a little, he was relatively articulate. He just looked a little happier than he should. She looked at the television. A boring show was on. She turned it off with the remote control. Suddenly, the room was silent. The three of them stared at each other for a moment without a word.

"I've always w-wanted to live in a house near a l-l-lake or ocean," the boy said.

She realized then that the boy had a stutter. She hadn't met anyone with a stutter in a while, so she was intrigued by the way he talked. Her husband stared at her, but she ignored him.

"It's a nice h-house," the boy said, turning his head.

In fact, their house was quite nice. The house had a lovely Asian-style outdoor terrace, and was located close to a lake, which was actually a little too small to be called a lake. Though the house had been built over ten years ago, her husband was still working on repairs to some parts of the house.

Just then, they heard a distant sound. She strained her ears. She could hear a car passing by. Then it was quiet again. Amid the silence, Mrs. Brown thought about the sounds she had heard during the day. A shallow tributary of the Mississippi River was located over the mountain on the other side of the lake, and all afternoon she had heard the sounds of guns coming from that direction. Someone was out duck hunting. Now the sounds had stopped. While listening to the gunshots all afternoon, she imagined countless ducks being struck with bullets and falling to the surface of the water.

Her husband used to go duck hunting. But she had opposed it for some unclear reason, and he stopped without any protest. He had even gotten rid of the gun. She suddenly remembered a story her husband told her about how Puccini had been addicted to duck hunting. She also recalled a strange law in Nebraska, which made it legal to hunt ducks from a boat in the river but illegal to hunt them from land. She even thought about the name Nebraska, which was a Native American word meaning "flat river," a thought that was out of place in the moment and one of those things that you can never remember when you're trying to.

"I envy you for l-living in this h-house. How m-much does a h-house like this c-cost?" he asked, looking out the window.

"A lot," her husband said.

"How much?"

"Over a million. This house was more expensive because of the lake down there. It also costs a lot to maintain, and there are other expenses as well. Because of that lake. If someone drowns in the lake, the people living nearby have to pay the damages, so there's also insurance. But the insurance premium is no joke," he said. She felt that he was giving more information than he needed to.

"If someone dies, the neighbors have to pay? I don't get it."

She didn't get it either. Despite having settled down there after coming to America to study and meeting her husband, there were a lot of rules she still didn't understand.

The boy walked to the center of the living room. He had a young, boyish face and thin arms and legs. If he weren't carrying a gun, the situation would have been very different. Her husband was old but still in great shape. She was suddenly reminded of the power a gun wields. Thinking about how such a simple object could give him so much control over them, she looked at the gun differently.

But he wasn't holding the gun properly. He kept moving the gun from hand to hand, as if it were as heavy as it looked. She doubted whether he really knew how to use it. Suddenly, she felt that the real danger wasn't in the fact that he had a gun, but that he didn't know how to use it. It looked like the gun had come into his possession by chance.

"I'd like something w-warm to drink," the boy said.

The weather wasn't that cold, but he seemed to be trembling. It wasn't clear whether it was because of the cold or because he was nervous. He told them to get up. Mrs. Brown led the way to the kitchen. Her husband followed, looking angry, like a person whose rest has been interrupted. She put water on the stove; the two men stood at her side. Except for the gun the boy was holding, the three of them looked like people preparing a cup of tea after a party. She realized that she wasn't really feeling any of the fear that a person in her situation should. It wasn't clear why, but the moment or opportunity when she should have felt afraid had passed, and now it seemed too late to feel that way.

"Have you heard this s-story? Somewhere around here in the Midwest, someone, a m-murderer, went into the forest and sh-shot some deer hunters," the boy said. He seemed to be having trouble talking at length due to his stutter, and it made her nervous.

"He shot th-three h-hunters. It wasn't an a-accident. He wasn't even a h-hunter." He looked at the Magnum in his hand and smiled.

She had no way of knowing whether he was the one who had done it. He didn't say whether the murderer was someone else. But he also didn't say it was him. He only said it was someone. But that someone could have been anyone. It wasn't clear whether he was just making it up. But if it were true, then it was clearly an impressive tale.

Nonetheless, neither the story nor the situation felt real to her. Everything felt too ordinary. The sound just then of the kettle whistling as the water came to a boil only heightened the feeling of normality. She poured three cups of herbal tea and gave one to her husband and one to the boy. Her husband took the cup of tea, still looking disgruntled, and set it back down on the counter. But just as she handed a cup to the boy, hot tea spilled out and splashed on his hand. The back of his hand turned bright red. He laughed awkwardly and shrugged as if to say it was nothing. She apologized. It was no one's fault, but she'd really meant it. She and the boy drank the tea while standing.

"Smells good," he said.

It was true. She had bought the tea in a store that sold organic products in a nearby city. She suddenly realized that she had been rather obsessed with organic products for some time.

She could feel the fragrance of the tea calming her down. After a while, the three of them returned to the living room. Mr. and Mrs. Brown sat on the couch again, but the boy remained standing. They could hear the faint ticking of the wall clock. It made them sensitive to other sounds. They could just make out the distant sound of the cars on the freeway and a small plane flying by. There was a landing field nearby. She had always wanted to try piloting a plane. She thought it would be wonderful to fly low over plains and hills and see flocks of sheep or horses running in herds from mid-air. Her husband had tried to dissuade her, saying it was too dangerous. But she figured piloting a plane couldn't be any more dangerous than driving a car.

"What do you want?" her husband asked anxiously after they had been silent for a while.

The boy didn't answer right away.

"Isn't there something you want?"

"I . . . I . . ." the boy said.

"You want money? If you want money, we'll give you money."

"Money isn't . . ."

"How much do you need?"

He sounded like he was pressuring the boy.

"Well, then, m-maybe you can g-give me the c-cash in your wallet?" the boy stuttered.

She got up and went to the closet by the front door, thinking that maybe what the boy really wanted wasn't money. She considered the fact that he had asked for the money in their wallets rather than for jewelry or the money in their safe. She took her wallet and her husband's from their coat pockets and removed all the cash. It was a little over five hundred dollars. She handed him the money, but he put it in his pocket without counting it. Then he thanked her. She almost said, "You're welcome."

He went to the window again and looked down at the lake. The moon, which had risen above the mountain, was visible through the curtains. He gazed steadily at the barely visible lake as if mesmerized. Mr. and Mrs. Brown looked at each other. Mr. Brown was frowning. She didn't like the look on his face and turned to the window. Sometimes, on nice nights when the moon was out, she would sit in a chair on the terrace and look at the lake. Some days she could even see fish leaping out of the water.

Just then, the doorbell rang. They looked at each other. But the boy looked calm. He went to the front door. She noticed that he was walking uncomfortably even though there didn't seem to be anything physically wrong with him. He opened the door. A young-looking girl with a disheveled appearance came in. She looked like she had just woken from poor sleep, as if she had been sleeping in a car parked nearby in the forest.

"Why are y-you so l-late?" he asked.

"It was hard to wake up," she said.

Looking a little embarrassed, she rubbed her eyes and stared at Mr. and Mrs. Brown in turn. Mrs. Brown wondered whether she was embarrassed because she had forced her way into their house or because she hadn't fixed up her face after waking up. The four of them stared at each other briefly without saying anything.

"Why didn't you tie them up?" the girl asked.

"I don't t-tie people up," the boy said.

"But shouldn't we tie them up?" she asked.

"It's fine."

"Tying them up is probably safer and more natural."

The boy didn't say anything. He seemed to be debating which would be more natural, and he seemed to think it was better not to tie them up. As Mrs. Brown listened to the two kids talking about them, she felt the situation to be more pitiful than absurd. She thought she had seen the girl somewhere before. Like the boy, the girl looked very clumsy. But that may have been why they suited each other so well. At any rate, they seemed more compatible than Mrs. Brown and her husband, who hadn't been getting along with each other very well recently.

"Have you done this sort of thing before?" Mrs. Brown asked, purely out of curiosity.

"No. It's the first time," the boy said.

"Actually, we didn't know we were going to do this," the girl said.

"Really? How do you think it's going?" she asked.

"I don't know," the girl said, smiling bashfully.

She could tell by their accents that they weren't from around there, but she wasn't sure where they were from exactly. Her English wasn't good enough to be able to distinguish between regional accents. She wanted to ask where they were from but thought it might be rude.

"Where are you two from?" her husband asked suddenly, as if he had read her mind.

They looked at him quietly.

"Do you think it's all right if we tell?" the girl asked.

The boy was quiet.

"They're only asking where we're from," she said.

The boy looked at Mrs. Brown as if seeking her advice.

"Tell us where you're from," she said.

"We're from Portland," the girl said.

"Portland, Oregon?" Mrs. Brown asked.

"No. Every time we tell people we're from Portland, they think we mean Oregon. We've never been there. But I've heard it's a really free city with a lot of hippies. I want to go there some day."

"We're f-from the Northeast. Portland, M-maine. Both of us," the boy said.

Mrs. Brown had always wanted to see the Northeast. On TV, it looked more like Europe than America. She hated the mild weather of the Midwest, where the seasons dragged on wearily, except for winter. She wanted to go some place where it was always foggy and rainy. She also wanted to see Nova Scotia, Canada, north of Maine. Nova Scotia was one of the places that always came to mind when she thought of travel destinations. Even the name, which meant "New Scotland," sounded wonderful.

"There's a place called Freeport, north of Portland, that's really beautiful. My grandmother lives next to a small inlet there, and when it's foggy in winter, it feels like you're far away from everything. I used to go there a lot because of that," she said.

"Stephen K-king was born nearby," the boy said.

Mrs. Brown had seen a movie based on one of his novels, set in a cornfield in the Midwest, but she couldn't remember the title.

"Bunkers were built on the coast of Portland during World War II. They were built to keep the Germans away, but the Germans never invaded. When I was little, we thought that the Germans would show up there one day, even though the war had been over for a really long time. We used to pretend we were fighting them off," the girl said.

"We w-went there a lot when we were l-little. We went fishing, wondering i-if the Germans were going to sh-show up," the boy said.

"There are a lot of nice lighthouses in Portland," the girl said.

Mrs. Brown thought that if they were to keep talking, they might even invite her to Portland. She also thought that if they had been planning to leave their hometown, they should have first headed for California or Florida and not the Midwest. Then she thought the same about herself. The conservative Midwest, a world of white people, was a stifling place. She had once gone to a national rodeo competition with her husband. The rodeo competition was held in a place several hours away by car. Entering the rodeo ground gave her the chills. The rodeo was full of nothing but white people. The moment she entered the stands, she could feel that all eyes were on her. The only other person of color was an African American man working as a rodeo clown—and he was a downright laughingstock.

She suddenly thought of a movie called *Kalifornia* that she had watched with her husband. She liked the movie, but he didn't. He was much older than she was, and she couldn't blame him for not liking the movie at his age. His tastes differed from hers in a lot of ways.

She wondered whether the boy and girl knew that they were in the Midwest. They seemed to know very little about geography.

"Aren't there t-tornadoes here?" the boy asked. That might have been all he knew about the Midwest.

"Actually, there was a tornado not far from here a few days ago. Two people died," she said.

"If there's one thing I want to see or experience here, it's a tornado," the girl said.

It was the same for her. When she'd moved there, she had wanted to see a tornado. She had seen an impressive documentary on TV about people who rushed into tornado zones to research and record tornadoes. But they weren't in a key tornado area, and there had been no more tornados after the last one that had come through quite some time ago.

An awkward silence unfolded in the living room. She thought that maybe now they would leave, unable to stand the silence. There didn't seem to be anything more that she could think of. Nevertheless, she wanted them to stay a little longer. She felt like an otherwise boring night had become a cheerful one because of them.

Just then, they heard a small plane pass by again. She had flown in one only once. But she hadn't piloted it herself. It was a two-seater single engine Cessna. She pictured the way the forest had seemed to bob beneath her as they skimmed over it. She might fly along the Mississippi River or one of its tributaries someday. There were numerous tributaries flowing into the Mississippi valley, including small tributaries with ill-fitting names, like Volga or Yellow River. Maybe there was even one called the Nile.

"Did he tell you about the murderer who went into the forest and shot the guys who were hunting deer?" the girl asked.

Mrs. Brown nodded. Mascara was smudged under the girl's left eye. She wanted to lend the girl some makeup.

"He tells everyone that story, like he thinks it's funny. But it is funny. It's a great story," the girl said.

She spoke without hesitation. Mrs. Brown looked at the girl's face, which was young and unkempt but very attractive, and she felt a little jealous. The girl's youth made her feel happy. Mrs. Brown suddenly remembered seeing a girl a while back, who was shopping for a coat in a store downtown, and becoming fascinated by her beauty. The girl put on the green coat she had picked out and looked at herself in the mirror, debating for a long time whether to buy it. The girl next to her now was wearing a green coat of a similar design. Maybe she had remembered the girl at the shop because of the coat. If the girl beside her were made up properly, she would look just like the girl she had seen in the store. Mrs. Brown pictured the girl differently and smiled, albeit faintly. The green color of the coat she was wearing was enticing. Mrs. Brown had never once worn a green coat. Almost all of her coats were black.

Her husband stared at her coldly. She was disappointed to find that he was so inflexible. He was having trouble accepting the situation he was in as his own. Perhaps he resented the fact that white people like him, rather than a person of color, had subjected them to this ordeal. Or maybe he was just angry that he couldn't get ready for his business trip the next day. He was supposed to give a guest lecture at a conference in Chicago. Anyway, what disappointed her most was the fact that she couldn't feel the value of having a husband in such a moment of crisis. Nevertheless, it was at least fortunate that her short-tempered husband hadn't lost his self-control and exploded with anger.

There had only been one time that he had been violent toward her. He'd punched her in the face, knocking her out. But it was probably for the better that she had lost consciousness. When she came to, she didn't feel any serious contempt or shame, and instead was able to accept what had happened as understandable to some extent.

"How many hunters did he say there were? Three? There were actually only two," the girl said.

"It was three," the boy said.

"It was definitely two."

They argued for a while about how many people were in the story, which they alone knew. Based on what they were saying, they could have been the killers themselves, but Mrs. Brown felt increasingly more skeptical that they could have committed the murders. They looked too naive to commit such a heinous crime. The boy looked at her shyly.

"Do you happen to h-have anything for h-hemorrhoids?" he asked, his face turning red.

She finally understood why he had remained standing and was walking so uncomfortably. He might also have been nervous about robbing someone for the first time, but the main reason was the hemorrhoids. They would have made it uncomfortable to walk or sit down. She felt sympathy toward him, as well as a sense of closeness. She realized that learning that someone has hemorrhoids can make you feel closer to them. It was different from finding out that someone has a heart problem or diabetes or high blood pressure. In fact, you have to be very close to someone in order to confess that you have hemorrhoids.

"We should have some medicine," she said.

She remembered that her husband had some hemorrhoid medicine in the bathroom cabinet. It was a popular suppository called Preparation-H. She had also used it once or twice. As she rose, she saw that her husband was staring at her unhappily. She felt that he was very deceptive and petty. She retrieved the medicine from the bathroom and gave it to the boy. It was a genuine, perhaps even the ultimate, favor that one person could do for another, and she was happy to be able to do such a favor for him.

The boy handed the gun to the girl and went to the bathroom. Mrs. Brown smiled, imagining the boy agonizingly inserting the suppository into his anus. His shit would be smeared with oil when he had a bowel movement. She didn't find the situation absurd at all, even though it could be thought of that way. The situation felt too ordinary. In comparison, other aspects of her everyday life seemed far more absurd.

When he came out from the bathroom a little while later, the boy looked more comfortable. The four of them resembled a middle-aged married couple and their kids, who were visiting after a long absence. They were sitting around awkwardly, as if they couldn't think of anything else to talk about after the initial greetings.

"Aren't you hungry? I can order us a pizza if you want. I'll p-pay," the boy said.

Mrs. Brown realized that he was stammering less conspicuously now. He seemed to be less nervous.

"They don't deliver pizza out here." Mrs. Brown said.

It occurred to her that she could have called for help on the pretext of ordering pizza, or even just called a pizza place. Then the situation might have turned out differently. Also, it was possible that they could deliver the pizza there. The Browns' house was some distance from downtown and they never ordered pizza, so she naturally assumed that they couldn't get delivery out there.

"But there is some leftover pizza in the refrigerator. Do you want it?" she asked.

The boy nodded, so she went to the kitchen and returned with the microwaved pizza. The boy and girl ate it hungrily. They must have been starved. The boy offered some to the Browns, but they declined. She felt bad that she couldn't offer them tastier pizza. The girl turned on the TV, and another boring show was on. It was one of those bizarre reality shows, but there didn't seem to be anything real about it. Plus, it was much less interesting than what was happening to them. While eating the pizza, the boy picked up a newspaper, opened it, and looked at it closely. He stared at it for a long time without shifting his gaze. He seemed to be reading one of the articles, but it was taking him too long. He looked like he was struggling to understand something rather than reading something seriously. She thought it was the science or arts section, but it was sports. He looked like he was having trouble reading the words and couldn't understand the story. Maybe he only finished middle school or was a high school dropout.

"Can you p-play the piano?" he asked Mrs. Brown. He finished eating and put the newspaper down.

She nodded. She had learned to play as a child and still played the piano in the living room from time to time.

"Can I ask you a f-favor?"

She nodded again.

"Will you p-play it for me?"

It was a completely unexpected request. She thought he would ask for more money or a change of clothes. Mr. Brown looked at his wife, dumbfounded.

"What the hell do you want? You have our money, so you can go now," he said.

But the boy ignored him. Mrs. Brown went obediently to the piano and sat down on the bench. She reminded herself that she was still a hostage. She wondered which song it would be nice to play. But the boy told her what he wanted to hear. It was a song everyone knew. She played "Under the Moonlight". To her surprise, the boy began to sing along. He looked like a choirboy as he sang. He didn't sing very well, but he did the best he could. The ambience in the living room changed while he was singing. It no longer felt like a house where people were being robbed.

After finishing his song, the boy asked if anyone else wanted to sing. When no one responded, he asked her to play another song for him. This time he requested "Heart and Soul". She had hardly been playing the piano recently and so made mistakes on certain notes. It bothered her a little, but she kept going. Anyway the singer didn't seem to notice her mistakes. The songs he chose didn't seem appropriate for the situation. They sounded too sentimental or emotional. But would any song suit the situation? Luckily, he didn't choose anything that would have been difficult for him to sing.

Mrs. Brown wondered if he was going to start dancing or try to get her to dance. But he didn't. That was fortunate. If one of them had started dancing just then, it would have been too far-fetched, like a stupid farce. He sang two more songs in the same way. He sang a total of four songs, as if singing one for each of them. When he was done singing, the situation, which seemed to have changed into something completely different, was once again an undeniable home invasion. Nevertheless, something had changed during that time, and they could all feel it. They seemed to have completely lost their clearly defined roles as robbers and hostages.

Mrs. Brown took a close look at the boy. He looked embarrassed. It occurred to her that he hadn't stammered at all while singing, and she idly wondered whether stammering could be cured through music, though she didn't say it out loud. For all she knew, that type of therapy was already in use.

"Is it all right if I ask a q-question?" the boy said.

She nodded.

"What do you do?" He turned to Mr. Brown and asked.

"I teach hydraulics at a university."

"What's h-hydraulics?"

"It's the study of water. I research ways of using the power of water and other liquids."

It wasn't much of an explanation, but he didn't ask any more questions. She knew that what her husband taught had something to do with liquids, but beyond that, she knew very little about what he actually did. He had once explained that hydraulics was used in the anti-lock braking system of the luxury car they had purchased, but that was the extent of her knowledge.

"That sounds like a g-great job. And what about you?" he asked Mrs. Brown.

"I teach middle school geography."

"That's great," he said.

She didn't think her job was that great, but she enjoyed it. Plus, since she was a geography teacher, she knew a lot of unfamiliar but fabulous place names. She liked to recite place names in her mind, not famous ones like Machu Picchu, Angkor Wat, Serengeti, Lake Baikal, but the ones hardly anyone knew. She was drawn to such places as Axel Heiberg Island or the Zemlya Franz Joseph and Severnaja Zemlya archipelagos, located near the polar ice cap in the Arctic Ocean. The four of them sat quietly for a moment. They looked like they were all waiting to hear the sound of another small airplane flying by.

"How about a pop quiz?" Mrs. Brown said.

She had no idea why she had suddenly asked such a strange question. Maybe she wanted to feel closer to the young strangers who had burst in on their evening. Her husband looked dumbfounded, but she ignored him.

"The name New York comes from the city of York in England. Same with New Hampshire and New Jersey. They all come from England. So where does the name New Zealand come from? Where might the island called Zealand be?"

"Isn't it an island in England?" the boy asked.

"Nope."

"Is there even an island called Zealand?" Mr. Brown asked, more loudly than necessary.

The three of them stared at him as if he didn't belong there.

"Is it in Holland?" the girl asked.

"Zealand is the largest island in Denmark too, but New Zealand is actually named after Zeeland, a Dutch province. James Cook subsequently anglicized the name to 'New Zealand.'".

The boy and girl smiled as if they were happy to learn that.

"Is it all right if I ask a q-question?" the boy said.

She nodded.

"What's your last name?"

"Brown."

The boy nodded as if it were what he had expected.

"Are you British?" he asked Mr. Brown.

He nodded. He was part British, but his lineage was complicated. He was still completely white, though.

"I have some German, Scandinavian, and Russian blood."

Mrs. Brown didn't know her husband had Russian blood. She envied the fact that he had these different ethnicities in him. She was a full-blooded Korean and was ashamed of this fact as if it were a stigma that could not be erased. But she didn't like her husband's family name. She had never liked the name Brown, which she thought made one sound like an easy-going, mild-mannered person. She didn't understand why so many names of colors were used for family names. Brown, white, black, green, gray. If you absolutely had to use the name of a color as a surname, then why not purple, indigo, or vermilion, she wondered. She had insisted on keeping her own name when they'd gotten married, but he wouldn't compromise. The surname Brown didn't suit her first name. She suddenly thought it was strange that she should be living with a man named Brown, and she thought about leaving her husband.

Mrs. Brown thought her young friends might tell them their names, but they didn't. Somehow they looked like they would have very common first names and unusual surnames. Since it was close to midnight, she thought she might have to prepare the guest room for them. They had a fancy guest room on the second floor overlooking the lake. The four of them continued sitting in silence, as if they were all waiting for someone else to get up first and excuse himself or herself and go to bed. After a while, the clock on the wall started chiming midnight.

"I want some chicken," Mr. Brown said suddenly, as if the clock had stimulated his appetite.

He must have been hungry. He usually had a midnight snack. Even when he'd eaten a full dinner, he still had a midnight snack. He glanced over at the boy, who nodded as if to say it was okay. The boy followed Mrs. Brown into the kitchen. Together, they walked from the living room to the kitchen and back again, like a hostess and an invited guest. She put a pot of chicken left over from dinner on the stove.

"What is that?"

"Korean chicken stew. It's very spicy."

"I can't eat s-spicy food. So you're from Korea. I don't know a-anything about Korea," he said, as if he were committing a huge breach of etiquette. It wasn't clear whether he was sorry that he couldn't eat spicy food or because he didn't know anything about Korea.

Her husband liked spicy food as much as she did. It occurred to her that liking spicy food might have been the only thing they had in common. She thought again that she might wind up leaving him. If so, the first thing she thought she would do was learn how to fly a plane. Once she knew how to do that, she would fill up the fuel tank and fly to Nova Scotia, or further north along the Canadian coastline, or even to the edge of the polar ice cap or all the way to the North Pole.

Now that she was alone with the boy, she wanted to say something to him but couldn't think of what to say. She wanted to ask more about the murderer in the woods, but it didn't look like he knew anything else about it. She also wanted to say that she hoped she would see him again even after they parted.

"You seem like a really nice person," the boy said.

She smiled in response. They went back to the living room while the chicken was boiling, and the four of them sat in silence. The girl seemed to be getting sleepy again. The boy looked exhausted and was getting drowsy. He began spinning the gun on his finger as if to keep himself awake. Mrs. Brown thought it looked dangerous and hoped the gun wasn't loaded.

Now and then, they could hear the distant sound of trucks on the freeway, which were criss-crossing the continent. She could also hear and smell the chicken stew boiling in the kitchen. She stood up. At that moment, a loud noise rang out. It was a gunshot. The boy's leg was bleeding, as if a bullet had hit it. Blood was dripping down his leg and pooling on the carpet. It looked like a red paint spill. She was a little concerned about her precious purple carpet being stained with blood, but she didn't really mind that much. The carpet could be cleaned. She rushed into the bathroom, brought out the first-aid kit, and wrapped a bandage around the boy's thigh. Then she ran to the phone and called 911.

Paramedics and the police arrived in about 15 minutes. When they showed up, Mr. and Mrs. Brown and the boy and girl were sitting in the living room. The room was filled with the smell of burnt chicken. Mrs. Brown liked the smell of the spicy, burnt chicken. She intentionally breathed in the smell while picturing the murderer who had gone into the forest and killed the deer hunters. She thought that the murderer who had gone into the woods alone armed with a gun must have been very lonely.

When I first met Mrs. Brown at a flight school in Nova Scotia, we quickly became friends because we were the only Asian students.

Soon after the robbery, she divorced her husband and moved to Canada, and she never saw the boy or girl again. The boy had asked for money, but only after Mr. Brown had pushed him to say what it was he wanted. The only thing the boy had asked for was something to drink, medicine for his hemorrhoids, and four songs on the piano.

Mrs. Brown and I talked about that. Smiling, she wondered aloud whether he had just wanted to sing a few songs. She never did find out what their motive was, and we decided that there didn't necessarily have to be one. Maybe they didn't know what they wanted. It may have been the same with the murderer in the woods.

Soon Mrs. Brown and I will finish the piloting course and take the qualifying exam. Then, after we get our pilot's license, maybe we will fly from Nova Scotia all the way to the North Pole. And maybe we won't have any motive for doing so. We will simply be flying toward a set of coordinates on the map.

Translated by So-Ra Kim Russel and the author

The Joy of Traveling

"It would've been nice if K had come with us," she said.

She was staring ahead, her hands on the steering wheel.

Their car was by the roadside next to a vineyard. Heavy rain had begun to fall half an hour earlier, obscuring their view and making it difficult to drive, so they had stopped for a moment.

"Are you sorry that we didn't come with K?" he asked.

"That's not what I meant," she said.

"Or are you sorry that you came with me?" he asked again.

Instead of answering, she shook her head as if unsure. Then, as if she felt that wasn't enough, she said no.

It was the second time on the trip that she'd said, It would've been nice if K had come with us. The first time, she'd said, It would've been nicer if K had come with us.

It was K, in fact, who had suggested the trip. The last time they'd gotten together, he had asked what they'd thought of the three of them going on a trip together. When they'd said nothing in reply, he'd said it would be a good idea. It was K, however, who hadn't shown up at the appointed place at the appointed hour. He'd called K at home, but there had been no answer. He couldn't tell whether K had forgotten his promise, or whether he hadn't been able to keep his word for some other reason. He and she had decided to go ahead, just the two of them, for the time being. They could try calling K again.

When he had called K recently, K had been drunk. It was

raining that day, and K had said that all he had done that night, when the rain began to fall and then inexplicably stopped, was to gently wrap in a tissue, under the influence of alcohol, a bug that had been sitting on the window in a charming manner, not a mosquito, but a bug that looked like a mosquito, although it was three or four times bigger than a mosquito, and flush it down the toilet.

K lived in a world of his own. It was self-contained, and in it, he lived a life that required no communication. K wanted to make a movie. He wanted to make just one movie. He wasn't making any progress, though. All he had were plans. Based on what he'd said, it seemed like it would be difficult for the movie to materialize. Seeing that his recent position was that not doing what you don't have to do is just as essential as doing what you can, he seemed to have given up on the movie, in a way. She was the only one who expected K to actually go through with it. She believed in K's talent, or his potential.

Maybe K was asleep. He had severe insomnia, and sometimes, he would go without sleep for several days, then sleep for two days in a row. Perhaps what had brought the three of them together was their severe insomnia. In any case, many of the significant memories they had in common had to do with sleep.

They were on their way to the T Peninsula, which was about forty minutes away by car. More precisely, it was forty minutes to the biggest town on the peninsula, and twenty minutes to the peninsula itself. The tip of the peninsula, however, was one and a half hours away. But it was still unclear as to where on T Peninsula they were headed. Whenever they went on a trip together, their destination was always only approximate.

He was thinking of a place he had visited with K sometime in the past. It was a small fishing port, and something small but memorable had happened as they stood on the breakwater there. A seagull had landed on the breakwater, and begun to regurgitate small fish. The seagull, which was in pain, continued to throw up. According to a fisherman who happened to be nearby, seagulls regurgitated what was in their stomachs in such a way from time to time if they had eaten too much. He hoped that something like that would happen on this trip as well.

Suddenly recalling the memory, he wanted to go back to the place and see a seagull throw up. It wasn't, of course, that he wanted to see a seagull suffer. And he wasn't even sure if the seagull back then had been suffering. The seagull disappeared, walking away slowly instead of soaring up suddenly, as if nothing had happened.

Now she was looking at the vineyard outside the window. They were in the middle of a low hill surrounded by vineyards on every side. He took a moment to picture in his mind the scenery that was before his eyes, and considered how he would depict it in a painting. He felt that it would be better to depict it in an impressionistic, rather than realistic, manner. There was something about it that went beyond realism, when you took it in. He had experienced many such vistas when he was in Europe, and had talked to people about it. Mostly, such scenery had been seen on rainy or foggy days.

It was in a provincial European city that he'd met her. At the time, he had been staying there without a clear purpose.

He ran into her one day at a café. She came over and sat down at his table. After exchanging a few words, he learned that they were from the same country, and that she, too, had been staying in the city without a clear purpose.

It was by chance that she had come to the city, which was close to the border. She was traveling on a train late at night when she saw a young man with a surgical scar on his head and a face that was nearly blue, sitting a little way off from her, staring at his genitals with his pants down. He wasn't exactly masturbating, just staring blankly as though he was perplexed that there was such a thing in such a place, or as though he didn't really care. Then in a moment, he buttoned up his pants, as though he had seen enough of something he had to see. When he got off the train, she got off with him. She didn't know why, but she did, in spite of herself. She couldn't, however, find him after getting off the train. She said it seemed that he had undergone a frontal lobotomy.

Thus, she had come to stay in the city. The two visited each other several times in their hotels. They also wandered around downtown, looking for the man who seemed to have gotten a frontal lobotomy. The city wasn't big, but he was nowhere to be seen.

Then late one night, someone knocked on his door, and when he opened it, she was standing there, looking frightened.

He let her into the room, and watched her gasping. After a while, she went to the bathroom, and then she told him what had happened.

On the way to her hotel was a small field, and a river flowing beyond the field. She had run into a robber while passing through the field. No, it wasn't clear whether or not he was a robber. Perhaps he had tried to rape her. The man approached her, and looked at her for a moment. He didn't demand anything from her. He had merely looked at her quietly from a distance.

Nevertheless, she suddenly felt afraid and began to run, and fell several times in the process of running across the field where potatoes or some other vegetables were planted. When she reached the riverside and turned around to look, he wasn't there. She ran across the bridge, and arrived at his door.

He asked her if she was okay. She said she was, except that her legs were trembling. It may have been in that moment that he felt a certain intimacy toward her. She was momentarily petrified because she had met a robber or a strange man, and was still trembling as a result. He saw her legs trembling. He felt that it took a somewhat strange or unusual process for him to suddenly become close to or intimate with someone. It was in the same way that he had come to like her. And they came to stay in that little European city together for some time, and had a good time, partly because of the people there, who seemed somewhat peculiar though it was difficult to say how exactly, like the man on the train and the man who had frightened her.

"I wonder where K went," she said as she watched the vineyard where the rain was falling, or the rain that was falling on the vineyard.

Suddenly it occurred to him that she liked K a lot.

He'd met K on an island before he'd met her. It was around the end of the summer one year, when a storm was raging. He had been staying at an inn on the beach for two days. K was there too. They were the only guests at the inn, and they naturally became friends.

Nothing really remarkable happened on the island. It was later on that he learned that K was bisexual. Not long after he returned from the trip, he met K again. K was a graduate student at a conservatory at the time, majoring in piano performance. He wanted to be a composer however, not a pianist.

They met in a practice room at the conservatory K was attending. K played for him a piano piece by Debussy, probably "Suite Bergamasque", and when he applauded after the performance, K stood up and embraced him, and told him that he was bisexual. He didn't feel any resistance in particular, and stayed in K's arms. K's hands gently caressed his chest. He thought that K's fingers were very pale and long. The hands seemed well suited to playing the piano. K's caress became rough. No, not rough. The caress was still gentle, but a little more persistent. He found it funny, and wanted to laugh but restrained himself. He felt that laughing might hurt K's feelings.

As K caressed him, he gently drew back the curtain on the window behind K, and saw a few people walking down the sloping hill on the campus. A sound came from the corridor at that moment, and K stopped. They stayed still for a moment, somewhat awkwardly, holding each other. He suddenly felt forlorn, thinking about the fact that two men were awkwardly embracing each other in a corner of a music practice room, and he scratched his thigh noisily, not to give vent to the feeling, but to neutralize it. At that moment, the faint sound of a string instrument being played came from somewhere in the building.

After a short while, the sound subsided and there came another sound, of someone blowing air into an instrument. He concluded without any basis that it was an English horn, and repeated the words in his mind. They sounded marvelous, as did the names of most metal and woodwind instruments. He made an effort to picture the specific form of the instrument. But the sound was very unfamiliar, and he had to conjure up something much more unfamiliar than the sound—mollusks, for instance, crawling very slowly over his flesh. At that moment, a sound came from the corridor again. K released him. And that was all. K didn't make any further attempts to embrace him. K identified the instrument, which he concluded to be an English horn or oboe. Then K said that English horns and oboes were nearly identical in form and fingering, as well as playing techniques, and that often, English horns were played when oboe players were needed. He also added that English horns were neither made in England, nor actual horns.

They became good friends. He liked that K was well informed about composition theory, which K tried to explain to him but which he couldn't understand at all. The study of harmonics, which involved the use of terms such as transposition, prelude, chromatic scale, and diatonic scale, sounded as difficult as higher mathematical theory to him. K said that it might be difficult at first but was surprisingly easy to understand once you grasped the principle, but for him, harmonics remained uncharted territory till the end.

Later, K told him about an experience he'd had as a boy. He was masturbating one afternoon on his bed in a patch of sunlight, thinking about a boy he liked. He didn't take his eyes off the sun while masturbating, and so after ejaculation, he was blinded and couldn't see anything. That was how he came to open his eyes to homosexuality.

The fact that K was bisexual did not create a problem in their relationship. Any relationship between people was just one of many different forms of relationships. Actually, he felt a little envious of the fact that K was bisexual. It seemed to him that bisexuals were a little more evolved, or that they were endowed with an ability which he didn't possess. Being bisexual was certainly nothing more than a matter of preference, but it also seemed to involve aptitude.

After that, K went to study abroad in Austria. After a period of no contact, he called and said he was staying in a city from which he could see the perpetual snow of the Alps. He also said that he had quit studying. He offhandedly wrote the name of K's city on his desk calendar with a red pencil. When he did, he suddenly became curious as to what K was doing there, and how the people there lived. At any rate, one thing was for sure—the people there saw the snow every day.

K returned not long after that, but he didn't say much about what he had done in the meantime. He said that due to climate change, the snow on the mountains soaring behind the city was gradually decreasing, as if that was all he could say about the place. He also said that a town not too far from the city had vanished completely under a landslide.

After that, she and K met each other through him, and the two soon took to each other. He took pleasure in the fact that she, whom he had once been fond of, and who was with him now, felt more fondness not for him, but for someone who was friends with him, too. Instead of feeling jealous, he felt a new emotion that was beyond love blossoming between the two of them.

"I had a dream about you a few days ago," she said. "You weren't doing anything in particular in the dream. Actually, you weren't doing anything, I should say. You came to see me, but you didn't say why, and you didn't suggest that we do something, either. You just sat by me for a moment, then left. One thing that stands out in my mind is that you were wearing your hair in a queue, like the Manchurians during the Qing Dynasty. Your hair was shaved in the front, and tied in a long braid in the back."

He couldn't quite imagine himself sporting a queue.

"Why do you think the Manchurians, or rather the Manchurian men, all wore their hair that way?" she asked.

"To feel a sense of unity with others? And at the same time, to differentiate themselves from other peoples?" he said.

"In any case, it's really strange, and funny, too, that all the man in a country would wear their hair the same way," she said.

"The hairstyle is really funny, but actually, they probably didn't think they looked funny, since everyone wore their hair in the same way. It probably only looked funny to strangers."

"Still, they could have secretly thought that they looked funny when they saw each other."

"Anyway, I think it's funny that all the men in the country could have looked at one other and thought they looked funny, or just to imagine such a thing, whether it's true or not."

"And it's funny, too, that they tried to conquer other people while sporting that hairstyle."

They knew where their conversation was going. It was sure to keep getting sidetracked, with no point to it whatsoever. That was the reason, too, why it was satisfying to talk to her. Their conversations never had a point, and so they never reached any point.

For a moment, he thought about the conquerors who had

gone around the Asian continent. It seemed sad that there were nearly no traces left of the Mongols.

"I feel sad sometimes when I think about the Mongol Empire. They built such a great empire, but it collapsed, leaving almost no trace. There are some traces of the Mongol Empire, not far from here. Even though there are nearly no remains. Still, the names of the places that show traces of Mongol rule are still there," he said.

In fact, K and he had visited the Mongol ruins on the island. The ruins, however, were very shabby. They could only guess from the names on the signs that Mongol conquerors had set foot there.

"I don't know why strange looking people keep appearing in my dreams. Recently, I dreamed that I went to some palace where all the maidens were limping. They were all limping as they went, carrying something. And then I learned that the princess there limped as well. So only those who limped could wait on her," she said.

"I like how you tell me such strange stories," he said.

"Something strange happened around here, by the way."

"What?"

"You see that hill over there?" she asked, pointing to a hill.

"Yes."

"I was going somewhere with someone, when we took a wrong turn and ended up going into some mountain. We followed the mountain path for a little while, and reached a dead end. There was a car idling there. It was afternoon and the weather was nice. But the car door was open, and the headlights were on. There was no one in the car. The windshield wipers were on."

"So?"

"I had a hunch. I couldn't shake off the feeling that something awful had happened. A feeling that the person who had been in the car had harmed someone else, or that something unfortunate had happened to them both."

"I can imagine."

"The wipers that kept moving from left to right added to the feeling. The wipers must have been old, because the sound of the rubber sliding on the windshield was quite loud."

"Why don't we go back there?"

"I don't know. And I don't even know if I can find my way back there. I arrived there after taking a wrong turn, after all."

"I want to go there, even if it means having to take a wrong turn. And I could leave the door open, the headlights on, and the wipers on the windshield running, then leave the car."

"And then?"

"I don't know."

In the meantime, dark clouds had filled the sky. They turned dark as though it were evening when it was actually midday. He pictured light streaming suddenly into the living room of a dark house, and a peacock standing there with its colorful tail fully opened. Somehow it seemed appropriate for the peacock to cry like another animal. Or for the peacock to be something that resembled a peacock but was something else.

"What are you thinking about?" he said.

"About the role something plays in something else . . ." she said.

"Like what?"

"The role of glucose in the body." Even after saying the words, she seemed unsure as to what the words were supposed to mean.

With the wind gradually growing stronger, the trees lining the street bent as if they might break, but they didn't actually break. The leaves of the grapevines shook frantically.

Suddenly he recalled the name Bianka Panova, and said it out loud. Bianka Panova, a legendary rhythmic gymnast from Bulgaria who took the world by storm in the 80s, occasionally came to his mind during obscure moments. He momentarily recalled her movements, so light, as if she were about to fly away. He liked the feeling of infinite lightness he felt when thinking about her.

"Or being a part of a part of something," she said.

He looked at her as if he didn't understand what she was saying. But it seemed that he could understand what she was saying well enough.

She rolled the window down a little. The sound of the wind came rushing in. He tried to hear the sound of the wind as two distinct sounds: the sound created by the wind itself, and the sound created by something else as it was shaken by the wind or crashed into something. But at that moment, she rolled up the window again. He didn't say anything about it.

"Sometimes when I'm sitting still in a car like this, I think of dummies. You know, dolls modeled after the human body, used in car crash tests. I saw one in a dream once. It was sitting in a chair at the end of a corridor in a two-story building. With electrodes stuck here and there on the body, and with pinwheel patterns near the ears," she said.

"Why are there patterns on them, anyway? The pinwheels are usually blue and white, aren't they?"

He thought about it, but couldn't figure out the reason.

"Anyway, I don't know why it looked so sad," she said.

"Dummies are made to crash and break, after all. That's probably why they look sad."

In the meantime, the dark clouds had begun to lift and the rain was slowly coming to a stop. He took his camera and went outside. He put up an umbrella. She remained in the car.

A warm breeze blew very slowly. Then shortly after, a cold breeze blew just as slowly. The breezes, it seemed, came from somewhere nearby. For a moment, he felt the difference between the two breezes that gently brushed past his body.

The grapes were big and green, but they weren't ripe yet. The vineyard wasn't full of the scent of grapes. It wasn't clear whether it was because the grapes weren't fully ripe yet, or because grapes didn't have a strong scent to begin with, unlike apples and peaches.

Anyway, it seemed that the scent was still trapped within the ripening grapes.

When he looked into the car, she was saying something on the other side of the closed window. He couldn't tell what she was saying. He tried to figure out what she was saying from the shape of her lips, but couldn't. She seemed to think he could understand, for she continued to speak. He smiled, and she smiled as well. After a short while, she turned her head and looked straight ahead.

Now the sound of the raindrops crashing against the ground had grown very faint. At that moment, she came outside.

"Look at that," she said.

A huge toad was crawling on the ground cautiously. They looked at it for a moment. The toad made its way toward the vineyard with slow hops, and soon disappeared. Then the weather cleared up and the rain stopped. The toad seemed to play a vital role in the weather clearing up. From somewhere came the sound of cicadas chirping. He strained his ears hear to the sound. He couldn't see them, but it seemed that the cicadas were on the trees. The sound of the cicadas rang out for the duration of a song, and then stopped for a moment, before starting up again. He seemed to be able to distinguish between the sounds of all the cicadas.

"Don't you think the sound of cicadas is too conspicuous?" she said.

"What's conspicuous about it?"

"I don't know, just something."

He listened carefully to the sound of cicadas chirping.

"Yes, now that I pay attention, it does seem that way," he said.

For a moment, they listened carefully to the sound of cicadas chirping conspicuously in the middle of the vineyard. He took a picture of the cicadas that were on the trees but invisible to the eye, then of the vineyard into which the toad had disappeared a moment ago. He took pictures as a hobby, and he mostly photographed animals, even though it hadn't been his intention to do so. The pictures he had taken included those of goats feeding on grass on an uninhabited island, a cat taking a nap, and fish swimming in a stream.

He wondered if the fact that they were at a vineyard was making them stay there longer. It didn't particularly seem that way.

"What is there to do at a vineyard?" he said.

"Wondering what there is to do at a vineyard?" she suggested.

It wasn't the answer he wanted, and he posed the same question again.

"Looking at a vineyard or picking a bunch of grapes. Or closing your eyes and picturing a vineyard," she suggested again.

"Or walking around the vineyard," he added.

They, however, did not stir from the spot.

"You could also leave the vineyard, couldn't you?" she said.

They looked at the vineyard for a moment in silence, then got back in the car. She took out a map and pointed to the peninsula they intended to visit. The map was small, and the peninsula was obscured by her finger.

She set off again. They left the vineyard behind, and after a while hill after hill appeared, but then in a moment, a vineyard came into view again. But when they went a little further, the vineyard disappeared without a trace and rice paddies appeared. Thick trees lined both sides of the road, and the sound of cicadas rang incessantly.

"Did you know, that the sunlight reflected off trees can cause you to black out momentarily?" she said.

"Is that true?"

"Yes. It can happen. When you're going very fast."

She drove the car slowly. The cars came from behind and passed them, honking their horns. He tried to black out while looking at the trees, without any success. He couldn't tell whether it was because the car was going too slowly, or because the sunlight wasn't strong enough. The nail polish on her fingers that were on the steering wheel caught his eye. It was blue. He liked the color, which didn't seem right for a nail polish.

An unfamiliar instrument was being played on the radio, which she had turned on. It sounded like Latin American music. He was suddenly pleased that so many instruments were in existence. Even instruments that weren't being played, ones that were just sitting still somewhere, were still pleasing to look upon.

"Lately I've been wanting to sing for some reason," he said.

"You should sing, then."

"I mean, I want to sing in a chorus, not by myself."

"You should join a choir, then. Are you a good singer, though? I don't think I've ever heard you sing."

"No, I'm not. That's the problem."

"Not being a good singer wouldn't matter as much if you sang in a choir."

"Wouldn't it matter even more? A little dissonance could ruin the entire choir."

"That's possible. I think you'd better not join a choir, then."

"Then I can't sing in a chorus."

"That's true. I don't think you have much of a choice."

"But wouldn't my singing improve a little if I sing in a choir?"

"It could, a little. But not beyond a certain level. There has to be a limit."

At that moment, they saw a farmer working in a rice paddy. He seemed to be shoring up the bank of a ditch that was crumbling away due to heavy rain. Standing next to the farmer was a woman with a baby on her back, and next to them, a wet dog was looking up at something, wagging its tail. The head of the baby, wrapped in a baby blanket, was drooping, but it wasn't clear whether the baby was sleeping or looking at the dog. He took a picture, seizing the moment. He hummed a song in his mind, and gave up on the idea of singing in a chorus.

"K told me an interesting story some time ago. It was horrific, but there was something remarkable about it. It happened in America—two men and a woman went to a summer house in the country. It's not clear exactly what their relationship was. In any case, they'd agreed beforehand that they would go to the summer house and have group sex, but for some reason, it didn't happen. It seems that the woman refused. Then somehow, the two men killed the woman, cooked her flesh on a barbecue grill and ate it, then ground up the bones into powder and scattered it out the window on the highway on their way back. What's remarkable about it is that they scattered the woman's ground up bones on the highway," she said.

He, too, had heard the story from K. The story sounded more sad than interesting. If K had been with them, they would have made up exactly the same kind of group as the one involved in the incident that occurred in America.

"Do you want to hear another story?" she said. "You could call it interesting or sad. A Scandinavian couple was traveling in a car to go on a vacation. They were headed to Spain, and were passing through France. They stopped at a rest area. But after a little break, the husband got into the car by himself and drove away. He'd forgotten that he had left his wife behind, and was driving alone. Only after he'd driven about two hundred and fifty kilometers did he realize that he had left his wife behind. He was very absent-minded."

"Maybe he felt troubled as he drove, sensing that he'd left something behind at the rest area without knowing what it was."

He found the story amusing.

"I think that kind of absent-mindedness isn't so bad."

"I think the two must've had a great trip. It's true, at any rate, that they had a trip they wouldn't forget for the rest of their lives."

He pictured someone driving away while the person he was traveling with stood at a rest area.

"I think the people in the anecdote were Danish. It sounds plausible that they were Danish. For some reason, it seems like the sort of thing that would happen to the Danish. I don't think it would've been as plausible if the people in the anecdote had been German or French," she said.

"I thought the same thing."

"Anyway, I hear that the Danish don't speak clearly and sound like they have potatoes in their mouths when they speak," she said.

"Is it that the Danish language itself is hard to understand, or that the Danish don't speak clearly?"

"I'm not sure about that."

"Do the Danish understand each other when they don't speak clearly?"

"I'm not sure, but it's probably just those who aren't Danish who can't understand, and the Danish probably understand each other well. It's hard to imagine that people who speak the same language would speak in a way that's hard for them to understand, and having a hard time talking to each other."

"It is hard to imagine, but I think it would be interesting to watch people who speak the same language have a really hard time understanding each other."

They crossed a bridge. The ornamental carving of leaves on the bridge, recently added, was almost unseemly.

"How hideous," she said. "They don't make anything right in this country."

"No, they don't. Actually, they make everything downright wrong."

"Did you know that there was a place I wanted to visit when we were in Europe, though I never ended up going?"

"Where was it?"

"Iceland."

"Why?"

"I don't know. I just wanted to go to Iceland. I actually went to Denmark, where there was a boat to Iceland."

He looked at her. He recalled the memory of them passing by a lake while traveling together in Northern Europe. The lake, beautiful and tranquil, and clear as a mirror, awakened a desire to plunge into its depths. It wouldn't be a bad thing, it seemed, to float on the cold surface without breathing. But if you did, someone who was passing by on a boat was bound to be shocked, as if they'd spotted a dead body.

They preferred lakes to oceans and rivers. In particular, there was something about a tranquil lake in the woods that was very alluring. During their stay in the European city, they'd spent much of their time lying by the side of a lake surrounded by trees, or swimming in the lake.

"I know. You want to ask me why I didn't get on the boat to Iceland, don't you? I'm not sure," she said. "Anyway, I really like the sound of the name, Iceland. I heard that even though it's big, most of it is wasteland, with a population of only three hundred thousand. But Iceland, a land of ice, isn't really that cold. There are countless numbers of volcanoes and glaciers and geysers, and in Devil's Kitchen, a volcanic area, water vapor spurts out of the ground, startling people."

"You sure know a lot about Iceland."

"And this is my favorite part—they say the Icelanders are very promiscuous."

"In what ways?"

"Over half the kids there are born out of wedlock."

"Really? How is that possible?"

"More than half the kids are born through extramarital affairs."

"I think it'll be fun to walk the streets of a place where more than half the kids are born out of wedlock."

"And they say that during a certain time in Iceland, it feels like the whole country has gone into hibernation."

"I think it would be great to stay in a place where it feels like the whole country has gone into hibernation, and go to sleep while others are sleeping, or to look out the window, unable to sleep."

"Wouldn't it be nice to learn Icelandic too? I think it'll be fun to use the language, which you really have no use for, to pronounce certain words and to create and say sentences by yourself from time to time. I think it'll make me feel really good to pronounce words such as 'sea lion' or 'active volcano', or say things like, I'm planning to go to Iceland this summer, or, Do you like watching ships entering a port? or, How many kinds of knives are there in the knife cabinet in your kitchen? or, Have you ever thrown your pillow out the window because you were angry or happy?"

Now she began to speak faster.

"When I look at the rearview mirror while driving fast like this, I feel like the road is chasing me. Quite frantically," she said.

He looked at the mirror on his side. It seemed to him, however, that the road was receding from them, not following them.

"It looks like the opposite to me. It feels like we're leaving the road behind quite rapidly," he said.

"It does seem that way, now that you say it."

Soon they reached the mouth of the bay where the peninsula began. A very straight road stretched out before them, with a lake on one side, formed when the embankment was built, and the bay on the other. She stopped the car for a moment by the roadside.

"A long time ago, someone I knew committed suicide in the sea. He was on a passenger boat, and he drowned himself one night. His body was found several days later, quite a distance from the spot where he jumped. He'd been swept away in the current. A lot of cuttlefish are caught in there, and what came to my mind when I learned that he'd been found there dead was the image of lighted lamps on the boats used for catching cuttlefish," she said. "Anyway, there was a composite picture in the wallet he left on the boat, a picture of himself wearing a suit, with only his upper body showing above the surface of the sea."

"That isn't a very original method of suicide."

Her face clouded over. It suddenly occurred to him that the man could have been someone she had known personally.

"There's a serviceman I know," she said in a more cheerful voice. "He's in the navy, quite high ranking. He's the captain of a warship. He says that if I come visit him this summer, he'll let me onboard his warship. Don't you want to go on a warship?"

"Sure."

He had never been on a warship. At any rate, it seemed that being on a warship would be different from being on a passenger ship or a fishing boat.

"Maybe we could persuade him to let us go far out to sea and fire at a desert island. Just for fun," he said.

"Do you think it'd be fun to do that?"

"I think it could be fun, if we just do it for fun."

"I don't think it's necessarily fun to do something just because you do it for fun."

"There was a time when I was little when I wanted to be a gunner. It wasn't a dream I had, just a simple desire. I thought it'd be fun to fire a gun."

"I read somewhere that a relative of an American president went deer hunting on the family's estate in an armored car. He wasn't all there, you see."

"I think the hunting must've been fun, at any rate."

They sat in silence for a moment. They tried to imagine the fun things they could do, which didn't come quickly to them.

But something fun they hadn't imagined could happen to them. Traveling made that possible sometimes.

He looked at the bay and the lake. Wind was blowing over both the lake and the bay, but the waves on the bay were much more violent. As he looked from the waves on the bay to the waves on the lake, it seemed that the waves on the lake were much more tranquil.

"I think it would be nicer with K here," he said.

"You think so?"

"Yeah."

"I'll try calling him later. Don't you have a feeling that somehow, this trip will be fun?" she said.

"Yeah, I have a feeling that fun things are waiting for us."

She smiled at him.

"Or maybe nothing special will happen," she said.

"That's possible."

"It'll be okay, though."

He smiled at her. It was dark around them, but he felt infinitely light, and he liked the feeling of lightness.

Translated by Jung Yewon

The Afternoon of a Faun

We were sitting at the edge of a lake one peaceful weekday afternoon. The branches of ash trees dangled in the water, some of them touching the water's surface, and the leaves of broad-leaved trees, that had been blown off by the wind, drifted on the water. Though the water was clean and tranquil, it was too cold to swim in. And though there were clouds to the west, in general the sky was clear.

There was a forest beyond the lake. It was not the kind of forest that stubbornly refused entry or seemed to lock people in, or the kind of dense, fierce forest where everything seems to be tangled. In the forest there was a small hill made up of boulders that looked as if a giant had tossed them wherever he felt like, and at the top of the hill rested a large boulder resembling a turtle. From where we were sitting it bore little resemblance to any animal, but viewed from the side opposite us, it did start to resemble a turtle if you thought about its name, which was Turtle Boulder. Anyway, this boulder was made up of two boulders of different sizes, resembling the head and body of a turtle. Like most boulders with names, this boulder probably didn't just derive its name from its slight resemblance to a turtle, but also because of some legend, though there was no way of knowing. He was sitting up straight with a pipe between his lips, she was leaning back against the boulder in a near-reclining position, and I was lying down on a mat. We were on a grassy area by the lake, in our own way like figures in a landscape painting. Beside us, we had an uncorked bottle of wine, a glass full of wine, and things to eat, like fruit. He was sitting erect because of a white straw hat he had on, which he rarely took off once he left the house. This unique hat had a small black bird that looked like a green linnet decorating the brim, which gave it a slight cheeky feeling, but it had nearly lost the appearance of a bird, since most of the feathers on its wing had fallen out over time, so it felt less excessive. His face was actually very tanned, and he really didn't need to shield his extremely dark face from the sun. His face looked like it couldn't get any more tanned, and more sun wouldn't have made any difference. Plus, the autumn sun's rays didn't burn, they were just strong enough to feel good on your face. Even then, he screened his face in the shade.

We laughed for a little while about something he'd just said. He then told us that when he was young, he had been standing by a riverbank when he was shocked to see his father being swept away by the flood-swollen river. It wasn't a very wide river, and he had taken a clear look at his father's face, which seemed to be turned toward his son as he was being swept away by the rapids, and he had looked slightly bewildered as well as radiant, the way he did when he had done something he was proud of. His father almost looked like he was smiling. What's more, it seemed as if his father was waving at him, and as a result, he also waved at his father without thinking, as if he were cheering someone on. He said that it was both a strange but gratifying sight. Anyway, instead of disappearing into the rapids, his father came home that night holding a stick with some fish hooked to it by their gills, shocking everyone once again, and that night his family had fish for dinner. Maybe his father hadn't been swept away by the rapids, but for some reason, he had jumped into the currents. He said, if it hadn't happened that way, his father wouldn't have been able to wave calmly from the rapids without looking bewildered.

My dad could've jumped into the rapids, he said. He smiled while looking at us.

I said, There might be people who feel the urge to jump into rapids, but few actually do it.

But there are people who do jump in, he said. And there's definitely something about rapids that makes people want to jump.

I think that's true, she said.

Anyway, he added, he might have looked sad as he was being swept away, but it made me strangely excited. He said this as if it were the conclusion he'd come to.

It was possible that he brought up this anecdote because a fisherman in a boat had arrived at a spot a little distance away from us a short while before. After drawing up a fishing net he had left earlier, the fisherman waved at us before leaving. We waved back at him. The countless silvery fish also seemed to be waving at us.

He then told us another childhood story. He had grown up in the countryside and had a lot of childhood stories, as if his childhood were somehow unusual. The day finally came when the circus arrived and gave a performance, he said. Toward the end of the performance, inside an enormous tent, I saw my father on the floor, bleeding, hit by someone after they'd gotten into an argument. They looked like the last circus act. I watched this scene with the rest of the crowd, feeling strangely excited.

He had told us this story before, but we smiled again while we listened. The elephants' stunt act, which was the last performance, had to be suspended, and the elephants also momentarily stopped to watch the stunts of the men. Finally, the two men were dragged outside. While I walked home that night with my dust-covered father, I felt him to be a colossal presence, and I suppressed these inflated feelings by silently, continuously singing a song, one I don't remember anymore.

According to him, his father was a dignified man; if he ran into his father while taking a walk, he would receive his son's greeting courteously, without speaking, then continue on his way as if he had just met a stranger. Sometimes, he said, after we'd stepped around each other, he would turn back as if he'd forgotten who I was, then suddenly, as if he'd remembered, he would turn to me and nod and I would also nod back.

His father was someone he had difficulty understanding, and there was a time when, just out of curiosity and in order to understand his father better, he had done some background research on his father's little known past. There was a rumor circulating in his family that his father had been an independence fighter during the period of Japanese colonization. However, there was no evidence to prove it. He had done some research but couldn't verify the rumor, and all he could prove, again, was that there was a rumor that couldn't be verified. Finally, he concluded that during a chaotic time in history, his father had departed for remote borders, not as an independence fighter, but to wander around as a horse-riding bandit or something along those lines—a conclusion he hadn't and couldn't verify. I think being a horse-riding bandit is more glamorous than being an independence fighter. It suits my father better, he said, looking at us as if seeking agreement. We looked at him without saying anything. And no matter what he did, he definitely didn't play a very important role, he said. That's what's most important when it comes to my father.

For a moment he turned and looked at the lake without saying anything, perhaps thinking about his father, who had drowned in a river a few years ago. His father, who had either been swept away or was swimming into a swollen river many years ago, who had been either an independence fighter or a horse-riding bandit, was discovered drowned in a river. When he brought up his father, he talked about these two memories as if they somehow explained each other.

We talked a little more about our childhood. She sounded as

if she had few stories about hers. I suddenly remembered being young and looking at a newborn calf in someone's shed, when the calf had approached and thrust its head toward me so that the hot air from its nostrils touched my face. The memory of that strange contact, which had happened without actual physical contact, was as vivid as the memory of touching fire. Whenever I recalled my childhood, that memory came back to me randomly without any connection.

It wasn't clear why we had gone on this outing. Near the house we lived in was a small grove of trees that made you somewhat feel as if you were in a forest, and we could have gone there like we used to. But maybe we needed to go somewhere that required hours of driving to get to, a place that gave us the sense that we had moved elsewhere. Also, maybe she and I felt that we should take a short trip together with him before it was too late. Recently, his health had rapidly deteriorated, and in the near future he might not be able to go on a road trip. Not too long ago he was suddenly in pain late at night and needed to go to the emergency room. But absurdly enough, on that day he had been home alone, and he wasn't sure whether he should be taken to the nearby hospital by ambulance or walk in crouched on his own two feet—he felt these two options were enormously different, and believed that he needed to decide with great caution—so he stayed up all night wondering which would feel more glorious, but thankfully, during that time he recovered.

Regardless, we wanted to have a day that felt as languid, indistinct, and long as a lifetime, so we decided to go on this picnic. But we started late, so by the time we arrived at the lake it was already late afternoon. On the way we were also rather restless with expectation, but by the time we arrived and faced the peaceful waters for a time, we had begun to feel a little gloomy and vacant.

Our friend, who had an unknowable side to him much like his father, thought of himself as an autodidact, though he wouldn't have used that term. Though he had a bit of a self-educated air about him, there wasn't much there. But he continued to delve into a number of obscure topics. Once, he became very interested in the wings and eyes of a certain species of fish and fowl, and read a number of books on the topic. But his interest never stayed that long on one topic, and soon enough he started following another topic of interest. It was no surprise that even if jellyfish and moss had meant nothing to him before, once he began learning about them, they would become a large presence in his life and would dominate his thoughts. As a self-educated man, his studies lacked depth and he sure wasn't opening up any new territory in the relevant field. As if an autodidact had to appear to stay under a certain level of learning, unlike a professional researcher, his interest stayed at a level which was just enough to satisfy his capricious curiosity. He had been studying *The Book of Changes* some time ago before his health deteriorated, and was now losing the little resemblance he'd had to an autodidact.

Recently, memory kept failing him, and he forgot who he was and even what he had been doing. Some time back, while he was traveling with a tour group on an island around the south coast, he had lost consciousness and was taken to the emergency room—he wasn't able to think about whether it would be nicer to be taken away in an ambulance or to walk on his own two feet, clutching himself. A few days later, he was able to return home. He had absolutely no memory of why he had been traveling with the tour group.

Even before that, he had occasionally done some startling things. One evening he picked a fistful of lettuce leaves and carried them in both hands as if they were a bouquet of flowers, then appeared shyly in front of us. He actually thought that the lettuce he had furtively picked from someone's garden were flowers. When she put the head of lettuce into a basket, he asked her, Why don't you put it in a vase? When she responded, They're not flowers, it's lettuce, he looked at the lettuce oddly. Afterwards while we were eating, he looked at the lettuce that she had put out and said, when did we start eating flowers? And after eating a leaf, he said, this flower tastes vaguely like lettuce. He actually believed that the leaves of the lettuce were flower petals. And afterwards, he uprooted vegetables like green onions and potatoes in gardens surrounding the house, as if he felt compelled to. But he never explained his behavior. I had a vague sense that he derived a certain pleasure that came only from digging up plants, roots and all. At least it was a relief that he no longer tried to pick at the flowers embroidered into the bedcovers, or tear them off all night long.

That moment, someone appeared on Turtle Boulder and shouted someone's name. He wasn't calling us, however; he didn't even seem to have seen us. He looked about momentarily, then descended from the boulder and disappeared into the forest. A little later, a magpie with three or four earthworms in its mouth landed close to us, then began walking toward the forest. It seemed as if three or four worms weren't enough and it was looking for more. The worms were twisting and moving their long bodies sluggishly back and forth. After the magpie disappeared, nothing else emerged. There were no wild animals from the forest that came to drink at the lake. They seemed to come only at night, as if they believed they could only drink at night. There weren't any snapping turtles either, as they had left the lake for the forest. As I gazed at the barren lake, an image of migratory birds walking on the frozen winter lake came to me. I thought that if the birds had a long neck and legs, it would be even more fitting. Before flying elsewhere, the birds could rest for a moment and even catch fish through holes in the ice. It seemed to me that the footprints of the birds scattered across the snow-covered lake, which might take on a particular shape when seen from far away, signaled the start of the oncoming winter, and so I found myself waiting for winter.

We sat without speaking for a while. The wine bottle was now half-empty. I watched the shadow of the ash tree's branches flicker faintly in the water. I felt bored, and thought dimly that boredom was saturated in nature and was one of nature's primary characteristics, and thus what a person would feel when they became a part of nature; I had the vague thought that the boredom of nature was different from the boredom of the city, the streets, or the house, because out of all the various types of boredom, the boredom of nature gives you the most dense and intense feeling. Then when I had this vague thought, everything else seemed vague to me too, and as I gazed vaguely around me, something caught my eye. I saw some birds sitting on a nearby boulder. They were black birds that looked like crows. They soon moved closer to us and it turned out that they were indeed crows. Then they let out a crow's cry, making it clear what they were. There's no need to go that far, I thought. Do we as people have to confirm somehow that we're human? There's no need to go that far. They walked back and forth for a bit as if looking for something to eat, but soon flew off into the forest, as if they hadn't found what they were looking for, and soon after, there was the sound of crows and other birds coming from deep in the forest. The birds' cries came from the forest, and it seemed as if they occupied the forest, but again I had the dim thought that it was not their forest. I tried to think even more obscure thoughts. I might have felt this way because the lake and sky's overly distinct contours and the hues of the forest seemed overwhelming to me, and burdensome. It seemed as if a dog was barking from somewhere but I couldn't be certain. I heard the cries of birds from the forest, as well as various other sounds.

She said, I'm thinking about the music coming from the opera company's practice room.

There was quite a famous opera company based in the house next to ours, and during afternoon naps, we would often be woken by the sounds of a tenor or soprano practicing. The sound was very close, and was usually quite piercing, and as a result, sometimes while I was in bed my ears would be drawn toward this music, and I would end up bursting with fury at both the music and completely unrelated things, then end up getting out of bed a little exhausted from suppressing my rage. Occasionally it was bearable, and on rare occasions, everything felt far away and I listened to the music in a languid, comfortable mood; and sometimes—I enjoyed these times—the sound was grotesque to me, and I was pulled into a grotesque imagined world. It felt good to be momentarily transported elsewhere. Once, in this grotesque imaginative space, I opened a strangely shaped door, and inside a large pit there was a pile of countless dead chickens, and pink baby pigs were walking slowly around the pit as if they were dreaming. Another time, I saw a countless number of birds on fire, flying up to the sky. And sometimes, when I was listening to the singing, it seemed as if the act of singing itself, and all the songs that existed in the world, were extremely strange. At rare times, the music exerted a power over me, but usually I found music very dreary and nearly intolerable. It had gotten to the point where I could only tolerate music at rare moments. Though she also played the piano, there was little music that she could tolerate, and she believed that something about peoples' absolute faith in music and its ability to touch the soul was excessive. She believed that, like religion, there were too many superstitions surrounding music. We both shared a certain hostility toward music. Instead, I generally preferred the sounds she made while working in the kitchen after she had played a few songs or a few notes on the piano, then audibly shut its lid. Random sounds and noises were often more splendid than music, and what attracted me were the sound of the grandfather clock in the living room, the sound of the bell ringing at the nearby temple blending with other sounds, and the sounds that birds or insects made, things which crossed the boundary of music and sound.

After filling our empty glasses with wine and drinking a little, we watched the mountains across the lake. Just then, smoke ascended from a faraway mountain like some kind of signal, and as the smoke thickened, it rose higher, as if there were a forest fire. The smoke couldn't have risen so high if it weren't a forest fire. The smoke got thicker and spread.

"It looks like a forest fire," she said.

"It looks like it," I said.

"A forest fire?" he asked.

His eyesight was weak, and he couldn't seem to see the smoke. As if this made him extremely dissatisfied, he looked in the direction she pointed. But as if he still couldn't see the fire, no matter how hard he tried, he said, It's natural for fires to start in mountains. Then as if implying that there was absolutely no need for smoke to be coming from a forest fire, he lit a pipe so the smoke drifted up.

It looks like there's a fire in the mountains, he said, looking at the mountains through the pipe's smoke.

At that moment a boat appeared, causing waves and foam as it went at full speed, until, as if the engine had halted, it suddenly stopped in the middle of the lake. I could see how many people were on the boat, but it was too far away to tell what they were doing. They appeared to be hurling something into the water, then drawing it out. Shortly after, the boat set off and disappeared toward the opposite shore. It was as if the boat had appeared and disappeared for no reason at all. We watched the smoke rising from the distant mountains and the still lake. The sound of birds came from the forest behind us, but in front of us, the lake was utterly tranquil. The world of noise and the world of silence tensely surrounded us—no, the world of silence was slightly dominant, and the world of noise seemed to be daunted. As if we were trying to give a little more strength to the world of silence, we were momentarily quiet.

He began to talk, asking if he had told us something before, and of course we had heard it before. He had been overseas and had happened to be standing at the edge of a perfectly quiet residential street in a village. He couldn't remember why he had ended up there. It was midsummer, and the streets, filled with dramatically contrasting light and shadows, were completely empty. There was a faint sound, which suddenly grew louder and shattered the enormous silence. A large motorcycle turned the corner and appeared on the empty street, careening down that short stretch in seconds, then it turned the corner ahead until its noise became faint again, and finally, silence filled the streets. As if he had been clobbered by something, he hadn't been able to move. Even though the new silence and the silence before the motorcycle appeared was the same, he said, I believed the two had very different characters. I felt like the motorcycle's noise had penetrated me, he said, and in the following silence, I felt like I no longer existed. If the dramatic contrast of light and shadows was a backdrop of the moment that he described, the silence that had been momentarily broken up and then recovered, might have constituted a particular theme.

I recalled a certain photo at his house that he had taken long ago while traveling overseas (he traveled a lot, and once, he had been bitten by many—at least over ten—leech-like creatures, ones that he said looked different from the kind you can see in dropwort fields.) The photo was taken in a place with an intense noon summer light, with a white horse standing against the backdrop of a white wall. This horse, which had no bridle or saddle on, was standing there as if waiting to be photographed. The horse looked rather artificial, as if it was aware of the camera and was posing. This horse looked like it was filled with resolve, yet it also appeared to be in a state of self-abandonment, enduring great difficulties. Depending on the feelings of each viewer, the horse evoked different motions. It seemed to have emerged from the white backdrop, but it also seemed as if it would disappear into the backdrop. I ultimately imagined the horse disappearing into the white background.

Two birds flew over and sat on the nearby branch of a tree, then cawed and flew into the forest. Suddenly she began quietly humming Debussy's "Prelude to the Afternoon of a Faun", then began reciting from the poem, "Sea Breeze": "I feel that somewhere birds / Are drunk to be amid strange spray and skies. / Nothing, not those old gardens eyes reflect / Can now restrain this heart steeped in the sea."

Then in a cheerful voice, she told us a story that we had heard before. It happened when she was young. One afternoon, she was naked and making love to a boy in a completely empty house when his father suddenly opened the door, and saw the two of them entangled. The boy had his erect penis in her body, and as they were both in shock, he hadn't been able to extract himself from her. Finally it ended when the boy's father grabbed him and mercilessly beat him until they were forced apart. Their first act of love had been halted absurdly. And that boy was none other than our friend—and her cousin.

He didn't have to tear us apart so savagely, he said, as he had said once before. He could have waited a bit longer until we were finished with what we were doing.

She said, After that, we had to hide from others and make love in the forest.

That might be why I feel so comfortable in the forest, he said.

Suddenly I wanted to make love to her in the forest. It could have been because of the poem "Sea Breeze" that she had recited or the love story she had retold, or it could have been the boredom

I was feeling, or it might have been the continual cawing of the two birds flying in the nearby forest, or it might have been the forest that looked chaotic and profane, and the sensual feeling of spending the afternoon in the forest. I imagined making love in the forest. It might happen that we would lean against a tree in an uncomfortable position and somehow caress each other, feeling the difference between caressing and being caressed, feeling a slight pleasure and displeasure at the same time, when suddenly while making love we would look up and see a bird in a branch, or a field mouse in the forest thicket, looking strangely at us, or looking shocked, nonchalant, indifferent or frightened, so that we would stop what we were doing for a minute and shout, this isn't a terrifying act so don't be afraid, we weren't trying to terrify you. It was a pleasant thing to think about. But I believed that actually putting this into practice was extremely troublesome. As for my fleeting desires, I might be slightly alarmed at watching its appearance and immediate disappearance, but I would forget about it, and I thought that if it were possible, it would be good if he made love to her in the forest instead of me, like they had long ago. But at the moment, as he recalled making love in the forest, he didn't seem to want to do it now.

We didn't say anything for a moment. It was clear from our absorbed expressions that each of us were caught up in our own thoughts. It seemed as if without our awareness, things that seemed to us like leaves floating on the water or clouds in the sky were leading us to certain thoughts or interrupting them. When I closed my eyes for a moment and imagined clouds drifting in the sky, I felt myself getting sleepy. She also seemed sleepy. My eyes kept closing, and I saw that hers were closing too. In front of my eyes, a winged insect lost its energy and fell to the ground, writhing. He was facing the lake with his back to us. His eyes were closed as if he were asleep, but he wasn't sleeping. When he scratched his head, as always, he didn't actually take his hat off, but instead, lifted it up slightly and put his hand between the gap and scratched, then put the hat back on as if he had never scratched his head. But as if that weren't enough, this time as he lifted the hat up, he combed his hair back as if he were melancholy, then put the hat back on. I wanted to take a walk but it was too much of a bother to get up, so I told myself that I would get up when someone else did, and stayed where I was. However, no one looked like they were going to get up, or even gave any indication of getting up.

When you are with someone at a certain location, there are times when the atmosphere of the place stands out in relief, and you forget the existence of the people you are with, or the people feel more distinct to you, so the place recedes and becomes even more indistinct than a background, but just then both the people and the place felt indistinct to me. I gave in to my drowsiness and gazed at the forest. Even if I suddenly saw a faun with the upper body of a man and the legs and horns of a goat stumble out half-asleep, or if primitive, near-naked tribespeople wrapped in animal hide came running out singing songs and dancing, I wouldn't have considered it at all strange. However, the forest revealed itself by allowing its branches be shaken just a little by the wind. I watched the trees in a dazed state.

Suddenly I had the thought that in general, animals have a symmetrical form or prefer a symmetrical form, but plants don't. It seemed that plants didn't completely ignore symmetry, but more or less disregarded it. And some plants even looked like they couldn't tolerate symmetry. I didn't know the reason why but it seemed to have something to do with the freedom plants could permit themselves, unlike animals that needed to maintain balance because they continuously moved around. In that sense, the vine plant expressed this aspect best. And even more, plants that were symmetrical would probably look abnormal. Even if this fact wasn't much, and was probably already known to many people, I felt better knowing that I had discovered this for myself, and I thought that perhaps this was the pleasure of being an autodidact. Thinking about this, I observed the surrounding trees and vines—they looked like arrowroot—climbing the trees, but my thoughts didn't develop any further.

At that moment, he suddenly got up, but as if he had forgotten why he had gotten up or as if he were uncertain of what he had been thinking about, he hesitated for a moment. He looked like he was about to sit down again. Though a little while ago I had told myself I would get up when someone else did, for some reason, I stayed put. It was as if in that time, my reasons for getting up had dissipated. Telling us he would come back after taking a walk in the forest, he headed toward the trees. I watched him walking unsteadily for a moment.

Eventually drowsiness engulfed me, and I watched my hand spread to my side through my closing eyes. Feeling as though my hand was falling asleep first, and feeling certain that I had uncertainly seen uncertain things flying about with an uncertain appearance, I fell asleep, and within moments I felt like the strength I needed to wake up could be drawn from these, so I first clenched and unclenched my hands—that seemed to have woken up first—a few times, until I woke up. But as my hand lay there, I felt as if it had a separate existence from me, and I had the strange feeling that my hand could walk to the lake on its own and dive into it, but when I thought that this wasn't possible, I recalled the dream I'd just had.

In the dream, I was walking somewhere when a stranger approached me and suddenly grabbed and twisted my arm, laughing loudly, and I didn't know why I thought this but I decided I had to say something that would make his shoulder unusable—and by making his shoulder unusable I felt that I could know why he did what he did—so I tried to think of something to say that would stop him from using his shoulder, but I couldn't think of anything suitable to say. But strangely enough, what the man had done gradually began to feel natural. I told her about the dream a little later when she woke up. We enjoyed telling each other our dreams, and though we did think that dreams could be analyzed for their meaning, and that the act of analysis could be meaningful, generally we just enjoyed the dreams for themselves. We enjoyed the feeling of dreams sending us one foot into the unknown world.

I also had a dream, but I don't remember it, she said. But thankfully I wasn't paralyzed during a nightmare. She frequently suffered because of this sleep paralysis. She then told me about a dream that she had had that morning. She was in outer space wearing the white clothes of a tennis player. She held an enormous tennis racquet and hit planets flying at her at frightening speeds, after they suddenly shrank to a size right for her racquet, and she sent them flying into infinity.

That's right, I should have brought scissors, she said in my direction. She meant that she could have given me a haircut. When we went to the forest near our house, she often brought her scissors and gave me haircuts. She would usually botch it up so I would normally have to get it cut again, but she and I both liked her cutting my hair, so it had become a small ritual that we acted out in the forest.

Beyond her shoulder, clouds bringing rain were crowding in. He came back from his walk. There was no way of knowing what he had done in the forest, but even if he told us, we still might not understand. He had stuck a small pinecone into the brim of his hat. Behind his shoulder, there were storm clouds that he seemed to have driven ahead closing in. The sky became pitch-dark within seconds as the sun was concealed, and for a moment through gaps between the clouds, two or three intense cylinders of sunlight were reflected off the lake, then immediately disappeared, and from far away, lightning struck and the sound of thunder came faintly but persistently, and as the wind rose the trees began shuddering, announcing an unusually heavy rainstorm. As if a phantasmagoric or majestic scene was about to unfurl before our eyes, we anticipated the coming of the storm, and as expected, in a moment large raindrops began to fall. We didn't escape the rain and instead, secretly awaited the drama of nature with boiling anticipation. The birds, which somehow knew that the rains would stop soon, began flying as they cawed uproariously, and the rains stopped, and just as before, within moments the clouds dispelled and the sky cleared, and again the sun shined. As the sun shone, nature's drama subtly unfolded, leaving us with an enormous, indescribable state of loss, and we had to comfort ourselves at least a little by not wiping off the few raindrops that had fallen on our faces. We watched the sky gradually clear. A moment later a butterfly flew over and sat on an apple we'd left half-eaten and began to drink its juice. No more butterflies flew over, and after the one butterfly had filled itself up, it flew away.

Then some man came out of the forest and appeared in front of us. He was holding a dog leash in his hand. He looked like the man who had been shouting something from Turtle Boulder a little earlier. He asked us if we had seen a large black dog. He spread his arm to show us how big the dog was, but based on the span of his arms, the dog didn't seem that big. He said that there was nowhere for the dog to go, but he couldn't find it anywhere. Where we were resembled a small island, a hill surrounded by a forest, at the center of which was Turtle Boulder, and the island was connected to land and to an elevated bridge, so if the dog hadn't swum across the water to somewhere, it had definitely crossed the bridge.

So the dog's vanished completely, I said.

As if it's evaporated, she said.

Or as if it's sunk into the ground, said her cousin.

He glared at us as if we were making fun of him. But the

atmosphere was such that it seemed natural for us to make this innocent man merely trying to find his lost dog the target of our joke. He held the leash tightly in his hands, as if by doing so, the dog would return. For that fact alone, I thought making fun of him was justifiable.

Are you sure it's a dog you're looking for? said her cousin.

He looked at us angrily.

A while ago, I heard something that sounded like a dog barking, she said.

I saw a dog that looked like a cocker spaniel jump into the water, but that was a long while ago, and that dog had really long ears and was cute, and it didn't jump into the lake but the river, but what kind of dog was the one you lost? I asked.

Though it was nothing much, the man looked furious. He was speechless, as if we were somehow connected with the dog's disappearance or had hidden it, and he tried to look at us suspiciously, but it didn't seem to be working, and as if he were offended, he looked at us for a moment, then he stared at the lake as if we were conspiring with it, then turned back to the forest he'd emerged from and disappeared into it.

I think I saw a black dog with something in its mouth, said her cousin.

It seemed to have a bird in its mouth, she said.

I saw a huge dog with a large carp in its mouth, I said. As soon as I said this, I suddenly thought of the carp living in a temple's lotus pond near our house. It was old for a carp, and occasionally came close to people. It had a face that seemed to understand everything—though there was no way to know what it understood—and looked plainly at a person with its mouth gaping open, then closed, as if it were about to say something. At those times, I would look at it as if I knew what it was trying to say. I thought to myself, when I return home, I can tell the carp about the outing.

Soon we saw the man standing on top of Turtle Boulder, and again he turned in our direction and shouted something. We didn't hear a dog barking anywhere. The next moment the man disappeared. Our conversation moved from the distant past to the somewhat more recent past.

I was thinking of keeping a vegetable garden, she said. If she did this, she could stop him from stealing things from other people's gardens. No, then he could pick as many vegetables or pull them out by their roots as he desired.

But who would take care of the garden? If you didn't want a garden full of weeds, then someone had to take care of it. Between us, there wasn't anyone who would be able to upkeep a vegetable garden. Ultimately the bugs would end up taking care of it. Even without thinking, it was obvious that it was of no use to think about the vegetable garden issue.

He had said, I don't know what to do with the Tibetan box I bought a few days ago. He had bought it at an antique store. This box that the owner said was hundreds of years old was extremely old but very beautiful. For a time then, the problem was the foul smell coming from it. Over a span of hundreds of years, this object that might have come from a Tibetan temple had absorbed incense and other smells, so that no matter how often it was washed, it continued to reek. He believed that the box, which had the odor of a coffin or a grave, had once held a dead baby's body.

That box looked like it held countless memories, and when opened, sometimes seemed to ring with the chanting of Tibetan monks. Anyway, he said, thanks to the smell, sometimes I feel like I'm in Tibet.

We sat for a while without saying anything. It seemed like it was time to go. The wine bottle was nearly empty, and the edges of the apple slices were tinged with brown.

She suddenly said, My problem is that I like the poppies far too much.

At our house, there were poppies in a clear blue vase that she liked very much, and she would lose track of time as she watched them. At a public park, she cut planted poppies that contained no opium. There was a notice that said not to cut the poppies, but she couldn't resist, so she took cuttings and brought them home, and on that point, I felt that was an okay thing to do.

We understood what she meant when she said, my problem is I like poppies far too much, and it was something that only we could understand. It meant that liking the poppy far too much was a problem, and it meant that it was a problem that wasn't a problem at all, and also referred to all the problems that we had. More than anything else, at that moment it was expressing the tedium she was feeling.

He said, There's a hot spring on the way. Should we stop by there?

Let's decide as we go along, she said.

And as if the crows were mobilizing for something, they flew to the lake and walked about restlessly while making exaggerated cries.

I feel like I can understand what they're saying, he said.

What are they saying? she said.

They're asking us to leave, he said.

There was something distinct in the sound that confused the mind, and it wasn't like the indistinct thing was actually there, but the sound made you imagine it was there. As soon as he threw away the now-brown apple, the crows pecked at it as they quarreled with one other. Then as if they wanted more to eat, they looked at us. Again, he threw them the apple skin. After they devoured even the apple skin, the crows waited for more, but he didn't have anything else to give them. Even then, the crows continued to wait, and we continued to make them wait. The crows seemed to be patiently waiting for that something, thought it wasn't clear what.

I heard this from someone else, he said. This person was on a picnic at a lake with his family when crows surrounded them during their picnic. They must have given the crows sushi with mustard, because the stinging taste made them so angry that they attacked the people, so they finally had to give up on the picnic and return home. They could have fought with the crows, but there were more crows than people, so they readily lost to those arrogant ones.

It's too bad we didn't pack food crows hate, I said.

That way, after we'd given it to them, even if we'd been chased away by the crows, we would have had a good laugh on the way home, she said.

The crows flew somewhere else again. We sat side by side, watching the lake as evening began to fall. In that time, the birds stopped their singing. Maybe they were resting for a bit, or were now singing elsewhere. The lake and the surrounding area were tranquil, as if this were one of the times the lake itself liked best.

He suddenly got up and went to the edge of the lake, took off his hat, and held it for a moment as if he were about to throw it in. I thought that it would be all right if after he'd thrown the hat in and we left, the pinecone-trim hat would float about in the dark night lake. Maybe after returning home, I would fall asleep imagining this. Deep down, I was hoping that he would throw the hat into the lake, but stayed silent. For some reason I believed this would be left to luck. But as if his hair needed to be neat, he combed his hair down with his hands and after he had smoothed it down, put the hat back on. Then he turned to us and smiled as if something wonderful had happened.

Maybe the dog has paddled across the lake and crossed by now, he said.

Or maybe it's still crossing the lake, she said.

We looked at the lake together. The lake was now so dark you couldn't tell it apart from the mountains surrounding it, so even if a dog was paddling across right now, you wouldn't be able to see it. That was when he took the pinecone off the hat and threw it over the water. The cone made a small sound as it fell into the water and floated as an indistinct dot, and soon after a fish jumped out of the water and fell back, then afterwards all was quiet. We sat and watched until the pinecone became one with the deepening darkness.

Translated by Krys Lee and the author

A Way of Remembrance

Perhaps I'd wanted to tell a story about frogs.

I think I developed the desire since I'd been spending a lot of time under the mosquito net after being harassed by mosquitoes all summer long, especially as they became more and more vicious at the end of the summer. The white mosquito net was fixed to the ceiling above the bed, enveloping the bed in a rectangular shroud.

This summer seemed particularly long, but then again, every summer seemed especially long. Perhaps the same could be said about how this summer seemed particularly hot, with a greater number of mosquitoes than usual. It was true, however, that I killed more mosquitoes this summer than I had any other summer.

The mosquitoes that bit me mercilessly stirred up a vague hostility that wasn't directed specifically toward them, but, failing to find another target, I took it out on the mosquitoes. Thus I waged a war with mosquitoes, and much blood was shed, most of it mine, in a war that went on without victors or losers. It was the mosquitoes, however, that died in countless numbers. I killed over ten mosquitoes a day, and their bodies usually remained intact on the walls.

Toward evening when the mosquitoes became active, I would leap to my feet, even after lying as if dead under the mosquito net, and begin to frantically kill the mosquitoes, which continued to reappear as though they'd reproduced on the spot, no matter how many I killed. I reflected on the number of mosquitoes I caught each day, and how I would write down my criminal record. "August 30, slapped to death twelve mosquitoes with bare hands," I could say. I could add something more, such as the way I felt after killing the mosquitoes, not just list the dates and numbers—"Felt unreasonably good today, despite killing countless mosquitoes," for instance—but I didn't.

On days when I killed over ten mosquitoes and had nothing else to do in particular, I felt that killing mosquitoes was the most important task of the day, virtually my only task, and consequently I felt that mosquitoes were important creatures which were indispensable to me. At times I lacked motivation, then found the strength to start the day by killing mosquitoes. By evening, the mosquitoes would be desperate to get a bite out of me, and I would be desperate to kill them.

At times I enjoyed lying on my bed, surrounded by the mosquito net, and watching the mosquitoes that were after me, sitting close together on the other side of the net, longing to suck my blood, nearly mad with desire, but suffering tremendously because they could not. At such times, I could almost hear them screaming in pain.

The mosquitoes were starved for blood, and I understood how they felt. Or I thought I did. I also sought to understand their predicament of being able to live only on blood. Occasionally, I allowed the mosquitoes to suck my blood, though it wasn't out of sympathy. The bodies of the mosquitoes that had stuffed themselves were filled with red blood.

Initially I'd wanted to write a story about frogs, but I'm not sure why. I heard frogs croaking in the small stream created by the trickle that came flowing down the mountain near the house, but I have never seen the frogs.

Frogs, of course, were something I liked, and when I was little, I used to amuse myself by catching frogs. And there might have been a time in my childhood when I'd seen a frog I'd caught and marveled at its features, and stared at it for quite a long time, and someone asked me what I was doing as I stared intently at the frog, and I said that staring at a frog for a long time made me feel quite strange. What impressed me more when I was little, however, were the toads that crossed the yard when it rained, not the frogs. Toads seemed to resemble frogs, but gave a very different impression. I want to talk about the difference between the two creatures as well, but I'm not quite sure what it is that makes the two appear essentially different.

Throughout the summer, I met nearly no one and did nearly nothing besides write this story. I spent a lot of time in the mosquito net listening to the sound of frogs croaking in the distance, which is perhaps why I wanted to write a story about frogs. Listening to the frogs croaking, I thought it came from just the right distance, not too near and not too far. The sound wasn't loud enough to demand all my attention, nor was it so quiet that it made me strain my ears. I would be oblivious to the sound one moment, then spontaneously start listening to it, then become oblivious again.

Or perhaps I'd wanted to write a story about a man who prepared a grave in the garden for the woman he loved. Or perhaps in the beginning I wanted to write a story about frogs, and at the same time, write a story about a man who prepared a grave in the garden for the woman he loved, and about the dead woman.

The two stories must have begun separately in the beginning, but merged along the way and became one story as the story about frogs became a natural part of the story about the dead woman. As always, my thoughts must have gone in an unexpected direction, and I must have let them slip, to whatever extent.

I thought about the things that could possibly appear in the story, and thought that it wasn't essential that a frog appear in the story just because I wanted to write a story about frogs. And the frog in question could be something metaphorical, not a real frog, but perhaps a thought that plunges into another thought like a frog that plunges or slowly creeps into a puddle. So something like a porcupine, for instance, could take the place of a frog, by all means (I actually knew a funny story about porcupines. After a mother porcupine died after giving birth at a zoo, the cubs lived huddled together next to a broom, mistaking it for their mother and rubbing themselves against the rough bristles). But I thought it would be all right to have frogs actually appear in the story, so they did.

In this story there will be frogs as well as other animals and plants (I thought I should make sure to say something about cucumbers while saying something about frogs, but in the end, I failed to say anything about cucumbers).

And above all, I want to write something in which words and sentences are endlessly repeated, as in some boring piece of music, a piece of music that makes you feel infinitely lethargic as you listen to it. Perhaps this sentiment has something to do with the fact that I did nearly nothing this summer besides endlessly catch mosquitoes and write this.

The story about frogs, or a certain dead woman, might begin in the following way.

Since she died, I've been living in her house as her replacement—so to speak, since nearly everything in the house belonged to her. Indeed, I view my face in the mirror in the bathroom she used, comb my hair with the comb she used, and eat my meals using the spoons and bowls she used. I also wear the pajamas she wore, sleep in her bed in her room, and live in the house she lived in.

The curtains that block out the sunlight so that not a single ray may enter, and the easy chair in the living room, which squeaks as you move, even if you move only slightly, are all things she used.

Sometimes I lean against the easy chair, rocking myself slightly, and listen to the sound the old chair makes, a sound that seems to indicate the chair is suffering a bit but which makes me feel quite good as I listen, and reminds me of a certain tone of voice she used to have. Inanimate objects mediate between the people who used to possess them in a mysterious way. My attempt to recall certain memories of her while combing my hair with the comb she used may have been inspired by an unconscious effort on my part to believe that there was something for which the comb was acting as a mediator, and to find out what it was.

Seeing that I show a certain affection when I view or touch the things she used with a certain affection, or view or touch them in a way that shows a certain affection, perhaps I had a certain affection for her as well. And perhaps there was something that could be considered something of a romance, of which I may have something to say, and so perhaps I could talk about the peculiar feelings or some thoughts I had about the romance through a story.

While sitting in the easy chair several days ago I suddenly thought of peaches, which led me to think of her, which led me again to think of peaches, which in the end led me to think of the actual peaches in the fridge, and so I ran to the fridge. There were several peaches in the fridge, and they were all half rotten, as if they'd made a certain agreement with each other. They may have been peaches left over from the ones we'd bought, several of which we'd eaten.

I stared blankly at the half-rotten peaches. The undeniable fact that the half-rotten peaches would not become fresh again, and that the rotten parts would spread and in the end make the peaches completely rotten made me sadder than her death, and the fact or the sadness brought to my mind the fact that she, who was buried in the yard and had begun to rot, would one day become half-rotten like the peaches in the fridge, and in the end, completely rotten. But it seemed that the half-rotten peaches before my eyes made me a little sadder than the fact that she would one day become completely rotten.

One morning I woke up and found her lying dead next to me—I was dazed for a moment, then came to my senses and confirmed that she was really dead, and took in the reality of it for a moment, after which I immediately thought of the peaches in the fridge, which did not explain anything about how I was a little more saddened by the fact that the half-rotten peaches before my eyes would rot completely, than the fact that she would decay completely one day, which saddened me in a different way. In fact, I wasn't really disturbed even when I saw her body, which may have been because I had fallen into a state in which nothing disturbed me, after the prolonged state of grief I was in had reached its climax. I didn't know what to do with her dead body. But I did not want to take the usual procedures—although I didn't really know what the usual procedures were—taken when someone died. I could not, however, leave the body as it was somewhere inside the house. In the end I decided to bury the body, and thought I would do well to bury it somewhere close, like in the garden, if I were to bury it anyway. In the end I buried her body in a shallow hole in the garden the day after she died, not because I wanted to be able to check on the process of her decay, but I was able to as a result. I could check on the changes in the state of the body at any time by digging it up, and in fact, I could see her lying in the ground by digging only a little. I carried out the task myself without any help. I spent an entire day digging a hole in the ground with a breadth and depth that would hold her, then lay her down in the hole and covered it up again. I had to work from early in the morning until late at night, and it was unusual for me to work all day like that. A joint inflammation, common in old people, certainly added to the difficulty of my task. If I had hired workers, they would have talked among themselves, even if they couldn't talk about it to my face, about burying a body in the garden, and about not burying it deep enough.

In any case, digging a hole, despite being a difficult task, brought me a peculiar joy, and I dug several more holes besides the one in which she was to be buried. When I saw the large and small holes in the garden, the garden looked like an historical excavation site. I was a little sorry that I hadn't been able to arrange the holes in a certain pattern, but they seemed all right as they were. And it suddenly seemed that digging holes of unknown use could be adopted as a hobby as occasion demanded. Holes were certainly something worth looking at, if one wanted to lose track of time. And holes were something you could keep on digging in any number, by digging a similar or quite different one next to the one you have already dug, for instance. I buried a half-rotten peach in one of the holes.

And part of the reason why it took all day to bury her was that I wasn't able to decide on the position in which to place her body. My first thought was to lay her flat on her back. I thought that would be the most agreeable position both for her, and for the people who saw her. But after placing her in the hole, I recalled that she had usually slept on her side, so I lay her on her side, thinking it would be more agreeable to her. But as I looked at her for a while, lying on her side, it occurred to me that it could also be disagreeable, so I had her lie face down, but then it occurred to me that she, who of course could not be breathing, could suffocate, so in the end I lay her flat on her back again. Then, for some reason, I absently opened and closed her eyelids a few times, but I wasn't sure whether I did so because I wanted to see her eyes, which could not see anything, a few times for the last time, or because I wanted to show her something. As I did so, however, I became uncertain as to whether her eyes had been opened or closed to begin with, and the fact that I would never be able to ascertain the fact of the matter made me feel at a loss. I also considered burying her so that a part of her body, such as a hand or a foot, for instance, was exposed. A hand or a foot protruding above the ground could give the viewer a shock from time to time, but that seemed extreme, so I abandoned the idea.

I thought for a long time about something I could bury with her, and the thought actually persisted even after I'd buried her. It seemed that I wouldn't be able to put an end to the funeral before I'd put an end to the thought. One by one, I examined the things in the kitchen, the bathroom, the living room, and the bedroom. There were quite a number of things I could bury with her. I could bury not just everything in the house, but things that weren't in the house that could be obtained somewhere. Above all, I wanted to get a few empty wooden boxes and bury them beside her. It seemed that empty boxes were things that could be buried with anything, without regard to themselves. I thought she, too, would be pleased to be buried with empty boxes.

I also considered burying her with all the things mentioned above, but that surely would be an enormous task. It would require heavy equipment. In the end I concluded that I had no choice but to make a drastic cut in the list of things to bury if I were to complete the task myself. I began to rule things out one by one, thinking, for instance, that it would be great to bury a brass bowl, which could accumulate elegant green rust over time, but I didn't have a brass bowl. I also considered burying something alive, according to ancient burial customs, or burying myself, even, but the simple fact that I couldn't bury myself rendered the task impossible. So I thought of burying a live crow or cat with her, but I was unable to obtain either a live crow or cat.

We had never talked about what I would do with her when she died. She had once said in passing that I should do with her body as I saw fit, and that was all. If I were about to die first, I, too, would have said the same to her. Her request that I do with her body as I saw fit was a sort of dying wish, and I did as she wished. If our situations had been reversed, she, too, would have done as she saw fit. And it was not difficult to do as I saw fit. In fact, there was nothing I could do besides doing as I saw fit. Whatever I did with her body, even if I neglected it, I would be doing as I saw fit.

So what I buried with her was a wide-brimmed summer hat, which she had worn not only in the summer but in the spring and fall as well. We had never discussed the things I could bury with her, but I had a feeling that the hat was something she might have permitted. I could not, however, bury the wooden chair in the kitchen, which had come to mind when I first thought about the things I could bury with her. I would have to dig a deeper hole in order to bury it, but that would be too much for me. So I came to a compromise, burying not the whole chair but just the legs, and for some reason, though not on purpose, I buried it not upright but at a slight angle and, and it looked even better as a result. The chair was situated above her stomach, and I placed her body between the chair legs so that the chair would not weigh down on her stomach.

After successfully completing the entire task, I felt a certain joy—I noted with satisfaction that the grave looked superbly finished—and ran inside the house, took a half-rotten peach out of the fridge, cut off the rotten part, and went back outside and sat in the chair eating the peach under the darkening evening sky. I thought of her lying beneath the chair, thinking what a good thing it was that there was a peach, though half rotten, and I could fall into a reverie about her while eating the peach, which called to my mind an image of her sleeping on a normal day. On a normal day, however, she had been unable to fall into sound sleep, because she often had nightmares. When she was having a nightmare, I would watch her for a moment, indulging in the pleasure of watching someone having a nightmare while feeling greatly pained at the same time, then shake her awake. When she was having a nightmare she would blurt out, with a frightened look on her face, something that wasn't coherent but sounded like, How does the blue rose that fell asleep in the red room look in its sleep? and I would say, It looks comfortable, and you need to sleep some more.

For some reason there was some dough in the fridge, but I had no way of knowing what she had planned to make with it. The dough, which she had probably planned to turn into bread or pasta, looked all right, and I could have made bread or pasta with it, but instead I shaped it into a ball, thinking of her as I did so, and named it after her. Then I shaped it again into a series of smaller balls, collectively naming them "A Hopelessly Diminished Smile", then lumped them back together into the shape of a mushroom and named it "The Unnamable", then again shaped it into a cube and named it "The Dough", then put it back in the fridge. Afterwards I took out the dough again and tried kneading it into various shapes in order to give it the name "Sadness" one way or another, but no matter what I did, I could not creates a shape fit for the name "Sadness". Nevertheless, when I recalled the dough in the fridge she had kneaded for the last time, I felt a certain sadness.

But the fact that I could take out the dough again whenever I felt like it and knead it into a shape I wanted, name it what I wanted or not name it at all, then put it back in the fridge, comforted me somewhat. I felt that she had left me with a task, which was none other than to take out the dough and knead it into a shape I wanted, name it what I wanted or not name it at all, then put it back in the fridge.

When I dug up the earth and took a look at her face some time ago, she was lying in the ground as if on a bed. She did not look at peace, though. She looked like a ghost, naturally leading me to picture a ghost, but she did not look like the ghost I pictured, perhaps because she was too real. And perhaps because of the vermin feeding off her dead body. Maggots were crawling around on her face, some of them wriggling in and out, and in the holes there were eggs laid by the vermin as well.

The body, swarming with vermin, reeked of an overpowering stench, but somehow, the foul odor gave off an abstract feeling, like a painting of a flame depicted in pure red, or a painting of yellow sunflowers.

The face, already partly eaten, was distorted as though she was startled or having a nightmare. The face naturally brought to my mind the other half-rotten peaches in the fridge, and I recalled how she had always loved to put a peach close to her nose and breathe in the scent. She could not smell certain things very well, but could smell the peaches well, at least. When she put a peach close to her nose and breathed in the scent, she said that there was nothing like putting a peach close to your nose and breathing in the scent. She said there was something about the scent of a peach that calmed the heart.

After she died, I had nightmares from time to time. Once, I dreamt that the hair of the woman buried in the garden, grew and broke through the soil and covered the garden and the house. After I had the nightmare, though, I thought it could be a wonderful thing. In that case, I could lie down and sleep for a little while on the hair of the eternally sleeping woman, which covered the garden, or after waking from sleep, I could gaze in a dazed state at the falling or already fallen leaves or at the azalea tree whose flowers she liked to eat, or wait for a bird to pass while gazing, through the branches of a persimmon tree which bore no fruit but whose leaves were thick, at the sky, where light was breaking through the clouds that seemed to resemble a certain thought of mine, and in the meantime, lapse into another memory of her and think about things she had suddenly blurted out which I did not really understand but did not ask any further about, or things that for some time had been troubling me, or in other words, things that were still troubling me, and things that recently began to trouble me.

From time to time, I sit on the chair that's buried at a slight angle in the ground above her grave, and reminisce about her, at which moments I feel that there's no place like the chair to reminisce. The chair, it seems, helps me to accept certain facts as they are in some cases, and in other cases, makes everything more obscure.

Once, when I was sitting in the chair in the garden, it crossed my mind that it may be nice to place another chair at the front door, which was some distance away, and I did. The two chairs, which had been in the kitchen, were now outside the house. I would alternate between the two chairs facing each other, one buried and the other placed, and think about her and recall certain things she had begun to say but had been unable to finish, and sort them out by completing them in my own way or leaving them as they were, or forget about her and think some obscure thought—a somewhat groundless thought, for instance, that the reason why peculiar thoughts come to my mind when I'm quietly gazing at the chair is because in a way, the chair with its four legs resembles the form of an animal with four legs—about the chair across from me, or after thinking some obscure thought, think that I had done quite well to place the two chairs in such a way, while thinking about the woman who was lying beneath the chair I was looking at. I would also sit in another chair in the house by the living room window and gaze at the two chairs outside, thinking about something I had meant to tell her but had never been able to, or watch a crow walk past between the two chairs, or think about things that could no longer be undone as I went from looking at the azalea tree in a corner of the garden whose flowers were gone, to looking at the cat passing under the azalea tree, which was the backdrop of the photo on the living room wall, taken with her standing in front of the azalea tree in bloom, then back at the azalea tree in the garden whose flowers were gone.

What caught my eyes in the picture I had taken some time ago was a stray cat, which had happened to pass through in the moment I took the picture. She had in fact hung the picture on the wall because of the cat between her and the azalea tree. The cat was looking straight at the camera as though the focus was on it, and as though it had been startled by something. She was looking up at the sky, her eyes unfocused.

The cat usually limped as though it had a bad right hind leg, and she, too, had continued to have a limp in her right leg after hurting it, somehow. The limping cat was always alone, whenever we saw it. For some time, the cat always came as if it had some business to attend to—though this didn't seem likely—almost always at the same hour, usually toward evening. I didn't feel much affection for the cat, and I thought the reason lay with the cat itself. It's wrong to make an issue of a cat's appearance, but its appearance was such that I didn't feel much affection for it.. It would turn its head first after stealing a glance at us, and let out a short meow as though it wasn't enough just to turn its head, then soon be off somewhere else where some trifling adventure awaited it. She, however, showed some affection toward the limping cat, but it wasn't clear whether this was because it limped like her, or because it always went around alone, and though it was impossible for her to express her affection toward the quite wary cat, she would look at it with affection whenever it passed through.

While looking at the photo of the cat and the azalea tree in the living room, I recalled that she'd liked flowers very much. Of course I hadn't been unaware that she had liked flowers when she was alive, but I realized that she had liked flowers even more than I was aware of. In fact, she liked to have flowers in the house at all times, and even after she died, dried flowers remained in vases or on walls, hung upside down, and the flower garden in which the flowers had withered or were withering seemed like a grave for flowers.

She always made me buy flowers, and with the money she gave me, I would buy some fruit I liked along with the flowers, since she never gave me money to buy fruit. If she'd given me money for fruit, I may have bought only fruit and no flowers—I never used to be much taken by flowers, but after I started to put flowers picked from the garden on her grave, I began to think of flowers in a different way. And when she gave me money to buy fish, I would at times buy some fruit and flowers along with the fish. At such times, she would smile and say that I always did as I pleased.

Anyway, when I bought fruit along with flowers with the money she gave me to buy flowers, she would put the flowers in a vase, then briefly look at the peaches or apples I took out of the bag and look at me, and she would briefly look at the peaches or apples as if to scold them, although she didn't scold me. She didn't eat fruit often, though she did eat them occasionally, and she liked to watch me eat even when she wasn't eating.

There were many things we enjoyed doing together. We enjoyed spreading a mat in the garden that was thick with weeds, and lying down. There was grass planted in the garden, but the weeds had outgrown it. In order to keep the garden well tended, you had to do nothing but tend to the garden, or do nearly nothing except this one task. We would ramble on, looking at some object of interest while lying in a garden thick with weeds, such as laundry on a clothesline, or leaves which swayed quietly in the breeze, or pumpkin vines and leaves that rose up the persimmon tree and spread out at a fearsome rate just as quietly.

For instance, having dreamt of a horse wearing a horse mask standing outside the window, she would say that one of the saddest things about the age we were living in was that you could no longer see horses pass through the streets on a daily basis, and I would agree. I pictured myself running into a horse standing quietly, resting or sleeping, in a little alley one afternoon, which would surely make my heart flutter more than anything else could. Anyway, it seemed that a horse standing still would fit into any painting's composition.

In the garden, however, something was out of place. It looked like a little hole that was under the pomegranate tree in a corner, which did not bear decent fruit. Even she hadn't known what it was for. It had been there even before she moved here. Perhaps someone who had lived here before had begun to dig a hole, thinking he would make a pond, but gave up halfway through, thinking it wasn't a good idea, then left it unfinished. But considering that a hole is likely to get smaller, gradually filling up with dirt, rather than enlarge on its own, and that it's natural—holes almost certainly get smaller unless someone keeps them from getting smaller—it had probably started out as a larger hole.

In any case, there were frogs living in the small stream in the mountain near the house we lived in, and so we could hear frogs croaking at certain times of the year. The croaking of the frogs, which would begin as solos sung by a few frogs, would eventually turn into a chorus. Then after some time, the chorus would turn into solos again, before coming to an end. But even though we sat in the chairs in the garden on summer nights, listening to the croaking of the frogs that lived in a stream, we never saw the frogs.

When heavy rain fell, the hole in the garden filled with water and became a puddle, and we hoped that frogs would make their way there, but no frogs did. Nevertheless, gazing at the puddle in a corner of the garden after rain, we could hear croaking. So we thought that the reason why the frogs didn't go there was because they didn't know that there was a puddle, and therefore, we should let them know that there was a puddle in order to make them go there, but it seemed that it wasn't something we could force them to know by bringing them over ourselves, but something the frogs should find out for themselves.

Nevertheless, we were disappointed that the frogs in the stream never became aware that there was a puddle nearby, one in which they could spend some time, even though it wasn't suitable for them to live in. But we didn't know how to help the frogs find out for themselves; neither did we know what we would do if somehow, an army of frogs actually made their way there, with an adventurous frog wheedling or pushing the other frogs that were hanging back. And we didn't know if the frogs would like pomegranates, either. But we believed, without any foundation, that the frogs, too, would certainly like the closely packed pomegranate seeds that resembled frog eggs, which could be seen when an unripe pomegranate was cut in half. So we cut an unripe pomegranate in half to expose the seeds and placed it near the puddle in case the frogs came.

Perhaps we were curious as to how the frogs from the stream had discovered that there was a puddle in our garden in which they could dip themselves for a little while, and made an attempt to find out. Or we could have taken some frogs by their backs and sat them down on our knees, or lightly stepped down on their legs with our feet and taken a look, and found out something new about them which we hadn't known when we hadn't been near them. Or we could have fed the frogs with sedatives or fever relief medication and watched their reaction as the effect spread throughout their bodies. Or, listening to the sound of the frogs that had begun to croak noisily, we could have realized that we had been oblivious to the sound of cicadas singing just as noisily in the meantime.

For quite some time in the summer, we were harassed by cicadas as well as mosquitoes. It seemed that somehow, the cicadas, which in the past had sung high up in the trees where they couldn't be seen, had lost their shyness, and come down to the lower part of the trees, revealing themselves without hesitation. Nevertheless, while the loud singing of the cicadas seemed to penetrate our eardrums, we entertained the whimsical thought that it would be all right to bury our feet in the ground as though dipping them in a puddle, amid the fleeting feeling that a certain sensation had come to us unbeknownst and vanished only after giving us a nudge; perhaps we buried our feet in order to grasp that sensation even as we struggled to shake it off. Perhaps with our feet buried in the ground, new and different thoughts would come to us, or we'd think about certain things differently.

But with the frogs actually making their way to the puddle and croaking noisily without returning to the stream, regretting terribly that they had come, they ruthlessly disturbed the peaceful evening, which shouldn't have been disturbed by anything, and didn't quiet down even when night fell. Not wanting them to croak at night, too, and having become even less sure of what we wanted from the frogs, and unable to tell them to stay since they were here anyway, we might have tried to come up with a way to chase them away, feeling as if we were engaged in a great struggle against them, but such a thing did not take place.

Nevertheless, we would gaze at the puddle to which the frogs could make their way someday, and listen to the sound of frogs croaking that came from a stream nearby, and continue on with our rambling summer night's conversation, saying things like if we really intended to make the frogs come, we may need a pond whose water did not dry up even when it didn't rain, but that there was no guarantee that the frogs would come even if there were a pond, and that perhaps the hole, which was looking less and less like a pond, should be filled up, but that there was no need to go to the trouble of filling it up when it was filling up more and more by itself, and that the hole could fill itself up on its own, and what we enjoyed was the feeling of certain words in the rambling conversation being repeated and reiterated so that a certain rhythm was felt, and the feeling of listlessness created by that feeling.

In this way, our conversations were ones that not so much broke free from reality as deviated from reality, and our reality lay in a place that deviated from reality, but that reality was more real to us than any other reality, and we knew that what made reality insignificant was none other than insignificant realism.

Naturally, many of the conversations we usually had were about our childhoods. Recalling trivial anecdotes from the past, at which we finally arrived by pushing forward certain thoughts in our vague memories, brought us delight. When I told her how I used to catch catfish in the summer with a spear gun by diving underwater in a river, she, in a like manner, would tell me how she used to go skinny-dipping in the river on summer nights. On summer nights, everyone in her village went skinny-dipping in the river under the moon. The bathing areas for men and women were more or less divided, with the men a little upstream, and the woman a little downstream. She said that the baths under the moonlight on summer nights were one of the most lyrical memories she had, and I could certainly relate to what she said. She said that when bathing in the river on a summer night, she could see many falling stars.

When she talked about such things, I, too, related that when I was little, as winter turned into spring, I had escaped from the throes of death while sledding in a frozen river because the ice broke, and she, too, talked about how she had escaped the throes of death when she was little. After talking about such things, I felt that we had remained alive thus far because we had escaped from the throes of death when we were little. There was something, however, that I never told anyone, not even her, which is that my first experience with fear as a child occurred when something with horns, or something with things that resembled horns, charged toward me, and ever since then, I've been strongly drawn to horns or things that resemble horns, although I don't feel that first fear return whenever I see something with horns or something with things that resemble horns, and I told her this only after she died, thinking it was something appropriate to tell a dead person.

Anyway, I still don't remember what that something was, that something with horns or things that resembled horns that had charged toward me, but it was probably a goat, and perhaps it felt very big even though it wasn't very big because I was very small.

The stories from our childhoods were usually about the countryside. We were both from the countryside, and though we lived in a city, we lived on the outskirts of the city at the foot of quite a large mountain that was in the middle of the city, that felt like the countryside and yet was closer to everything in the city than it was to everything in the countryside, and we, in a way, always longed for the countryside, and assumed that we would return to the countryside someday, and always harbored a longing for the countryside, saying it would be nice to see a certain spot on the beach while traveling in the countryside and to build a house and live there, but in the end, we were unable to return to the countryside. Perhaps it was because we lived in a place that wasn't in the countryside but felt a bit like the countryside. But more importantly, we liked to talk about doing certain things that weren't possible for us to do, even when we knew that they weren't.

I spent much of the summer staring quietly at things in her house, thinking about her buried underground, and thinking this was a way to remember her. I felt that the blue fish she had kept in the little fishbowl by the living room window was her alter ego, and at times I would talk to myself while looking at it. And toward evening, I would sit in a chair in the garden in a state of despair, thinking about despair while eating something, like grapes for instance, which I kept eating because I kept reaching for them in spite of myself, and in such moments, it seemed as if my despair came from the grapes I kept eating in spite of myself. I would become lost in despairing thoughts while slowly, very slowly, chewing and swallowing the grapes, seeds and all (and at times, when I became lost in a certain thought while slowly, very slowly, chewing and swallowing the grapes, seeds and all, a great sense of despair came over me). In those moments, however, it occurred to me that this was not the way to remember someone who was dead, and make the person stay alive in my heart, but more of a way in which I made myself go on living even while steeped in memories.

Not long after she died, her fish died as well. Together, her fish and I had watched her burial. When she was being buried, I took the fishbowl containing the fish and put it down on the grass so that it could get a last glimpse of her. It didn't seem to matter whether or not it could comprehend the death of its owner.

All summer, I fed the fish the mosquitoes I'd killed, and it seemed to like eating mosquitoes more than anything else. The fish, which leaped out of the fishbowl and nearly died several times, would occasionally hit its head against the fishbowl, but I couldn't tell whether it did so for the same reason that people hit their heads against the wall. Or perhaps it had something to do with how the fish ate too many mosquitoes. After the fish died, the idea of my own death consumed me at times, but in the end, I came to the conclusion that it didn't really matter.

Now I'm sitting on the chair above the spot where she's buried. One of the armrests of the chair is shaking as if it's about to fall off soon, and I'm resting my arm on it as gently as possible so that it won't fall off. I look at the chair, and the garden surrounding it, and the wall surrounding the garden, and the mountains surrounding the area beyond the wall, and the sky surrounding the mountains, then slowly narrow my view, looking at last around the garden I'm sitting in, then look at the empty house. The house looks abandoned, and will probably remain abandoned forever, as long as I don't go inside. And when I look at the house thinking such thoughts, the house looks completely abandoned, and it seems that the fact will not change even if I do go inside. Perhaps I, too, could remain abandoned forever in the abandoned house. One day, two bodies, one in the house and the other buried in the garden, could start rotting slowly away. In the silent house, a picture hangs on a wall, and in the picture a woman is looking sideways at something invisible, be it a bird flying in the sky or simply the empty sky itself, and a cat is standing under the azalea tree behind her, looking straight ahead, seemingly startled, and the gaze of the cat could be directed at me and also at her, lying outside in the garden.

Translated by Jung Yewon

Together with a Chicken

It was early dawn when I was woken up by the sound of a cry. The cry continued in several long stretches, and only after listening to it for some time after I'd woken up did I realize that it was the crow of a chicken. I think at first I thought it was the sound of someone quietly tapping a triangle in the dark, and then the sound of someone's muffled scream, and then the sound of a bird crying—a long-necked bird like a red-crowned crane, for instance. It became clear, however, that it was the crow of a chicken.

Listening to the crow of the chicken, which continued for quite some time, I found it strange yet wonderful that I could hear a chicken crowing from my home in the city, but I thought there was nothing odd about hearing a chicken crow at dawn.

Slowly coming to myself, I lay still and listened to the crowing, thinking that although a chicken crowed several times a day, there was no crow like the crow at dawn, and that the chicken itself, knowing that better than anyone, probably put the most effort into the first crow at dawn after a night's sleep. Like someone who was facing great danger and thinking of a way to get out of it, I quickly thought a somewhat silly thought, that it could be very disappointing for a chicken to hear another chicken crow at dawn before it did, and that it could be very disheartening for a chicken to hear another chicken crow louder than it did. It seemed a little funny that I had a thought like that as soon as I woke up at dawn, which pleased me quite a bit. Still lying down, I looked out the window with a smile on my face.

I assumed from the crow that the chicken was a rooster—hens don't crow in such an arrogant way, parading themselves around—and the rooster was probably quite large. I opened the window so that I could better hear the sound that had awakened me. It was dark outside and a thick mist reached the windowsill, which made the window in my room look like the window of a ship, and it seemed that it would be appropriate if a whistle hooted somewhere in the mist. The moment I threw open the window all the way, however, the crow of the chicken, which had been continuing in long stretches, came to a complete stop, as if by magic. It was as if the act of opening the window had led to the closing of a door, shutting out the sound completely. I could no longer hear the chicken crowing after that, no matter how long I waited. I muttered, that chicken has failed to make a lonely man at early dawn focus all his attention, as though to receive a signal sent from an unknown being in a distant, unknown world,.

I looked at the thick mist, and for a moment was tempted to walk out the window of my second-story room, and fall lightly into the void. A moment later, I closed the window after filling my lungs with the dawn air, which had been full of the sound of crowing, but as I expected, I didn't hear the crowing. That was all. It was the same throughout the day, and the next day at dawn. Still, I couldn't stop myself from thinking all day about the crowing that had gently shaken up the dawn for a little while.

Maybe someone was rearing a chicken at home, or a friend had asked him to take care of it for a little while, and then taken it back because the neighbors complained too much when it crowed at dawn. Or maybe a friend who always brought his chicken around with him because he couldn't bear to be apart from it, had visited him for a night and then left. (The chicken could have nagged him to return home quickly.) Though the last scenario wasn't likely, it made me feel good just to imagine that there was a man who traveled around with his pet chicken. They could travel and look at the scenery unfolding outside the window together, or look at each other as though they had read each other's thoughts, or fall asleep together, or wake up and feel happy that they had each other by their side. Or maybe the chicken was still at the house, but for some reason didn't want to crow ever again after dawn that day.

In any case, I was quite sad that I couldn't hear the chicken crow again. To ease my sadness, I removed a snapshot of a chicken from my desk drawer and looked at it, and I had to spend some time during the day sitting on the windowsill for quite a while, looking at the birds flying over to the branches, but they only chirped, none of them crowing like a chicken. Only chickens cried as though to blow off steam. Other birds only spoke, and didn't shout like chickens. The cry of a chicken was like that of an elephant or wolf. It also had something in common with the sound of a bell.

Still, I considered the rooster's dawn crow a good omen for a trip I was planning at the time—it would be more precise to say, a trip I was vaguely imagining, or to say that I had allowed vague thoughts about a trip to gently stir in my mind. The trip I was thinking of, however, could be something like a vague story whose plot grew more and more vague, with the characters disappearing as well, or something that was close to something like that, not an actual trip.

The next night, a female friend of mine came to visit. She said that she no longer experienced the hallucinations she had been having for some time, and I said I was sorry. From time to time, she had heard a muffled sound, like a sound from the other side of the wall. I told her how I'd heard a chicken crow at dawn the day before. She said it had been quite some time since she'd heard a chicken crow at dawn, and I said that a chicken that crowed at the top of its voice like that may have crowed thinking that no other chicken could do it better, and that and the task could not be entrusted to any other.

She said that someone she knew had left a mynah in her care. The mynah was quite arrogant in a way, and tended to look down on people. She said that the bird, which was also clever, would throw back the latch on the birdcage and go out into the living room and walk around for a bit, then quietly go back into the cage as if being out of the cage didn't change anything, and as if it hadn't been aware that it had left its cage, and as if that was why it had to quickly go back inside the cage, and then close the door by throwing back the latch again, and sit on the perch as if nothing had happened and quietly look at people with scorn, as if that was all there was for it to do as a mynah. I said that I wanted to see the mynah that looked at people with scorn, and that I hoped it never lost or abandoned that attitude. She said that the mynah, which had already grown into the attitude, would not change.

We went on talking about birds, and became curious as to why chickens and other birds bobbed their heads incessantly as they walked. We weren't sure, but we concluded that maybe they did so in order not to forget the fact that they were birds, or to maintain their balance, which could easily be lost as they walked on their two legs.

As I was in a good mood, I asked her to tell me about an experience she'd had while traveling in China. I had heard the story several times before, but it put me in a good mood whenever I heard it, so I always asked her to tell it again. We began to drink beer together, and she began the story.

She once went on a trip to China with a friend, and had an unforgettable experience. They were traveling on the Yangtze River on a ship, when three robbers disguised as passengers tried to rob the passengers, but were found out and jumped into the river like frogs and swam away. She said that they looked quite fabulous as they swam away casually like cormorants, and she later learned that they belonged to a family of robbers that went back generations, maybe even to the era of the Chinese classic, *Water Margin*, and had been carrying on their family business ever since, possessing great pride in what they did.

The story was fabulous enough, but the story I wanted to hear at the time was one about chickens, not robbers. I wanted to hear the story about chickens more than anything.

She and her friend arrived at a little village in a remote area of China. They saw a rooster standing at the entrance to the village as if it had been waiting for them. It looked quite dignified, holy even, and before long, they readily followed the rooster—guided by the rooster, to use my friend's words—to a house, and a woman greeted the visitors her rooster had brought. They, however, were so tired and hungry that they wanted to eat even the dignified rooster, and they let the woman know. The woman said without hesitation that she would prepare the chicken in return for some money. She caught the chicken and began to prepare it, and in the process tried to use spices they didn't like, so they had to stay by the furnace to keep her from adding them, but she used the spices when they weren't paying attention and so they couldn't eat it. In the end, the dignified rooster wrapped up its life by filling up the stomachs of the woman and her family.

Afterwards, I saw a picture of the chicken my friend had tried to eat but couldn't, which didn't look at all holy as she'd said, or dignified, either, but it did seem to be keeping up certain appearances, appearances that could perhaps be kept up only by all the chickens in the world. Still, when I saw the picture of the dead chicken, I had an odd feeling, as if I were looking at the picture of a distant relative I never knew, who had died long ago.

She felt terrible that she had made the dignified chicken die just to appease her hunger, but afterwards, she saw another rooster along with several hens in the woman's backyard, a rooster that looked just like the one that had died, as though it had been reincarnated. She said, however, that her guilt did not go away.

The picture of the rooster, which was the picture I had taken out of my desk drawer and looked at on the day I heard the chicken crow at dawn, was not the only thing she showed me at the time. She took pictures of many chickens she encountered while traveling in China, and chickens were the only things she took pictures of on that trip. No, to be precise, some of her photos of chickens did feature humans or other animals. The focus, however, was always on the chickens, making them the central figure of the pictures. She said that she didn't know why she'd decided to take pictures of so many chickens, but that once she began to take pictures of them, she didn't want to take pictures of anything else. I looked at the different chickens in a variety of poses, seemingly lost in different thoughts, and they were more impressive than any other travel record. She said she could recall vivid memories of her trip while looking at the chickens in the pictures. She also said that she'd had a wonderful trip because of the chickens, and because she took pictures only of them. In the same way, she could take pictures of only cows if she went to India, and of camels and donkeys if she went to Central Asia. A dignified or contemptible looking chicken, walking around or standing quietly in the garden or the ruins of a grand temple, could actually be much more impressive than the temple itself.

While drinking, we continued to talk about raising chickens, and because we didn't actually intend to raise chickens, we could speak more freely for instance, about how many chickens it would be good to raise—the number of chickens we could raise could theoretically start from one and increase infinitely, but we could always maintain a certain number of chickens, a hundred and forty-two, for instance—and whether we would raise just chickens—we could raise along with the chickens animals that could blend in naturally with them, such as ducks and geese, or ones that had a hard time tolerating each other, such as dogs and cats. We talked about how it was animals and not humans that usually made us smile, but we couldn't be sure what the reason was exactly.

I fell asleep for a little while after she left late that night, and I had a dream about chickens.

In the dream, which was somewhat impressive, my friend and I opened the door to a house we had somehow entered, and walked into a room to find a vast desert stretching before us. There was majesty to the desert that stretched out endlessly, even though the desert was in a little room.

In a moment, however, a gigantic sandstorm began to rage in the tranquil desert. Struggling through the sandstorm for a while, I thought that the storm, which was slowing us down was somehow losing its force, after which the storm subsided, and at last, the tranquil desert reappeared. Spread out before us was a majestic and marvelous view, created by the simplest, and in a way, the smallest unit of particles—sand. The view, made more impressive by the most extreme contrast between light and shadow due to the location of the sun, evoked ancient times, as well as the end of the world. The tranquil desert looked like a scene in a photograph, and by processing its lines and surfaces, I could fold the desert in half like a photograph and put it in my pocket. In this way, I put several deserts in my pocket. And I realized that the sky there, too, had been painted. The sky was blue paint painted on a broad canvas that went on infinitely, and the sun was red paint painted at the center of the blue. The sky, however, was too big to fold into a few layers.

After walking for some time, we came across a small oasis, and Arabian music floated in from somewhere. A record was playing on the turntable of an old phonograph under a palm tree, and that was where the song was coming from. I thought that

Arabian music was pleasant to listen to at any time, but that it was perfect music to listen to in the middle of a desert. Anyway, there was something standing languidly in the languid scene—it was a rooster with a vivid red comb, standing with one foot raised and gently folded, and looking quite brawny. It looked like a figure created by the slow and soothing Arabian music as if through a spell, and it seemed that anything could be created by such Arabian music as if by magic. I thought that the rooster would step up onto the record that was playing at any minute, but for some reason, it didn't.

We stared at the rooster without moving as if we'd been bewitched by the rooster, which was staring fixedly at us. I felt as if I would fall into a strange kind of hypnosis just by staring back at the rooster, and in fact, I did almost fall into a state of hypnosis once, after staring too intently at a chicken. At any rate, you could fall into hypnosis by staring intently at anything long enough, and that could be the principle behind hypnosis.

In the shadow of the oasis in the middle of the desert where the sun was beating down mercilessly, the rooster looked like a riddle, with the brazen attitude of a sphinx. And it seemed that the rooster would pose a curious riddle to us, but it didn't say anything. It seemed that if the rooster opened its mouth, it would make a sound that would sound quite strange, either for a chicken or that of anything else, but it didn't make a sound. It seemed to me that under the circumstances—I couldn't guess what kind of circumstances they were—it was trying to show that it would be better for it to keep its mouth closed. The rooster thus stood still, bewitching those who were looking at it, and as if bewitched itself, it looked quite enchanting, as though absorbed in itself.

At the same time, we were reminded of a rooster that belonged to a musician in Marrakesh, an old city in Morocco, which had been on a TV show we happened to watch together some time before, and talked about it. The musician's rooster would let out a long cry from time to time, as though accompanying its master's guitar playing while it stood precariously and continued to rock to and fro on the head of the guitar on its master's shoulder, which it had been trained to do. The rooster, however, wasn't very bright and cried when it wanted to, not when it was supposed to, so its master had to force it to cry from time to time by rapping it lightly on the head, but at times, it wouldn't cry no matter what. People liked watching the master playing the guitar while his rooster sometimes cried out, and gave the master a bit of money. I couldn't tell how the chicken felt as it stood precariously on the guitar, singing as it continued to rock—it seemed very nervous— but the master looked very happy to put on little performances with his rooster.

In any case, my friend, probably reminded all of a sudden by the rooster next to the oasis, said that she was going to go see the musician's rooster in Marrakesh, as if Marrakesh were a place she could reach just by climbing over a hill or something. I thought it would be nice to go to Marrakesh to see the rooster and its master sing together in the square. Marrakesh was far away, but seeing them would be reason enough to go there.

I saw her walk toward the sand dune before us and climb over it. The dune was very big, and her body looked very small in comparison. Somehow, it really seemed that Marrakesh would be on the other side of the hill, and that there would be a rooster singing on a guitar on the square there. With her back toward me, she waved at me, and I waved back at her. At last, she climbed over the hill, and could no longer be seen. I smiled, picturing her invisible lips smiling. I was sad that we had parted ways because of a rooster, but soothed my sadness by thinking something else about the rooster. When I turned my eyes back to where the rooster had been, however, the rooster of the oasis had disappeared. It seemed as if it had vanished along with the incantatory, lethargic Arabian music that had come to a stop in the meantime.

And after I had that dream, I was somewhat surprised and pleased at the same time that the more I thought about chickens, the more there was to think about. It was very pleasant to have continuing thoughts about something, especially about chickens. And they had to be thoughts by thoughts, and for thoughts.

One of the things I liked to do as a child was to sit blankly on the floor watching the chickens roaming around the yard. I never got tired of watching chickens. They didn't seem that interesting at first glance, but the longer I watched them, the more interesting they grew. And one of my favorite moments was when I was lying in my room at midday in hot summer, watching through the open door the chickens quietly roaming in the yard, or a rooster suddenly attacking a hen for some reason, getting up on its back and pecking it on the head. The chickens would peck at the feed or sit still, doing their thing, but then suddenly chase other chickens away ruthlessly, as if they couldn't stand the fact that other chickens were there, or that the other chickens were their associates. Anyway, as chickens were the only things moving in the yard, I would always grow drowsy after watching them for a while. Seemingly dazed from the midday heat, the chickens made me, unable to take my eyes off them, dazed as well.

Sometimes, I would watch the chickens that were walking around the yard while giving myself up to drowsiness, and hear my mother and father talk loudly to each other somewhere unseen, and what they said sounded bizarre at times. Once, I heard my mother talk about a squirrel and sand and a letter, and my father talk about a barber shop and a post office and a butcher shop, and their words got mixed up from time to time and sounded like, I'd like a squirrel to get a haircut at the barber shop and buy some cow intestines with sand in them at the post office and take them to the butcher shop (I think I'm always drawn to my childhood memories because of such strange yet fascinating scenes that could be pictured only during my childhood.). At such times, I would think of the mailman who rarely came to our house, and fall asleep, thinking that I didn't need any news that would make me happy, but that it would be nice if he brought me an orphaned squirrel every time he came. He had an old pouch that looked as if it could carry anything and everything, including several orphaned squirrels—and I thought that I was ready to set out with a squirrel, and should tell him that the next time I saw him, but I never made such a request.

I also wondered, after dozing off and waking up from a dream, what chickens dreamt about. If they dreamt at all, they must dream about the people they lived with. They would surely not dream about whales or tigers or turtles, which they had never seen. But it was possible that they dreamt about cats, which often tormented them. Dreams about cats could be nightmares for the chickens, and after having such dreams, the chickens could lament the fact that they couldn't live in a world without cats, or at least in a world that was separate from the one in which cats lived, even though they wanted to, and peck at other chickens with their beaks for no good reason.

Afterwards, I remembered how even when my grandmother died, I just stared at the chickens in the yard amid the sound of people crying. The chickens, quietly roaming the yard, helped me to feel the sorrow I should feel, and at the same time, endure the sorrow. My grandmother had once bought me a bicycle with the money she had gotten from selling the chickens she had raised.

Now awake, I stayed in bed, but I didn't have an easy time falling back asleep. Somehow, I felt that I'd be able to fall asleep if I heard the sound of a chicken crow at that moment, but no such sound came. I let out a very quiet yelp that could make even a flower flinch, if there had been a flower by my side, but I stopped.

I had some beer again after tossing and turning for quite some time, but it was no use. Another sleepless night had arrived. At moments like that, even a tangled string on the floor could look quite tragic, but I didn't feel anything. I didn't feel either good or bad. I felt indifferent. If I left the earth and went to some place like Saturn, maybe I would feel a little different. I couldn't really tell what I was thinking, either. It was as if I were fumbling with a Braille book I couldn't read with the tip of a finger. Nevertheless, it seemed that my thoughts vaguely touched upon something.

I took out about five sleeping pills, put them on a plate, and swallowed them one by one with some beer. The pills, which came in different colors—white, yellow, and pink—had similar effects. From time to time when I couldn't sleep, I put some sleeping pills on a plate and slowly swallowed them with some beer, as if they were snacks.

Once, I took a few sleeping pills so that I could get some sleep, but I didn't fall asleep, so I kept taking them to see what changes would come over my body and mind depending on the amount of sleeping pills I took, and found it interesting to feel myself gradually slipping out of consciousness, and ended up taking nearly fifty pills. What I had taken, however, was only half the lethal dose. In any case, I hadn't taken the sleeping pills to end my life.

After taking about ten sleeping pills with beer, I felt a little befuddled, though I couldn't tell whether it was because of the beer or the pills, and the blanket, crumpled up on the bed, began to resemble the Tien Shan Mountains or the Kunlun Mountains, and it seemed that in the darkness beyond them under the bed, there would be a desert like the Taklamakan Desert, and that fish and birds would be flying or swimming together in a place that could either be a lake in the desert or the sky, and that a fisherman at a lake there would fish out with a fishing net a horse that was white all over. I pictured flamingoes flying under the bed, and it seemed that where I was lying could be anywhere in the world. I could be lying on the grass on a grassy plain, or on a rock in the woods, or in the middle of the desert. I thought of some names of deserts, such as Taklamakan, Gobi, Namib, Sahara, Mojave, Kalahari, and Negev, and the names seemed to quietly call me to some place very far away.

I was floundering in a semiconscious state. I thought that if I were lying on the grass, it would only be natural for me to picture a snake crawling on the grass where I was lying, and that there should be a pillow or a die or a kettle, as well as the countless shards of a shattered mirror. They may not be necessary for the snake, but at any rate, the snake, too, would prefer that countless pieces of shattered mirror, quietly reflecting the sunlight, be with a pillow or a die or a kettle on the grass, than something that made a sound that could startle it, which was poisonous. And it would be nice as well if on the grass there was a little ball, such as a baseball, that had nothing to do with the snake and had come flying from somewhere. The snake could pass through the grass at leisure or coil itself up or shed its skin, giving no heed to the things that had nothing to do with it. And if I were lying in the woods, I could think about how one of the greatest things about the woods is that you can lose your way there, and that the woods always held the possibility of you losing your way there, and that a wrong path could turn out to be a wonderful path. And I thought that if I were lying in a desert, it would be nice if there were countless camels' feet, cut around the ankles, stuck upside down around me. I once heard that that's the way Mongolian nomads hold funerals when their camels die.

Suddenly, I thought of the chair in the mirror that had appeared in a dream I had. There was a chair reflected on a mirror, and I tried to sit on the chair in front of the mirror, but there was no chair on which I could sit. The chair existed only in the mirror. Curiously, the grassy plain and the woods and the desert that had come to my mind also seemed to be something without substance, just like the chair.

I went on taking the sleeping pills one by one, as if I were savoring their taste, and I grew more and more befuddled, and my mind was dizzy with thoughts about the play of thoughts. Something inside me seemed to move, but I didn't. I felt sadness for a very brief moment, but after letting go of the feeling as though letting go of a fish I'd caught with my hands, I didn't feel much of anything. Nevertheless, it seemed that if I moved at all, something long and thin inside me, perhaps something that took up a great part of me, would come flowing out like strands of noodles. The more it seemed that something inside me was being stirred up, the more still I remained. And after some thought, I told myself that now wasn't the time to meet a ghost or to lie still in bed, becoming a ghost myself or wearing a coat that made me resemble a ghost. Then it seemed that everything grew quiet.

I thought of the names of the tranquilizers I'd taken, such as Stilnox, Xanax, Ativan, and Halcyon, and the names felt as awful as their effects or side effects. The names of deserts, such as Taklamakan, Gobi, Namib, Sahara, Mojave, Kalahari, and Negev, would be much more appropriate as names of sleeping pills or sleep inducers. It would be fabulous to fall asleep after taking sleeping pills named Taklamakan, Gobi, Namib, Sahara, Mojave, Kalahari, and Negev. Even when I tossed and turned, unable to fall asleep even after taking the pills, I would be able to imagine that I was wandering around deserts with such names. And the thought would make my sleeplessness a little less painful.

Anyway, as I sat still, leaning against the bed, opening and closing my eyes repeatedly, unfamiliar scenes slowly unfolded before me. They had to do with dreams, and reveries in the form of dreams, and a perspective outside of reality, through which reality is perceived in a strange way. Various scenes were spread out before me, and there appeared rooms in which languages roamed about capriciously, and thoughts rushed in and out like waves, and I passed slowly through the rooms, which were full of picturesque scenes from an engraving made up of only blue and white.

When I went into what looked like someone's living room, a nature scene unfolded. There was a huge river in the middle of the vast landscape. Suddenly I recalled a childhood memory. Whenever I saw a river, I used to picture a frozen lake, or more often, picture myself skating endlessly as it grew dark on a frozen lake which stretched out as far as the eye could see. There seemed to be fish nearly made up of ice in the cold water beneath the thick ice, at rest as though frozen. Curiously, I pictured a frozen lake whenever I saw a lake, perhaps because I imagined that at the end of it, there was a world you could reach only by endlessly skating away on the frozen river.

It wasn't winter, however, and the river wasn't frozen. The river was flowing slowly, and on the slowly flowing river there was something that was drifting down just as slowly. It was a large tree, pulled up by the roots, and it seemed to be drifting down comfortably. With my eyes fixed on the tree, I walked for a little while at the same speed at which it was drifting down. I was walking side by side with a tree, and felt happy because it was the first time I felt that I was walking side by side with a tree since I'd had a dream about walking side by side with a little tree, holding its hand. (The tree, of course, was reaching out its branch like a hand.)

It seemed that you could make possible a series of impossible things just by chanting a spell in your mind or snapping your fingers lightly. It seemed, for instance, that it wouldn't be such a big deal to run into squirrels sitting with their legs crossed, or having a serious discussion with their arms crossed, and that it would be nothing for a bird, sitting on a tree, to fly up into the sky, uprooting a tree and taking it along with it.

I continued to pass by rooms in a house, and imagined traveling with a chicken the whole time. Considering that when people traveled in the past, countless animals such as horses and camels served as their companions, comforting them, and enriching the journey in a way that wouldn't have been possible without them, imagining a journey with a chicken wasn't anything remarkable.

I imagined that any minute, a chicken might appear and we might experience a brief moment together, or be on our way together. Perhaps I would come across a rooster standing on someone's grave, looking like a sculpture as if it has forgotten that it's a chicken, or I might walk on the sandy beach with it. Then I could say to the chicken walking by my side, There's an island beyond the clouds in the sky touching the sea, and you can see it from here when the weather is fine, but the weather isn't very nice right now, so it's all right if we can't see the island. But somehow, I felt as if a chicken, which hadn't revealed itself, were already guiding my way, and I pictured a chicken that was with me.

I kept on walking. I gradually came to understand the joy of walking, and realized that I only had to let my body understand the joy. No, I only had to let my body pass on the joy it already knew to my mind. I was headed to a realm of ideas, however, rather than a specific place, and I was feeling the joy of wandering in the midst of ideas with my body and mind.

And when a hill unfolded beneath my feet, I ran into a flock of sheep. One of the sheep came toward me, and I, too, went toward the sheep. We looked at each other for a moment, as if waiting for the other to say something first, and took part in a silent conversation for a moment. I realized once again through the conversation with the sheep, as well as my own monologue, that there's an element of monologue in every conversation.

When I opened another door and entered, a forest opened up, and when I continued for a little while to follow the path leading into the forest, I saw a brook running, and heard the booming sound of water beyond the brook, and then in a moment, a waterfall appeared before me. Huge fish were swimming against the strong current in the quite large waterfall that exuded a certain energy and spouted a strong current of water, and I watched the fish going up the waterfall with envy.

When I was little, too, I used to watch the fish in the river for long stretches of time with envy and admiration, and it seemed that in those moments, I could live with a sad face at all times, if for the fish that looked sad for some reason, that lived in a place where I couldn't live—once, when I was little, I became curious as to how long the fish that lived in a world that was different from mine could stay out of water, and wanting to find out, I caught a fish and placed it on land, and to make it fair, I myself went into the water and stayed there without breathing, and I think we came out even.

And once, I became fixated on the question of why fish had that fishy smell, and continued to think about it on my own. Was it to protect themselves through the smell? There must be predators that are repelled by the smell. But the predators, also fish, would probably not keep themselves from eating other fish because of their smell, even if they're repelled by it. Plus, the predators themselves could have a fishy smell. Anyway, I wonder how fish feel about each other's smell. Are they drawn to it, or repelled by it? I think they're probably drawn to it, since it's hard to imagine so many fish living in water being repelled by each other's smell. And maybe it's impossible to detect the smell in the water.

Anyhow, such thoughts were appropriate while looking at fish, and perhaps they were one of the first serious inquiries I'd had about something in nature.

Most of the fish failed to go all the way up the waterfall in one attempt. They all succeeded, however, after some trial and error. But it seemed that even though they didn't require that much practice—perhaps they had trained themselves sufficiently while swimming toward the waterfall, that going up such a waterfall had become no big deal—they enjoyed going up the waterfall for the sake of it, and that's why they jumped up to the top of the waterfall, falling back down, repeating the act several times, then heading upstream. It seemed that the fish loved jumping up over the strong current, then falling back down.

I could see why. And when I saw the fish going up the waterfall, looking so splendid, it seemed that there was nothing in the world as splendid as going up a waterfall. It wasn't something that just anyone could do. Only some fish, that had the amazing capacity to go up waterfalls, could enjoy such a blessing.

And somehow it seemed that the waterfall would be much less interesting if it weren't for the fish going up the waterfall. The fish, it seemed, made the waterfall even more wonderful, and even more vibrant. And as I quietly watched the fish going up the waterfall, I was even deluded into thinking that it was the fish that were making the water cascade down. It seemed that the phenomenon occurred under the same principle in which caged squirrels spin their wheels. I said that to the invisible chicken next to me, which agreed.

Anyhow, I saw something circling around in the whirlpool created by the waterfall, and upon closer look, I found that it was an unpeeled onion. The onion continued to sink and rise, trapped in the whirlpool and unable to drift down any further as if someone had thrown it there for an experiment, and now, as I quietly watched the onion, I felt as if the onion were making the fish jump up the waterfall. The strong current of falling water and the violently jumping fish and the thrashing onion seemed to be moving through a physical, organic force, which created an optical illusion effect.

I took a small path next to the waterfall and went up toward the upper part of the waterfall. There were many fish there that had already come up the waterfall, swimming toward their destination upstream. I walked for a little while along the brook, moving together with the fish that were swimming toward their destination.

As I went upwards, there appeared other waterfalls of various sizes and shapes. I gave each waterfall a fitting name, and it seemed that waterfalls would continue to appear as long as I kept giving them names. At the same time, it seemed that I would be able to turn each waterfall into a shape I wanted. I could, for instance, make a waterfall that looked like a comet with a long tail. And it seemed that the waterfalls, while they were actual waterfalls, were at the same time waterfalls in my mind.

When I opened another door and entered, I saw enormous trees I'd never seen before, bent strangely like a person with distorted limbs, with a huge knot that looked like an eye of a giant on the trunk. The trees looked like lunatics, and it seemed that they would suddenly go berserk, or at least block my way. I walked among the trees, quite nervous that I may have to take part in a strange fight against the insane trees. The trees, however, stood still, looking ominous rather than flaunting a splendor fit for their great size. Nevertheless, it seemed that the trees were twisting their limbs almost imperceptibly as I passed by among them.

Incidentally, there was something on the branches. At first I thought they were birds, a kind I'd never seen before. But sitting on the branches were children, all naked. The children didn't turn their heads away or anything, even when they saw me. No, they didn't seem to see me. Their eyes were all closed, and they were gently rocking as if they were dreaming. I felt an urge to wake one of them, but stopped myself. Above all, I felt that the children shouldn't be disturbed, whatever they were doing.

Children should be tying up birds they catch onto tree branches, or spinning tops, or rolling down a hill, or running across a field against the wind with their mouths and arms wide open, at the speed of a bird soaring high up into the sky and in a like manner, or lying down in a barley field like barley stalks bending in the wind, or knocking down an ant tunnel and raising up another in a similar shape, but they're not, what's wrong with them, I muttered.

I could see, however, why the children were in such a state. I recalled a memory from my childhood which involved throwing live rats, which I'd caught with other kids, into the river. I couldn't remember, though, why I'd done such a thing at the time, or whether the rats had swum safely out of the river in the end, or whether they'd drowned. We were playing a game, catching rats and throwing them into the river, which was a suitable game for children to play. The children on the trees were clearly playing a game of their own. And it seemed that I, too, was engrossed in a game of my own.

I thought that the children would wake up suddenly and ask strange questions, and if they did, I would be able to give them answers that sounded strange to my own ears. Or they might wake up slowly and turn into chickens or some other birds. But they grew faint, as shadows do, and in the end they vanished completely.

At that moment, there seemed to come from somewhere the sound of a chicken crowing, which had awakened me the day before at dawn, and which I'd listened to for a while even after I woke up. I began to walk in the direction of the sound. Somehow, I seemed to be returning to the oasis in the desert where a chicken had appeared and then disappeared amid the sound of Arabian music. But I found myself marching in place. I felt my eyelids droop under the weight of sleep, and felt my body grow fainter and fainter, thinking I was learning how to travel together with a chicken.

Translated by Jung Yewon

At the Amusement Park

I went to the beach. No, I went toward the beach. But it wasn't the beach I arrived at. There was no beach to be seen, only land stretching far out toward the sea, and new buildings.

But the amusement park I'd once been to was still there. It was closed, however. I went to the ticket office at the entrance. A notice on the ticket office window announced that the amusement park had closed down and was off limits. It was written in language that was easy to understand, but I stared at it for a long time as if I couldn't believe what it said. It seemed that the amusement park hadn't been closed for a long time.

I stood there for a moment, not knowing what to do, and a little later, I began to knock on the window of the empty ticket office for some reason. Naturally, no one answered. Still, I knocked halfheartedly on the window several times. At that moment, someone said something to me. I turned my head. An old man, sitting on a bicycle, continued to speak while looking at me.

But I couldn't grasp what he was saying. I couldn't tell if he was speaking in a manner that was difficult to understand or if I just couldn't grasp what he was saying. But it wasn't as if I could make him speak more comprehensibly. Outrageously enough, he seemed to be scolding me.

Summer had passed but it was still hot, and I was irritated, and would have punched him if he were close enough. But he didn't ride his bicycle toward me, or get off his bicycle and drag it along with him, or leave the bicycle behind. But I couldn't go up to him. I thought I couldn't go to him if he didn't come to me, and I clung desperately to the thought.

The old man had stopped speaking. Still, I had something to say to him—no, I didn't have anything to say to him, but I thought of something to say. As I was about to reply, however, the old man took off, pedaling away. I stared quietly at the old man who was leaving on his bicycle. Taking off like that is a terrible way to treat someone, I thought. I felt an urge to run after the old man, knock him down and snatch his bicycle away. But the old man was cruising down a ramp now, and the bicycle was speeding along even though he wasn't pedaling. He seemed to be running away from me. Even if that wasn't what he'd wanted, that's what happened. And as a result, I returned to the amusement park entrance in a very bad mood.

Next to the entrance was a little gate for pedestrians. I gave the gate a push, not with all the strength I had, but the gate still didn't budge, as if it had made up its mind not to budge with all the strength it had. The gate was letting me know that I couldn't enter. I could climb over the gate, but that wouldn't be like me.

I went around the ticket office to another side of the amusement park. I thought there might be a hole somewhere in the barbed-wire fence beyond some brambles. And just as I'd thought, there was a hole. I was able to make my way in through the opening—it was one of those so-called dog holes, but it seemed to have been made by people coming and going, not dogs—trying to keep the thorns from pricking me and failing. Entering the amusement park turned out to be easier than expected, so much so that it seemed pointless.

The amusement park was abandoned. But it didn't look ridiculous or absurd. In fact, it didn't look any different from the amusement park I had known. The amusement park was slowly falling into ruin, and had been somewhat shabby the last time

I'd visited, too. The facilities were plain, and so were the visitors. People who worked at the nearby factory and who weren't very well-groomed often came to visit. Occasionally, there were groups of people who were wheelchair-bound or hearing-impaired, and the trip must have been a rare treat, because they loved it there. In addition, Chinatown was nearby, so a lot of Chinese people came to visit as well. They always talked a lot and created a big scene. They never spoke quietly. And it wasn't difficult to spot poorly dressed workers from far-off countries, either. The amusement park, in fact, was so run down even in its heyday that it looked like it belonged in a small town in Central Asia. The workers didn't talk much, and when they did, they spoke quietly.

No one was there in the amusement park. No dogs or cats, often found in abandoned places, could be seen either, no matter how hard I looked. They were so hard to spot that I mumbled, Where are all the dogs and cats? But none showed up as in response to my query.

The amusement park was a compound consisting of a boating area, a forest lodge, and rides. A lake stood in the middle of the park that was too small for a lake and too big for a pond. But it would be more acceptable to call it a lake than a pond.

I looked at the lake for a moment. I had ridden a boat on it once. I recalled who I had ridden the boat with, and frowned. My companions were a pregnant woman and her young son. The baby in her womb was not mine. Her son, too, was another man's child. Her son was fond of me. I didn't know why. He was cute, but very naughty. He couldn't stay still for even a moment. He loved to play tricks on me, and even got me into trouble several times. She didn't say a word about her son's behavior.

She had approached me on the street and said hello as I was walking. She said she knew me. I didn't remember her. She tried to refresh my memory, but to no avail. Nevertheless, we went to the amusement park together, and we got on the boat. And that was all. No, that was not all. I don't want to say anything more about her for the time being. No, I never will.

The restaurants and souvenir shops in the amusement park were empty but still had their signs on them. Flowerbeds stood before them, and the flowers, which had been in bloom that season, were withering away. I couldn't tell if the plants were perennials and the time had come for them to wither away, or if they were dying for another reason. I wondered if I should uproot a few, but restrained myself.

There was a little zoo off to the side, but now only the cages remained. Upon closer examination, I saw balls of hair that had been shed by the animals, and could guess what kinds of animals had been in the cages. But no guesses were required, for the signs were still there, in full view.

I used to like the enormous polar bear from Alaska. The zoo wasn't fit for such a big bear, but it was there nevertheless. The bear, tamed into docility, had lost its wild nature. Having left home, it did not seem to be adjusting well and was going through a difficult time. The bear pounded its head against the wall now and then, as if in pain.

I was on friendly terms with the zookeeper. I used to go there quite often. Sometimes, when he was free—no, he was always free, and I never saw him busy at work—he would tell me amusing stories. He told me that in Alaska, it was legal to hunt bears, but it was against the law to wake a sleeping bear. After telling me that, he looked at me as if to ask if I knew the reason why. I couldn't figure it out, no matter how hard I tried. But I didn't tell him that I didn't know. Admitting something frankly was difficult for me to do. I went on thinking, and in the end, he told me what the reason was. When a sleeping bear was awakened, the bear could chomp the person to death.

He also told me that in one of the states in America, it was against the law to hunt whales, which wasn't strange in itself, but the state was landlocked, which made it impossible to hunt whales even if you wanted to. If a law was founded on the impossibility that it could be violated, it would be an unreasonable law.

The zookeeper told me some other things as well, which I no longer remember. They were mostly about hunting, but I don't know how he knew such things. He told me that he had been a cyclist once. But he didn't look like he'd been a cyclist. He was as fat as the bears he took care of. It wasn't clear whether he had indeed participated in a race. Nevertheless, he went around the zoo, which wasn't very big, on a bicycle from time to time.

I was sad that I wouldn't see the zookeeper again. I was just as sad, of course, that I could no longer see the Alaskan bear. Were they living together at another zoo? Or had they parted ways?

I moved on, trying to soothe my sorrow over the bear that had come from the Arctic, and the man who looked like the bear. All around me there were various kinds of rides, soon to be torn down, and I pondered for a moment which one I should turn my attention to first. Nearby was a ride that children liked, which looked like a pirate ship that made your head spin after you rode it, but I avoided that one.

I made my way over to the merry-go-round that was next to the pirate ship. A number of wooden horses were suspended from long beams. Each looked slightly different from the other, and there were carriages as well. I mounted a horse that had been lowered. I kicked it, for some reason. As I did, I imitated the sound horses make when they're startled. I continued to kick, imagining that the horse was going very fast, and I was careful not to fall off, my hands tightly clutching the reins. The wooden horse seemed to take me beyond the amusement park and the landfill that lay beyond it, to the beach.

The horse sped up even more. I felt I could easily fall off. Still, I let go of the reins I had been holding to make the ride feel more realistic, and sat up and shook myself. Before I knew it, I reeled and fell to the ground. I dived, with my shoulders hitting the ground first, but I laughed as if I had anticipated the fall

I got to my feet and slapped the buttocks of the horse that hadn't taken me to the beach. I thought about riding another horse, or a carriage, but didn't.

I made my way over to the dock. In the past, an elephant used to pass through the trail I was on. The elephant, which had been the only elephant at the park, would carry people on its back.

I arrived at the dock, where duck shaped and regular boats still remained. The floating bridge had nearly collapsed, and was full of holes here and there. I crossed the bridge carefully, and went toward the duck-shaped boats. There were many boats, but all of them, made of plastic, were partially damaged.

I could have gotten on a duck-shaped boat, but I got onto an ordinary boat. I didn't like the look of the ducks. The boat felt as thought it would sink any minute, but it didn't sink easily. In any case, I probably wasn't heavy enough to make the boat sink. And although there was a hole, it was on the side, not at the bottom. As long as the boat wasn't tilted sideways, no water would leak in through the hole.

Now I was ready to set off, but I couldn't find any oars. And the boat was tied to a rope, which couldn't be untied no matter how I tried.

I gave up without making much of an effort. There were times when I made something work out of pent-up anger, almost, a kind of peculiar perseverance, but I didn't do so at that moment. It wasn't because it wasn't worth it. I submitted to the voice within myself that told me to give up when I tried to do something.

There wasn't much to do on a boat that couldn't go anywhere, so I lay down in an uncomfortable position. I looked up at the sky for a moment, and even before I got tired of looking at it, I turned my gaze to the surface of the water. Birds that appeared to be seagulls were floating on the surface, or paddling around. They seemed to be enjoying a peaceful moment.

Just then, I saw something floating nearby. But I couldn't tell what it was. There are things whose identity can't be determined at a glance but can be determined after a moment. Thus the hat revealed its identity to me. There are, of course, also things whose identity can never be determined.

The hat wasn't right side up. There was no person in the water, of course, wearing the hat. I made the hat drift toward me. I didn't call it over, of course. No hat comes just because it's called. I stirred the water with my hand to make it come. In this way the hat, having no choice, came toward me.

The black fedora looked like something that belonged to an old gentleman. It was floating on the water without its owner. It suddenly occurred to me that the owner of the hat may be bald—a thought that wasn't completely without grounds, but could not be guaranteed. Some people wore hats to stand out, but others wore them to conceal a part of themselves—their bald head, for instance.

I picked up the fedora. But I didn't put it on my head. It wasn't because the fedora was wet. I already had another hat on my head. Nevertheless, I shook the water out of the wet fedora, took off the hat that was on my head, and put the fedora on. But the fedora didn't fit. It wouldn't go on my head. It wasn't that the fedora was too small. It was that my head was too big. To be honest, my head was exceptionally big, so big that it felt too heavy to carry around on my shoulders. I've never seen anyone with a head as big as mine. On rare occasions I'd run into other people with big heads, and we'd recognize each other at a glance and stare fixedly at each other's heads for a moment, trying to estimate whose head was bigger, but every time, the other guy would lower his eyes as a mark of respect, as if to say he was no match for me. When he did, I would nod my head lightly or decisively, as if to say I understood. Average-sized hats didn't fit my head, and I always had to get my hats tailor-made, since I couldn't reduce the size of my head to fit a hat.

I flung the wet fedora into the water with no regret whatsoever. The fedora looked better than my own hat, but it was of no use to me. Hats are for putting on your head, not for carrying around in your hand.

The fedora floated, intact, right beside me. I had to stir the water again with my hand to return it to its original spot. In this way the fedora, having no choice, returned to its original spot.

Something else was floating near the fedora. It was obvious that it was a doll. But this time, I didn't make the doll come my way. Looking around, I noticed many other things floating in the water; they had no choice but to float because they were too light to sink. And though I couldn't see them, many other things might have sunk—things unable to stay afloat, things that had lost the ability, things that couldn't float again once they'd sunk. A bench or a bicycle, or even a ship, might have sunk to the bottom. Things that had sunk had to stay where they were, with no hope of returning to the surface.

Insects that were born with the ability to walk on water, or with organs that enabled them to do so, were nowhere to be seen. I tried to come up with examples of such insects. First, a water skipper came to my mind. But nothing else did. It wasn't that there weren't any others—I just couldn't think of them. So I mumbled, It would be nice to see a water skipper. It wasn't something I said because there were no water skippers. I recalled that I'd once enjoyed watching brown water skippers crawling around on the water in a reservoir. The water skippers, which had been black, turned brown as they grew older. The reservoir was one of the places I liked to visit. I also recalled diving beetles. But diving beetles didn't exactly walk on water. They swam. I didn't like diving beetles as much as water skippers.

Looking down at the water, I noticed how dark it was, deeper than I'd expected. I was a little frightened, but I pretended I wasn't. Still, it was true that I was frightened, and so I didn't hide the fact. I came right out and said, How frightful!

As I stirred the water with my hand, ripples formed, giving rise to distorted images. The water calmed down, but the reflections on the surface, too, seemed distorted. I repeated the act several times, paying very close attention. But I didn't get anything out of it.

I lay back down on the boat as if I had lost interest in everything. The boat was uncomfortable to lie in, so I had to put up with the discomfort. I recalled a memory in order to forget the fact that there was dark water beneath the boat.

The memory was a pleasant one. Some memories well up like a wave of nausea, but this one wasn't like that. It came from a newspaper that had been sitting on a bench in some park. It was a story about an old woman who had gone to a reservoir near her house to drown herself. She jumped into the water, but curiously, before jumping, she'd called the police on a public phone and said that someone had jumped into the reservoir and hadn't come out. Having jumped into the water, however, she suddenly changed her mind and came back out of the water. It wasn't clear why she had changed her mind, or if she had swum or walked out because the reservoir wasn't deep. The paper never goes into such details.

Anyway, the police and firemen arrived in the meantime at the reservoir, and divers went into the water to conduct a search. But there was no body to be found, of course. After a while, the police and firemen were about to give up and leave, when one of the policemen noticed an old woman who had been observing the search effort from the sidelines, and asked her what was going on. She admitted that she had filed the report, and that in fact, she was the one who had jumped in the water. Curiously enough, she hadn't just gone home but had been watching the commotion she had caused.

I don't know what happened to the old woman after that. I don't know if the police wrapped up the case by giving her a scolding, taking her age into account, or if they took her to a nearby police station to interrogate her and determine the extent of her crime, which wasn't serious since all she'd done was file a false report. I don't know why she attempted suicide, either. Perhaps she'd told the police that she couldn't tell them. That it wasn't the kind of thing she could tell them. As if to say, why should I tell you such a thing? It was understandable. There are some things you just can't explain to other people.

I felt a sudden urge to use the old woman's tactics, but repeating something that had already been done wasn't my way of doing things. I needed to come up with a method that no one else had thought of. That was a principle I valued.

After that, I wanted to meet the old woman. She lived in an area not too far from where I was staying. We seemed to be kindred spirits. Like me, she had a curious side. I thought we'd be able to make interesting plans together, plans which would be somewhat absurd according to other people's standards, but which were exciting to us. We would rejoice in secret as we carried out our plans. But I didn't actually go and see her. It seemed like a troublesome thing to do.

I lay in the boat a little longer. It was the kind of place where you could sing by yourself as much as you pleased, but I never sang. I didn't sing whenever I felt like it. At least, I didn't sing while thinking I should sing whenever I felt like it. At such moments, I would stop singing even the song I had somehow started to sing.

I came up with a way to free the boat, but it wasn't a good one. I had recently lost a knife I always carried around with me. I thought I'd be able to at least carve a hole at the bottom of the boat if I had the knife, but then I realized I didn't have a knife so I wouldn't be able to make a hole. With nothing else to do, I wanted to get out of the boat, but I felt like I needed an excuse to get out. If excuses were something that cowards sought, it was possible that I was a coward. I looked for a lame excuse. It's all right for excuses to be lame. The lamer the excuse, the better.

Although I generally liked myself thinking in this way, at that very moment I didn't. I had to think differently. So I thought, An excuse wasn't absolutely necessary here. Excuses weren't necessary at moments when excuses couldn't be made.

I got off the boat. It wasn't that I didn't have the desire to stay longer, but I got off anyway. The conflict between my desire to stay and my desire to leave wasn't severe, and neither was the difficulty in observing it.

I went to a bench nearby. I sat erect for a moment, but soon lay down. There was no need to worry about what anyone else thought. Since there were no passersby, I couldn't watch someone else watching me. It felt like there were bugs crawling around, but I didn't see any. Instead, I saw flying bugs. They might have been bugs that both flew and crawled. Watching them, I thought that I wasn't with something that wasn't with me. It wasn't an important thought.

Suddenly I recalled a photographer who used to take pictures of people around the area. He always took mundane pictures. There were always couples and families smiling against the backdrop of the amusement park rides. He once took a picture of me. I looked very stupid in the picture. I carried it around in my pocket for a while, but before I knew it, I lost it. If I hadn't lost it, I probably would have thrown it away.

Gradually, sleep came over me, and I gladly gave in to it. All the benches in the world made me sleepy, just like that. I seemed to have fallen asleep without even having to close my eyes. But I must have closed my eyes, as I'd fallen asleep. I never slept with my eyes open, as some herbivores do.

After some very sweet slumber in which I didn't have any

unsettling or fabulous dreams, I sensed something strange. It wasn't the fact that I was at an abandoned amusement park that felt strange. Something strange seemed to be happening to my body. My arm was quite itchy, and when I took a close look at the arm with my sleepy eyes, I found that some parts were swollen and red. But whatever had bitten me was nowhere to be seen. I frantically scratched the swollen parts before finally coming to my senses. There were times when I would come to my senses only after doing something senseless like that.

I saw something crawling on the ground. To my surprise, they were caterpillars. No, I wasn't surprised. Having been bitten by various things before, I wasn't surprised that a caterpillar had bitten me. What surprised me was that countless caterpillars were moving in a line from where I was toward a nearby pine tree. It was as if the caterpillars had come out of me. But it wasn't so. Under the bench, I saw that the line of caterpillars was connected to a pine tree across from the other one.

Having risen from my spot, I lightly squished a caterpillar with a stick and watched it squirm, staying still as if the scene were something to consider quietly in my mind. Naturally, I didn't feel anything. I didn't want to touch the caterpillar with my hands. I wasn't that close to the caterpillar. The caterpillar continued to squirm, and I squished harder. A blue liquid trickled out. Only after that did I remove the branch, as if I had confirmed something.

I amused myself briefly by pushing away several caterpillars with the stick and blocking their way. The caterpillars moved about in confusion for a moment, but soon regained their order. I tried to come up with a way to drown them all by luring them to the nearby waterfront—it seemed that I'd be able to do so just by luring one of them over, since caterpillars tend to blindly follow other caterpillars—but I couldn't come up with a good way to do it. And trampling them to death seemed too cruel.

I persuaded myself that the best thing to do was to leave them alone. I couldn't decide whether or not I should leave the area swarming with caterpillars.

Fortunately, however, I saw something that drew my attention more than the caterpillars. An airplane ride that children liked, now neglected, stood nearby. I made my way over to it. The airplane was slightly raised, but not at a height I couldn't reach. I could crawl up to it, though I couldn't jump.

I got on the airplane with more difficulty that I'd expected. The seats were too small since they were made for children, and a little uncomfortable as a result, but I sat down anyway. No one made it move, so I sat still. When I got on the airplane, I couldn't see the ocean in the distance.

I began to rock my body little by little. Gradually, I applied the force of my body, and slowly, strength came from somewhere, strength that could perhaps be useful in some way. Strength, to an extent, comes in the same measure as that of the force applied. After a while, of course, that isn't always the case. For there comes a point when strength leaves. Force can still be applied, but not as much strength will come, and it can't be used in any way. That was something I was well aware of. Sometimes lacking strength, I had to be well aware of how to use my strength effectively. I had a good grasp on all the different kinds of forces I had applied to things or which had been applied to me, including forces that had been used differently from what I'd intended, because they'd manifested themselves differently from what I'd intended, but the knowledge rarely helped me when I was actually applying a force or struggling against a force.

The airplane didn't rock as much as I did, but it did rock slightly. A little later, I began to shake the airplane frantically, with all the strength I had. I did it out of an urge to bring on a disaster caused by some kind of greed. My greed, strange little thing, always got worked up over petty things.

I wondered why I liked to shake things frantically, but couldn't come up with a reason. It could have been one of my morbid desires. Anyway, it seems that among the many things I'd shaken, there were many things that weren't shaken as much as I intended to shake them. No, there were things that didn't budge no matter how I shook them. In any case, shaking something, and shaking myself along with it, was something I was quite familiar with. Once, I shook something so frantically that I nearly passed out.

Frantically shaking the airplane didn't make me feel like I was on cloud nine or anything, but I shouted, I feel like I'm on cloud nine! The feeling was quite good.

Long ago in my childhood, it seems I had been taken by someone to an amusement park and ridden such a ride. Had it been my father? Had he taken me there to humor me? I didn't want to remember such things, so I shook the airplane hard enough that I got really worked up. Hard enough that I began to grow dizzy. Even so, I did not stop. The airplane squeaked, and looked like it was about to crash. It seemed that it would be all right for us to crash together. I wanted to make the airplane crash. But no matter how hard I shook the airplane, it didn't crash. My strength alone wasn't enough.

I stopped the shaking. All the strength in my body had left me. I sat still, as if I were sitting in an airplane whose fuselage had gone through severe turbulence for a moment, and then gotten back on the right track. I didn't feel as if all the repressed feelings in my heart had left me or anything.

I scolded myself for a moment, as if scolding a child who had played a mean trick. But I didn't scold myself harshly, as if to say that what I'd done could be overlooked to an extent. I'd do it again, if only I could regain my strength.

The clouds in the sky were gradually expanding. They didn't look like rain clouds, but it could rain. In some cases, clouds that looked like they wouldn't bring rain did bring rain. And the opposite case could often be seen as well. As long as we made the effort to learn, nature taught us all kinds of things.

I sat quietly for a long time in the plane. The boats were floating quietly on the water. Things that appeared to be seagulls were also floating quietly on the water. Rides that had stopped working stood still on the ground or in the air.

I was surprisingly calm. I didn't think further, delving into thoughts that had already been delved into as much as possible. There were times when I was alone in this way and felt as if I were a complete being, or in other words, a being that was completely nothing. When I was with someone else, I felt at times that I was incomplete. But at that moment, I didn't feel that way.

As evening fell, the amusement park and the rides gave off a different feeling than they did during the day. The different feeling wasn't easy to describe in words, but it was a different feeling at any rate. I felt sad somehow. Perhaps it was because there was no one around me.

Beyond the amusement park, in the direction where I thought the ocean was, I saw a high-tension wire hanging in the air. For a moment, I imagined a current running through the wire. I felt pleased to think of the flow of electricity that would light up many houses and streetlamps.

The clouds were now thinning. Evening was falling quietly. The day was drawing to a close just as quietly.

Outside the amusement park, people were probably heading home. I told myself that it was time to go. But I didn't want to hear something like that, even if it came from me. I quietly told myself to be quiet.

I saw the moon, risen early, beyond the high-tension wire. Birds that looked like seagulls were flying overhead. An airplane was flying very high up in the sky without a sound, leaving a long contrail in its wake. It was probably a reconnaissance plane. I looked at the long contrail, which remained in the sky even after the plane had disappeared. Before long, the contrail, too, dispersed. In the meantime, I continued to fly in the sky in the little airplane in the amusement park.

Translated by Jung Yewon

Animal Songs of Boredom and Fury, Part One:
The Sound of the Alarm in the Water

"The eyes of singing animals and their songs of boredom and fury have forbidden me to leave this bed. I will spend my life here."
—Paul Éluard

The eyes of singing animals and their songs of boredom and fury have made me leave my bed, which I haven't left in a long time, and come to this riverside. I don't even remember the reason now, but at least when I first came here, that's what I thought. I never saw the eyes of the singing animals, but I'd heard enough of their songs of boredom and fury, and I'd had my own fill of boredom and fury.

I lived by a river, but I didn't bother to build a house there. Nevertheless, I drew a line on the sand by the river to mark that someone lived there. So that no one would trample on my house in passing. In other words, the line was the boundary of my property that could not be trespassed upon. The faint line, however, grew fainter after a day, and I had to once again draw a faint line to indicate that it was the lot for my house. I didn't know at the time, and neither do I know now, why I did such a thing, which wasn't necessary, and which didn't seem necessary at the time, either. Anyway, drawing a line wasn't difficult to do. In any case, it was much easier than building a house. But that is not the reason why I drew a line to indicate that there was a house there, instead of building a house. And neither was the reason

I didn't build a house because it was much more difficult than drawing a line. And it wasn't because I didn't need a house. If I had a house, I could have lived in it. I once built a mud hut and lived in it, but the maintenance and repair were not trivial. And with it came the problem of cleaning, which was a complicated and serious matter.

At times I drew the lines so they enclosed a larger space; and at other times, a narrower space. As a result, I sometimes naturally had to spend time in a space barely big enough for me to stand in, and at other times, in a space large enough to invite many people to. I would watch what took place in the part I considered the interior of my house, as well as the part I considered the exterior of my house.

It was a good place to write, but I didn't write anything. Somewhere in the sand, there was a piece of paper I had buried. And written on the paper was something I had written. But I forgot what I had written on it. Maybe I'd written, "Probably no one knows that in the sand, there's this piece of paper with someone's writing on it."

I've forgotten who it was that sang, "The eyes of singing animals and their songs of boredom and fury have forbidden me to leave this bed. I will spend my life here." He was probably a poet who felt boredom and fury more acutely than anyone else.

I lived on fish I caught in the river. I used a primitive but sure method. I built an embankment with rocks in order to catch fish. I ate a lot of fish of various shapes and sizes. The fish all looked different, but they generally ended up tasting the same, for I cooked them using one recipe, so it was difficult to create different flavors. I skewered the fish on a stick and roasted them over the fire. The fish, while roasting, would burn black, and I had to eat the burnt parts as well, but gradually I learned to cook them so that they didn't get as black. I ate everything except the bones. The fish generally had similar bone structures. I was deeply impressed upon discovering the not-at-all-new fact that the bones were very efficient for the fish. On some days I ate over ten fish a day. On other days I ate up to twenty fish a day. When I say this, it may sound like I lived only on fish. It sounds that way even to me. I did, for a while. I even thought, People could live only on fish like this. Could they, indeed? The issue, of course, would be the duration of time. They could do so for ten days, or a month. But could they for almost a year, or more than a year? The reason why I ate only fish wasn't to see if I could live only on fish. It was just that there was nothing else to eat. Fish was my staple food, as well as my snack. But soon, I came to eat other things as well. Wild berries grew in the nearby forest, but not in abundance, so I could only eat a few. And after a little while, the berries no longer grew. Still, at any rate, I lived on fish and wild berries for some time. I didn't know if fish and wild berries went well together. Still, I thought that wild berries were perfect for eating after blackened, charcoal-flavored fish. At any rate, I made an effort to think so.

I discovered that there was another mammal that lived on fish from the river, and felt inspired by the fact. I had never seen it with my own eyes, but I thought it might have been an otter. The footprints on the riverbank and its excrement suggested that it was an otter. Several times at night, I saw an animal I thought was an otter climb out of the water. But I couldn't hear the sound of its cry.

It was mostly an owl that let me hear the songs of boredom and fury. It lived across the river and at night, it would sing songs that let you know how great its boredom and fury were. Listening to its cry, I felt my own boredom and fury to my heart's content. With the river between us, we each felt boredom and fury that were similar in some ways, but different in others. I felt that the owl's boredom and fury weren't much greater than my own, but trickier and tougher.

Listening to the owl cry, I thought of Polly and Molly, who were dead. Polly and Molly were parrots kept by a woman I used to live with. Polly was male, and Molly female. Polly was mute, and Molly was a chatterbox. Polly wasn't interested in anything, and Molly was interested in everything. The two were somewhat eccentric. Polly had a habit of staring at people without a word, and Molly, of kissing a cross every chance she got, and making the sign of a cross with her head. When my girlfriend said to Molly, You must kiss the cross and make the sign of a cross, Molly would do so, as if she had been waiting for her chance. Polly and Molly's relationship was just so-so. The two were ill at ease with each other, and ignored each other. They had no interest in each other's lives. They seemed to have forgotten, even, that they were both parrots. My girlfriend favored Molly, so much so that it was obvious to everyone. Polly was always a little low in spirits, and particularly liked my girlfriend's red shoe. The world was too difficult a place for Polly to live in, so Polly would stick his head in my girlfriend's red shoe. Molly would occasionally say, Run, Polly. It wasn't directed at anyone. Molly talked to herself from time to time. My girlfriend, in a good mood after returning from church on Sundays, would sing a song from church, and stare at Molly and say, What do you think, tell me what you think, show me that you think, too, and Molly would think for a moment and say, Crazy bitch. When she did, my girlfriend would be very happy and pat Molly on the head. My girlfriend went to church only on Sundays, and did cross-stitching when she had some free time. I kept two goldfish in a small fishbowl by the window. Polly and Molly, and my girlfriend and I, lived together for some time this way.

The tragedy of Polly and Molly began when Polly chewed up the red shoe that belonged to my girlfriend after she returned from church one Sunday. Furious, my girlfriend slapped Polly, and Polly, who had always been docile, suddenly attacked her and pecked the top of her foot until it bled. Not one to back down, my girlfriend attacked Polly and strangled him, and as Polly heaved his last breath, she also strangled Molly, who had witnessed the scene. Polly and Molly struggled for a moment, but that was all. Polly had been punished after doing something that deserved punishment, but Molly's death had been unfair. But it didn't matter. After their deaths, Polly and Molly each lay for a while looking at the ceiling and out the window, Polly on the bed and Molly on the windowsill. Polly looked low in spirits, even in death. My girlfriend regretted killing them, and stayed up a whole night kneeling at the foot of her bed like someone who was deeply penitent for her mistake, with the birds on the bed and the windowsill. She talked to herself as Molly used to when she was alive, saying, I thought wrongly, all of this is due to wrong thinking. She wished that Polly and Molly would come back to life and enjoy her shoe, and kiss the cross and make the sign of the cross. But it was in vain. I listened to the song of the owl, thinking of Polly, who had committed one brave act, and Molly, who had died unfairly.

For some time, I hadn't had to live only on fish. An old man living nearby brought me things to eat. The things he brought were edible, but not very palatable. They were mostly leftovers. He said they were freshly cooked, but they didn't look fresh. Perhaps the freshly cooked food went through a change as he brought them so that they looked like leftovers. He couldn't bear that I lived on only fish and wild berries. He wanted me to eat what he ate, too. I gradually came to depend on the things he brought me. But in my position, it wasn't necessarily desirable. He came irregularly, and when he didn't come, I starved. When he didn't come, I thought that he was doing it on purpose in order to starve me, and to respect his wishes, I didn't eat anything.

He never invited me to his house, so I thought that his house must be unfit to invite people to, or that I must be unfit as a guest.

Still, I thought about what I'd do if he did invite me. I thought it wouldn't be easy to accept his invitation.

He also told me stories. His stories were generally boring, but some were all right. One story he told me about a parakeet in England was interesting. A parakeet that belonged to a woman in England, which nearly died of an allergic reaction to the wrong kind of birdfeed, sat on the woman's shoulder after being resuscitated and learned how to cross-stitch. One day, when the woman was taking a little break, the parakeet took the needle in its beak and began to cross-stitch. The parakeet, skillfully poking the needle in and out of the fabric, enjoyed cross-stitching. It liked gold needles and showed great interest in dragon patterns. An English cross-stitch magazine selected the parakeet as the young cross-stitcher of the year. The old man said that the parakeet must have been of royal Chinese descent in another life. Then he said, The English seem to be interesting people. In reply I said, Not just English people, but English parakeets as well.

The old man wore dentures. He usually kept them in his pocket, and took them out and put them in his mouth when he spoke. He said he had to, for proper pronunciation. But the dentures were shaky, and his pronunciation wasn't always correct. And sometimes, the dentures fell onto his lap as he spoke. When they did, he picked them up quickly and put them back in his mouth. I wondered how he would sound without dentures, but he never spoke without them. I heard him speak only with his dentures on, so it seemed to me that his dentures were speaking. When he wasn't speaking, his dentures sat quietly in his pocket.

The old man carried around a little portable radio. The radio, originally made for people like hunters and fishermen, was a marvelous invention. It would play for an hour after the lever attached to it was spun frantically for about a minute in order to recharge the battery. I liked to spin the lever. After spinning it, I heard about things that had taken place very far away. It was through the radio that I heard an anecdote about a goldfish that fell through the chimney of an old man's house in England. The old man revived the goldfish that had fallen through the chimney onto a frying pan by putting it in a fishbowl, and it was presumed that the goldfish had been dropped by a heron that had caught the fish for dinner and was sitting on the chimney,.

I saw long-legged birds, such as herons and cranes, landing on the river at dawn where wet fog descended. For some reason, they arrived not in groups but alone or in pairs. So I was unable to see the magnificent spectacle of them landing in many numbers on the river. I recalled a crane I'd once seen in a dream, standing motionless on a frozen lake in a very cold place, perhaps Siberia. The crane, which seemed to have fallen behind its group, stood there with one leg folded, as if its foot had suddenly frozen to the ice, as if it would stand there like that forever.

One morning, I came across a boat by the river. It hadn't washed up in a flood or anything. I would have known if there had been a flood. If there really had been a flood, I, too, may have been washed away by it. No matter how much I thought about it, it didn't seem possible that there would have been a flood without my knowledge. There was no one in the boat. So no one had been washed up in the boat. Perhaps the boat had been in a spot a little way off from the riverside where I had set up a base, and that was why I hadn't noticed its presence there. But how could I not have noticed it, when it wasn't far away from where I lived, and was so conspicuous? The boat had sunk in the shallow water. Upon closer examination, I noticed that there were holes at the bottom, which would have made it impossible to be washed up in the first place. The holes in the boat hadn't been my doing. There were three little holes at the bottom of the wooden boat, and a bigger hole on a side. Actually, the holes were more like cracks, but it was difficult to conclude that they were cracks. They were in between holes and cracks. In light of the fact that holes are likely to be the result of someone's deliberate doing, and cracks are likely to form on their own, they were probably cracks. But upon reflection, I couldn't be sure. There are holes that form on their own, as well as cracks that are made deliberately. I could have tried to plug up the things that were neither holes nor cracks, but didn't. I couldn't be bothered. Instead, I pondered whether to destroy the boat completely. But it could not be destroyed, even though I tried. Destroying it would require the help of something, or someone; I couldn't do it with my strength alone.

After coming across the boat, I spent a lot of time in it, lying still and watching the herons and cranes from time to time. They didn't pay attention to me. The boat, which had essentially lost its function as a boat, made me question whether or not it could even be called a boat. After all the water had been scooped out, it could be used as a boat momentarily. But only until it sunk completely, which would happen before long. At any rate, the boat wasn't completely submerged in the water, and I spent time on it as if I were someone in a boat. But I didn't make the boat my home base.

Children from the nearby village came to the riverside now and then, but they didn't come to play with me. Even if they did, of course, I wouldn't have played with them. I didn't feel a desperate need to spend time with people. They played in the sand. There was a little sandy beach there. It couldn't be called a sand hill, not quite. If it was a sand hill, you'd be able to slide down from the top as if you were sledding, but you couldn't. There was a bit of an incline, but you wouldn't automatically slide down just by sitting there. Once, I sat at the top of the sand mound, waiting to slide down, but I found myself in the same spot. When the children played in the sand, I, too, played in the sand. There is no child who doesn't like playing in the sand. Grown-ups don't like playing in the sand. Grown-ups only play in the sand when children pester them to. No grown-up ever pesters anyone to play in the sand. You could say that if you no longer like playing in the sand, you are no longer a child. But that's a difficult generalization to make. I've always liked to play in the sand. Does this mean that I've always been a child? Or is my case unique? And although the children played in the water and swam, I didn't go in the water. This is strange, since I loved the water more than anything else and once swam across a wide river. Anyway, the children could have found pleasure in harassing me, but they didn't. They seemed afraid of me. We played separately. The sound of children playing noisily didn't stir any emotions in me.

As far as I knew, there was one owl that lived in a nest in a tree across the river. I never saw the nest. The owl flew across the river and returned at night. Listening to the owl's cry, I sometimes felt sorrow instead of boredom and fury. I also thought about a playwright who, as he lay dying by his window, confused the passersby in the street with the characters in his play. When I lived in my girlfriend's house, I would look at the faint forms of the people passing by the curtained window, feeling that they were phantoms.

One night, listening to the owl's cry across the river, I named the forest the Forest of Owls. Sounds of other birds, such as magpies and scops owls and unknown birds came from the forest as well, of course, but that didn't stop me from calling the forest the Forest of Owls. Listening to the owl's cry after that, it seemed natural that it came from the Forest of Owls. Sometimes, as the owl settled on a tree, it made a sound as if it were bumping into a wall. At times the cry of the owl in the forest sounded to me like the sound of a pendulum clock. Though it wasn't at all similar to the sound of a pendulum clock, it sounded that way to me.

Polly never spoke, but he liked the sound of the pendulum clock on the living room wall very much. The sound of the clock rang dull and long. Every hour when the clock struck, Polly stopped what he was doing, even though he didn't have very much to do, and went to the living room and perked up his ears while looking at the clock. Polly's favorite hour was midnight, when the clock struck twelve. Molly, however, who was different from Polly in every respect, was indifferent to the sound of the clock. Molly sighed when the clock chimed on monotonously. To me, at least, she looked as if she were sighing.

Besides me and the otters, which lived on the fish in the river, there were other animals. The fish also became prey to birds. Some birds dropped suddenly from the sky to strike, and others, which were mostly long-legged, strolled around in the shallow areas and grabbed the fish in their huge beaks. At times, I would watch a fish swallowed by a crane go down the crane's neck, and feel choked up. But it had nothing to do with sorrow.

One day, I saw a watch in the water, which hadn't always been there. The watch I had been wearing on my wrist fell into the river when its strap broke. In other words, I didn't take off my watch and hurl it into the water. I'd failed to come up with such an idea. If I had, of course, I could have done so. My girlfriend had bought me the watch. From time to time, I used to compare the time on the watch I was wearing with the time on the pendulum clock on the living room wall.

I'd seen a number of objects in the water. I'd seen shoes, spoons, forks, scissors, glasses, pots, etc., and I'd even seen a bicycle. I'd also seen a little fish swimming in a glass jar in the water. But this was the first time I'd seen a watch.

The watch was lying right side up. The water was shallow and I could see the hands of the watch clearly, so clearly that I could tell the time. I looked at the hour. It was a little past three. I saw the second hand, thin as a hair, delicately and gracefully drawing a circle as it turned. Anyway, the watch didn't look distorted or enlarged, as objects often do in water, and looked exactly its actual size and shape. The water was only ankle deep, after all. Nevertheless, I thought that there should be a distortion of time, but no such phenomenon occurred. I didn't know why certain distortions occurred when you saw something in the water while you were underwater, or saw something out of the water while you were underwater, or saw something in the water while you were out of the water. I didn't take my eyes off the watch. And I thought that the watch wasn't allowing me to take my eyes off it. Several minutes passed. The watch was working properly. At that moment I realized that it was waterproof. Perfect! I cried. I raised my eyes and looked around me. There was no one around. There was a bridge nearby, but there was no one standing there either, looking at me without being able to take his eyes off me, as I looked at something mysterious in the river without taking my eyes off it. The bridge was empty. Completely empty. It's perfectly empty! I cried. But the perfection was short of the perfection I felt with the watch that was working properly. At that moment there came a sound. It was very faint, practically inaudible. Nevertheless, I heard the sound. In other words, the sound came so that it could be heard. The sound came regularly at fixed intervals. It was the sound of the alarm on the watch. I stopped and stuck my head underwater, so that it touched the bottom. I shoved my head into the water with my right hand, as if forcing someone else's head into the water. For a moment, it felt unpleasant. No, I can't say that it was unpleasant. Considering that I smiled at that moment, I may have done so with great pleasure. In any case, I shoved my own head underwater. In other words, I was siding with my right hand, not my head, at that moment. But I failed to shove my entire head in. As I said earlier, the water was only ankle deep. I put my head closer to the watch. When I did, I could hear the sound of the alarm more clearly. It felt like some kind of a revelation. But I didn't believe in revelations as such. I stayed where I was with my ears submerged. I suddenly recalled that I'd once had a desire to get baptized. My desire to get baptized, of course, wasn't due to some kind of religion. I wanted to get baptized for the pleasure of baptism itself. I wanted to enjoy baptism without even really knowing what kind of a pleasure it would give me. Thinking such thoughts, I stayed for a long time with a part of my head underwater. I could stay that way for however long. In any case, my nose was out of the water. I had no problem breathing. Still, I stopped breathing as I do while underwater. But I couldn't go without breathing for long. I wondered if I should wait for the sound of the alarm to stop on its own, or if I should turn it off. I wondered for quite some time. It wasn't something that could be decided easily. But the problem was resolved on its own. The sound of the alarm came to a stop while I was wondering. It wasn't because the watch was broken, though. The watch hand was still moving. The sound of the alarm had come to a stop because ordinarily, it automatically comes to a stop after a certain amount of time has passed. The alarm rang twice a day. At that hour in the morning, it woke me up, and in the evening, it rang to put me to sleep. At that hour in the evening, I tried to sleep wherever I was. Without exception, regardless of where I was—on a bench, on the grass, on the stairs, on a rail, on a tree, under a bridge, on the rooftop of a building, or by a railroad. When I heard the sound of the alarm in the evening, sleep came over me. But that day was an exception. No sleep came over me. The sound of the alarm that day chased sleep away. I could see sleep running away with my eyes, almost. I regretted that the watch had no other function. It was waterproof and had an alarm, but it didn't glow in the dark. If it had a glow-in-the-dark function, I could wait till it got dark, till night fell, and see the watch glowing in the water. For some reason, it had become difficult to find glow-in-the-dark watches of late. From time to time, it was quite enchanting to see the hands and the twelve little sticks marking the hours, glittering in the dark.

Although Polly didn't speak, he liked the sound of the alarm as well. We would listen to the sound of the alarm on my watch. When the alarm rang, I didn't have to shout, Come here, Polly, listen to the sound of the alarm with me! No matter where he was, he'd come flying as soon as the sound of the alarm went off. And then he would listen to the sound of the alarm, looking as if there was nothing in the world more astonishing. When the sound stopped, he would quietly go off, as if very disappointed. Molly, however, had no interest in the sound of the alarm. Instead, Molly would sit by my girlfriend while she cross-stitched, watching the flowers and trees coming to life on the fabric, or other things that didn't seem to belong on fabric.

I raised my head. I felt as if someone was watching me. I saw a shadow cast over the quietly flowing river. I lifted my head toward the bridge. I saw something there, but I couldn't tell what it was at first glance, and had to take a closer look. There are things, of course, whose identity couldn't be determined even upon closer examination, but this time, I could tell. But what I saw wasn't what I had imagined. I had imagined a child. From time to time, a child would stop and pee in the middle of the bridge while passing through, then go on its way. The bridge was downstream and there was no chance of the urine flowing my way, but I would get furious when I saw a child peeing over the bridge, and yell. I got furious despite the fact that I myself often peed in front of other people. Of course I didn't do it deliberately. It's just that people happened to pass by while I was peeing. Children, however, didn't hurry even when I yelled, and went on their way only after taking their time. I tried to understand why children peed on the bridge, of all places, and thought I understood, to some extent. It was understandable. But it's difficult to say how I came to understand. Perhaps it was something that could be done, something that could be encouraged, even, as occasion demanded. Watching the transparent yellow liquid draw an arc and fall over the river could be satisfying to the person in question. Considering that, you could say that women, who always pee sitting down, are fundamentally deprived of one of the great pleasures of life. I'm not sure, of course, if women pee sitting down because they can't pee standing up. I've never talked to a woman about that matter. Anyway, among animals, there are some that excrete as they walk, and others that come to a stop when they do. Ducks, geese, and the like do not stop to defecate. Dogs and cats, however, always stop. Though I haven't seen it myself, I've heard that beetles, too, stop and raise a leg when they excrete. This may be irrelevant, but I once saw someone defecate in front of a large building on a busy street in a big city. I was on a bus. On the ground was a huge heap of feces. Still, he was straining himself to excrete more. I cheered him on. Now that I thought about it, he seemed to have the face of an otter. I also remembered another story about feces. This is something my girlfriend, who had come home from church one Sunday, told me. Someone defecated during mass that day. Apparently, he felt so ecstatic while singing a song praising God that he had defecated before he knew it. Oh, the grace of God is everywhere.

I took a good look at the form on the bridge, and realized that it was a cow, of all things. A bull. The bull was alone. There was neither a child nor an old man steering the bull. The bull's owner may have been lagging behind. The shadow reflected on the river belonged to none other than the bull. Firmly embedded in the bull's head were two horns that indicated that it was a bull. It was impossible to pull them out. There was a story about a man who pulled out a bull's horn with his bare hands, but the story was a lie. A bull's horns cannot be pulled out with bare hands. The horns are very useful when a bull fights another. The horns can inflict a fatal injury on the other bull. And sometimes, a bull can bunt a person with its horns. It could get in trouble by doing that, of course. It could also bunt something else. I had seen a bull bunt a wall, or a tree, for no good reason. The bull in question looked in my direction instead of looking at something far away. But it looked at me without showing any sign of curiosity. But considering that you couldn't really say whether or not a bull was showing any sign of curiosity as it looked at you, it was difficult to say that it didn't show any sign of curiosity. I couldn't even say for sure whether or not the bull was looking at me. Still, it was looking in my direction, because there was nothing besides myself to look at, so you could probably say that it was looking at me. I was probably attractive enough to attract the bull. Looking at the bull, I suddenly wondered how and what bulls saw when they saw something. When they saw a person, for instance, did they see the eyes? Was the cow looking at my appearance now, or at my form in general?

I recalled another bull I had seen before. They were two distinct bulls, for I had seen them in two completely different places. Anyway, that other bull had been quite angry. But how had I been able to see that it was angry? You couldn't tell at a glance that it was angry. The bull wasn't kicking the ground with its hind leg in a fit of anger or anything, as bulls do when they're extremely angry. Neither did it attempt to bunt someone with its horns as if ready to attack. And it didn't have a defensive posture, either; it looked a little cowardly. Nevertheless, the bull was angry no matter how you looked at it. In any case, it made me think, It's quite angry. It didn't look as if it were hiding its anger. But you couldn't say that it was manifesting its anger fully, either. Still, I couldn't rid myself of the feeling that it was angry.

I went near the bridge where the bull was standing. The bull was still standing in the same spot. I looked into its eyes. We looked at each other for a moment. The bull's eyes were full of boredom and fury, but somehow, they looked exhausted. Suddenly I felt exhausted, and felt an urge to go back to my bed, where Polly had lain dead. But the eyes of the bull weren't quite enough to make me do so. I thought that there wasn't much to expect from the bull. Suddenly, the bull yawned as if it were no longer angry. Then the bull raised its head and let out a single cry, its mouth open as wide as it could be, then went on its way. After a short while a child passed by, but it didn't seem honorable to stop the child and ask if he was the owner of the bull that had just passed by.

I went back to my watch. It was still ticking. I left the watch where it was in the water. I might be able to hear the sound of the alarm after about twelve hours. I went to my boat and pushed it deeper into the water. But the boat didn't get swept away; its bottom was still touching the riverbed. I made up my mind not to leave the boat, lying submerged in the water on a boat that was submerged, with only my face out of the water. I wasn't sure if it was because of the eyes of singing animals and their songs of boredom and fury. I suddenly wanted to hear the sound of the owl cry, but no sound came from the forest. I thought of Polly who never said anything. When had Polly stopped speaking? Even my girlfriend, who had kept Polly for a long time, didn't know. And when had Molly started kissing the cross? According to my girlfriend, it started when Molly saw her one Sunday after she'd returned from church, taking out the cross from her bag and kissing it, crossing herself, and putting it on the table. Had she been crazy, as Molly said? Was I crazy too, as she said? And did she still go to church on Sundays? I thought about the goldfish in the fish bowl by the window. They often gnawed on each other's fins. Were they still alive, their fins torn?

Translated by Jung Yewon

Animal Songs of Boredom and Fury, Part Two:
The Cave Dweller

The entrance of the cave faced west, so from time to time, I could see a magnificent sunset as evening approached. The sun became larger and redder as it neared the horizon, and sunk majestically and disappeared under the water. Watching it, I would imagine myself walking quietly into the water and disappearing into the sea.

The entrance of the cave was the size of an ordinary door, and the exact depth of the cave could not be determined. Beyond a hall-like space whose ceiling measured about three meters in height, the cave gradually diminished in height and breadth, to the point where it would be difficult for a person to pass through. Still, there was a hole at the end, and there seemed to be a larger space beyond the hole, but it could not be confirmed. According to my estimation, the cave was quite deep. I felt the wind blowing from the sea enter the hole and disappear into the cave. But I couldn't tell for sure if the wind entered through the hole and died out somewhere deeper, or if a part of it reached a dead end and came back out again. I tried to be sensitive to the movement of the wind in order to find out the answer, but I couldn't tell for sure. Sometimes, a weak breeze that had nothing to do with the wind from the outside seemed to come from the inside.

There was no special reason why I'd come to live in the cave. I'd settled down there after going through a period of wandering, so to speak. My settling at the cave was half out of my own volition and half not. Actually, no one's will was involved in the matter. Perhaps you could say that the will of nature was involved, if such a thing exists.

I came to see that the cave was quite a decent place for me to live. The cold and humidity posed problems at times, but the cave was a shelter from the storm, as well as a safe haven from the threat of savage beasts—there were no savage beasts in the area, of course, and thus there was no threat, but I liked to think that the cave was a safe haven even from the threat of savage beasts.

The cave, millions or tens of millions of years old, must have been the oldest house in the world. There was a time when most of humanity lived in caves. In those days, caves were the best places to escape from the threat of savage beasts.

There was also a Greek philosopher who spent his last years in a cave, and though I didn't know why he spent his last years in a cave, I thought a cave was a decent place to spend one's last years in. But that wasn't why I decided to spend my last years in a cave.

There were no bats in my cave, but there was something that appeared to be bat feces, suggesting that bats could have lived there before. I thought that if the flock of bats returned, we could live together.

When I began to live in the cave, I survived on various canned foods. Cans were stacked up high in a corner of the cave. I alternated between eating canned sardines, mackerel, mackerel pike, herring, and tuna. It was a difficult task to eat canned sardines, mackerel, mackerel pike, herring, and tuna day after day, but I endured it relatively well. Curiously enough, I craved canned sardines, mackerel, mackerel pike, herring, and tuna again when I grew hungry, which in a way was admirable. Some cans were well past their expiration date, but I never got sick of eating them. One of the canned sardines had neither the shape nor taste of a sardine, but I could still think I was eating a sardine, and think I had eaten a sardine after I was done.

I did not have many possessions. I had a rabbit skin coat that might seem somewhat unexpected, and I used it as a mat when I slept, put it on when I was cold, or used it as a cushion to sit on. The rabbit skin coat went well with the sable hat I never took off, but looked a little funny because its length was a bit awkward. But I didn't dress that way on purpose. I had no choice as I had no other clothing. The coat was black. It was made of dozens of rabbit skins that probably hadn't always been black. They were probably white and grey rabbit skins that had been dyed black. And the coat didn't include the skin of the white rabbit I'd once kept. The coat wasn't something I'd made, nor was it mine. It belonged to a woman I'd once lived with, and I'd taken the coat from her. Incidentally, I didn't know the whereabouts of the woman. Not only was I unaware of her whereabouts, I didn't know whether she was alive, either. During the last days of our living together, she played the cello hysterically and incessantly, and she, in fact, had been hysterical. The song she most enjoyed playing was "Fingal's Cave Overture".

I once had a white rabbit, whose name was Ramsey. I often held Ramsey in my arms. And she liked to be held in my arms. That's what I thought, at least. When I held Ramsey in my arms, she never looked uncomfortable or struggled to free herself. She sat quietly in my arms, and I would pat her on the head. When I did, she looked at me with a bit of fear in her eyes, and even though I looked at her with kindness in my eyes, she still looked at me with fear. When we were quietly looking at each other, I felt that we were indispensable to each other. No, rather, I felt that we understood each other to an extent.

Ramsey wasn't a very active rabbit. She usually lay face down, looking dejected, in the grass off to one side of the house. Insects such as beetles roamed around on the grass. And Ramsey would occasionally sit quietly by the pond in the yard and stare at it. Ramsey, who looked somewhat sickly, died at an early age. She was found floating dead in the goldfish pond, but I didn't know what had happened. It didn't occur to me to fish Ramsey out of the pond, and I watched her body floating on the water for days. Ramsey's eyes remained closed. One day, as I was watching it, I suddenly recalled that I had caught a rabbit on a hill with my father when I was a child. But we didn't actually catch the rabbit. When we found the rabbit, it was already dead, caught in a snare someone had set up. In other words, we stole the rabbit. As we walked home, holding the dead rabbit by its ears, my father sang a song, which seemed inappropriate for the journey home.

My father smiled as he skinned the rabbit before me. Watching the scene, I, too, smiled, perhaps finding it genuinely amusing. My father skinned the rabbit expertly from one end to the other—I don't remember if he started with the head or the tail—revealing the skinned rabbit's red flesh. My father may have wanted to teach me how to skin a rabbit. Perhaps teaching his child how to skin a rabbit was the best thing a father could do for his child. And with the rabbit skin, my father made me a little hat, which still had the rabbit's ears on it. I didn't dare go outside wearing the hat, but I would try it on in secret when I was alone in my room.

On the wall of the cave, there was a wall clock. I found the clock, which must have once hung on a wall in someone's house, on a rock on the beach. The wall clock was no longer working. But the three hands, consisting of the hour hand, the minute hand, and the second hand, were moving. But they didn't move on their own. They moved randomly when I shook the clock. Then after a short while, they came to a stop as if nothing had happened. I would look for a moment at the hands which were now still, and hung the clock back on the wall. The seemingly useless act allowed me to pass time, and also allowed me to have some vague musings about time, and things related to time, and thus wasn't so useless after all.

Living in a cave, passing time was the biggest task for me. Making time pass, thus making my time expire, was the only thing that mattered. What I did where did not matter. In general, however, I passed my days not knowing what to do, yet knowing that it wouldn't matter what I did, and yet I couldn't bear to stay as I was.

I spent a lot of time in the cave watching the sea. Small fishing boats sometimes passed by and I watched them appear and disappear without taking my eyes off them. In particular, watching the lit fishing boats passing in the dark of night was quite exciting. They were catching squid. There were no huge oil tankers or battleships to be seen.

Once, I saw a bird with a large beak flying through thick fog, and I thought it was similar to a pelican but was probably something else.

I thought about a lot of things, one of which was that I spent a lot of time thinking about a cat I'd once had. The cat died presumably of cancer, living out its last days in pain. It also looked as if it had gone a little crazy, but I don't think I drove it crazy. At least, I didn't intend to make it go crazy. The cat, which had lost its sight, would look at me with strange eyes, like those of a stuffed animal. It resembled a visually impaired person—do visually impaired people know that when they look at something, they look at it with strange but striking eyes, as if looking beyond what is seen? Anyway, when the cat looked at me with those eyes, I sometimes felt that I could not bear its gaze.

The name of the cat, too, was Ramsey, and I called it Miss Ramsey, but its full name was Little Miss Colorado Jon Benet Ramsey. Ramsey was murdered when she was six, but the identity of the murderer still remains unknown. After learning about the case, I gave my cat the name Miss Ramsey, which seemed natural and just perfect for the white, odd-eyed cat. It was as natural as the Little Miss Colorado crown was for Ramsey in the picture in the newspaper. Ramsey was also the name of a forgotten gifted mathematician.

The cat had another name, given by its previous owner, but I didn't like the name. Until I began to call it Ramsey, the cat's name was up in the air for a while. But Ramsey, who was used to being called by its old name, refused to be called Ramsey. When I called it Ramsey, it didn't respond. Even when I said, "Come here, Ramsey," it wouldn't look my way. It was the same when I said, "Ramsey, don't sit there looking like that." The relationship between a cat whose owner called it Ramsey but which didn't think of itself as Ramsey, and an owner who still called it Ramsey even when it didn't think of itself as Ramsey—that was the relationship we had. In general, our relationship was one of indifference to each other. When passing by, we just stared at each other like strangers.

Ramsey, whom the Little Miss Colorado crown had suited so well. Occasionally I put some of my girlfriend's lipstick on Ramsey's lips. But I wasn't successful in putting her nail polish on the cat's toenails. The cat's toenails were too small to put nail polish on. Incidentally, at a certain time of the year, Ramsey would shed its toenails, and grow new ones. I picked up the shed toenails, wrapped them in paper, and kept them in a drawer.

Once in a while, the cat would do mysterious things. The most mysterious thing it did was to walk back and forth from one end of the living room to the other. It went back and forth at very regular intervals for a long time. Viewed through the open bedroom door, it looked as if many identical-looking cats were endlessly walking back and forth.

I called Ramsey "Marie Antoinette" as well. That's who came to mind when I looked at cats. The French palace of the 18th century where Marie Antoinette lived was a paradise not only for cats but for pets in general, and there were cats everywhere. Versailles swarmed with cats, parakeets, monkeys, and dogs, and when I pictured Versailles, I always imagined animals, suddenly frightened by something, barking or howling in panic and running through the mazelike interior. I also thought that things were probably that way not only in Versailles, but in all the palaces of the past, including ancient Egyptian and Persian palaces.

Ramsey spent its last years as a blind cat. I had lived my entire life in fear and anticipation that I may go blind, but it was actually my cat who went blind. I felt envy, the kind that was appropriate to feel against a cat. But the cat lost its sight gradually, and was not too inconvenienced in life.

Once in a while, I sang a song to my blind cat called "Nero, the Black Cat."

You're my cute black cat, the red ribbon looks so good on you
But when you're pouting you hurt my feelings by scratching me

Nero, the Black Cat, Nero, Nero, my cute friend is a black cat
Nero, the Black Cat, Nero, Nero, the fickle little cat
La la la la la la la la

When you walk with light steps, a scary cat comes after you
If you fall for the sweet talk, there's nothing I can do

Nero, the Black Cat, Nero, Nero, my cute friend is a black cat
Nero, the Black Cat, Nero, Nero, the fickle, naughty little cat
La la la la la la la la

The world may turn dark at night, but your eyes sparkle like stars
I feel safe even in the quiet and lonely darkness as long as you're here

Nero, the Black Cat, Nero, Nero, my cute friend is a black cat
Nero, the Black Cat, Nero, Nero, the fickle, naughty little cat
La la la la la la la la

I feel safe even in the quiet and lonely darkness as long as you're here
Nero, the Black Cat, Nero, Nero, my cute friend is a black cat

But if you're too naughty, I won't give you any canned mackerel
La la la la la la la la

I sang the song, thinking it was inappropriate and yet appropriate to sing to a blind cat. When I sang the song, the cat would look at me or not look at me with its blind eyes. Singing the song, I thought it would have been a good song for my father to sing while bringing the dead rabbit home from the hill, but to my disappointment, he never did.

What I liked about "Nero, the Black Cat," was the repetition of the lyrics and the variations. I wanted to write something with repetition and variations, about leeches in a water dropwort field, or a centipede suddenly spotted in the house. In my opinion, repetition and variation were the most fundamental underpinnings of existence and consciousness.

While living in the cave, I also had a tennis racket and several balls. The old racket had a wooden frame and several broken strings, but the rest of the strings were curiously taut, and the balls, though a little flat, were still somewhat bouncy. From time to time, I served a ball against the cave wall, as if exercising. It wasn't easy, however, to hit the ball that bounced off the wall, for the wall was bumpy and it bounced off in an unpredictable direction. But that made it fun to hit the ball, and I felt as if I were overcoming a great challenge.

One day, I grew tired of hitting tennis balls, and threw them all out into the sea. I watched the green tennis balls get washed up by the waves and gradually disappear. Perhaps the little balls are still floating around in the sea. No, I believed they were. If I had the chance, I wanted to throw more green tennis balls out into the sea.

From time to time, I lay in the cave humming a melody. I always ended up humming "Fingal's Cave Overture" in my heart. When I did, I could picture white foam surging on the cold sea over which seagulls flew, as well as a black cave, its mouth open toward the sea, under a steep cliff. "Fingal's Cave Overture" was one of the few songs whose melody I could recite by heart.

I also had a telescope that I used to look out at the sea. I would focus on something, adjusting the zoom this way and that, but the lens was broken and it was no use. Still, I would look at something, adjusting the zoom as if I were trying to focus on something. The telescope failed to magnify things for me, but allowed me to focus on them.

Also on the cave wall were paintings. But they weren't rock paintings carved by someone long ago. It was graffiti done by someone in the not too distant past. And they weren't things that would generally be painted in a cave by the sea.

At times, people, mostly fishermen, came to the cave. It seemed that they came to take shelter from sudden storms, or because they'd taken a wrong turn. Some of them were startled to see a man, wearing a rabbit skin coat and a sable hat, crouching in the dark. They tried to initiate conversation, but I didn't say anything. Still, some of them would give me something to eat, such as canned food. One fisherman kindly gave me a fishing gut with a hook on it as a present, and I cast it into the water. But no fish bit the hook, because I hadn't put any bait on it.

At times, I drew things on the cave wall to pass the time. But the things I drew were closer to ideograms, such as Chinese characters and Egyptian hieroglyphics, than actual forms, but they weren't exactly ideograms or hieroglyphics, either. They were somewhere between drawings and scripts, or in other words, drawings evolving into scripts, but not quite evolved yet. They were my own written language, created by me, but there was no system to it.

I'd once had the preposterous idea that I would write something. But what I wanted to write about was nothing at all. I wanted to write something about leeches in a water dropwort field, or a centipede suddenly spotted in the house. It seemed like a fabulous idea to describe their movements. I also wanted to write about the various hallucinations I had experienced.

I think it was during one summer that I began to live in a cave. But nothing told me that it was summer. Neither the ships passing by the coastal waters, nor the birds flying in the sky, told me that the seasons had changed. I would have been able to tell what season it was if I had more accurately observed the location of the stars in the night sky, but I didn't know how to determine the seasons by the location of stars. Nevertheless, it felt like summer to me, and I passed the season like someone who enjoys summers, or painfully endures them.

What I liked the most about my cave was the sound it made. In general no discernable sound came from the cave. But when the wind blew outside, the cave turned into a natural instrument. The cave made different sounds depending on the wind. At times the cave made a sound like that of a harp, and the cave itself seemed like an enormous harp.

Once in a while, I took a walk. But I didn't go far. On the beach near the cave, there was a ruin that appeared to have been some kind of fortress once, with the rocks all crumbling and dirt piled on top. I went there, then turned around and came back. Although it wasn't easily recognizable as such, the ruin had the atmosphere of a fortress, whether real or imagined. Utterly destroyed, it was now covered in weeds and wildflowers. At any rate, I liked to think that the place had once been some kind of a fortress, and called it my fortress, and stood there at times as if I were guarding it.

Once, I had come out of my cave and was on my way to my fortress, when a group of people appeared before me. The group consisted of an old man with a deeply wrinkled face, a boy with freckles, and a dog with many spots on its body. They didn't look as if they were out on a picnic. In other words, they weren't dressed for a picnic, and weren't carrying anything that people on a picnic would carry. Actually, I was dressed like someone on a picnic, and carrying something that someone on a picnic would carry in his hand. I wasn't wearing the rabbit skin coat but I was wearing the sable hat, and carrying a sardine can. What caught my attention was the dog. It was a speckled dog with randomly distributed spots all over its body. I tried to find some kind of symmetry in the spots, but to no avail. There was nothing remarkable about the dog, except for the fact that it had randomly distributed spots. The dog began to bark at me all of a sudden, but the old man did not stop the dog. He left the dog to bark as it pleased. The dog stopped barking only after it was satisfied, and stood still. Then the old man patted the dog. Very slowly, as if the dog were good for patting. The dog stayed still as if it didn't feel anything. It showed no response to the man's patting. It neither wagged its tail nor pricked its ears. Or maybe the dog expressed its good mood by staying still. We looked at each other for a moment. I, alone, had to bear the gaze of two people and a dog. At that moment, the old man suddenly raised his cane, and I ducked, thinking that he was about to hit me, but he put his cane back down. It appeared that he hadn't been about to hit me. Still, I couldn't tell why he had done such a thing, which could cause misunderstanding. He was small, and seemed coarse. He had moles on his face, which were very small compared to the spots on the dog. And he was wearing a hat, which had a slightly tilted brim to begin with, at an angle. The old man and his hat really got on my nerves. He looked quite absurd. I thought about making him fix his hat, but restrained myself. Right then, he said something. But I couldn't understand what he was saying. He was missing several upper teeth, and his pronunciation was off so it was difficult to understand what he was saying. The boy didn't step forward to assist him. I shook my head to let him know that I couldn't understand anything. Then for some reason, he took off the hat and held it in his hand. The foul odor released from his head, which had been trapped in the hat, was carried in the wind and reeked for a moment. I thought to myself that we could put our faces close together and get our fill of the foul odor from each other's heads. But he put his hat back on, as if all the foul odor had been released. At that moment, I briefly thought about the foul smell that would come from my own head if I took off my hat, which I hadn't removed in a long time. While I was having these thoughts, he turned around and continued on his way. The boy and the dog seemed to want to stay longer, but he ignored their wishes, and they had no choice but to follow him. I wasn't sure if I wanted them to stay longer, so I just stood there. I watched them until the group of spotted humans and a dog became a little spot and disappeared beyond the hill. And that was the end of our encounter. It was the second human encounter that I'd had while I lived in the cave. After returning to the cave following the incident, I couldn't forget about it for a while, and wondered if I still had some lingering desire for human contact, but came to the conclusion that I didn't. I soon forgot about the incident as well.

I didn't neglect the condition of my body. In a way, you could say that I was quite fastidious about it. For one thing, I had too much time on my hands. Since I didn't have much else in the way of distractions, it was a wonderful diversion.

No emotions stirred within me, other than a certain indescribably unpleasant sensation—all the more unpleasant because it was indescribable—that came over me and roused me, then left.

I felt as if I were growing distant from anything human and gradually becoming something closer to an ape, an animal.

After the supply of cans had been depleted, I caught fish with a net I picked up at the beach. The net, which must have belonged to a fisherman, had little holes here and there, but I could catch fish that were bigger than the holes. I also collected shellfish, such as oysters and mussels. I had a magnifying glass, and I used it to light a fire and cook the shellfish.

At times I would light a fire on some rocks outside the cave in broad daylight and quietly watch the flames. Lighting a fire, not to cook or escape the cold, but just to look at the flames, resembled some kind of religious ceremony, or an act of sorcery, but that wasn't the reason why I lit fires. Perhaps it was akin to what a poet did when he burned a rose and watched in seriousness all night to see if the spirit of the rose would appear.

I liked to check that all the joints in my body were working, whether properly or improperly. It was similar to checking if heavy equipment such as the arm of an excavator, for instance, was working properly. Some of the joints in my body worked marvelously. My right arm and right hand, for instance, were wonderful at picking up things, a pebble, for instance. I watched in awe as the fingers on my right hand made the preparation necessary to pick up a pebble, and my right arm made the preparation necessary to lift the right hand that picked up the pebble, and in the end pick up the pebble. I also watched in awe as my left arm and left hand, which weren't healthy, failed to pick up even a pebble.

My left eye wasn't completely blind, but the sight was awfully weak compared to that of my right eye. With my right eye closed, I could see nearly nothing. I couldn't hear very well, either. The hearing in my left ear, however, was better than in my right ear. I listened to various sounds with my relatively good left ear and relatively bad right ear, blocking the two ears in various degrees.

For instance, I would listen to the sound of a seagull crying with my left ear completely unblocked and my right ear completely blocked, and listen to the sound of another seagull crying with my left ear completely unblocked and my right ear slightly blocked, and listen to the sound of yet another seagull crying with my left ear completely unblocked and my right ear completely blocked, and listen to the sound of still another seagull crying with both my left and right ears completely blocked, and listen to the sound of another seagull crying with my left ear completely blocked and my right ear slightly blocked, and listen to the sound of another seagull crying with my left ear completely blocked and my right ear completely unblocked. And the process would continue with my left ear and right ear blocked or unblocked in various degrees, and further, with my eyes and ears open and closed, or blocked or unblocked, in various degrees. I conducted this complex experiment on the reception of images and sounds in all seriousness. Through the experiment, I once again confirmed the fact that although my left eye wasn't completely blind, the sight was much weaker than that of my right eye, as well as the fact that the hearing in my left ear was better than my right ear.

The sound of seagulls crying, which suddenly cut through the fog and disappeared on mornings when the thick fog was the only thing that could be seen, put me in a kind of hallucinatory state at times. While listening to the sound, I felt as if I would soon be turned into a seagull and fly into the fog.

As the days went by, I grew increasingly thin, to the point that my skeleton almost showed through my skin, and my body looked as if it had been shaped with a certain kind of care. I had various visions when I was sick with a fever. I saw things such as a stone statue lying on the grass, a polar bear walking alone toward the North Pole, and a crow sitting on a grave. I also saw the black and white keys of a piano floating on a pond, and gigantic wooden chairs, whose height I guessed to be a good five to ten stories high, lying around in countless numbers. I thought I was taking a walk in a forest of chairs, actually strolling about under the long wooden chair legs, feeling the strange little sensation that I had become very small.

For some unknown reason, I was always touched when I saw the arrangement of a great number of chairs. Once, I even had a dream about countless chairs arranged in an orderly manner on a flat plain, and it was one of the most pleasant dreams I've had.

I sensed that my end would come soon, but it didn't matter to me. I pictured myself lying as a skeleton in the cave. Perhaps bats would be living in my cave then. I also pictured myself lying, already a corpse, on a little ship floating on the sea. The ship could reach the South or the North Pole, as long as it didn't get stranded midway. I considered leaving my cave, but never did. I thought it would be nice if the cave turned into my grave.

Ramsey, my lethargic rabbit, would lie face down, looking dejected, in the grass. And in the grass, insects such as beetles would be roaming around. Ramsey would lie face down in the grass, looking dejected, as if hypnotized. But had Ramsey really been looking at the insects that were roaming around in the grass?

The woman I'd once lived with played the cello hysterically and incessantly during our last days together. Thanks to her, I suffered endlessly from the image of myself taking the cello from her and beating her to death with it. Even so, I found myself becoming as meek as a tamed beast when I listened to her play "Fingal's Cave Overture," which was the song she most enjoyed playing. Perhaps I had found the cave because of the song she played. But had she, in fact, been crazy, as I'd thought? The music she played sounded to me like animal songs of boredom and fury.

Making time pass, thus making my time expire, was the only thing that mattered. What I did where did not matter.

The entrance of the cave faced west, so from time to time,

I could see a magnificent sunset as evening approached. The sun became larger and redder as it neared the horizon, and sunk majestically and disappeared under the water. Watching it, I would imagine myself walking quietly into the water and disappearing into the sea.

Translated by Jung Yewon

Animal Songs of Boredom and Fury, Part Three:
The Forest of Owls

The warm sun is shining down, and an old man is passing by a rock on the beach, with a black dog at his side. The dog is running around on the beach, sometimes ahead of the old man, sometimes behind, its feet sinking into the sand. The dog is running with all its might and hurls itself to catch the little ball that the old man throws, not very far because he doesn't have much strength. How the dog loves the green tennis ball! The old man keeps throwing the ball, which the dog catches in its mouth, even as the man frowns, clutching his stomach as if he has peritonitis.

But how funny the old man looks! He's wearing at an angle a hat with a tilted brim, and yellow rubber boots, the kind that children wear. He always wears yellow rubber boots, regardless of the weather or his mood. As if to make the point that he's the only person in the world who wears yellow rubber boots regardless of the weather or his mood that day, as if to make the point that wearing those boots distinguishes him from all the other people in the world. I nearly burst out laughing the first time I saw him.

It was in a scene like this or one that reminds me of this scene, that we first met. I appeared before them at the moment the old man threw the ball and the dog ran after it. The old man acted as if he was surprised at my sudden appearance and glared at me. As if he had seen a beast that had come down from the mountain.

At least, I felt that he felt that way about me. He looked at me as if he'd seen a beast. And I did look like a wild beast, due to the many days I'd spent homeless. The dog barked as if it, too, was flustered by my appearance, and came up to me a little later and began to sniff my groin. But it soon turned its head away, as if it had failed to find what it was looking for, or anything that drew its attention. Then it ran toward the ball, which the old man had thrown once again. After casting a brief glance at me, the old man began to walk on, again throwing the ball. As if he was done with me.

But for some reason, I began to follow the old man who was following his dog. After a short while, he turned around and saw that I was following him, but he paid no attention. His dog, however, which had been merrily catching the ball in mid-air and looked quite docile, suddenly took on a different attitude and growled at me, looking at me in a menacing way. But the dog merely growled, and did not stop me from following it.

I continued to follow them. We went past the sandy beach, through the brambles, took the narrow path leading to the village, and after a short while, climbed over the hill that overlooked the village. They were moving slowly, but the distance between us continued to widen. I was walking very slowly, so slowly that it almost didn't feel like I was walking. But I could follow them without letting them out of my sight. After a short while, they disappeared into a house that was standing alone, apart from the village. I arrived after a while, and stood outside the fence of Hardy orange trees surrounding their house, and looked in.

The old man, who was in his garden, looked at me with surprise as if he'd seen a zebra standing beyond his fence. I reached out and widened the opening in the loose Hardy orange bush between us, and made an attempt to say something that would be appropriate, or something that would be alright even if it made no sense. But he just looked at me without saying anything, with a look that seemed to mock me in an odd way. Humiliated, I unknowingly picked one of the well-ripened Hardy oranges on the tree that happened to be in front of me. He quietly glared at me.

It occurred to me that what I had in my hand was a Hardy orange, so I put it to my nose but all I could detect was a delicate fragrance, not the strong scent characteristic of Hardy oranges. In order to smell the Hardy orange better, I gently dug a hole in it with my fingernail and smelled it—how I enjoyed carrying around the Hardy orange in my pocket, and taking it out whenever I could to smell it! When I did, I could smell the scent I had anticipated, and in my excitement I cried out, in spite of myself, like a monkey with a banana in its hand. The old man looked at me as if to scold me. I wanted to put the Hardy orange in my mouth and bite it so that the tingling sour taste would fill my mouth, but I resisted, taking into account what you could call my dignity.

Right then, he motioned to me with his hand. I interpreted the gesture as an invitation to come around the hedge of Hardy orange trees into the yard, which I did. But he came up to me and drove me out, gesturing to me in the same way he had just a moment before. It seemed that he had meant to drive me out. But as I made to leave, he called out to me. I went toward him. But he told me to stay where I was. I stayed where I was. He approached me. He looked me over from head to toe, and told me to follow him. I followed him into his garden.

His house was small and shabby, covered in ivy that seemed on the verge of engulfing it. Growing in his garden were plants that had fully matured, and others that hadn't grown fully. Some of them had chosen to shrivel up instead of thriving. Plants that grew near the ground, such as China pinks and hollyhocks, spreading out low above the ground, had withered away, and their flowers which had come into blossom the previous season were drooping and tangled, though not yet dead. The garden was full of more weeds than flowers and trees. Things that had been carried in the wind and sprouted, or things that had broken in through the loose hedge of Hardy oranges and grown at a furious rate, were in greater abundance than the things he had planted. But weeds grew even when neglected, or as long as they were neglected, and the old man seemed not to care about them. They, too, had to live, and some had to be spared.

The old man, looking around his garden, seemed to have great pride in it, and I, gawking at the garden, interpreted his pride in my own way, thinking that a garden was something you could have considerable pride in, no matter how sparse and insignificant it was.

For a moment, we looked around his garden without saying anything. Various fruits which were in season, including the Hardy oranges, were ripening in his garden. But they didn't look very tempting, as they were so small. Off to a corner, there was a tree that looked like a quince tree, which had no fruit on it whatsoever.

The old man took a quiet look around the garden, and began to trim some of the trees and flowers in a rather absentminded way. I quietly watched him as he went about his business. After a while, he straightened his back and gently pulled and let go of some branches that were touching each other or were about to touch each other. They seemed fine and should have been left alone, and in the process, a leaf fell even though he hadn't pulled at it, as if to reward his efforts. In the meantime, the dog was running around among the green weeds, showing off the blackness of its hair.

After a while he took me to a corner of the garden. There was a birdcage there, with a bird inside. It was a little brown bird of unknown species, and it lowered its head as if it were shy. The bird did not fly around the cage in freedom and happiness. But when the old man fed it a little, as if to suggest that it sing for a little food, it sang reflexively in a shy little voice. We listened to the song of the bird. In general, the sound of animals crying sounded to me like the laughter of animals that were actually furious or in despair, as if mocking the fact that nature's creatures could laugh. For a moment I became absorbed in, and was moved by, the little performance of the bird. The feeling tugged at my heartstrings, and I went into a trance. When the song of the bird came to an end, the old man fed it a little more, as if to get it to sing another song. Anyway, the old man made me leave even before I had allowed the feeling to spread throughout my entire body. And the dog barked, as if to tell me that I'd better leave. In the end, I had to leave his house, saying goodbye to his garden and his birdcage.

After that, however, I would follow him when he was returning home from a walk, and he would let me into his garden. We would go to his birdcage and listen to the little bird sing. But the bird didn't always sing for food. I understood. Even birds have moments when they don't want to sing at all, or want to sing in their hearts, if they do sing. Or it could be that they don't know how to express in song a fear that only they know, or no longer want to sing after singing for a bit, or deeply regret singing after finishing a song.

Thanks to the birdcage, the bird was safe, but it trembled in fear at the appearance of birds that were bigger than itself which would fly over. The old man, for some reason, was not pleased that other birds came and sang in his garden. Other birds had to go to other places if they wanted to sing. But he didn't go out of his way to chase away the birds that came and sang in his garden. It was tiresome to chase them away one by one. And it was tiresome just to think that the birds you chased away could return and you'd have to chase them away again. He just watched the other birds that came and sang, looking unhappy.

Now the old man is disappearing over the hill with the dog. The dog is still hurling itself at the ball he throws. They may come to me on their way back from their walk. For a moment he may look down on me, asleep on this rock, and wait for me to wake up, or wake me up and take me to his garden. He may want to show me his shabby garden again. I may follow him, looking bothered.

Children from the village are approaching. There are five of them in all, and they're all carrying something in their hands. Three are holding sticks, and two are holding fishing rods. And one of them has a net for catching fish as well. They're singing a song they probably learned at school, and the ones with sticks are brandishing them in tune with the song, or without heed to the song. The sticks are something they use to scare seagulls from time to time.

I'm watching them from the top of a rock on a low sand hill, a little ways away from where they're passing by on the beach. I'm hiding myself, lying flat on the rock. But maybe it's just in my head that I'm hiding. No, my body may be hidden, but my head, the top of my head, may be exposed. Even when you think you've hidden yourself completely, your head may be exposed. One of the children, in fact, waves at me.

Watching the children go, brandishing their sticks fearlessly, I mumble, Children today have no fear. Maybe it was because owls, which used to make children tremble in fear at night, have disappeared. That's why they're scaring seagulls now, fearlessly brandishing their sticks. And by scaring seagulls, they're bracing themselves for the misfortune that will befall them in the future. That's also why they fall asleep in cabbage or spinach fields. No, maybe children today don't do stuff like that anymore. Isn't there a way to scare these fearless children? The shrewd seagulls, though, weren't at all scared of the sticks, and only showed their annoyance by flying up into the air for a moment, then coming back down.

In a while, the children will pass by, carrying a net with fish, or perhaps a small octopus. Having a hunch about its fate, the octopus in the net may be sticking its tentacles through the holes in the net and flailing them around in the air to express its unhappiness, right? Because there's no way that it would be happy.

I could tell the children to stop and ask them where they're going and what they're doing. They could ignore me as if to say it's none of my business, or they could answer me politely, saying, We're going fishing, you see these fishing rods? and I could say, Oh, so you're going fishing, I wonder why I find it hard to believe you, it's probably because you're holding your fishing rods high up into the sky, but anyway, if you catch any fish, show me the fish you've caught on your way back, and then the children could say, But the fish will be dead, and then I could say, So show me the dead fish, and then the children could say, What's the point in seeing dead fish? And then I could say, firmly, I want to see dead fish, and then I could say, a little less firmly, I want to see how they look when they're dead. I enjoy having heart to heart chats, or having our hearts open as we talk. But soon enough I think, What's the point in that? The children are going fishing because grown-ups have told them to, or because they enjoy fishing, and I don't care at all where they're going and what they're doing. The children glance my way as they pass quietly before me, as if they're somewhat afraid of me, and I look at them with warmth in my eyes and let them pass. One of the children looks dismal, as all children should look.

I live in a lighthouse a little distance away from here. The lighthouse, which isn't too big, hasn't been in use since a bigger lighthouse was built in a more suitable spot. The lamp that lit up the night sea and the power generator, which must have been there before, have all disappeared, and the interior looks as if someone for some reason lit a fire long ago, and now, with the soot peeled off, it looks like an unadorned black room. And the room, which could look bleak, was made much richer in atmosphere thanks to the geometric house of a white web made by several spiders working together. The lighthouse no longer serves its function. It does, however, serve a different purpose—above all, it serves as a wonderful house for me.

Do I see myself at that age in those children? I do, in a way. I, too, used to go fishing in the river with other children. But what I recall now is lying flat and still on an old pine tree with bent branches on the hill in the back of the village, or sitting on the tree, carving something—probably a fish or a bird—in the bark with a pocket knife that all Boy Scouts carried around as a matter of course. I spent many days this way, without realizing that the sun was going down, caught up in something with a strange passion and devotion. And I think it was while I was carving something on the tree one day that I decided to run away from home. Not long after that, I carried out the first of countless attempts to run away from home. Dressed from head to toe in my Boy Scout outfit, and having packed several kinds of equipment necessary for survival given to Boy Scouts, such as a compass. I felt excited, like a boy summoned by the emperor. But it was deep into the mountains, not the city, that I was headed. I wanted to go where no humans lived. In search of this solitude, I went to the Forest of Owls, for I had told myself, You're going to the Forest of Owls now, it's time. And I convinced myself by saying, The place that's waiting for you is the Forest of Owls. Without knowing what it meant, but it didn't matter. If it was for such a reason, there was no reason why I couldn't go anywhere, whether it be the Forest of Owls or elsewhere. But what happened to me after I went to the Forest of Owls? What happened after that, what I must have gone through after reaching the Forest of Owls, doesn't come easily to my mind. But my memory of it could surface naturally as I think about something else.

Two women from the village are going diving now under the rock. They'll catch abalones and sea urchins and other things deep below the surf that children can't catch. They'll go down to the seabed, holding their breath, enduring the water pressure that presses down on their chests. And they'll swim around the seaweeds and corals like sea otters, collecting things that sea otters like as well. Perhaps on their way back, they'll give me one of the sea squirts or sea cucumbers they've collected with much effort, if they have a good harvest.

People may think it's natural to see me sitting on this rock, like a bird in its nest. Perhaps I have become a part of the scenery on this beach. Like an otter resting on a rock on the beach. Or they may think that a uniquely shaped rock is sitting there, the rock and I having become one. Nearly no one, aside from the villagers, comes to this beach where there's nothing but sand hills, with nothing special to see besides a few wild flower trees. But although there's nothing much to see here, it's not completely devoid of attractions. People from other areas, who happen to take a wrong turn and end up here, turn away thinking, There's really nothing to see on this beach, though the scenery would be a surprise for someone who wants to see nothing much, and then suddenly sees a part of me, exposed above the rock. They might wonder, What in the world is that? and then think, I must have been mistaken, and go off somewhere else.

When I lie still on the rock for a long time, or for a long enough time, I come to feel that the rock and I have merged, that I am helplessly fettered to the rock, and I fall into a strange state in which I harbor a secret desire to become a mythological figure and for an eagle to come swooping down and peck at my heart. And at times, I get caught up in a hallucination in which something immobile, something silent in the rock infiltrates me, and ideas, either familiar or unfamiliar, or reveries, rise with wings up into the air, grasping me in their claws like a hawk. It was also on this rock some time ago that I combed my hair with my hand and had a hallucination in which some creatures very small and black, which looked like ants—or like lice, since they came out of my head—fell to the ground in countless numbers, and became bigger and bigger till they became the size of my thumb, and when I took a closer look, they looked like the Huns or the Vandals, armed with swords and spears and shields—but why did they look like the Huns or the Vandals, of all people? All I know about them is that they, too, are one of the many tribes that have vanished into history. They were soldiers on horses, and they fought each other, shouting, and then suddenly attacked me, all of them at once, and I thought, All kinds of things come out of your head when you don't wash your hair for a long time. But most of my ideas or reveries soon crumble like the ashes of burnt paper. Perhaps it's because no fact in my life—which I have lived to this day thinking, This is only a bad dream, let's just imagine that I'm having a bad dream, as I'm having a familiar nightmare which begins with some unfamiliar but quite lyrical scenes and then changes almost imperceptibly—is unquestionable, and I haven't found my own language with which to capture the facts that are not unquestionable.

At times I lie on this rock, watching the calm or undulating sea which looks dejected somehow, and I become just as dejected, and fall into a pleasant reverie about a character in a novel, who swims with a knife in his mouth. I've pictured this character so often that I seem to be the character himself—was he, too, a Boy Scout? But I do not remember whether the boy swam across a river or a sea where an island could be seen, and why he swam across it with a knife in his mouth.

On this beach, there are several pleasant things I can do. When the sky and the sea change into a majestic and unusual shape, fit for their size, and demand of me an appropriate response, I smile reluctantly. And I gaze endlessly at the scene as if the scene itself renders the attempt to describe the change useless, as if I am trying to find out what it is.

One of the things I like to do is to catch little slugs in the bamboo forest nearby, take them to the lighthouse, and set them free there. Waking up the next day, I would see them clustered together on the wall in the lighthouse, and watch them in wonder as they climbed up the wall, unable to comprehend for the life of me why they were there, having completely forgotten that I'd brought them there. Though my intentions actually lay elsewhere, it gave me great joy to watch the slugs, which must have been climbing up the wall all night, continue to climb up the wall, as if I'd been captivated by an enchanting scene. And how heartrending it was to watch the slugs that have climbed up to the ceiling become exhausted at last and fall to the ground and die! I, who at such times experienced a complex change of emotions brought on by compassion, would pick up the dead slugs and take them to the bamboo forest and release them, and then take live slugs from the forest and set them free in the lighthouse—in other words, I would switch the dead slugs with live ones—and watch them climb up the wall with great effort—by doing so, I could think that we had undergone some kind of ordeal together, that although the ordeal they were going through wasn't the same as what I was going through, the two weren't all that different from each other. But I take starfish from the beach and set them free in the bamboo forest for somewhat different reasons. It's because as I set them free, I think, Everything in my life has fallen into ruin, so it's alright for starfish, that have nothing to do with me, to go through this kind of ordeal. But the starfish I set free in the bamboo forest looked comfortable even when their lives had come to an end due to my vicious desire and cruel hand. They looked so comfortable, in fact, that I added dead starfish to the list of things that come to my mind when I feel a pure and blind—blind because it's so pure—and desperate and quiet longing for death.

And from time to time, when I'm in the mood, I take a walk

around the lighthouse. Sometimes I even make my way over to the pebble beach, which is quite a distance from the lighthouse. It's very pleasant to step on the sparkling black pebbles that have been washed clean in the seawater, and hear the sound they make as they bump against each other, and at such moments, it feels as if my pleasure emanates from the pebbles, sparkling as they bump against each other—but why was it that the pebbles, which brought me pleasure, threw me into extreme confusion now and then? And the silver grass field, situated further away where the river and the sea meet, is one of my favorite places. How pleasant it feels to walk briskly through the silver grass, letting the grass lash my face and chest with their tough stems! And how calming it is to lie down on the field, panting from exhaustion, and watch the grass swaying in the wind! Strangely enough, such useless acts made me feel that I was one with nature, or at least that I was a part of nature, and I came to realize anew how wonderfully useful uselessness is to me. Nature, however, makes me feel as if I've been abandoned, rather than making me feel that I'm part of nature, and strangely enough, when I feel this way, I feel as if I understand what nature is thinking.

And occasionally, I go to the village and observe the things that go on there. A mother comforts her child, who is startled by the menacing force of the clothes she has hung out in the yard as they flap in the wind. The father of another child, not realizing that the child has reached the age of rebellion, yells at the child when he says something, demanding if it's something a son can say to his father. And the crows that come flying from the pine grove at the back of the village, which I have named the Forest of Owls even though I don't hear the sound of owls coming from it, quietly land on the roofs and walls of the village houses, and watch the empty yards as if awaiting the misfortune that is about to befall this peaceful village, and other children are running back and forth through the alleys, and above their fluttering hair, white cirrus clouds pass by, and on the village coast, a fishing boat, after a struggle against a small storm, makes its way, cleaving the water, into the port to join other ships at rest. What I like most of all is the view of a cow plowing a field.

How touching it always is to watch a cow plowing a field, pulling the plow, quietly and patiently! The docile cow lets you know that it can be scary when it's angry, but it isn't angry now, and when it's not angry, it just lets you know what a docile cow it is. The master shouts at the cow in a firm but affectionate voice. Whoa, and giddyup, are the only two words required for the master and the cow. No other words are necessary. Words such as, Now that the long winter is over, bustling spring is about to begin, we'll endure the spring by plowing fields together, it won't be easy, but we plowed fields even in the heavy rain of summer, and there's nothing that we, together, can't do. The two express and accept each other's affection and trust with the two words, whoa, and giddyup. Between the two, there's no place for a third party. They have become one through hard labor. And they feel a sense of unity as they look at their achievements: the neat furrows on the field that they have plowed together. The master looks at the furrows, thinking, The furrows look quite pretty, and the cow, in agreement, lets out a moo. And with that, the cow's fatigue is washed away, not completely, but in some measure.

I went to the old man's house several times after that, and each time, I found him pacing along the hedge of thorny Hardy orange trees, as if to summon certain emotions at the edge of certain thoughts, or sitting in a chair in the garden, quietly reading a book. He said there was nothing but books in his house, but he never took me on a tour of his house.

Each time he saw me, he stared at me as if he'd never seen me before, but would soon invite me into his garden as if he remembered who I was. One day, he, for some reason, assigned me some tasks I could do in the garden, and I, too, for some reason, carried out the tasks he assigned me. First, he made me sweep the yard. He was loath to do anything that required him to hunch over. He personally taught me how to do the sweeping. But that wasn't necessary since I, too, knew how to sweep. It was something that could be done without special instruction. He seemed sorry that he couldn't teach me something he knew.

Little by little, it was decided what we each had to do in his garden. He pruned trees and left the fallen branches on the ground. It was my job to remove what had fallen on the ground. He climbed up the ladder leaning against a tree in the garden—when he did, I had to watch his two legs quivering on the ladder—and after pruning the tree, he stood on the ladder looking down on me as I picked up the branches that had fallen to the ground, as if to clearly demonstrate how different our positions were, like someone looking very far down from very far up.

Anyway, he would make me sweep up the fallen leaves, but didn't let me burn them. He did that himself. He liked doing that. He said everyone could do his assigned tasks better through division of labor. I wasn't sure if that was true even as I carried out my assigned tasks, but I tried to think it was.

Nevertheless, we breathed in the smoke that rose from the burning leaves together, and laughed together. We smoked a cigarette, which he handed me, together as we breathed in the smoke, and laughed harder as we coughed. And we spent time together in his garden, pruning what needed to be pruned, picking up what needed to be picked up, and sweeping up what needed to be swept up.

I gradually came to learn about him, and I also found out that his ears, with their curiously shaped earlobes, were hidden under the hat he wore. And I discovered several of his bad habits. Without taking his hat off completely, he would reach underneath and scratch his curiously shaped head, but in my opinion, that wasn't a habit that needed changing. Being considerate enough not to show others his unsightly head was something to emulate, even.

He also had a habit of taking off his hat once in a while and sticking his finger into it, and twirling it around and around, and even I couldn't say anything about that. Sometimes I took the hat away from him and put it on my head. The hat, whose brim was tilted to begin with, could only be worn at an angle, no matter how I put it on. When I laughed in jest, looking at his ugly, bald head, he would cover his head with his hands. He knew that his head was ugly.

I took the old man on a tour of my lighthouse. He seemed to prefer it to his own house. He seemed to be considering if it would be better to live in my lighthouse than his own house.

Striking upon an idea, I made a fairly reasonable suggestion, asking him what he thought of setting his house on fire and burning it down, but he rejected my idea. We could be delighted like children, or overwhelmed with emotions, while watching his house burn down. He failed to let go of his attachment, which would have been alright to let go of. Being foolish, he failed to realize that as hard as it was to let go, it was nothing compared to the greater joy to be gained. I should make him realize that truth. For it was true. But I shouldn't tell him that I'd be pleased if he abandoned his house and came to live with me at the lighthouse. For it wasn't true. And I should tell him that his cherished quince tree was nearly dead, and that it would be difficult for it to come back to life. I do not know if that is true or not, but that's how it looks to me, at least. I should also tell him that we can no longer hear the song of the bird that didn't always sing for food. It suddenly died recently, but was left in the cage because he couldn't accept its death—my sorrow following the death of the bird wasn't great, but nevertheless, I plucked a few wild chrysanthemums and cast them over the sea.

Perhaps it's because of the cigarettes the old man gave me that I have hallucinations from time to time on this rock. He would only say that it was an herb. He grew them in a corner of his yard. It was also to the herb that he gave the most devotion. We shared a smoke now and then, and when I did, my entire body relaxed and my eyes seemed to lose their focus. Perhaps it was because of this cigarette that I saw soldiers resembling the Huns or the Vandals—had they come out of my hair, or had my hairs turned into them? When I came to, I saw that what was crawling on the rock were nothing but ants. And once, I hallucinated that amid the sounds of something that sounded like a lute, foul-tempered but playful monkeys suddenly appeared before me and led me by the hand to a sinister forest and danced in a circle around me, in not very graceful movements that befitted them, and then suddenly spit on me, and when I came to, there was nothing before me but the wind blowing.

Anyway, it isn't easy to break away from an urge that comes over me out of some fantastical thought that has nothing to do with hallucinations. There are moments when I have to pluck red camellias or purple Chinese milk vetches or yellow sunflowers and cast them over the sea—the first time I did so was after I had spent several days wallowing in sorrow over the death of my cat, and by plucking the yellow petals of sunflowers and casting them over the sea, I was able to free myself from the sorrow, or the feeling that came across as sorrow, resulting from the death of the cat—or stick a finger in the belly of a dead fish and gently stir up its intestines—it's something I do to add more weight to my heart, or to turn a moment that's given to me into something that isn't mine—or noisily chew, and then spit out, some tough plant, such as plantains, as herbivores do. In such moments, I try to stop myself, thinking I shouldn't do such things, but it's no use. So at times, I must allow myself to do such things. Sometimes there are things you shouldn't stop yourself from doing. There are times you must allow yourself to do something, if you insist on it.

It is almost evening now. The children and the women may all have returned home in the meantime. But I don't see the old man taking a walk with his dog. Because I'd made them up. The old man died some time ago—a little after his bird died—and his dog has disappeared somewhere. It was in my imagination that he took a walk on the beach with his dog every day at a certain hour, and it was his phantom I saw in my imagination.

A passage from a novel by Virginia Woolf that the old man, who died of a terminal illness, quoted to me by the nearly dead quince tree in the garden remains in my memory of him. "The real flower on the window-sill was tended by the phantom flower. Yet the phantom was part of the flower for when a bud broke free, the paler flower in the glass opened a bud too." I chanted the sentence like an incantation after that.

The old man said that after he died, he would probably live on as a phantom for a while. And I believe that he still takes walks with his dog on the beach as a phantom, and paces around his abandoned garden. At least until the ivy covering up his neglected house swallows it up.

I hear the cry of a forest bird coming from somewhere. But it isn't the cry of an owl. It seems to be the cry of a crake. The cry of a crake isn't the sound I need right now, and I don't pay attention to it. Flying overhead are migratory birds that fly in a formation, and behind them, the moon has risen, looking faint and tinged with blue, like the phantom of a moon. The moon looks like the moon I saw long ago when I went to the Forest of Owls in my Boy Scout outfit. What happened to me in the forest then? I may have continued to move into the deeper recesses of the mountain, and upon hearing the ominous cry of mountain beasts instead of the cry of owls coming from the larch forest in the valley that was growing dark before I knew it, I may have felt inexpressible fear and tried to get out of there but in the end, I lost my way. And I may have gone deeper and deeper into the forest while trying desperately to find my way back out, thus feeling that the forest was like a swamp into which you sink deeper and deeper the more you try to free yourself, and feeling afraid as I watched things growing faint in the thickening darkness. But I may have overcome the fear, sitting on a rock and thinking about the phantomlike larches bathed in the faint light of the moon that had risen over the mountain, and rocks and invisible beasts, and thinking that I, too, was a phantom no different from them, and while groping the hard surface of the rock upon which I was sitting, thinking that in a forest of phantoms, everything from larches to rocks and invisible beasts and humans was a phantom, and was no different from each other. And I may have been living like a phantom to this day, ever since I made my way out of the forest of phantoms.

Even though it might not be possible, the thought of living another life as a phantom after this life is over has always fascinated me. A phantom could exist without getting involved in anything in life, like the sound of ivy leaves, quietly swaying in the wind, that briefly and lightly startles someone who has lost his way deep in the mountain and entered the larch forest that is dark even though it's midday, by making him feel a chilling sensation different from the kind felt in a dark larch forest at midday, or makes your eyes briefly rest on them as you enter an abandoned garden, or exist as a being like myself now, who merely gazes at everything from the top of a rock on the beach, making children who are passing by turn around and look back, and then grows fainter and fainter in its formlessness until completely disappearing in the end, like a dead body decaying after several years. Then the phantom, listening to the sound of its own voice that resembles the cry of an owl coming from a darkened forest in the evening, or a low mumble, could feel that it was still living on as a phantom.

Translated by Jung Yewon

The End

Tonight, while sitting next to the window and gazing at the stony darkness outside, I feel that the end has arrived for me and that my feeling this way somehow assures me of it. And any sobbing won't be necessary. It's simply that my turn has finally come. How thankful I am. It will be over and done with in no time, and what I need to do is merely wait for my eyes to close by themselves. I'd once wished for my end to be a fabulous one, or the absolute opposite, but I'm not so sure now as to which it will be.

It's over, everything, a clear-cut end. Of course, I worried somewhat that the end wouldn't come, but it was a minor concern since I knew my end would surely come. To be exact, though, the end hasn't quite arrived yet. Nonetheless, it's so close to the end that I can safely say this is it. There shouldn't be any obstacle preventing me reaching the end. I can even see the end. Something that I once thought was the farthest thing from me has now become the closest. It's close enough for me to almost touch the tail end of it, and I can even sense it on my fingertips. Yes, I knew for sure it would happen. How strange, considering that I don't remember the beginning of it, but, nevertheless, the end has come. Maybe the ending was there from the beginning, and it's been a long ending. This is not exactly the ending that I had wished for, but it's still a decent one. Yes, I think I can say that. And what a stroke of luck for me to have this ending. I don't have any strength left to continue going any further. It's been like this all the time. I don't remember a time when it wasn't this way. But how could I have come even this far in such a state? Well, that's not important. All I have to do now is wait for the last moment, with hands overlapping, as if all the necessary preparation for this moment were already completed.

Tonight, while sitting next to the window and gazing at the stony darkness outside, I feel that the end has arrived for me and that my feeling this way somehow assures me of it. My turn has come. The opportunity that had seemed so far away and inaccessible has finally been given to me. How thankful I am.

I wish I could recall the name of the potted plant on the round table by the dusty window, but I can't. I bought it one day at a nearby flower shop, wanting to have some kind of living thing in this house where nothing alive existed. It wasn't an easy name to remember and I wasn't able to, so the shop owner had to repeat the name three times, but on my way home with the plant, I forgot the name and I still can't remember it. Since then I have taken good care of it, but, nonetheless, it has withered. The plant continues to shrivel up, as if that's the best thing it can do for itself and as if it was doing its best. As time passed, its small and unusual pouch-shaped leaves gradually dried up and faded to yellow and its vines no longer grew. Contrary to the shop owner's explanation that the plant blooms every now and then, it has never blossomed at all. But the plant hasn't completely died, either. Rather, it's been hovering between life and death. So I often utter nasty words to it, saying it would be much better off if it just died, but even after all this it continues to live. But after my lady had died, I brought her ashes home and sprinkled them in the pot of soil, thinking it would make good fertilizer. I thought that I had done what I could for the plant and wished it would fulfill its part. But it couldn't do it alone.

While I was looking at the wilted plant and deciding that I wouldn't call her my lady, memories of her suddenly returned to me. When did all that happen? It's not easy to find an accurate coordinate in time, when everything is jumbled together like a smear. But I vividly recall certain anecdotes and I also recall that our relationship never reached the point where we said we loved each other; it was a relationship that from the beginning lacked the possibility of reaching such a state. Well, it wasn't that long ago anyway. It started at the beginning of this spring. And spring hasn't ended yet; it's still late spring.

On that day I was strolling along a path in the hills behind my house. It was a path I had trekked numerous times and thus I was so familiar with it that I could even walk it with my eyes closed. It had been made by people treading through the undergrowth and was so entangled with so many other small paths that people would easily get lost, though they would all soon find the right path. I myself took a number of trips around the hill that day.

It was drizzling, the kind of drizzle that one only experiences in the spring. The raindrops were so fine I couldn't feel them. And the rain made no sound when it fell; it was silent. I knew I was getting wet but pretended not to notice; yes, while I was clearly aware that I was getting soaked, I continued walking. No one was in sight. It seemed to me that people who were about to take a walk must've stayed home once they saw rain falling outside their windows and thought, Darn, it's been a long time since I took my last walk . . . well, I'll let it go, it's raining. I saw myself walking in the forest, the only person there. If somebody else had been there, that person would've thought I was a little crazy, as I was walking to and fro with an unstable gait as if I was lost. But I didn't think I looked strange at all.

After walking like that for a while, I wanted to pee. Strangely enough, I often peed more frequently in the forest. The biological instinct by which mammals mark their territories with their urine seemed to be coming back to me, there in the forest. I stepped off the path a little and found a bush and started peeing. I thought that would be a good thing to do for the forest. It would enrich the soil.

Suddenly, at that moment, something pulled at my pants and interrupted my peeing. I turned around. A brown puppy was tugging at one side of my pants and it wouldn't let go. So I asked the dog to let go of my pants and said that it would be a good thing to do for its own sake and that I wouldn't be responsible for the consequences if it kept holding on to my pants with its mouth, and I thought my words were clear enough for the dog to understand. But the dog seemed unable to comprehend what I had just said, even though I thought I had been clear. So I eventually decided that I had no choice but to kick it away. But kicking it away while one side of my pants was being held in its mouth wasn't technically an easy thing to do. So I stopped pissing and bent over and tried to hit it with my fist.

Right at that moment a woman appeared in front of me, apparently the owner of the puppy. She looked old and gave me a strange feeling. Right then, to make things even more strange, she called out to her dog, "Pepper, Pepper." Pepper? At first I didn't understand what she was saying. I even thought she was a little batty. But surprisingly enough, the dog let go of my pants and ran over to her. Meanwhile, I had to zip up my pants in front of her before I stepped out from the bush. "Did you get hurt by any chance?" she asked. But I didn't say anything, as I rarely open my mouth when I'm mad. But she seemed to interpret from my silence that I didn't think it was a big deal. "I'm so sorry," she said to me. Still I said nothing. I was in such an unpleasant mood because I could feel the piss held in my bladder.

Seemingly unaware of my uncomfortable state, she first gently admonished the dog and then apologized to me on its behalf, and following this she scolded it once more, this time instead of me, blaming it for everything that had happened, after which she completed her apology to me, which was so polite that not to accept it would've been rude.

The dog looked very dispirited. "Maybe it's had enough," I told her. I thought that possibly she had deliberately released her dog on me in order to embarrass me, but I said nothing. She leaned forward and petted her disheartened dog so that it immediately became cheerful, as if it had forgotten everything that had just happened. I didn't like the dog acting that way, but again, I didn't say anything. To me dogs are all like that.

I was about to resume my walk when suddenly I wanted to ask her something. "I think I heard you say Pepper—did I hear correctly?" I asked her. "What does it mean?"

"It's my puppy's name," she answered.

"A dog's name!" I said. She nodded. I thought what a name for a dog and how strange it is to call a dog Pepper.

As if reading my mind, she said, "Isn't it a pretty name? My dog loves pepper and she never touches food without any pepper sprinkled on it, and that's how she got her name."

"Your dog certainly has a strange eating habit," I said.

"Isn't she cute?" she asked me. The dog wasn't cute at all, but it did indeed have a strange look. No dog ever looked cute to me, but her dog had a particularly ugly face. Every part of it was squashed, wrinkled, and all crumpled up without even a trace of cuteness. It was such an ugly breed. "Pepper usually doesn't bite anyone, and I wonder why she acted like that," she said. I thought about what she had just told me and wondered what the dog must've thought of me in order for it to bite my pants, and this somewhat irritated me.

I lifted my head and gazed at the woman's face directly in front of me. She was smiling. She was an old woman who must have been attractive in her youth. She might have reached that age when youth's beauty became irrelevant, but she still retained traces of her former beauty. To me, she now looked as old as I was.

Everything was going okay so far. What looked really unusual was her outfit. She was wearing a tight, yellow knitted hat that reached right above her eyebrows, which were nearly hairless. I later discovered that she had lost almost all the hair on her head. She was in what looked like a pretty picnic outfit, a brightly colored dress. Even though I tried to find something unappealing about her, she didn't look bad at all.

She stared intently at my face. I dropped my gaze to the ground and looked at the dog. The dog looked up at her while she looked at me. When I looked at her again, she was looking down at the dog and the dog was looking up at me. Without turning our heads the three of us looked at each other for a while from different angles. And right then, I realized that the dog had a strange habit. When it looked at people it tilted its head slightly to one side. As I don't like either dogs or people looking at me this way, I wanted to end my time with the dog and its mistress, so I lifted my head again and, as I turned to leave, I said goodbye to her. She looked at me as if we had spent too short a time together and as if she wanted me to be with her longer. I wished I could've vanished in front of her like magic and hoped she would close her eyes. But her eyes remained wide open and she continued to look at me.

I started walking again. And as I moved far away from her I came closer to a nearby mineral spring on the hill. Lifting my head after taking a sip of the spring water, I found her standing in front of me as if she'd been transported by magic. I wondered why the woman had followed me. I finished drinking the water and was about to put the gourd down, but I didn't, and instead I scooped up some water and offered it to her. She took it and drank it and then courteously thanked me.

She pointed to a bench by the spring and suggested that we sit there, as if we had already become friends, and then she walked toward it. I realized she had some difficulty walking, but it was too minor to be called a limp. I stood still. There wasn't any reason for me to follow her and do what she wanted me to do. She sat on the bench first and then motioned for me to come over. Not knowing what else to do, I slowly approached her. But I didn't sit down on the bench. It was all wet with rain.

Feeling awkward, I continued to stand there, undecided as to what to do next. "A man shouldn't care too much about getting his pants wet," she said to me. I could've gotten upset, but when I gave it a second thought, it wasn't such a bad thing to say. And so I finally ended up sitting next to her.

Her dog found a spot between our legs and sat on the wet ground. The dog wagged its tail while looking up at me, but I wasn't sure if the dog knew that I wanted to keep my distance. I could barely suppress my urge to put my foot on its tail and keep it there so it wouldn't wag around. "Pepper seems to like you, and she doesn't like many people," she said to me. I not only disliked the dog but I also disliked the fact that the dog liked me, since being liked by someone or something that I don't like is annoying. I've never felt close to dogs, even though dogs are supposed to be the animal dearest to humans. I can't say that I've never tried to have a close relationship with dogs, but it just never happened. At that moment I thought to myself that a cat would make a far better companion, but I didn't tell her this. The dog seemed very happy to be in the drizzle with us.

The rain fell steadily, neither growing heavier nor subsiding. I could feel the rain seeping into my clothes and wetting my body. Raindrops slid down my neck and tickled my chest. I felt as if my body was swelling because of the humidity. All the while I couldn't hear the shouts and labored breathing that I usually heard from people when they exercised on sunny days, and I liked that. This was the reason I took a walk on such a rainy day. It was a warm day in May and I smelled the Acacia blossoms' pungent fragrance strike my nostrils. Acacia trees, which don't like to mix with other kinds of trees, surrounded us and covered the entire mountain so that no other trees were in sight.

"I've seen you before," she said. Surely she hadn't seen me when I'd walked around with a stick, whipping golden-bell flowers for no reason, I thought. "I stole a glance at you sitting on a bench, sleeping soundly, and you looked peaceful, like a sleeping baby," she said.

"Were you only looking at me, nothing else?" I asked her.

"No," she answered.

"Which means?" I said.

"While glancing at you I also thought you looked attractive, too," she said. "You must've been loved by many women when you were young," she said, while gazing at me.

"This woman sure has eyes," I thought. "But I wasn't a playboy as many people seem to think," I told her, while wondering what I was talking about.

"You must have had a nice body when you were young," she said.

"Could be," I answered, smirking, with my shoulders puffed up like a high school boy.

"You look like you were a boy who often did bad things," she said, while looking at me and smiling.

"How did you know? Well, as a matter of fact I have committed a bad deed," I said.

"What kind of bad deed," she asked.

"I don't know if I want to talk about it," I said.

"I want to know," she responded. Strangely enough, I felt that I could tell her anything.

"Long ago I was imprisoned for injuring a person." I didn't

know why I was telling her about such a thing. For some reason it seemed that it would be okay with her. She seemed to possess some kind of power that put a person in a defenseless state. Words that had been held back by my firmly sealed lips began to spill out of me all at once.

"At that time I was working at a butcher shop in a village; it was a job that my younger brother had gotten for me. I liked working there. The different sections of dead animals that were cut up and exhibited in the showcase soothed me and made me feel comfortable. One day an old woman who lived in the village came to buy some meat. She was an old hag who I really didn't like. She was the kind of woman who was hard to please and who was also obnoxious. When I handed her the meat that she had ordered, she looked into the bag and said that I had shortchanged her. So I put the bag on the scale again and had her read the weight that showed the exact amount she had ordered and then I gave the bag back to her. She now looked into the bag and said the meat's color wasn't normal and that the meat looked spoiled. So I told her that the meat had come in that very same day. She then looked right into my eyes and this time asked me if a sick cow had been butchered and then told me that my face showed that I was capable of doing such a thing. So I told her that as long as I could remember I've never deceived others nor myself at the same time. And then I told her to leave if she didn't want the meat. She said it was rude of me to say that to a customer. She then flung the meat on the floor. At that moment and without realizing what I was doing, I struck her shoulder with a knife that was lying next to me on the counter. The knife pierced her shoulder and she fell to the floor, bleeding profusely. She looked as if she had lost consciousness because of the shock. So I called the police and waited for them. But the police arrived much later than I had expected, and so meanwhile I had to spend a boring time waiting. Leaving the old woman there on the floor, I took a big chunk of meat from the refrigerator and began to slice it into pieces. The feeling of meat on my fingertips calmed me down. And I didn't regret what I had done to the old woman at all. And I also didn't think that it was something I couldn't imagine doing.

Sitting next to me, she quietly listened to my story. Since I wasn't used to that kind of earnest, heart-to-heart dialogue, I felt somewhat awkward. But that doesn't at all mean I didn't like talking to her about such things.

"And when I was in court charged with inflicting bodily injury, I didn't defend myself. I said to the judge that I didn't regret what I had done and that statement worked against me, resulting in a longer jail sentence. Yes, I deliberately missed a good opportunity to receive a lighter sentence."

She had a tranquil expression while listening to me. "I'm trying not to pity you," she finally said. Like an obedient student, I listened to her silently. "I like you, not because you were honest enough to tell me about such a thing but because you did such a thing," she told me. Feeling awkward, I petted her dog's head. The dog then began to wag its tail again. Realizing that I was petting a dog, I felt embarrassed, so I withdrew my hand. Examining my face, she said that I looked pale and that I looked as if I had an ailment. I asked her how she knew. She said that she used to be a nurse and took care of sick and injured people but that now she was one of those who needed care. And it was the only thing about her past she revealed to me that day, even though I wanted to hear more stories. Instead she talked about her future in a weak voice. "I don't have many days left; it's getting close to the end." I looked at her face and it clearly revealed that what she said was true. But I didn't ask her what her illness was, not because I thought asking such a question at our first meeting would be inappropriate but because I thought the right thing to do was to wait until she told me herself.

We sat there for a while without exchanging any words. "What are you thinking about?" she finally asked me. I answered that I was thinking of all the Acacia trees' roots that must be entangled together under the mountain. I told her that I was feeling the unyielding power of the roots and that it seemed dreadful to me. As a matter of fact, I was frightened of it. I wasn't afraid of the roots' imagined shapes nor was I afraid of their monstrous vitality. No, I was just scared of something. Yes, I was scared of something and I didn't know what it was or why. To get rid of my fear I tried to think of something that would bring me greater fear, but I could think of nothing else. She was now silent. I quietly looked at her profile as she sat still with her feet on the ground. Strangely, it seemed to me that she was feeling what I was feeling then. Yes, I felt that she and I were linked by some unknown power and that we had entered a space that enabled us to get closer to each other. I tried not to be fooled by such feelings, but it wasn't easy at all.

At dusk we finally left the hill together. When we parted she told me where she lived and asked for my address. Well actually, she first asked me if I had a home and when I answered yes, she then asked me where it was. Where I lived wasn't far from her house, but I explained where I lived as if it was far away from her place, giving her all kinds of contorted directions. It didn't mean I absolutely didn't want to meet her again, but without having any clear reason I thought maybe it would be better not to see her again. "You live close to me and I think I know where your house is," she said. We then said goodbye to each other. With her dog standing next to her, she watched me walk toward my house. When I did turn around after walking some distance, she was waving at me, as if she had been waving since I started walking toward my home.

I returned to my shabby house and to my even shabbier life. I was at a point in my life where any improvement seemed impossible. It was a hopeless life, actually worse than hopeless. I couldn't stand being awake, so I desperately tried to sleep most of the day. And I ate almost nothing. And because I ate almost nothing, I had almost no energy, and because I had almost no energy, I slept most of the time, and because I slept most of the time, I didn't have any energy, and because I had no energy, I ate almost nothing. I didn't have any zest for life. But it wasn't anything new, since I had been that way all my life. But as the days passed like that I wanted to see her again. This wasn't what I had imagined I would want at all. So after several days I purposely went to the place where I had met her the first time and saw her there again. She looked paler and was now so emaciated that I hardly recognized her, but I eventually did by remembering her emaciated condition.

When we met again her dog recognized me first and ran up to me. The dog still looked ugly but not as ugly as before. That day I realized it couldn't look at things properly unless it tilted its head to one side because of its unusual body structure—its head was almost directly attached to its body. It was obvious to me that the dog's appearance and bodily functions must have evolved in this adverse way. After realizing this, the dog no longer looked like something I could never get close to.

She was a couple of years younger than me. The reason she looked older was because of her illness. "It's uterine cancer," she told me, as if telling me the make of her clothes. "It isn't too late to do something, but I'm not doing anything about it," she said, with her hands in her jacket pockets.

I had met her only once before, but she had already become the closest person to me. It seemed as if I had known her for a long time. We spent the day together and that evening we went down the hill. And as before, when the time came to part I left the spot first while she and her dog watched me walk away.

After our second meeting we often met on the hill. No plan was ever made to meet, but, nonetheless, that was a place where

I could meet her. She was always at the same spot. We liked to lie down together, side by side, with passersby glaring at us. Sometimes we went into the bushes to lie down and while there overheard people's conversations, often hearing the person who had fallen behind say he or she couldn't continue walking any longer after their companion had asked them to hurry up. I often rested my head on her lap and took a nap. When I opened my eyes I could see her looking down at me with a smile on her face. It brought me a strange though not uncomfortable relief.

Now and then she told long stories that didn't have a clear plot and now I don't remember what they were all about. I listened to her stories without paying much attention since they were not stories that required my full concentration. She usually spoke out of turn. But, nevertheless, each time after finishing her tales she would ask me, "Did you hear what I just said?"

I would say, "Sure, from beginning to end, without missing anything."

She would ask me, "How was it?"

Then I would answer, "It seemed like a story you would tell and it seemed, well, somewhat strange . . . no, it really wasn't strange to me at all."

She would then ask me again, "What did I talk about? After talking I can't remember what I've just said, but I know whatever it was I talked about something for sure."

I would often tell her, "It was just an incoherent tale."

She usually asked, "Was it really incoherent?"

Then I would answer, "Yes, it was. There was no coherence at all."

She would then say, "That's why I could say such a thing."

I would say to her, "But it was good anyway."

She would say, "I don't know why I told you such a story. But thank you anyway for listening to it till the end."

I told her, "Thank you for telling me the story." Yes, without fail, whenever she finished her story, we would have a conversation like that.

Maybe our relationship was one where we were both just thankful, nothing more, nothing less. I think the expression "nothing more, nothing less" would be a good one to sum up our relationship. I was aware of the nature of our relationship and also knew it was all in vain. One thing was for sure: it wasn't love that brought us together. Speaking of love, I believe no such thing exists—what exists are only people who believe that love exists, like all other ideals in this world.

Anyway, I didn't have any reactionary feelings toward her. Unlike so many others, she didn't say things like, "Try to see the world more positively." She also didn't try to make me choose a better path in life. And because of all this I think I was able to bear her. She also left me alone to be the way I was, even though it wasn't a good way to be. I treated her the same way she treated me. And how she was spending the last moments of her life wasn't much different from what I was doing. All this enabled us to have sympathy for each other and to bear it all. And so between us there wasn't any conflict like what I'd experienced with other women. I was able to bear those other women only after our relationships had cooled off. Above all, what those women gave me was compassion. I would've endured them much better if they had approached me with more impure intentions.

One day, while sitting in the bushes we had designated as our special spot, she asked me whether there was anything I wanted from her, telling me that whatever it was, she wanted to give it to me. I thought about it for a while. I wanted to ask her for something that would either be impossible or too difficult for her to give. "I want to have your bones," I said. I don't know why I suddenly said that to her. She sank deep in thought for a moment, and then said, "You'll have them, but not right now." And I knew what her reply meant. "But how about this for now?"

she said, as she thrust her lips toward mine. Her lips felt unreal as they touched mine. That's how our somewhat blundering, gawky kiss happened unexpectedly. Her lips were tasteless. And the kiss was neither good nor bad. It was such an empty experience that I wondered how it was possible for me to feel that way. And it seemed she felt the same way, too. With our lips touching we looked at each other from such a close distance that the other person's face appeared blurry. And while we were kissing we didn't experience anything like eternity passing. The kiss, where no tongues were extended and no excitement was shared, was so dispassionate that it didn't provoke or reject any reaction—it was a kiss of cessation. I felt like I was kissing the trace of a kiss. I felt her shallow breathing on the tip of my nose. We realized that we couldn't get any closer to each other, couldn't go beyond the border created by our lips and that if we did so it would go against our deepest wishes.

Our lips soon parted, and after our kiss we both felt that everything was over with and had passed by. We saw an unembellished sadness on each other's faces. Our sadness, unaccompanied by any intensity, hovered on our faces for a moment and then disappeared behind our smiles. Our sadness was the kind that could be transferred but was not contagious. We both knew that certain words shouldn't be spoken, such as the fact that we wanted to die by each other's hand while in each other's bosom, and so we didn't say them. After that day we did kiss one more time and that was no more than our lips touching. Apart from those two kisses, we didn't even hold hands.

For a while we remained still, without exchanging any words. A silence surrounded us. Speechless, we continued to sit in silence. It wasn't the stillness that follows after a gust of passion has swept by, but, nonetheless, what we felt was something similar. And we entrusted ourselves to the stillness. After some time had passed she finally opened her mouth and, as if murmuring to herself, she said, "I've never had this feeling of barely existing before." Until she said those words I didn't even realize I was there with her at that moment.

The hill was covered with red azalea blossoms. Spring was in full swing. Trees and plants that had waited for this time of year were all in a frenzy. I suddenly thought that spring flowers were all too persistent in asserting their joy and their moment in time. "It would be so good if this whole hill caught on fire and all the trees burned down to their roots," I said. She didn't say anything in response. She looked as if she was deep in thought. After a while she looked at me and asked, "What are you thinking about?"

"Your uterus and what is happening or not happening in it," I answered. But as a matter of fact that wasn't what I was thinking of at all; I made it up on the spur of the moment. She remained silent. Soon she lay down gently. I lay down next to her, pressing my large body against her tiny one.

After a while she began to hum a song that I hadn't heard before, but, strangely enough, it wasn't foreign to my ears. "What song is that?" I asked.

"It's not a song you would know; I just made it up," she said. "And if I had to make up lyrics for it, they would go like this: 'One day, when I was sitting by the window, a bird flew into the room through an open window and entered my uterus, and there it built a nest, laid eggs, and soon baby birds were born, and the mother bird pecked at my flesh to feed its offspring, and now the mother has died but the babies are still flying about in my uterus.'"

"It would sound like a sad song to some people, but it doesn't sound sad to me," I said. But she said nothing. She looked as if she was thinking about other things. For some reason I thought that the forest we were lying in was her uterus. "This thickly wooded forest seems to have a dense regularity, and I feel like I'm confined in it," she said.

And again, without any words spoken and like people who

were already dead, we lay together. We felt that everything was done and had been erased, feeling that even our feelings no longer existed, feeling that everything had reached rock bottom, and feeling that we ourselves were the bottom. And our hopeless situation, which was too obvious to require confirmation, gave me pure satisfaction. That day, after a full moon had emerged, we finally walked down the hill. The full moon that night looked as if it was traversing a different path from its usual one.

That evening for the first time I went with her to her house. One surprising thing I found there was an incredible number of painkiller ampoules and injectors stacked in a cupboard. While drinking coffee at her kitchen table she said, "When I look at those drugs I feel a kind of providence that I shouldn't fight against. So I use as little painkillers as possible."

"It may sound silly, but aren't you in a lot of pain?" I asked.

"I can endure it," she said, "and feeling the pain isn't a bad thing, since through my pain I feel like a whole person."

After a couple of days we met again at the hill, but she didn't look well at all. When I gazed at her face she asked me how she looked. I told her she looked funny. While saying that I felt a lump form in my throat.

When we found a place to sit down she repeatedly rolled up and released weeds with her right index finger until she finally said, "I have no strength to hold myself up, and I just can't find the energy I need to continue living." She looked as if even saying that was too much for her. "Ending it won't be easy, but I think I can do it," she said. I nodded twice, once for my consent and the other one for my support. "I won't help you there, since any help from me would be useless," I said. "Thank you for understanding and accepting me the way I am," she said.

It was the last time I saw her alive. Several days have passed since then. During those few days I was bedridden with a very bad flu. And one evening, barely able to gather myself up, I wanted to go to her. I was in a state where I couldn't move unless something forced me to. But that day I went to her house out of my own volition.

I found her dead, and next to her body I saw a needle and potassium chloride. She was wearing the same clothes she had worn the day I first met her. She even wore the yellow knitted hat she had worn that day. Surprisingly, she looked very neat and tidy. And she looked peaceful, too. Her dog was also dead, with its limbs sprawled out. And it was true that for the first time I thought her dog looked cute. So I sat down next to it and even petted its head for a while. Its loose hair stuck to my hand, but I didn't bother to brush it off.

I believe her last moment of pain didn't last long, just as she'd wished. That is one good thing about potassium chloride. It is fast and infallible, so to speak. And I'm so grateful for this potassium chloride I now hold in my hand, waiting for it to be dissolved in my body.

Without any reluctance, I did all that needed to be done after her death, and afterwards I brought the ashes of both her and her dog to my house. Actually, most of the ashes I sprinkled in a forest near the incinerator and only brought a handful of it home. I tasted the blackish powder, but the taste was insipid. I put the powder in an empty coffee jar and placed it on a cupboard. After that I sometimes added some to my coffee, but it didn't make any difference to the taste. And one day I had an idea of what to do with the powder, so I sprinkled it in the plant pot. But the plant didn't come back to life. And it will never revive itself, since I uprooted it completely. This is the memory I have of her, of our encounter, an encounter that never reached the status of love and which, from the beginning, lacked the possibility of ever reaching love.

Even though I now wonder whether all this actually happened, I know that in fact it did. It's over, fortunately, everything, a clear-cut end. Of course, I worried somewhat that the end wouldn't come, but it was a minor concern since I knew my end would surely come. To be exact, the end hasn't quite arrived yet. Nonetheless, it's so close to the end that I can safely say this is it. There shouldn't be any obstacle preventing me from reaching the end. I can even see the end. Something that I once thought was the farthest thing away from me now has become the closest. It's close enough for me to almost touch the tail end of it, and I can even sense it on my fingertips. Yes, I knew for sure it would happen. How strange, considering that I don't remember the beginning, but, nevertheless, the end has come. Maybe the ending was there from the beginning, and it has been a long ending. This is not exactly the ending that I had wished for, but still, it's a decent one. I think I can say that. And what a stroke of luck for me to have this ending. I don't have any strength left to continue going any further. It's been like this all the time. I don't remember a time when it wasn't this way. But how could I have come this far in such a state? Well, that's not important. All I have to do now is wait for the last moment, with one hand over the other, as if all the necessary preparation for this moment has already been completed. And since I have recited these words countless times to myself, I can even remember all of it by heart.

Tonight, while sitting next to the window and gazing at the stony darkness outside, I feel that the end has arrived for me and that my feeling this way somehow assures me of it. And any sobbing accompanying this feeling won't be necessary. It's simply that my turn has finally come. How thankful I am. It will be over and done with in no time and what I need to do is to merely wait for my eyes to close by themselves. I had wished for my end to be a fabulous one or the absolute opposite, but I'm not so sure now which category my ending will fall into.

Translated by Inrae You Vinciguerra and Louis Vinciguerra

Volume Without Weight

Forgetting its own weight, a shape composed only of volume. As if the volume is composed of sadness, I feel sad when I hold the balloon in my hands; it's a sadness that isn't easy to attune myself to, a sadness I can't feel without becoming uncomfortable, a sadness that isn't of good quality, a chaotic sadness. But the weight of the volume that seems unaffected by gravity seems to me so heavy that I can barely hold it up. The lightness of what I'm holding now is heavy enough to press down on any matter with weight.

He's sitting in an old wheelchair by the second floor window of a luxurious country house, wearing what looks like a woman's colorful, floral patterned pajamas. He's motionless and appears to be asleep, and actually, he is asleep. Now and then he twists and turns fitfully, as if he's having a bad dream. His disheveled white hair covers his head and is blown about by the wind coming through the open window. Soon he slowly opens his eyes. With a blank look, he gazes about for a moment.

"I must've dozed off. Falling asleep without realizing happens to me more often nowadays. Maybe this is part of a process where I gradually adjust myself to eternal sleep. I've already reached the stage where I can accept my death at any time, even though I don't know for sure if death is worth waiting for," he murmurs.

After some seconds pass, he wipes his mouth. "Luckily, it seems I didn't drool while sleeping, which usually happens to me.

My mouth is always half open and usually remains open while I sleep. Who knows, maybe I drooled but it dried up. It doesn't matter, though, because I don't care about things that happen without my noticing; and even when I notice they're affecting me, I usually ignore them. Of course, this takes place when I'm able to ignore them, or when my concerns have no effect on them."

As if his neck has stiffened, he kneads it a couple of times and then sinks into thought. "Since it feels like someone is gripping my neck while I sleep, I always end up massaging it after waking up. And I know I do this all the time, not because of my stiff neck but because it's become a habit." He smiles. "I like to think that I do everything for a reason. Yes, the important thing is to find a plausible excuse for whatever I do, as though having no excuse is something that can't be excused. Having an excuse is very crucial, whether I'm doing something or nothing at all."

He slowly raises his head and looks up at the ceiling. "Luckily, there're no bats hanging from the ceiling. Recently when I awake from naps I often see a flock of black bats dangling upside down from the ceiling with their wings folded, bats that can usually only be seen in caves. While clinging to the ceiling and seemingly focused on me, all the bats are quiet—at least I can't hear anything. Since I know they're not going to harm me, I leave them alone, and then, after a moment or so, they become numerous in front of my eyes. But I don't feel anything like horror. The real horror comes when they fall on me as they lose their power to cling onto the ceiling. At those times I have to pretend I'm plucking them off my body. And I wonder why I can so clearly see those non-existent bats while at the same time I don't see real things happening right in front of me."

He looks around the room, as if it's new to him. "Everything is as it was, nothing has changed, and there's no reason to change, and no reason not to change as well. But how can I say nothing has changed? That's because I examined everything in this room in minute detail before I fell asleep. Everything in this room is subject to my protection and surveillance, a surveillance that isn't much different from my protection. Things in this room have no meaning without me; the desk can be a desk and the wheelchair can be a wheelchair because of me. In this way I can be superior to things and control them—at least in my mind. And because I know that this superior capacity can only be sustained in my mind, I try so hard to maintain it."

"Even though I might not be aware of it, things must be getting old and worn out. And I wonder why I feel that the things in front of me look absurdly exaggerated: in their bigness and in their smallness, in their hardness and in their softness, and in their brightness and in their darkness. Maybe they're not actually real. Maybe they're nothing but my feelings. My feelings create such differences. Yes, I think it's better to trust this world more than myself; in other words, relying on the solidity of physical properties rather than on my sensations would be better for me."

For a short spell he sinks into thought. "I think my thoughts are reasonable. Anyway, nobody seems to come into this room, and, of course, no one goes out because no one comes in. Who knows, though, maybe my son came in and quietly looked at me sleeping and then left. I know he's often done that when he's home to check on whether I'm dead yet or not. At those times he would silently leave my room after giving a look-see, saying, 'Well, more time seems to be needed for him to die, and, of course, I can wait, since everything takes time.' But nowadays he rarely comes into my room, and I guess that's because he's realized I'm not going to die as soon as he wishes. Well, I can feel his disappointment. I want to die soon enough, but so far I don't see any signs indicating I'll be gone that soon. But I also know that having no signs of approaching death doesn't mean it's impossible to die soon enough."

He pricks up his ears. "How silent it is. It seems my son isn't home. Recently, he hardly stays home and pretends to be busy or to seem really busy. Well, when you pretend to be busy long enough, maybe you actually become busy. My daughter-in-law seems to be taking a nap in her room. During her naps she hates to be bothered by any noise I make. But I don't care about that. I'm not the kind of person who cares about what someone else thinks regardless of what I'm doing. I can't say, though, that I'm totally free of concerns. Anyway, I try to be as quiet as possible when she's home. And, as a result of my effort to be quiet, I sometimes let out a cry. At those times I scream at the top of my lungs, but in reality my screams don't have any sound."

"Or maybe my daughter-in-law got bored and went shopping. There's nothing better to kill time with than shopping—I, though, have never gone shopping to pass time but everybody says this is the case. Regardless, she is still immature, unthrifty, and lazy. Although she has a cute side that my son doesn't possess at all, I don't prefer either one of them, but if I had to make a choice, I would say that my heart tilts in favor of my daughter-in-law. But it doesn't mean I don't like my son, either. I just need more patience when dealing with him. My daughter-in-law, though, is somewhat nice and tries to be nice to me even when she doesn't have to, something that doesn't work for me anyway."

He strains his ears to make sure there's no sound. "I still don't hear anything. Also, nobody seems to eavesdrop on me. And that's because I've never said anything that's worth listening to. I always talk to myself, whether I'm being spoken to or not. Therefore, I know there's nobody to eavesdrop on me—except myself. Fortunately, or maybe unfortunately, I don't hear the unidentified voice at this moment that nowadays I hear whenever I'm about to sleep or to awaken from sleep, a voice in an urgent tone that silently calls my name and makes me somehow feel shameful. Anyway, where does the voice come from? Maybe it's better not to know the identity of the unidentified voice."

With his palms, he covers his ears. "When I block my ears, I can hear all kinds of sounds, sounds I couldn't hear with my ears open, sounds that disappear when my palms are removed, sounds that don't disappear even after I remove my palms, sounds that I can't make out any meaning from, sounds that come from my inner self, sounds that are nothing but noise, sounds that are all rushing into me at the same time. But it doesn't mean I care about them, since they're nothing but mere sounds. They may threaten me but they're not able to harm me. I'm now, to some degree, familiar with them. Yes, I became familiar with not only these sounds but also all the sounds of this world, sounds that are nothing more than mere noises."

He glances at the door. "The door is slightly open. My son always leaves the door ajar to show that he hasn't locked me in here. Of course, he doesn't confine me to this room, even though I like to think that way, since thinking that I'm suffering because of my son somehow consoles me. Can I, though, leave this room whenever I want to? Oh well, sure I can leave this room, but it'll only be a short distance before I reach the steps. That means I can't get downstairs unless I tumble down in my wheelchair. The stairs actually prevent me from getting downstairs. Sometimes a sudden urge rises in me and I feel like doing it and ending it all . . . but to completely loosen the reins of reason is much more difficult than you'd think. It's not a novel thing at all, though. The problem is that I need help from reason even when I lose it. The strange thing is that reason is as tenacious as a leech; yes, there's nothing that clings so strongly to itself than reason. I think that bastard reason is sitting stubbornly with hands interlocked, refusing to loosen its grip while only listening to its own voice . . ."

"When I really want to go downstairs I ask my son to help me, and, of course, this happens only when he's at home. He carries me downstairs in his arms and acts as if he's carrying something heavy, but actually, I'm not heavy, since my body has only bones and skin left on it. But such things happen very rarely. And even then some kind of whim beyond my control usually rises up in me and I'll insist that he take me back upstairs,."

"For some unknown reason I seem to be afraid of leaving this small room. The thought that this is the only place I should be crosses my mind. If I'm out of this room for even a bit, I feel like a fish removed from its fishbowl, and, of course, I'm not sure if a fish out of its bowl feels as I do when I'm out of my room. My mind hardly wants to go anywhere I can't reach without someone's help, which is, I think, a good thing. And when I'm somewhere else, I shout to my son to take me back to my room. At those times, even though he doesn't complain and obeys my order, I can read his mind by seeing his different facial expressions—a face filled with discontentment followed by some discontent, then one with just a little discontent, and finally, a face with no discontent. And he seems to think that I ask him to do one thing and then another in order to give him a hard time, but, as a matter of fact, I rarely do it on purpose. At times, without any good reason, I feel repulsion toward my son and begin plotting against him, but I rarely put my plans into action. Putting thoughts into practice seems somehow dull to me. I feel satisfied enough when those thoughts remain just thoughts."

"But this doesn't mean I dislike my son at all. Comparing my son to any other son in the world, I can't say my son is bad . . . if I had a son with a nasty heart, I would've been kicked out of this house long ago. Well, maybe that wouldn't be such a bad thing. I wonder why my son doesn't take me somewhere and abandon me; I'm ready to easily forgive him if he did so. The notion that a son is not supposed to do such a thing to his father prevents him from doing it. Oh yes, my son values righteousness and duty above everything else. The more I think about my son, the funnier a bastard he becomes."

"Anyhow, my son takes care of me, and he's also busy with

some kind of business to support his family, a business that's suspicious and involved in criminal activity. He's capable of that. But he never talks to me about his dishonorable business, even though I might be able to offer some valuable advice if he asks for it. I think he considers me a useless person. Well, it's true. I'm the kind of human being who wouldn't disturb the world in the least by disappearing at any time. As a matter of fact, the world would be better off without me. But I don't want to disappear, even if it's a good thing for this world."

"And repulsively enough, my son still maintains his formal respect for me. It's nauseating. When I get mad and irritated without any reason, he, with a shameless face, says he wants me to realize that I'm still his father, regardless of whatever I say or do to him. He also says he wishes I would treat him as a son from now on. He just doesn't realize that there are certain things you can't get, regardless of how much you try . . . I can't say I'm doing my best as a father, but at least I think about my obligations all the time . . . oh, no, that's not true. It's been a long time since I discarded such things as righteousness and obligation . . ."

"But my bastard son always looks so energetic and confident, as if he's confident about his confidence. I think that's maybe why he always looks unreliable to me. There's nothing more stupid than being convinced of one's own power. All kinds of power entail inconsiderateness and imprudence. But my son doesn't understand such things yet. And the bastard thinks he can achieve anything if he directs his efforts to whatever he wants, not knowing that there are things you can't do regardless of your efforts, and there are also people who just can't do certain things. And my son's overflowing confidence always makes me uneasy—I don't like it at all. If I say to him, 'You look full of energy today,' the bastard glows happily, without catching my cynical tone. What a dope. Actually, he's not that simple but is rather shrewd. I don't know who he takes after in that regard, but I'm pretty sure it's not me. And that's why he's been doing well, even though I don't know how long it'll last. For instance, this house isn't cheap. It's a pompous house, though I can't fully appreciate its pompousness while only dwelling inside. The interior is gaudy enough, but it seems to me that he has even more regard for the exterior. Yes, just as I thought, my bastard son is remarkably sly . . ."

"He has some lackeys around him, too. And they all look like gangsters with robust bodies; probably, they all go through life using only their muscle power. They also seem devoted to my son. It appears to me, too, that to them my son is someone to fear. But I wonder why people around that bastard fear him. Well, as a matter of fact, I'm also afraid of him, and I only have to look at his face to fear him, so I can say my fear isn't unfounded. My son, though, has never beaten me up. But he has threatened me; oh, that's not true either, since I'm already afraid of the bastard without him having to actually intimidate me. As a matter of fact, I'm ready to be smacked any time, a beating being the best solution when words don't work."

"Maybe the malice existing between us is not as deep as I think. The enmity hasn't grown as much as I expected . . . although I understand the feelings of the people around my son who are scared of him. One time, when one of his underlings betrayed him, he calmly broke one of the guy's fingers in the living room of this house, telling him, 'You don't seem to understand the consequences of your betrayal, but this will teach you, and remember, next time it'll be your neck, not a finger.' The guy turned ghastly pale and trembled, with the scene being somewhat spectacular to me. Another time, while he and his lackeys were all plotting in the same room, he took down a sword that was probably once used by samurais and peeled an apple that his wife had brought him. That's quite a skill, I thought. That blade must harbor the memory of someone disemboweling himself—the blade was impressive enough for me to think this. Maybe that's the reason he always says no whenever I ask if I can touch it. I think peeling an apple with a blade that somebody once used to cut open his own belly would be fun ...."

"My son believes that he needs power to live in this world. And he, without doubt, thinks that power is beautiful. And in this respect he takes after his grandfather, my father. There are not many people like my father, who possesses everything I detest. What was desirable to him was rarely desirable to me. He would say that only the powerful survive. To him other people were always means to achieve his goals, a ladder to step on to reach what he desired. In other words, he would ask me to try standing in the shoes of the strong, that is, in the shoes of wrongdoers. To me nothing is funnier than the logic of the strong. Honestly, exploiting other people is one of the most natural things for us human beings to do. But at the same time, the logic of the weak is also funny; their logic exists only in their hope for the future, believing that someday justice will materialize, even though in reality such a thing won't happen . . . actually I might have to thank logic for enabling me to express all this ingratitude toward my father. And who knows, maybe this kind of ingratitude is one way to repay his kindness."

He touches his legs for a moment. "I can't feel anything as usual; no sensation is left at all. But I can still do things while pretending I have sensations, as if they exist without existing. This has been going on a long time. Well, my back is stiff after hours of sitting in this same position. Compared to the stomachache that has just started, though, my backache is nothing but a piece of cake. The ache is caused by this damn inflammation of my stomach. Groaning would be natural, but I would rather bare it, since groaning all alone without any listeners would be a dull thing to do. When my bastard son comes home, I'll share my fabulous moaning with him, for they're too good to be heard by just me alone. Yes, even groaning can sometimes be bracing, but at other times it brings me little joy. Usually groaning with somebody next to me seems to perk me up while groaning alone has the opposite effect. And I can now say that there's no one who exploits this better than I do, to the point where I can defeat anyone at exaggerating pain. And that's why I'm not even thinking of groaning for now."

"By the way, my dangling feet are starting to feel tight. That's because they have socks on them, which the housemaid patronizingly slipped on even though she didn't have to. She did it because I have cold feet and they get cold easily without socks—and I'm not good at tolerating cold feet. One of the socks, though, is only half on. They were both fine at first, but it slipped off without my noticing, and the fact that I didn't notice gives me an uneasy feeling. But there's nothing I can do about it, since I can't reach my feet with my hands even though I can bend over a little. And I can't move my feet up to my hands, either. My feet are beyond my reach. They're so far away from me that I feel pathetic. But regardless, my feet feel closer because of their tightness. I wish the housemaid would come soon; usually I don't want to see her, but today I want to see her more than any other person."

He stops speaking to himself and sits still; he seems to be thinking about what to do next. "There are few things I can do in this room other than sitting still like this. Nonetheless, I don't stop thinking of what I can do. I begin speaking aloud about what I'm supposed to do and what I'm thinking of doing, about what I can do or about what I'm not necessarily supposed to do, and about what I can do patronizingly. And then after a while I naturally reach the conclusion that I can do nothing about what I'm not able to do, and from then on I take doing nothing to the extreme. No one can compete with me when it comes to doing nothing, since I've been familiar with doing nothing for such a long time. Well, I'm not going to do anything, even though there are things left that I can do. I won't allow myself to do anything, and I'll stay here and do nothing. And even when I do something, I will consider it not done by me. Actually, it's unusual for me to have nothing I can do, and it's rare for me to have nothing to do. The problem, though, is that the few things I do usually end up causing damage. For instance, I prove that everything within my reach is under my control by toppling or breaking them. So I try to put things out of arm's reach. But at the same time, I can't restrain my hands which, without my realizing it, reach out for things. And now and then when I think it's necessary, I abuse myself. It's not full-scale self-torture but rather more like going crazy. By doing this, I can be a witness to what my mind can do to my body. And I can see what my impaired body can do to my tarnished spirit . . ."

"Sometimes I pull at my thinning hair with my fingers. This is a funny thing to do. And when I notice my head leaning toward my hands, I feel somehow satisfied. The fact that my upper torso is the only part of my body subject to my will is a good thing. The lower half of my body has been doing nothing but propping up the upper half ever since it became paralyzed long ago—since then it's had the role of being weighed down by the upper body. And maybe it's because of the numbness of my lower half but almost always I feel that my upper body is full of energy. My two halves feel like diametric opposites. Anyway, maybe I should cut off my useless legs. But if I cut off useless parts of my body, eventually not many parts will be left. My head, probably the most useless of my body parts, should be gotten rid of first . . . yes, by all accounts my situation is hopeless. Maybe, though, to experience despair is the most human ability, since the gods are not blessed to enjoy it. But I no longer want to depend on my despair, which I've become so reliant on and which can be a kind of strength for me. Despair and my reliance on it only irritates me, though."

Without saying a word, he sits for a while. "Well, my stomach inflammation seems to be going away. I know, though, without a doubt, it'll be back; whether I'm anticipating it or not, it's going to cause me more or less the same pain. But why do I always think aloud instead of thinking silently, spewing out undigested thoughts, even when I'm alone. Perhaps the reason I speak to myself out loud is because I don't want to believe what my heart is saying or because I don't want to listen to it. Of course, I'm not sure if I really have such a thing in me, that is, if I really have the truth in me."

He again sits still for a moment without saying anything. "The suffering of human beings exists where God's mercy and warm breath reaches." He speaks slowly, as if reading a quote. "I don't know why I'm saying this, and I don't know its meaning, either. Even though I maybe don't know the meaning of what I'm saying, I want to say it anyway—God could be referred to as having an absolute ability to be completely indifferent or callous to all things in existence."

He sinks into silence once more. "When I sit silently like this I become anxious for no reason. But I also know what to do when this occurs—I think about the object of my anxiety or I think about what my anxiety is urging me to do." He looks around the room, assailed by misgivings. He then glances toward his desk and opens his eyes in a flash, as if something he can do has crossed his mind. "Oh, that's right—I should finish recording my will, since I've already decided to create one. Well, that's a surprise—I didn't forget about it. Yes, I'm going to pretend that all of a sudden something fabulous to do popped into my mind."

Turning his wheelchair around, he begins rolling it backward toward the desk. "This wheelchair only moves backwards; moving backwards is much easier than moving forwards, though not that much easier. And I don't know why this wheelchair does such a strange thing. It began after my bastard son fixed it. It needed some repair work after I had used it for a long time. Maybe the bastard did it on purpose. But I was the one who insisted on leaving it that way when I realized the wheelchair wouldn't move forward. By doing so I felt I was more esteemed by others. Anyway, by moving backwards this wheelchair somehow faithfully reveals some aspect of my life situation to me."

He reaches the desk and takes out a videotape. He then connects a camcorder—placed on a tripod by the desk so as to capture his profile—to a TV set on the desk and inserts the tape into the camcorder before pressing the play button. But nothing is seen on the screen. "Everything has been deleted. No wonder, since I erased everything I recorded. And that's because nothing was worth saving. I just couldn't make a will that fully satisfied me."

He rewinds the tape to the beginning. "My bastard son bought me this camcorder for my birthday. He buys whatever I want, as if there's nothing else he can do for me." He remains thinking for a moment with his finger on the record button. "Beginning is always difficult, and, of course, what follows is difficult, too. And beyond that, there's the more difficult part waiting for me—ending it . . . the ending that ultimately can't be ended . . ."

After a while he looks up at the ceiling, as if some idea has crossed his mind. He sees some fully inflated balloons attached to long strings hovering near the ceiling. He pulls down on one of the strings and then holds it for a moment before letting the balloon float toward the ceiling. The balloon reaches the ceiling again. "My son bought me these balloons knowing how much I like this kind of thing . . . for some unknown reason I wanted to have balloons . . . my son doesn't treat me very well, but I know he tries to be nice to me; nonetheless, he's not trying so hard that I'm touched by his efforts. Yes, I shouldn't be moved by such a trifling matter . . ."

"Regardless, I like these balloons because when I don't know what to do, I can pull them down and let them soar while thinking if there's anything I can do with them, or to them, or without them. And sometimes I do this endlessly while wondering what I'm doing. I would stop if somebody advised me to stop, but no one asks me to stop, so I keep doing it. Of course, I can't bear people meddling in my affairs, either. And, strangely enough, after playing with the balloons, I feel lighthearted—but not all the time. Incidentally, when I hold a balloon I feel like the whole world is held in my hands. And at those times I press the balloon harder without even realizing it. After this, when I release the balloon, the whole world escapes from me, leaving me behind all alone, and I feel I'm left in a place where the world has disappeared. But, at the same time, I feel all my feelings are false."

After freeing the balloon, he gazes at it on the ceiling. "The way the balloon floats in midair, like it has forgotten where to fly to, looks as if it's submerged in deep, silent water . . . and besides balloons, there's another thing my bastard son buys me—candy. Even though he knows I have diabetes and eating candy is not good for me, he buys candy as often as he can. That's because I can't tolerate running out of candy; first, I solicit him for candy, then I unreasonably demand it, and finally, I get angry and berate him." He smiles. "Sure, I know my getting mad and scolding him over the matter is brazen enough. But, at the same time, there's some lesson here to learn—you can't get something just by wanting it . . . to obtain something you sometimes have to be aggressive and persevering. Of course, getting what you desire after all the fuss is not a big deal, either. Well, since I've been thinking of candy, I might eat one."

He takes a piece of candy from his desk drawer and puts it in his mouth. "One strange thing about candy is that I don't crave it until I think of it; regardless of what I'm thinking about, I end up thinking about candy, and eventually I'm unable to resist. I don't have strong teeth, and nothing is easier than sucking on candy. Of course, nothing is worse than candy for my diabetes. Hum, this time I put a melon-flavored candy in my mouth. Whenever I have one I feel like I just finished eating a melon, a fake one . . ."

He begins sucking on the candy. "I think I eat too much candy nowadays. So I made a rule in an attempt to restrict the number I eat daily—the rule being I will punish myself whenever I violate the rule. And I hope the punishment is strong enough to eradicate my desire to eat candy by merely thinking about the penalty. But I don't think the punishment works well on me. For instance, as a punishment I have to eat three more candies than the three I'm allowed to eat. As a matter of fact, no worse punishment exists for my health than eating more candies. But I don't believe this is an appropriate penalty, since this is some kind of silly ploy. For example, I try to take something bad from someone after giving the person something good . . . well, I'm not sure if I just used an appropriate example. I think I need to think of some other penalty . . . wait a minute, how about calling it a prize, not a penalty? As a way to coax me, awarding a prize would be a better way than punishing me; I award myself more candy if I don't exceed three per day . . . a prize that allows me to eat more candy! But what a stupid thing to do at best . . . I think I see the limitation of my mental capacity, the ultimate end of my intelligence . . . well, that's me. Unfortunately, I've never thought of anything that makes me admire myself. I'd better stop thinking about candy and get back to what I was thinking about before . . ."

For a moment, he's in a reverie again. "I can't think about anything but candy. I'd better find something else to indulge myself with which I can resist . . . well, the candy has already melted in my mouth. No wonder, since I've sucked on it so fervently . . . it probably couldn't withstand my vigorous sucking . . . the fact the candy melted due to my body temperature and body moisture is somehow amazing, since my body seems all dried up and hardened and cold."

He sinks deeper into thought. "I can't think of anything else but candy. And when I try to block out the thought of candy, all other thoughts are blocked out as well. In this case, there's only one solution." He put another piece of candy in his mouth. "And now I'm finally free from thinking about candy. Yes, as I imprison the candy in my mouth, it frees me."

He's lost in thought once more. "I must have some problems in the way I speak, and, furthermore, in the way I think, since no ideas cross my mind and since I think in a way where no thinking ensues. But at the same time, so many disconnected thoughts swarm wildly in my mind that I feel as if I'm dancing to the tune of my thoughts and words while they cajole each other."

He changes his posture. "Fortunately, I don't feel like taking a pee yet—but holding it back isn't an easy task at all. I can postpone the decision of whether to take a pee or not, since I have time until the housemaid comes in and changes my diaper. Wearing a diaper at my age should be a cause for shame, but I'm not ashamed at all. I was the one who came up with the idea of wearing a diaper; I asked them to put a diaper on me since I would eventually wet my pants if I didn't wear one. Pissing in a diaper, though, is pleasant. Nothing else gives me more pleasure than the moment when warm urine flows from my crotch, even though I abhor the cold, wet feeling of urine after it cools. I must have some sensations left in my lower half since I can still feel warmth, coldness, and wetness. How strange that the same urine can offer such different sensations to the same person. How marvelous."

Pressing the record button again, he listens to its winding sound without uttering a word. "I like to listen to the soft winding sound of magnetic tape that records both images and sounds, sounds I can barely hear and sounds that seem to be devouring all the thoughts in my head. But it's not so good that I'm able to say no better sound than this exists."

He presses the stop button, rewinds the tape, and then presses the record button once more. But he's unable to say a word and only glares at the camcorder. He presses the stop button on the remote control and then presses the zoom-in button. His face becomes so large that it almost covers the whole TV screen. "Well, my face has become too big. And it doesn't look very good, so now I can regard it as my own face."

He then presses the zoom-out button. As one whole side of the room now appears on the TV screen, he sees himself at one corner of the screen. "Well, this time I've become too small." His hands tremble while he maneuvers the remote control. "I'm sick of my shaking hands; unlike my paralyzed legs, they shake as if they're full of energy while I remain still." After struggling briefly, he finally succeeds in making the whole upper half of his body appear on the screen. Silently, he looks at his profile. "Somehow I look more innocent on the TV screen. It doesn't look like me, since there's nothing wicked or sly about it. Well, this purity is also the other side of my artfulness." He presses the record button.

"In my life, fathering you was my biggest mistake among all the mistakes I've made in my mistake-ridden life. This mistake was a monumental one, as it was made in a situation where no single mistake was permitted at all. You've become the human being I never planned or dreamed of."

He presses the stop button and rewinds the tape and then presses the play button and watches what he just recorded. "I thought there would be nothing to say, but I see I had something to say after I started speaking. Words are things that can arise and be created while we speak. Without emotion my voice doesn't sound bad, but my face doesn't look very good . . . it's completely contorted."

After pressing the stop button, he changes his expression. But his face becomes even more contorted. "It's not at all easy to create an expressionless face." He sinks into thought. A big smile fills his face, but then gradually he stops smiling. His face soon reaches a point where it's almost free of any expression. "Yes, now it looks okay. After my facial expressions have disappeared, I'm left with only my ugly, wrinkled skin." He then zooms in all the way. Now his coarse lips cover the whole screen. "Well, by doing this, I don't need to care about my facial expression." He presses the record button.

"As you might know, your mother and I didn't love each other. Well, maybe we loved each other in the most exhausted sense of love. Yes, it was a strange relationship. Anyhow, we accidentally got to know each other and kept on seeing one another, like a habit you can't easily abandon. While together we would treat each other in a causal and disrespectful way . . . although no serious ill-treatment occurred at all between us, I couldn't help feeling insulted."

He stops recording. An unpleasant look crosses his face. "Have I ever truly loved anyone or anything?" He shakes his head. "I was always ready not to love anyone or anything. Love was something beyond my capacity. So I've tried not to love anything, even a trivial thing. I thought loving somebody was the most horrible thing I could do to myself. And now I can allow myself to admit that I don't have the ability to truly love someone, and I'm also now able to recognize the fact." After smoothing his face, as if to iron out his facial expression, he presses the record button again.

"Here is my memory of the day you were conceived. Your mother and I were in the city cemetery lying down in a lonely spot between tombs, there where souls who had given their lives in vain for a falsely beautified image of their country were resting. The cemetery was the place where I didn't feel any rejection, something I felt in many other places. It was a warm spring day, and it felt good to be lying still beneath the warm sun with my eyes closed. While lying there I was thinking of the people who threw their lives away for their country, thinking no stupider emotion exists than patriotism and that nothing is worse than appealing to people's patriotism. Suddenly, at that moment, your mother said, 'What a lovely spring day it is, with all the leaves sprouting everywhere.' I didn't even turn my face toward her. 'Don't you think so?' your mother asked me. And I answered, 'Well, it looks that way to me, but even though something looks lovely, you can't trust what you see.' She looked a little disappointed at my reply. She then talked to me about something else, but I didn't listen to her. Your mother kept babbling to me, even when she knew I wasn't listening . . ."

He stops recording. "But why do I remember all these things, even though I don't try to? Whenever I recall the old days, the memories I don't want to remember cross my mind while the memories I want to recollect don't come. Well, actually, I've no memories worth recollecting . . . the times past, the dead times, the times not totally dead but still writhing about, the times that didn't belong to me at all, and the times I wish were as distant from me as possible. Anyway, fortunately I'm unable to go back to those times." He again presses the record button.

"I was listening to something else in the cemetery. I was listening to the dreadful sounds of a cuckoo bird that would have made any listener fall into a defenseless, sorrowful state. And the more I tried not to be taken in by the sounds, the more they trapped me. I opened my eyes and tried to discern figures in the sky's drifting clouds. But the clouds didn't create any forms and just floated by. I closed my eyes again, feeling drowsy and wanting to sleep. I couldn't sleep, though, since something was disturbing me. I opened my eyes again and saw that your mother was lying next to me. I had forgotten she was there. At that moment, as if she was thinking of something fabulous, your mother, with animated eyes, began touching my body without my consent, without my telling her to do so, and without my permission. 'Stop it!' I told her, saying, 'Even though we're in a relationship, it doesn't mean you can touch me or do whatever you want.' But it seemed no words could reach her, since her hands became more aggressive. I'd never felt so alienated from her, such distance between us. Suddenly, for some reason, she flinched for a moment. I heard someone approaching, but soon it became quiet again. And, after she had made sure no one was around, she went back to what she was doing. I was lying still with my eyes closed, thinking of all those dead people lying in the graves while I inhaled the air filled with the faint odors of corpses. But the air had something about it that made me feel cozy and snug."

He again presses the stop button. A smile that was about to appear suddenly disappears. He presses the record button.

"After a while your mother said, 'Open your eyes and see what I'm doing.' 'You must be doing something useless as usual,' I said, with my eyes still closed. 'Well, I don't know if you're right,' she said. After she said that, I felt her hand slip into my pants. She did it as if she was retrieving something hidden in there. But since I was enjoying the warm spring sun, I remained still. There was something in the spring sun that dulled my senses. And then, a moment later, I realized that your mother was trying to unzip my pants. The zipper, though, wouldn't go down easily. I stayed still without thinking of helping her. I didn't help nor hinder her since I didn't think it was worth bothering with. Well, to tell the truth, at that moment I had a stomachache after eating lunch. I didn't feel a bowel movement coming then, but, nonetheless, I felt uneasy and tried to remain still. Of course, I worried about diarrhea, but actually I couldn't really think of anything else since I was trying so hard not to fart."

He presses the stop button on the remote control. A smile forms around his lips. "The memory of that day, though, which I still remember even though there's nothing worth remembering, still amuses me. What a comedy. Oh, you, give me a share of your smile, even though it's a sour one." His smile turns into laugher. "I feel that laughter that occurs in the presence of no one else is genuine. And I also feel I'm not the person who's speaking. I always like feeling that I'm speaking through somebody else's mouth, that is, the feeling that I'm someone else speaking about me." He presses the record button.

"Anyway, after opening my pants' zipper, she succeeded in taking out what was inside. Upon accomplishing what she intended, her face beamed brightly."

Once more he's absorbed in his own thoughts after pressing the stop button. "Well, I don't think anything is inappropriate for a will. I don't think there's anything unreasonable, as I only spoke of things that should appear in a will. Anyway, is this some form of self-censorship? Well, I don't think I need to be censored. I'm going to allow myself, or the person who is close to me but not really me, to speak freely. And he's going to say anything he wants, something I didn't ask for." He presses the record button again and then the zoom-out button. His whole body and the wheelchair now appear on the screen.

"Maybe you think I'm fabricating this story, but I'm only speaking the truth, even though I'm not quite sure whether what I remember is the way it happened or not."

He presses the zoom-in button on the remote control. His face fills the whole screen.

"After a while, she mounted me. She did this as if she had something inevitable to do. 'What are you going to do?' I asked her. 'Wait a minute,' she said, while putting the hardened part of my body into her. 'You're heavy,' I told her, as she was sitting on me with all her weight. She then said to me, 'It's too loose.' Yes, she wanted it to feel tight. I laughed. The word "loose" made me laugh. The word, indicating an incompletely fastened screw or a slack string, took on a new meaning. Wanting her to finish quickly, I asked her to hurry up, but I remained still because she'd already started doing what she wanted to do. She seemed to hurry up a bit at my request. I felt something like an insect crawling on my leg, but I ignored it. And then everything was over in the blink of an eye ... what caused you to be born after ten months happened just like that. I couldn't do anything to prevent it. There wasn't even time for me to consider the consequences of that incident. And then something unexpected happened ... what was it ... oh yes, an insect stung me on my thigh. I tried to catch it but failed. I didn't intend to kill it even if I had caught it ... I just wanted to see what kind of insect it was. Oh no, as a matter of fact I was going to kill it without thinking of killing it. Well, maybe I wanted it to reach the point where it was almost dead. I always reciprocate without fail, especially when something bad has been done to me. The spot where I was stung became swollen and red in an instant. It was sore and stinging. I got mad, and I wasn't sure who I was mad at—the insect, your mother, or maybe both. And your mother asked me why I was so angry over such a trivial thing. I told her it was impossible for a person to avoid getting angry about such a matter. Your mother then moistened her finger in her mouth and applied her saliva to the insect bite. She also laughed while saying the swollen spot looked pretty. I laughed, too, even though I didn't want to. 'It'll be alright soon,' she said. 'It's stinging more,' I responded. Your mother then asked me to give her a hug. I told her I didn't want to. But then I said, 'I'll allow you to hug me.' Instead of hugging me, she again asked me to hug her. Reluctantly, I extended my hand and brought her closer to me, and when she was close enough, I reached out with my other hand to prevent her from coming any closer and then said I wanted to end our relationship. She looked at me straight in the eye but I avoided her gaze. 'Are you seeing another woman,' she asked me. I shook my head. 'Why do you want to end our relationship then,' she inquired. 'Oh, no reason, and I don't think I need to give you any reasons,' I said. 'Yes, I don't think there's any reason to give a reason, and I hope you understand,' I told her. 'Of course, there's nothing I can do even though you don't understand me,' I said. She couldn't continue speaking. And I tried to think of something that would totally have her at a loss for words. She looked at me as if she couldn't understand me. 'Don't give me that look,' I told her. 'What do you think happened to us just now,' she asked. 'What did happen to us?' I retorted. She glared at me. 'Oh, that thing, but let us assume nothing happened between us, and then I can only think of my insect sting, and, of course, I'm the one who was stung,' I said. 'I'm ovulating,' she said. I couldn't continue. 'Yes, it's true,' she said. 'You've made me speechless . . . did you plan all of this,' I said to her. 'And, if so, what a vile intention you had . . . if you have a baby, abort it, and I will go to the hospital with you if you want me to . . . oh no, you go alone, I'm not going to the hospital because I dislike hospitals,' I said. 'You must be kidding,' she retorted. 'My heart is telling me to say what I just said to you,' I told her. 'Don't we love each other?' she asked. I laughed at her remark. 'I couldn't help laughing,' I said. 'What kind of relationship do you think we have?' she asked. 'I don't know what role you want me to play in our relationship,' I replied. 'You selfish bastard. You always think badly of others, and you do what is bad for other people, even though it's not good for yourself,' she said. 'That's me,' I said. She burst into tears. 'Don't cry, it's not going to make any difference,' I told her. And then I got up, since I don't like people crying in my presence. As a matter of fact, I detest it. Also, I couldn't hold back my bowels any longer. 'If, by any chance, we meet in the future, I hope it's an even more disappointing situation for you,' I said. After saying this, I left the graveyard, leaving her there alone."

He stops recording and reviews what was just said and then sinks into thought. "I don't like this. I'd better speak about something that would move my bastard son, a story that would disgust him." He presses the record button.

"Ten months following this incident, you entered this world. Your mother and I couldn't part, even after we parted ways at the graveyard. Our connection was a slovenly, tenacious one. When you were born I was drinking at a bar while earnestly wishing one thing—that you wouldn't be born. And I hoped that if you had to be born you'd be born in a totally different form, far different from a human or any other living thing in this world . . . then I could tolerate you, I thought. But regardless of my simple wish, you were born an extremely normal baby. Your weight was more than average for a newborn and you were round and good-looking, but I didn't like the way you looked. As a consequence of a moment's carelessness, the result wasn't that bad. As a newborn baby, though, you were weird and greasy. But the unbelievable shape in front of me was real enough for me to believe in your existence."

He stops recording, pulls down one of the strings and holds a balloon in his hands, a balloon that has forgotten its own weight and that exists only with volume. "Forgetting its own weight, a shape composed only of volume. As if the volume is composed of sadness, I feel sad when I hold the balloon in my hands, a sadness that isn't easy to attune myself to, a sadness I can't feel without becoming uncomfortable, a sadness that isn't of good quality, a sadness that's in a chaotic state. But the weight of the volume that doesn't have any gravity seems to me so heavy that I can barely hold it up. The lightness of what I'm holding now is heavy enough to press down on any weighty matter."

Without realizing it, his hands press the balloon harder and harder until it finally bursts. Startled, he begins cursing. "I wasn't going to burst it . . . why the hell did you have to burst?" He picks up the crumpled balloon from his knee. "I should pretend there's nothing provoking me, even though I've been provoked . . . I'd better compose myself." He pulls down another balloon and releases it after holding it for a while. At one point he strokes it and says, "Be careful so that I don't burst you." After awhile he says, "Well, finally I can calm down. Touching the balloon soothed me, and how amazing that a balloon is so useful and that I believed it was useless." He lets the balloon float back up to the ceiling and presses the record button.

"When I saw you for the first time I didn't think you were a precious being that I wouldn't give up for anything in the world. At that time your mother and I weren't even married. As a matter of fact, I didn't want to get married. Of course, your mother thought differently. Yes, you were born as a bastard. And your mother attempted to trap me by using you as a pawn. But I escaped from you and your mother, since she was a damnable woman. Well, maybe I can't exactly say that, but at least I felt that way."

He stops recording and smiles. "This smile seems like a fool's smile. And I know that only a blockhead would smile like this—I must look like a dunce." Angrily, he presses the record button.

"When you were a baby, your smell was enough to make me gag. Looking at you in the cradle, I pledged that I wasn't going to do anything for you. And I vowed to keep my oath, since I'd already made it."

He stops recording and sinks into thought. "Oh, I feel shitty. Well, when my mood reaches rock bottom, things usually take a turn for the better." He now begins to repeatedly curl and spread his fingers. "Strange, I always do this when I'm down, as if I'm helping my shitty feelings pass through my fingers . . . I don't know why I even try to leave a will when I know it's useless." He again becomes lost in thought. "That's right, I do this to kill time, to delete time. Oh, what a drag, always reminding myself of what I do and why I do things." He presses the record button once more.

"Soon after you came into this world I left that women, your mother, and after a long time had passed, you ended up visiting me. I was lying in my room when I heard somebody knock on the gate. Opening the gate, I saw you standing there. I probably wouldn't have opened the gate had I known who you were. You tried to get into the house and I tried to push you out. Finally, while you stared at me without saying a single word, I asked you what you wanted. You then took out an old faded photograph of me as a young man from your wallet and shoved it in front of my nose, and after seeing that photo, I couldn't deny anything. I just gazed blankly at the photo that renewed our connection and then gave it back to you. When I asked you why you had visited me, you said that your mother had asked you to do so on her deathbed. While trying to control my unpleasant emotions, I told you that this couldn't be a reason to come looking for me. You made a sad face upon hearing that. I asked you how your mother died, and you said she got into an accident. 'What a lucky woman,' I mumbled. But at the same time, I felt sorry for her, though in a different way than I felt sorry for myself. You looked into the house and checked out the shabby existence I was living at that time. And I stared at you with a blank face that matched my miserable appearance, though it wasn't completely miserable. I was glad to reveal everything to you, and that excited me. My life during those days was worse than I realized then. Well, come to think of it now, nothing was that bad, I mean, nothing was completely bad. My pathetic life wasn't desirable, but at the same time, it somehow fit me. Of course, I can't say it was a good situation for me to be in, but it was tolerable, since I had adapted to it. My life has been peppered with my useless efforts to narrow the gap between what I wanted and what actually happened to me. You see, I tried to construct a perfectly bad situation, one so watertight that there was no way to escape from it and one where my life would end. I had lived my life in a way that neither I nor anybody else could understand. Throughout my life, I didn't make any effort to do anything and I considered things mine that I was given or attained without any work. Of course, I knew you wouldn't be able to understand all this. And to let you know that our meeting was over, I tried to shut the gate. At that moment you said, 'Father, come live with me. I'll take care of you from now on.' So I said, 'If that is what you want, I won't grant your request.' You said, 'I can't leave you like this. I'll provide you with everything you need.' So I said, 'I wouldn't be satisfied even in that situation. And you wouldn't get anything out of living with me, anyway.' 'Oh, it's no problem for me at all. And it's the right thing for a son to do,' you said. 'If that's how your moral sense works, you'd better discard it,' I retorted. I saw you glaring at me, with eyes that only so-called successful bastards could have, and I was so embarrassed I didn't know where to turn my face. And your deep and tranquil eyes fueled my humiliation. But even now what happened after that is shameful enough. Unfortunately, I was in a pitiful situation and desperately needed somebody's help, so I was easily swayed by your words. And then the comical occurred: while sobbing and without giving me any time to stop you, you embraced me in your arms with an emotionally charged face, and I was rocked in your arms without knowing what else to do . . . and from that day onward everything was too perfect, but I wasn't quite comfortable with it. The dues I had to pay by living with you, you for whom I did nothing, was horrible enough . . . but you really tried to do your best for me as a son. And I now realize that you didn't do all those things for my sake. You did it to fulfill what you believed was a son's role, and you did your best to bolster the satisfaction you gained from your actions."

He stops recording and closes his eyes and again becomes lost in his thoughts. "I don't think I need to thank my bastard son because I'm alive in this condition. No, I'd rather believe I wouldn't be alive with this pitiful torso if I didn't have a bastard son, even though whether I'm alive or dead doesn't make a big difference." He again presses the record button.

"Maybe I could've done something without your help, and, if so, you should've let me do it. And even if there was nothing I could do without your help, you should've left me alone. After all, you performed the crucial role of concocting the worst possible situation for me."

Looking angry, he presses the stop button and gazes out the window. "I can see a lake from this room, but it isn't a great comfort to me. I see it as a rather minor consolation. Beyond the huge lake there's a thick field of reeds. The reeds have probably been bent by the wind. But no wind is blowing. Nevertheless, the lake water is rippling. I have a hunch that something is going to happen to the quiet lake. Maybe a flock of wild ducks will fly down to it or fish will leap out of the water." Like a hunter, he holds his breath and stares at the reeds beyond.

He bursts into laughter and continues to laugh for a while. "The view of reeds by the lake is nothing but a photograph hanging on the wall. This photo is the only relic of my father's that I still have. There's no reason for me to keep it—I just lost my chance to throw it out and have ended up keeping it. It's a decent picture, except for the fact that it was taken by my father. He took this photo on a duck-hunting trip. My father wasn't a professional hunter, but he ran a firearms store and would go hunting in his free time, sometimes taking me along. When we arrived at home, the trunk of the car would be filled with dead ducks. At that time the walls in our living room were covered with stuffed wild animals. It was a ghastly scene, and I had a hard time while walking to the bathroom at night, what with their glaring eyes staring down at me as if the animals had returned back to life. And as time passed, the number of mounted animals grew. My father said that looking at the dying animals lying in their blood invigorated him. I now can finally understand what he meant. And I think that my suffering, caused by the bats after I awaken from my sleep, are related to this memory."

"I should stop talking about this. It's not a cheerful thing to talk about. I'll return to the present. Actually, this house has a yard and beyond it I can see a hill. The only thing that attracts my attention is a tomb on the hillside, but I don't know who it belongs to. It's just a perfect view from my room. Getting a house with a full view of a tomb enables me to believe in my son's consideration for me."

He moves his wheelchair to the window and looks through a telescope. "Yes, for sure, there's nothing to comfort me except the tomb. Sometimes a squirrel appears on the pine branch behind the grave and draws my interest, but I hardly give my full attention to it. Of course, I know it's not there to attract my attention. And at other times three squirrels come out, probably two of them are male, and they quarrel to gain the female's love or to prevent her from being taken away from them, and sometimes their disputes become heated. It's a funny thing to watch. There's nothing that bewilders me more than the mating ritual. And I can't think of anything else that is more laborious. By the way, on this beautiful spring afternoon, it wouldn't be a bad thing spotting a young girl picking wild vegetables. In such a case, giving in to my better nature, I would wave to her, even though she doesn't see me. Never mind a young girl, I've never even seen a hunched hag, either. At one time I would sit like this by the window and look outside from morning till evening without interruption. And, as if there was something I was longing for and without realizing the time passing by, I would spend the whole day with my eyes fixed on the hillside scenery, which over time would change a bit as it brightened or darkened, grew luxuriant or withered but, essentially didn't change at all. I don't do it any more now since I've lost interest in what this window has to offer me, this window with its view of the tomb. Yes, I no longer want to see the grave. And that's why I only glance at the unimpressive scenery now and then. At times, though, when it seems to me that there's no way to eliminate the abominable scene, I just close my eyes to it, that is, to something that can't hide itself from me."

He closes his eyes. "When I close my eyes, I can feel myself receding and becoming detached from everything. I often do this as a way to make sure of who and where I am." He keeps his eyes closed without saying anything. "How empty everything is," he mumbles. "With my eyes closed like this, I can fully feel a vast emptiness in the darkness." He moves his body around. "I see I'm twisting around, as if rubbing my body against the emptiness, an emptiness that fills me and surrounds me as well." He soothes his body. "By the way, there's nothing more physical than this great emptiness. And at the same time, it seems that everything turns into nothing but a mere name in this emptiness. I can't actually feel anything real: neither physical things nor circumstances nor events—everything just merges into nothingness."

At that moment he hears sounds coming from downstairs. "It seems my daughter-in-law has gotten up. The housemaid must be arriving soon." He opens his eyes and moves his wheelchair toward his desk. "Soon my daughter-in-law will come upstairs with the maid to see me. And then she will go downstairs after ordering the maid to perform some lousy chores. I don't think many women with such good fortune as my daughter-in-law exist. Her only work is to lounge around most of the day until she takes a shower, puts makeup on, dresses up with pretty clothes, and waits for her husband to come home. And since she eats such good food and leads such an easy life, she also has a lovely, fair complexion. Her shiny skin is really bewitching. Strangely enough, I've never harbored any lewd thoughts about her, even though she's the kind of woman who can arouse any man's desires and I'm the kind of man who usually can't resist having lewd thoughts about her kind of woman. Maybe that's because my sex drive has shrunk to the point where nothing is left. So I'm thankful for having absolutely no sensation in my lower body and am free of erotic feelings for my daughter-in-law. A healthy body is always subject to lewd passions. And the important thing is to prevent the mind from dreaming of things that are impossible to attain in reality and to prevent it from pursuing phantoms and yearning for things in vain. Well, I know it's not as easy as I think."

He listens to the sounds in the house and hears the toilet flushing. "What my daughter-in-law does isn't always disagreeable, though I don't like her using polite terms when referring to me, which she always does regardless of my repeated requests not to do so. She does this whenever possible. I can bear it, though, since she's my daughter-in-law. One thing I'm sorry about regarding my son and her is that they don't have a child. I wonder who has the problem. I suspect it's my son. Thinking of my son as a eunuch, though, makes me feel at ease somehow, and satisfied. But if they had a child, I would take care of it, as any grandfather would. I think I could look after it well in my clumsy inexperienced way. We would play together, me in a wheelchair and the child in a baby carriage, all the while being aloof and indifferent to each other. Or I can allow the child to play with me. Well, even if they had a child, they're definitely not going to let me take care of it, since they wouldn't feel safe leaving it with me. But on the other hand, I might have prevented the child from coming under my care, even if they wanted this to happen, as my bad energy might affect the child."

He hears the doorbell. "That's probably the maid. She comes twice a day and I don't like her. She doesn't know her place and scolds me every time. She tells me not to litter the room with things, not to make unreasonable demands, not to stare at her, and to obey her. But I have no ulterior motive when I stare at her. And when I don't look at her at all, she complains, asking me what kind of person I am, a person who doesn't even glance at someone he's with. Come to think of it, I can't blame her for this, as I have a strange tendency to either totally ignore someone or to glare at the person to the point where the person feels embarrassed, which is another way of ignoring them."

"And when she changes my diaper she asks me how it's possible for a diaper to stink so much. As a matter of fact, it stinks a lot to me, too. But, nonetheless, I can't stand this maid any longer. And when I tell her that as a maid she shouldn't treat me in such a way, she laughs at me. She even threatens me by saying she will punish me if I act like a child. I think I'm going to ask my daughter-in-law to fire her and get someone else easier to tolerate or to get anyone else even though she might be as hard to bear."

He stops speaking and becomes lost in his thoughts. "Since I have time until my daughter-in-law comes upstairs, I'm going to continue what I've been doing." He presses the record button. When he presses the zoom-in button his lips become so enlarged they lose their recognizable shape.

"One time you asked me if we could reconcile. I will give you the same answer I gave you then if you ever ask me the same question again: our relationship isn't one that can be reconciled. You can trust me on this matter, as I won't change my mind. I don't even have the will to struggle with myself to establish a good relationship with you, since it's such an impossible task to begin with. I can clearly say this without any emotion. Well, at least with a firm pledge not to be swayed by my emotions."

He watches what he has just recorded and then deletes it. "My bastard son will be embarrassed if he sees this film after my death. But I'm not doing this to bewilder him. I'm also not doing this because I like doing it. Well, anyway, I don't think I am." He presses the record button again.

"Come to think of it, I believe I've said everything without any qualms or hesitation. The only thing I don't like about this tape is that I couldn't convey the full force of my negative thoughts and feelings towards you. In other words, in this tape I've failed to fully communicate my disgust toward you."

He presses the stop button while thinking. "I guess I need

an ending statement, like a period at the end of a sentence." He again presses the record button.

"I believe you may now realize how insignificant you are to me. If you still don't realize that, well, I don't have any way to help you. And even though you'll never have the chance to realize it, I still can't help you. Yes, I've never considered you my son. And because of this, the relationship we've had ought to be nullified, is nullified, and, therefore, I announce that it is null and void."

He presses the stop button. "But I wonder if I can actually negate our relationship by telling him all this." He shakes his head and rewinds the tape to the very beginning and then presses the play button and reviews the whole tape. "Oh no, this isn't what I wanted. It's the same stuff I deleted yesterday because I didn't like it. I can't help thinking that what I really wanted to say is what I couldn't say. There's no progress. It's too slow even if there is any progress. Well, at some point thinking itself is too slow and not able to progress without being slow. Yes, using tautology is my particular grammatical style."

He suddenly presses the stop button, rewinds the tape once more, then presses the record button and remains still without saying a word. Meanwhile, his emotionless face is being recorded as the other previous recordings are erased. His face now becomes distorted while his two hands slowly rise up to cover it. After a while he puts his hands down and looks at his peaceful face.

"Sometimes I think I know what I want." He approaches the desk and pulls open a drawer. Taking out a candy, he puts it in his mouth and begins sucking on it. "I wonder how much candy I've eaten today. The number of wrappers in the drawer doesn't indicate anything because I unwrapped all the candy in advance. What a slick old bastard I am. Anyhow, I've something to ask: is there any real melon contained in this melon candy? I can't be free of this question whenever I eat melon candy." His head tilts slightly. "Well, I see myself saying, I really don't know." He says this with a smile. "And there's one more thing I want to know. How much longer will I stay in this room?" He then sinks into his thoughts once more. "Probably until all the melon candies are gone," he mumbles while smiling, as if he's thought of something good. "Well, as long as melon candies are still here in this room it may be worth it for me to stay alive. And I don't really know whether this would be a good excuse or not for my being alive. Well, at least I can pretend it could be . . . and now I have my last question: why are all candies, as far as I know, sweet? Why isn't there any sour, salty, astringent, or bitter tasting candy? It wouldn't be bad here with all that candy." He again sinks into his thoughts. "But for some reason, I think I can taste all the flavors in this melon-candy . . ."

Translated by Inrae You Vinciguerra and Louis Vinciguerra

Drifting

It wouldn't have been a bad idea, I thought, if right about then I'd turned around and walked back, but I didn't, since it didn't seem like a good idea. The place I'd left wasn't far away, though at that moment it seemed too far away.

It was a bitter cold, midwinter night. I was drifting along the street to avoid the numbing coldness, but all the doors on the street were locked tight to prevent uninvited people like me from breaking in or trespassing. It was already close to dawn, but I wasn't able to find a place to rest. While trudging along it seemed to me that my body, which couldn't get more stiff in the bitter cold, would crack and shatter on the street like plaster flung on cement. The street itself was completely deserted. I had probably seen such an empty street before, but I felt as if I was seeing one for the first time.

Standing for a while on a corner, I gazed at the desolate street scene. At that moment a drunkard, who seemed to have momentarily set his foot on the shores of euphoria, stumbled along the sidewalk while dragging along his own shadow. To catch his attention I took a step toward him, but, as if I was invisible, he passed by me and disappeared around the street corner. I didn't feel like following him, so I stood still and gazed at the street corner where he had vanished, gazed as though for some reason I needed to do it, all the while feeling that I had missed something.

I saw no one else on the street. It seemed to me that some kind of tyrannical monster, which only appears in the dead of night, had chased all the people into buildings or wherever they all were. I wanted to see lovers tightly hugging each other to stay warm and clinging to the walls like shadows, but they weren't anywhere to be seen. I would've rooted enthusiastically for them, or I would've chased them into a nearby motel and even given them some money if I had any. I also looked for somebody, or even a shadow of somebody, who was in a similar situation as me, and even though we couldn't offer any actual help to each other, we would, nonetheless, at least try to help each other—but there was no such person in sight.

A few cars, mostly taxis, mercilessly raced down the streets, teeming with dim, dopey-looking streetlights. In the approaching darkness just before dawn, the streets revealed their shadowy contours. To my eyes the streets and the buildings looked as if they would simply collapse in the morning light instead of revealing their solid contours. The streets were dead, so much so that the simple act of night turning into morning wouldn't do any good to liven them up. It was bizarre.

"It wouldn't be a bad idea for me to turn around and walk back right about now," I thought, but I didn't do it, since it didn't seem like a good idea. The place I had left wasn't far away but at that moment it seemed too far away. Right then, as if on cue, heavy snow suddenly began to fall. Far from being delighted, I grudgingly glared at the snowflakes. To me at least, shivering in the cold, the snow wasn't something I welcomed. "I wouldn't have left my shelter if I'd known about the weather in advance," I thought. But I still didn't want to return to the place that I had left after having considered it for quite a long time. My hideaway, which was only a temporary dwelling when winter began, only had part of its walls and roof remaining and wasn't able to properly shield me from the falling snow.

The snowflakes grew larger. They were swirling and dancing about everywhere and scattered my thoughts in every direction. I closed my eyes. I was cold again, something that I had been able to forget for some time because I was thinking of other things. The cold weather had reached the point where I couldn't endure it any longer. In order to stop thinking about it I pressed against my sunken tummy, which hadn't had any food that day, and tried to focus all my attention on my hunger. As a result of my attempt the cold weather wasn't forgotten. In fact I could now feel both coldness and hunger at the same time, and with the combination of the two I suffered even more, so I attempted to find a different kind of pain that would make me forget my hunger and the cold weather, but it was no use. So I mumbled to myself, as if I had arrived at some kind of conclusion, "Controlling pain by manipulating my thinking is a more difficult thing to do than I thought."

Even after deciding to resume my walk I needed quite some time before I could actually put my decision into action, and after roaming about for a while I found a lit underpass and walked furtively down the stairs. But just a couple of steps before reaching the bottom I slipped and tumbled down. I cursed at the stairs, even though it hadn't actually tripped me, but still, I wouldn't have tripped if it hadn't been there. I slowly raised myself up, since I knew there wasn't anyone who would come to help me. Fortunately, I wasn't badly hurt. I took shelter from the winter wind in the underpass, but I still felt cold. Anyway, I thought that there I could avoid the chilly air being blown about by the cold wind. Nonetheless, there was nothing that really protected me from the cold weather. In the underpass, even though no one was looking at me, I hid myself behind square pillars that were lined up like the colonnades of a shrine, and I looked like a person who had sneaked into the place. My behavior made me feel as if I'd taken sanctuary there after committing some kind of crime. And my legs were shaking, but there was nothing that I could sit on other than the cement ground, so I didn't squat down. Once more I thought of my shelter, even though I didn't intend to think about it. At least there I had a couple of cardboard pieces that I could lie down on and other things that could be used as a blanket. Knowing it was useless, I, nonetheless, began to regret what I had done that day. Turning around, I put my forehead against a cement pillar. I smelled an odor coming from the pillar that I had often smelled before and which was quite familiar to me. As if it was something I could drink, I inhaled the smell deeply. Of course it didn't happen all the time but the cement odor did sometimes help to clear the cobwebs from my head, which was never completely clear. Right then, from somewhere nearby, I began to hear faint rustling sounds that gradually became louder until I could hear them clearly. I thought a mouse living in the underpass must've made them. The noise continued. "It must be coming from a mouse that became nervous when it realized that a human being was here," I concluded, since I thought that I was familiar enough with the various noises mice make and was able to distinguish between each sound. In actuality, though, I didn't have this ability, but I often thought I did. "If I ever sleep here my body could be bitten by mice," I thought. Thinking it would be better for me to leave instead of chasing away the mice, I stepped forward like a person who was ready to exit the place, but before completing my first step I again placed my feet together and stood still.

For some reason what then appeared in front of me was not a mouse but a dirty-looking man who resembled a mouse. A handful of his wet hair formed a spike that stuck out above his forehead. He seemed to be a mouse disguised as a human. Emerging out of nowhere, he gave me the impression that he hadn't seen

me, and even though I was now very close to him, he didn't pay
any attention to me at all. I gazed at him. Right then, he suddenly started spinning around one of the pillars, as if somebody
had asked him to do so. I approached him. "Good evening?" I
said, in such a hospitable manner as to feel the pleasure that one
can derive when meeting somebody at such a time and place. But
he didn't even look at me. "Good evening?" I said again. He still
ignored me. I soon realized that saying such a thing under such
circumstances was inappropriate. He didn't appear to be having
a good evening at all. "Are you all right?" I asked. He again said
nothing. Actually, he didn't even glance at me. I realized that he
looked unusual. It soon became apparent that he was missing
one eye. "He's one-eyed," I mumbled to myself. "He's one-eyed,"
I said again, this time louder, as if mumbling didn't satisfy me.
And his other eye was either half-open or half-shut. To me his
being one-eyed didn't look as if it would bring misfortune to an
onlooker. "What are you doing?" I asked him. He still didn't answer me. "This guy also seems to be deaf," I mumbled. It appeared
that he not only couldn't see me but also couldn't hear me. For a
while I watched him spin around the pillar. "Did you eat something bad?" I asked him. Once again he didn't answer me. "Or
are you out of your mind?" I asked. Again he didn't answer me.
I wondered why he had to behave like that, but I couldn't come
up with a reason. And I really wanted to know the reason for his
behavior. "Maybe, if I do exactly the same thing that this guy is
doing, I'll be able to know the reason," I thought. So I did what
he was doing. I circled around the pillar in the opposite direction, making larger circles than he was. As if performing some
kind of religious ritual, we circled around the pillar for a while.
But instead of religious symbols drawn on the pillar, there was
only some obscene graffiti. As I spun around I became dizzy, and
my mind became confused as well. And I couldn't control my
mind, which was becoming even more confused. I had learned

that leaving my confused mind alone was one way to handle it when it became impossible to control, and so this is what I did. But I was still unable to figure out why he was spinning around the pillar, and I also couldn't understand why I was now doing the same. But anyway, doing so definitely distracted me from the cold weather. "Hum, the cold weather was the reason," I thought. He stopped spinning abruptly and stood still and looked at me. "Are you done with your spinning?" I asked him. At that moment his face contorted as if he had seen a ghost. He took something out of his pocket and threw it at me, yelling, "Get lost, you nut." And after saying this he turned around and disappeared in a flash, the same way he had appeared. I ran after him, but, while looking at him between the pillars, he quickly walked up the steps and vanished from view.

I gave up following him and went back to where I was. I couldn't help feeling sorry, though, that I was unable to catch him and punch him. But it was no use thinking about such a thing after he was long gone. While trying to calm myself down I looked around for what he had thrown at me. Next to some drains I found two pebbles. The round pebbles were worn and smooth, as if they had been rubbed in the palms of his hands for a long time, or maybe nature had created them that way. The pebbles were useless, nevertheless, I put them in my pocket, as if they would become useful someday. Suddenly I remembered what he had said to me a short while before. It was a word that I hadn't heard recently but one that I was long familiar with. People had always told me that I was somewhat nutty. I didn't exactly understand what they meant by the word, nonetheless, judging by the way they treated me I felt that there must have been something abnormal about me. Anyway, because of that or some other reason I've had to spend time in a place that was far removed from normal society.

I stopped thinking and slowly moved my feet up the stairs.

Snow was still falling outside. Searching for a cozier place to rest, I started to walk. "Just a little more time to bear before morning comes as usual and then everything will become much better," I thought. But soon, out of nowhere, two policemen approached me. Strangely enough, everyone I met that night seemed to pop up in front of me out of nowhere. And it seemed to me that they appeared not because of anything I had done but for their own reasons. Of course, during my usual walks in the street I was often stopped and checked by the police. Actually, it wasn't just the police that questioned me. Considering that anyone in uniform, such as guards, park rangers, nurses, and bus and train conductors, seemed to enjoy engaging with me by giving me orders and threatening and persuading me, they must've liked me. The policemen asked me what I was doing there at that time of night. I wasn't able to answer immediately. I wanted to come up with a marvelous response that would surprise even me. They again asked me the same question, only phrased differently this time. They asked me what I was doing, or what I was going to do there at such a time. I brooded over their question. The question seemed to require contemplation. It was a difficult one to answer without much thinking. But the words that came out of my mouth were totally unexpected. "What are YOU guys doing here at this time?" I asked. But they ignored what I said and asked me the same question. "I don't know," I replied. I was disappointed by my reply and disappointed that I hadn't given myself enough time to think of a better answer. They asked me for my identification card. "What did I do wrong?" I asked them. They said that they needed my ID card because I looked like a person who was likely to commit a crime, even though I hadn't committed any crime and hadn't broken any laws. "Is that my fault?" I asked. But soon I realized what I had just said contained something that people could easily misinterpret, so I kindly enough offered them an explanation by saying that I didn't intend to ask if it was my fault but rather meant to ask if I was responsible for them thinking that way and for looking the way I looked. They appeared unable to understand me, and, as a matter of fact, even I couldn't fully comprehend what I had just said. They again demanded my ID card. I never did comply with their request. It seemed to me that I shouldn't acquiesce to their demand. And it was natural for me to do my best at everything. They said that my attitude would cause some trouble. So I told them that I didn't want them to get into any trouble. They said that it wasn't they who would be in trouble but me. They said that what they had wanted to say to me from the very beginning was the very thing they had just said: I could get into trouble. Sometimes my words, as soon as they poured out of my mouth, became jumbled and came out totally differently from what I had intended.

They asked me questions like who I was, where I was from, where I was going, what my occupation was, what I'd done before, where I lived if I had a place to live, and if I had ever broken the law. While assessing the situation and being guided by my intuitions, I replied with simple or general answers to their various questions. I told them that I didn't trust the legal system. But they didn't seem to understand what I had said. So I asked them if they wanted to listen to my thoughts about the legal system, but they didn't really look interested. I assumed that my words were beyond their intellectual ability. I drew another conclusion, too— that I, who had made a statement that was incomprehensible to them, was also beyond their understanding. Everything seemed so natural. I suddenly thought of the basic human right of all suspects, the right against self-incrimination, and I sunk into a deep silence. I haven't fulfilled any of my duties as a citizen, but I've always practiced my rights without exception, thinking it a legitimate thing to do as a citizen. My abrupt silence, something that actually surprised me, seemed to have startled them, too. I didn't offer them any excuse and didn't complain about their improper questioning of me. They said that there wasn't any other course of action but to take me to the police station. Hoping that they would arrest me, I thrust my hands out in front of them. Right then, one of the men lifted his index finger and drew circles in the air next to his head. And I knew what that meant, too. "Well, he doesn't look like a lunatic to me . . . but something is missing up there," the other policeman said. I didn't make any effort to convince them that contrary to their assessments I wasn't a lunatic and I wasn't missing anything. Envisaging the detention room where I would be locked up and imagining myself grabbing the bars with my head between them, I waited for them to take action. But they were neglectful of their duties and were going to let me go. So I insisted that they shouldn't do it. And I beseeched them to take me to the police station. Above all and by any means, I wanted to avoid the unbearable cold of the night. I didn't mind going any place, even into the flames of hell, if and only if I could avoid the cold. I wished that I was able to fabricate a case against me that would be too solid for them not to arrest me, but I couldn't think of anything. Right at that moment one of the policemen read my mind and said to me, "If that's what you want, sure, I can arrest you and take you to the police station." Without resisting, I submitted to the arrest. I was grateful for their kindness. There was a naturalness to my actions that can exist only when one entrusts oneself to others, knowing in advance what will happen. Wishing they'd handcuff me, I stuck out my hands, but they didn't do it. They didn't seem to know how dangerous a person I could be.

We all headed for the police station, with me walking in front of them. While walking I thought that once I got there I would ask them to provide me with a place to rest. I had been to police stations before and so I knew I could make such a request. "Well, I might ask for something to eat first . . . oh no, maybe I should ask them if I could warm up in front of their stove," I thought.

Strangely enough, I felt that everything would go as I wished, and I was in such a hopeful state.

The police station wasn't far away. I knew well enough how to act in a police station, even if they didn't instruct me. As I entered the gate of the station, I stiffened up my neck muscles more than I needed to, since I had a tendency to flinch involuntarily when I met people with authority. The policemen delivered me to a detective who was snacking at a table. "What's this?" the detective asked, while putting his sandwich down on the table. Lifting up my eyes, which had been staring at the sandwich, I looked at the detective. "Unidentified, and I can't make any sense of his chatter," one of the policemen said. "Unidentified?" the detective asked. I nodded. "I didn't ask you," he said to me. "Who are you?" the detective asked. I looked at the policeman who a moment before was asked by the detective if I was in fact unidentified and I had nodded yes in his stead. With the tip of his chin the policemen motioned toward the detective, indicating that I had to pay attention to him. "This question is for you," the detective told me. I looked at him again but said nothing. Not responding to his question seemed to me extremely natural. I had always maintained an ascendancy over anything that was natural. By this time I felt that my sitting on a chair would also be natural, so I sat down on an iron chair by the table where the detective was sitting. "Who told you to sit there?" the detective said to me. I stood up from the chair. I wanted to sit back again after obtaining his permission. "Sit back on the chair," the detective said. But I didn't sit. Now it didn't seem natural at all. "Are you going to stand around like that?" the detective asked. I hesitantly sat back down on the chair. And this also didn't seem natural to me. "Sit straight up," the detective ordered. I realized that my body was tilted and so I straightened myself up. "You don't have to sit so stiffly," the detective said. He gazed at me . . . well no, "observed" would be a better word. I, who was familiar with people looking at me this way, didn't feel uneasy at all. Behind the detective I noticed a stove with wheels on it and pushed my chair near it. "Who said you could come close to the stove—go back to where you were," the detective said. I returned to my original spot. "Are you cold?" the detective asked me. I nodded. "You look cold," he said. He then pushed the stove toward me. "You don't have any ID card, do you?" he asked. I nodded again. Without his noticing it, I gradually moved my chair once again closer to the stove. "Name?" the detective asked. So I gave him the name that I remembered. "Good name," he said. "I don't like it," I said. The detective looked at me with curiosity. But I couldn't show him as much curiosity as he did toward me. At that moment I smelled something burning, and I soon realized the smell was coming from my singed trousers, since I had gotten too close to the stove. As if I'd been burned, I sensed a sharp pain on my knees. I quickly drew back from the stove. Amused, the detective burst into laughter. "Are you all right?" he asked. While soothing my throbbing knees with my hands, I nodded. "Good, what do you do?" he asked. "I was brought here for walking the streets at night," I answered, wondering if this was the right answer to his question. "I know, but what I meant was - who are you?" he asked. I contemplated his question. I failed, though, to think of a proper answer. He soon asked me the very same question again. Above all things, I detested being interrupted by someone's impertinent remarks when I was deep in thought. I didn't answer. "Answer my question," he snarled. "I'm thinking of the answer," I said. To be honest, at that moment I had already forgotten what the question was. "Who are you?" he again inquired. "I really don't know," I said, giving him an answer that was faithful to the truth. It was the very question I had been asked by people throughout my life whenever I introduced myself, and without fail I never knew what to say. He asked me to speak louder and to be more articulate. I could barely hear my own voice. And it was muffled by the noise of a chair being dragged across the floor. I had to force myself to even open my mouth to speak. I was exhausted. "Speak louder, understand?" the detective said. So I shouted that I understood and would do so. Everyone stared at me. He asked me to lower my voice. My voice returned to being weak and almost inaudible. "Open your mouth," the detective instructed. Even though I couldn't understand why he would ask me such a thing, I did as I was told. "Hmm, I don't see anything in your mouth, so why is your speech unclear . . . it's as if you're chewing on something when you speak," he said. Feeling ashamed, I dropped my head. But my inarticulate enunciation was caused by the unusual structure of my mouth and I could do nothing about it. Anyway, I felt I was fortunate that the odd structure of my mouth couldn't be seen. "Your job?" he asked me. "I don't have one," I said. He gave me a very pitiful look. "Place of residence?" he asked. "I don't have such a thing," I answered. He now looked a bit annoyed. But I understood. I don't mean that I could understand why he was annoyed and that it was therefore justified; rather, I understood the fact that he was annoyed. "It's been a long time since I've had such things," I said. I made sure that I didn't hide anything about my identity. I honestly told him all I could under the circumstances, and I also didn't say what I couldn't. In other words, I was honest and didn't fabricate anything. And I was deeply touched by my honesty. "Everything I've said is true," I told the detective as further explanation, thinking that my words failed to convey all I had intended to say. He asked me if there was anybody behind me. I turned around but found no one. "I don't see anyone," I told him. "I didn't mean that, I meant whether you're a front man for somebody," he said. "Oh, I see," I said. I now understood what he meant. So I talked to him about something I had been feeling— that I had always felt someone unidentifiable controlling me from behind. As if dumbfounded by what I had said, he stared strangely at me. He then asked me an assortment of questions which I couldn't comprehend, not even half of them, and so I haphazardly answered the questions with either a yes or no, and that was the best I could do. It seemed to me that whatever I said to him wouldn't have mattered anyway. While missing the point of my own words and having no point at all, I was speaking gibberish. Even I was aware of it. And I was doing it pretty well and without much difficulty. "It's like speaking to a wall," he said. I nodded to him. He then stopped speaking for a moment. So I stopped thinking about things that were unclear to me. But soon other thoughts doggedly poured forth that were even more imprecise and fragmented, so that to connect them was a difficult thing to do. "What are you thinking about?" he asked me when I was silent for a moment. Right then, I was thinking of my buttocks which had started to ache, something that I couldn't avoid thinking about. "Could I sit on a more comfortable chair?" I asked him. My desire to sit on a cushier chair was becoming an ardent wish. "Listen, you're not in your house. Stay there," he said, as he began pushing a chair next to him with a plastic cushion on it toward me and allowing me to sit there. I knew he would, judging from his somewhat gentle gaze. The new chair was a little more comfortable but not that much. He continued asking me questions. Instead of feeling good about his interest in me I now became annoyed. And I felt drowsy, too, but I managed to overcome it by repeating his words in my mind in order not to miss what he was saying. But because I paid too much attention to repeating his words or because I paid too much attention to his words, I couldn't comprehend their meaning. He asked me again about something. I said nothing. My thoughts were scattered and receding to a place where I wasn't able to recall them. And these thoughts also took me to where they were heading. "This is like speaking to a wall," he said. I thought he had uttered the same words a little before, but I didn't say anything. My body was now slouching enough so that even I was aware of it. And I began to derive some satisfaction from my languid state. It was something that one wouldn't be able to feel without loosening the reins of consciousness, and so I loosened the reins even further. By whatever means, I now wanted to just lie down and do nothing else. Of course, I didn't have such a thing as a daily plan, but it was still long past my bedtime. He sat up and asked me to do the same thing, and then he looked straight into my eyes and asked me to look straight into his, and then he spoke to me. He tried to have me understand that walking around without carrying an ID card is illegal and tried to have me admit the seriousness of my transgression and to have me promise him that this wouldn't occur again, all the while sounding as if he was almost pleading with me to help him. I also asked myself to help this man who was asking me for help. But we both seemed to know that all our efforts were useless. "What is going to happen to me?" I heard myself asking him, as if I actually wanted to know and was concerned. "I'll discharge you," the detective said. I looked at him. "I said I'm going to let you go," he said again. I could now vaguely understand that my mental state prevented them from freely punishing me. The detective stared at me as though he wanted to make sure that I had understood all of what he had said. For a moment I was silent. But what I soon said to him was something that surprised even me. "Please, do to me what your laws dictate," I told him. He looked as if he was somewhat touched by my words, since he and the two other policemen, who for some time now must've looked at me with some curiosity, all burst out laughing. "I wish I could do it, but I can't," the detective said, as if he was sorry about not being able to punish me. "And that's because you're not above the law, you're beside the law . . . well, to be more exact, you're outside the law," he said.

After a while the detective talked with the policemen about what to do with me and I just listened to them. I wasn't able to understand all of what they were saying but the gist of it was something like: Considering this guy's mental condition, we shouldn't punish him, so let's send him to a welfare facility, instead. The detective opened his notebook and copied down a phone number. But I doggedly resisted. I never wanted to go back there. "I'll contact the place and when their staff arrives please go with them," he said. I wondered about myself when I soon became calm for no apparent reason. The detective then picked up the sandwich that he was eating before and took a bite out of it. I stared at him as he ate it. "Are you hungry," he asked. After thinking for a moment, I shook my head. "So, you're not hungry," he said. I again shook my head. "What do you want to say—are you hungry or not?" he asked once again. This time, instead of shaking my head, I said, "I'm not that hungry, but . . ." "You mean you're hungry but not that hungry," he said. It seemed like a long time since I'd last eaten something, that is, since I began not eating anything. These two ways of saying this are the same, but to me the latter seemed to consist of a much longer time than the former. He thrust his half-eaten sandwich toward me. Regardless of my intention, I grabbed it from him. I started eating it from the side that his mouth hadn't touched. I wasn't going to bite that part of the sandwich where his mouth had been. But right in front of me the whole sandwich, including the part I hadn't intended to eat, disappeared into my mouth. He gave me a pitiful look and I felt I should pretend that I was indeed pathetic. "You must've been hungry," he said. I couldn't say anything because I was choking on the sandwich I was devouring. I feigned grasping my neck with my hands. I knew he knew why I was doing so, but, nonetheless, he looked at me as if pretending not to understand, and then he took out a carton of milk from a drawer and handed it to me. "Drink this," he said. I resented the fact that he didn't give me the milk with the sandwich in the beginning. "Do you want more food?" he asked. This time, without any hesitation, I nodded. "But I don't have any more," he said. Why then did he ask me if I wanted more food, I thought. "I know you're wondering why I asked you when I didn't have any more, right?" he said to me. He seemed to have a talent for reading people's minds. "I just said it, since most people say no, they're okay, when they're asked such a question," he said. Gazing at me, he smiled.

I finally began looking around the inside of the police station. Everything appeared peaceful, with only a couple of night duty policemen around. A detention room located at one corner of the station was empty. It looked like the perfect place for me to rest. "Could I stay in there?" I asked the detective. He shook his head. "Not everyone can go in there, and, unfortunately, you're not qualified to stay there," he said. He then went back to something that he had to do. I remained silent. He stopped what he was doing, then glanced at me and asked, "What are you thinking about?" I told him I was thinking that if by any chance aliens visited our earth I would be the first human they would approach, but I wasn't thinking about how to welcome them when it happened." He gazed at me as if I was strange. I, too, thought it was strange for me to say such a thing and understood why the detective was giving me that look. He stared directly at my face, as if he was waiting for me to say something else. I, too, stared directly at him and waited for what I was going to say. But I said nothing. "What are you thinking about now?" he asked me again. He seemed to enjoy talking to me more than doing his work. Or he must've disliked his work more than anything else. He waited for a while, but since I didn't say anything he turned his head toward his desk. "Excuse me," I said. He turned his head around again. "What's up?" he said. I said nothing. Actually, I didn't have anything in particular to tell him. "From now on keep quiet, even if you have something to say," he said.

Meanwhile, it was already dawn and the police station gradually became busy. As if his night duty was over, the detective began to get ready to leave. Another detective came in. My detective handed me over to his replacement and gave him the note with the phone number on it and talked to him about me. Throughout my life I have heard so many people talk about me that now I can't distinguish between what I know about myself from what I've heard. The new detective glanced swiftly at me and then turned his head, as if I wasn't worth his time, and began working at his desk. Pretending to be busy, he flipped through some papers. I quietly looked at what he was doing. Soon I felt pain in my loins. The pain wasn't new to me; in other words, I was very aware of it and it was something that I didn't have to worry about while feeling it. The pain gripped me. It wasn't anything more than simple pain, though it still wasn't nothing. Fortunately, the pain lingered only around my loins and didn't spread to other parts of my body.

The new detective seemed to have no interest in me at all. It looked to me like he even forgot that I was there. I wanted him to know, though, that I was there or at least that I wasn't absent. I cleared my throat. But he didn't react at all. Clearing my throat wouldn't accomplish anything, I muttered. Next I pretended to blow my nose. But he didn't even look at me. "Failed again, but I have other ways," I said to myself. I punched my head with my fist. For a moment he turned his head, but not to toward me. With my fingernails I started scratching the back of the chair I was sitting on. The scratching sounds annoyed even me. It was one of the things I did when I wanted to grate my nerves. But, as if he hadn't heard anything, he began to scratch his head. I again sat in silence. Right then, the detective finally glanced over at me, but he soon turned his head away from me again. After a while I wanted to say or do something. I didn't want to stop myself from doing or saying whatever I wanted. I stood up. "Remain sitting and don't stand up unless I tell you to," he said, without even looking at me. So I tried not to rise until he ordered me to. As a result of my effort it seemed that I wouldn't be able to stand up even if he asked me to. But gradually I felt an itch on my belly. I tried to ignore it, but it was no use. I scratched it. This lessened the itchiness but now I felt an itch on my side. This time I scratched my side. And now the itch moved to my back. Regarding having an itch, one interesting thing is that if you scratch one itchy spot then the itch spreads all over the body and the whole body itches. Having an itch was something I had been afraid of my whole life, almost as much as going hungry, which I feared the most. While twisting my whole body as much as I could, I began to scratch everywhere. "What are you doing, are you making fun of me?" the detective asked, while glancing at me. I told him that I wasn't doing that. "You can make fun of me but don't make me feel like you're doing it," he said, after which he turned his head away again. I tried to track down the itchy spots only in my mind now instead of actually scratching them.

Soon a man was dragged in by a policeman. Barely lifting up my eyelids, which kept closing involuntarily, I looked at the new catch. He looked like the bastard I had met in the underpass who had done strange things and then disappeared in a flash from my sight. But since I first saw him in dim lighting and since my mind now felt dull, I wasn't sure whether this guy was the one I had seen in the underpass or not. His face was covered with his disheveled hair so I couldn't make him out clearly. Real handcuffs had been firmly placed around his wrists and the back of his hands were stained with blood. I soon had to stand up and give up my chair to the guy. Yes, I had to take a backseat now. "Stay over there," the detective said to me, pointing to a chair in the distance. The detective then asked the guy some questions, but his mouth was firmly sealed. Judging from what I overheard, the guy seemed to have broken into somebody's house to steal something. And judging by the bloodstains on the back of his hands, there must've been a scuffle when he was being arrested. Of course, no face exists that automatically brands someone as a thief; nonetheless, he didn't look like a thief. The detective kept inquiring about something, but the man remained silent. "Could I stand up for a while? I've got pins and needles in my legs," the guy abruptly asked the detective after sitting silently. "Thieves are supposed to have pins and needles in their legs," the detective said, "So, no, remain seated." The thief now looked as if he was in pain. "If you confess to everything, I'll let you stand," the detective said. The thief gradually began to confess to his crime. To eavesdrop on their conversation, I leaned my body forward. Gradually, the thief's face began to look like a thief's. Right at that moment, while I was looking at them, my legs were attacked by pins and needles, too. So I stood up and did some stretching and then sat back down. No one paid attention to me at all. They seemed to know that I had failed at being a dangerous person. I repeatedly stood up and sat down until finally I sat down on the chair and remained there. The detective's interrogation of the thief continued. The thief now submissively confessed to all his crimes. He appeared to have given up on everything. But all the crimes he had confessed to, even though I wasn't exactly sure what they were, didn't seem like a big deal to me. He looked to me to be a mere petty thief. And I wasn't sure what he had stolen. I no longer heard what he was saying. After the itchiness had swept through my whole body, I didn't sense anything else at all. Things that I had either made contact with or were near me were losing their reality, too, so that I could only barely sense their existence by tracing them with my dim consciousness and not by touching them. My boredom swelled, little by little. I couldn't think of anything that would make me shudder, something that would've jolted me out of my doldrums. I fortuitously stuck my hand into my jacket pocket and found that I had two pebbles there. I put one pebble into each of my pants pockets and fiddled with them. I didn't think these pebbles would be useful, but for sure, it had something to do with that, I said to myself. I then put both pebbles in one pocket and played with them. The detective looked at me. "What's that sound? What do you have in your pocket?" he asked. I didn't respond. He approached me and took the pebbles from my pocket. "What's this?" he said. "Pebbles," I said. "What do you do with them?" he asked. "They're just pebbles," I said. They were pebbles that couldn't do anything by themselves, I thought. "Why are these pebbles in your pocket?" he asked me. I didn't answer. He gazed at me suspiciously and then at the pebbles, but he seemed to conclude that there wasn't really any reason to doubt me, so he gave them back. This time I put one pebble in each pocket. It seemed that with my help the stones were finally in a place where they were supposed to be. I then felt that there was nothing left for me to do. And I was now unable to think of anything at all. "Yes, I can't think of anything any more," I thought. But I knew that was just me thinking, since I also knew that numerous thoughts were hovering about, thoughts that were capable of stirring up my whole mind. The detective went back to his work. I stood up. Actually, I stood up automatically, as if somebody had raised me up with their hands. Since I was so familiar with living a passive life, I now was able to regard even voluntary actions as passive ones. No one stopped me. I walked to a spot a short distance away from them. And still no one paid any attention to me. I again went back to my chair and sat down. I soon stood up again and this time walked farther away than before. The same thing—no one cared about what I was doing. I returned to my original spot. No one in the police station minded my walking to and fro. I seemed to be invisible to them. I could only see my shadow, not myself. I felt as if I was a ghost. "I should know by now that I'm a phantom . . . I should let myself know that," I murmured. I was a being whose presence or absence didn't make any difference. I wasn't making any difference. Witnessing my astonishment at such a place and at such a time, astonishment over the fact that I myself failed to make any difference in this world, didn't surprise me at all. I no longer needed to stay there. So, as if I had nothing to do with anyone there, I got up, passed between the desks, and walked out of the police station.

It wasn't snowing any longer. But the world had turned snow-white because of the thick layer of snow that had fallen during the night. As if I enjoyed such a scene, I gazed at it, and this made me actually begin to like it. I set my feet down on the snow-covered street. And even though the layer of snow was as high as my ankles, my steps didn't make any footprints on the snow. Yes, I didn't even need to bother erasing my footprints. All this seemed so natural to me. Like an alien who had just arrived on earth or like a human on the way to greet an alien, I broke into a gallop.

Translated by Inrae You Vinciguerra and Louis Vinciguerra

Losing the Olfactory Sense

Something was unusual. He couldn't taste the flavor of the familiar food he was eating. So he stopped eating after a couple of spoonfuls. Bending over the dish, he sniffed at the food while trying to recall what it smelled like, but it was no use. He paid the bill and then stepped out onto the street and took some deep breaths. But he couldn't smell any of the street's familiar odors either. He felt as if everything he saw had been bleached white. He stuck out his tongue and tasted the strange atmosphere.

After taking several steps, he suddenly stopped. The trees along the street cast dark shadows under the summer's late afternoon sun. The sky was blue and clear, with clouds floating lazily by. And in the bright sunlight, he frowned.

Many things had changed. He felt that things had become more contentious than before. To him it seemed that everything was revealing itself at its worst. He was standing in the center of town but just a few people were there. And they were mostly old folks resting in the shades cast by the trees.

He resumed his walk and soon saw several people gathered on the sidewalk. It turned out to be a bus stop. Joining them, he stood there for a while. The people were standoffish and would occasionally turn their heads towards where the buses would come from. Probably because of the hot weather, they all looked weary.

He casually glanced up at the sky. Butterflies were flying in every direction. He chose one of them and followed it with his finger wherever it flew. But he felt nothing on his fingertip. Standing still, he lifted up his hand, with his palm facing upwards, and let the butterflies hover above his fingertips. He felt something was weighing him down, and so he gathered up that feeling and placed it on his shoulders.

Soon a bus arrived and people began to board it. He was in line, but, as if he had a sudden change of mind at the last moment, he didn't get on. Leaving him alone and belching black smoke from its exhaust pipe, the bus drove off down the empty street. And after the bus had vanished from sight, he still stood there motionless, as if waiting for another bus.

But before long he started walking again and soon entered a store and bought a pack of cigarettes and an ice cream. The goods on display at the store were all white with accumulated dust. And before he asked about anything, the owner of the store told him that a huge dam was being constructed outside of town, near the lower reaches of the river, and that once it was finished the whole town would be underwater, and for this reason most of the people had already left. He imagined the town submerged in water. And in his mind he saw the drowned town undulating underwater.

Stepping out of the store, he took a bite of his ice cream. But the ice cream had no taste at all. He only felt something hard and cold in his mouth. So after taking a couple of bites, he flung it on the ground. He then lit a cigarette and took a puff, but soon he threw that away as well. He couldn't taste it, either. With his foot, he crushed the still burning cigarette.

He started walking again. But walking on a scorching summer day wasn't an easy thing to do. For him it was like burrowing into a gigantic, porous sponge. After walking a little further, he saw a boy in an empty lot kicking a deflated ball around. He watched the boy for a short while. Not knowing that he was watching, the boy continued kicking the ball. It seemed to him that the boy was kicking it because he didn't know what else to do with it. He closed his eyes for a moment and tried to remove the boy from his field of vision, but when he opened his eyes the boy was still there.

He began walking again and soon turned a street corner. A new street appeared before him, but it was so similar to the previous one that he was almost unable to distinguish one from the other. He stood still at the intersection, as if he was lost and needed help. Only a yellow traffic light was blinking. The streets looked as though they had toppled to the ground from a great height.

He crossed the street and continued walking, but this time in the opposite direction. As he was walking, though, he felt that he was deviating from his path. By taking smaller steps, he delayed his detour. He soon stopped walking again. He felt that the world spread before him was stuffed inside his belly. And it seemed to him that the streets spread out in front of him were his intestines spilling out of his body. With his gaze he gathered up the streets and then placed them where he couldn't see them.

He began walking again. Further down the street he saw a lumber mill that had closed down. Tall weeds were growing between rotting timbers in its yard. Regardless of the "No Trespassing" sign on the gate, he pushed it open and entered. But before taking many steps, he felt something sharp pierce his shoes and sting his foot. It turned out to be a large nail protruding out of a wooden board. When he took off his shoe, blood oozed out from his sock. But he didn't feel any pain at all. After pulling out the nail from his shoe, he walked out of the mill yard. He then took down the "No Trespassing" sign, which came down more easily than he had expected. He then re-hung it upside-down.

He continued walking along the street. Even though he was clearly stepping forward, it seemed to him that he was walking over the same spot. And he also felt that all his movements weren't actually made by him. Although he was experiencing difficulty while forcing himself to move forward, he, nonetheless, continued to take one step after another. But he felt he barely managed to touch the ground.

Soon he stood in front of a restaurant, which, with its dust-covered front and its broken sign, appeared to have been closed for quite some time. In front of the restaurant a dog lay flat on its belly. The dog didn't block his way, but he stopped as if the dog was doing so.

No wind was blowing, as though it had been blocked from flowing freely. He felt stifled. He bent down over the ground where hot air was rising up. And as the prostrate dog was breathing, dust repeatedly rose and fell. With his head tilted slightly, the dog was looking vacantly up at the sky. He bent over the dog. It was making some strange sounds. Without any clear reason, he felt some kind of hostility toward the dog. As if trying to shake off his antagonism toward the animal, he stared at something in the distance. He then looked up at what the dog was gazing at and saw a butterfly flying around.

He got to the town's restaurant and leaned against the side of the building. He stood still, looking as if he was plotting something. Nothing was moving on the street. Without a doubt, everything before him looked completely disjointed. The yellow road divider was worn off in places and this made him feel somewhat nauseous. At the opposite side of the street a truck, with flat tires and broken windows, lay abandoned. Indeed, everything on the street appeared to have been abandoned or was about to meet that fate. And he felt that everything he saw was preparing to do battle with him.

Right then, several shabby-looking dogs appeared, and the dog that was resting on the ground followed them. He closed his eyes and imagined making the dogs disappear around the street corner, and after the dogs had in fact finally vanished, he opened his eyes and confirmed it.

Like a machine that had been overused and was now out of order, he remained there, standing motionless. Nothing moved for a long time. Suddenly, a booming motorcycle emerged from down the street and passed him by, tearing down the empty street. A cloud of dust rose from the ground. The motorcycle passed by so fast that it almost seemed like some kind of illusion, and after it was gone, an unmanageable silence filled the street. He stared at the empty space in front of him, stared as if he was expecting something marvelous to unfold. But nothing appeared or happened as he'd hoped. Without knowing why, he felt uncomfortable and wanted to get out of there. Right at that moment, he heard faint buzzing sounds in the silence. He pricked up his ears and realized it was coming from a cluster of flies circling above a pile of animal excrement. As if fascinated by the sight, he watched the swarming flies hovering above the dried feces. The flies persistently circled around the pile of shit, circled as if they were maintaining their bond in order to fulfill a common goal. Strangely enough, the scene excited him, but he couldn't figure out what part of the scene had that effect. He was unable, though, to overcome a feeling that something was pressing against him. Lifting up his head, he saw a flock of birds flying overhead and waited for them to pass by. The birds flew in a formation along a seemingly specific route, and he watched this like someone who had made it all possible. After the birds had vanished and as if being a consequence of their disappearance, he finally resumed his walk. But as though he was weighing himself down, it was difficult for him to continue walking.

After passing through the downtown area, he arrived at the end of the street and then began crossing a bridge. The bridge had collapsed halfway across. And right there, he stopped walking. Looking down at the river flowing under the bridge, he saw a sunken tire in the rippling water. Absentmindedly, he stretched out his hand over the water. And also seemingly absentmindedly, the river kept flowing, undisturbed by his outstretched hand. Like a person displaying an excessive interest in what they were seeing, he gazed fixedly at the water.

A crazy woman soon appeared out of nowhere. Smiling and twisting her hair with her fingers, she approached him. Her hair was extremely disheveled. He wanted to say something when the woman passed by, but she burst out laughing and he couldn't say anything. Having passed him by, the woman continued laughing loudly. He fought off an impulse to follow her. Stepping on his own shadow, he stood there for a while, and this gave him the impression that, for some unknown reason, he had been reborn.

Soon he reached the riverbank. In the shade beneath the bridge a little boy was repeatedly scooping up water with a glass cup and emptying it into the river, as though he was baptizing the river. Ignoring the boy, he turned his head away and then began walking along the riverbank.

Further on, an object in the sand captured his attention. He saw the roots of a tree trapped in the sand. The roots were all entangled and rotting. But what really drew his attention was something else. Looking like a fanciful creation intended to excite his imagination, a wooden leg was half buried in the sand next to the roots. Some mishap seemed to have taken place there. Unintentionally, he let out a loud groan. As if angry, he picked up the artificial leg. Once a part of someone's body, it was heavier than he'd thought. And it was all covered with mold. Not knowing exactly what he was doing, he put his arm into the hollow of the leg. The leg swallowed up his arm. And he barely managed to free himself, and then, with all his strength, he flung it into the water. But doing so failed to free him from the feeling that his body consisted of many artificial parts. The fake leg floated a bit in the water before sinking to the bottom, and it was clearly seen through the shallow water. He imagined himself lying down on the river bottom.

After a while he lay down on the sand by the river. The heat rising from the hot sand wasn't easy to bear. He scooped up a handful of sand and then let it trickle down between his fingers. The falling sand piled up next to him. He imagined something light being built out of sand.

He got up and slowly circled about while stomping on the sand, as if he was trying to compact it, and he finally stopped when he was exhausted. Soon, as though drawn by the water, he slowly stepped into the river. He looked down at his legs and saw that they looked like they had been cut at the thighs by the water's surface. And below the surface, he felt as though he had artificial legs. For a while he didn't turn his gaze away from his thighs. It seemed that he had entered a place where it wouldn't be easy for him to escape. Right then, the water swelled up rapidly and reached his chest and then neck, until finally it reached over his head and he was submerged under water. He floundered like a drowning person. Gradually, he sank to the river bottom. But all of this was nothing more than a figment of his imagination, as the water level remained at his thighs.

He walked further down the riverbank. There he saw an old man drawing in his fishing net, and so he watched him for a while. Only a few fish had been caught in the net. The old man cast his net several more times, but it seemed too strenuous a thing for him to continue doing. Soon the fisherman gave up on catching more fish; he collected his gear and prepared to go home. Walking up to the old man, he bought three catfish. The fisherman put the fish in a transparent plastic bag and handed it to him. The old man then left and he remained there alone. He stared at all the things around him that would soon disappear from his sight. And the margins of his sight gradually widened.

The sun was setting. Regardless of whatever else was happening, the sun as usual was setting on time. And that day's unusual sky was a blazing blood red. By closing his eyes, he trapped the sunset's blood red color in his eyes, and once there, the red color began fluctuating and permeating throughout his body. He could even feel the sun and its red color in him.

After it became dark, he headed downtown and went into a restaurant and ordered some food. A flytrap was dangling from the ceiling, with many dead flies stuck to it. And the food he ordered came so late that when it was served he didn't immediately begin eating but instead stared down at the dish. He soon realized that the restaurant owner was staring at him, and so he began eating his food. Something was unusual, though. He couldn't taste the flavor of the familiar food he was eating. So he stopped eating after a couple of spoonfuls. Bending over the dish, he sniffed at the food while trying to recall what it smelled like, but it was no use. Sitting by the window, the restaurant owner was busy chasing flies away with her arms. He paid the bill and stepped out onto the street and took some deep breaths. But he couldn't smell any of the street's familiar odors. And he felt that everything he saw was bleached white. He stuck out his tongue and tasted the strange atmosphere.

He realized that for some unknown reason he had begun walking in a certain direction. The town now looked even more desolate in the darkness. It appeared to him to be an ancient archeological site that had been discovered by chance and excavated after being forgotten for ages, and he felt that he himself had long ago disappeared with the town.

Before long, he entered a fruit store and bought a bag of apples. He took an apple out of the bag and smelled it, but it didn't offer up any scent at all. He then finally realized that he had a problem smelling. Yes, like other people losing their visual or auditory senses, he had lost his olfactory sense. A world where he could no longer smell anything seemed quite different from the one he had experienced when his sense of smell was functioning. He now felt like he was standing in a snow-covered wilderness. He tried to figure out how he had lost his sense of smell, but it wasn't clear. He had caught a cold some time before, but he had since totally recovered. It must've happened for some reason that he wasn't aware of. And it also seemed to him that he shouldn't try to figure out the reason.

He resumed his walk and realized that he was traveling toward his mother's house. But even though he was walking forwards, he felt that he was moving backwards, away from his mother's house. His body seemed to be malfunctioning.

After walking for a while, he finally arrived at his mother's house. But his mother wasn't living there any longer. The gate was firmly shut and a thick layer of dust concealed any trace of human habitation. He stood there blankly for a moment. Right then, the gate across the street opened and an old woman appeared. She scrutinized him cautiously, with a look that someone wears when meeting a stranger. He had never seen her before. She told him that no one lived at the house across the street from her.

Walking away from the gate, he dumped the apples on the ground that he had bought for his mother. He felt that his mother had become irrelevant to him, and even if there was any relationship left between them, it seemed too late to rekindle. He actually felt that he and his mother hadn't had a relationship from the start.

He went into a shabby motel nearby to stay the night. The motel was on the second floor of a building that was located in the middle of a marketplace. Once he was in his room, he opened the window and looked outside. The scenery in front of him felt familiar and guided his eyes to a nearby building. It was at one time a shop that sold all kinds of cooking oils and when he was a kid he would sniff the various odors, but the store was closed now. He continued looking at the building. But recalling a past long gone wasn't an easy thing to do. Even though he succeeded in remembering the smells of the different oils, it didn't help him to recall anything else. The past was isolated in a discontinuous world, one with absolutely different dimensions. And the building itself gradually began receding from his sight. While keeping one eye on the fading building, he kept his other eye on something else. The outer world he was looking at through the windowpane was motionless, as if it was trapped in the glass. The world looked like a picture drawn on a square sheet of paper, and in his mind he smashed it to bits and then stared at the pieces. But suddenly, as if something had startled him, he stepped back from the window and looked at the world within the window frame. The scene soon became blurry and so finally he turned away from it.

Sitting on his bed, he waited for some clue that would tell him what to do. But soon he realized that he was confused and didn't know what to do. He abruptly stood up and went to the bathroom to fill the sink with water, and then he brought the plastic bag to the sink and released the catfish. They were sluggish and weak but still alive. In the sink they lay on their sides. He picked up one of them and held it in his hand, as if he was weighing its value. But leaving a slimy feeling in his palm, the fish slipped out of his hand. As though wishing to retain the slimy feeling, he clasped his hand but felt nothing. He opened his hand with his palm facing upwards, and, as if trying to decipher something he didn't know, he gazed quizzically at his palm for a while. But when he realized he was only looking at his palm, he finally stopped gazing at it.

Lying in bed, he closed his eyes. He heard sounds coming from outside, and as if this jolted his awareness, he opened his eyes. And he then concentrated all his attention on his auditory sense and listened intently. But this time he heard nothing. He could only feel the hot summer night air in his ears. Soon he covered his ears with his hands and looked around at the things in the room. They looked as if they contained all time within them. He now began tossing about in his bed, and when he was perfectly curled up, he finally fell asleep.

That night he had a strange dream. In his dream he was sitting in the dark living room of a house when suddenly he heard something boiling in the kitchen. He ran over there. In the kitchen he saw a pot boiling on top of the stove. But strangely enough, when the water was boiling and spilling over, he saw that human hair, resembling long noodles, was spilling out of the pot. When he opened the pot he saw that his own head was being cooked inside; it wasn't easy though to make out that it was his own head, but, for sure, it was his. He again began tossing about while talking to himself in delirium. Among the incomprehensible things he shouted out was, "It's different from what you think." That night, he managed to get only a little sleep.

When he got up the following morning, he saw that the catfish were all dead, with their bellies protruding out of the water. And this seemed to him unavoidable and destined, and, at the same time, it also seemed to be some kind of ambiguous ending. He picked up the dead fish, threw them into the toilet, and then flushed them down. The dead catfish swirled and circled down the toilet bowl while seeming to push against each other. But they didn't completely disappear; rather, with their heads stuck in the toilet, their tails were left sticking out. For a while he gazed at the tails but soon turned away. Harboring a certain expectation, he sniffed his hands but couldn't smell anything.

He hurriedly exited the motel. It was already afternoon. The motel owner was nowhere to be seen. His foot, which had been pierced by a nail the previous night, now began hurting. And it wasn't easy to continue walking. He stopped and ate at another restaurant, but again he didn't taste or smell anything. Thinking there was a chance that the loss of his sense of smell could last a long time, he got a bit worried, but, at the same time, he felt a certain expectation, too. And it seemed to him that it revealed a condition of his life. He quickly left the restaurant.

The street was filled with trash. He inhaled the air deeply but again smelled nothing. He missed smelling the foul odors. He went to the bridge where he had been the previous day. And before long he saw the crazy woman again, the one he had seen that day, approaching him from far away. She passed by him while laughing and twisting her hair with her fingers as she'd done before. He remained there, standing still, with his whole body rigid. He then realized that he was twisting his own hair unconsciously. And when she had vanished from sight, laughter burst out of him. All this made him feel as though he had some kind of connection with her.

He stood there for a short spell and then, as if he had thought of something, he began walking again, walking the same streets he had traveled the day before. Although walking wasn't easy for him, he doggedly continued on nonetheless. After the sun had set, he went to the outskirts of the town to visit a woman he had lived with once. Her house wasn't too far away. And when he arrived at the spot it was still there. When he knocked on the door, a plump, middle-aged woman opened it. Seeing him, she expressed disbelief and astonishment. "Can I come in," he asked. Without saying a word, she let him in. She looked baffled at his sudden appearance.

The interior of the house was even shabbier than its exterior. And it felt more like a temporary dwelling than a home that had been lived in; it was a home without much life and vital energy in it. In the yard he saw a nearly dead flower that was barely able to prop up its already dead stalks. Nothing in the house looked as if it had been well cared for, either.

"Where are the kids," he asked, once he was in the house. "Gone," the woman answered. "What do you mean—gone? What are you talking about," he asked. "They've been adopted," she said.

He looked as if what she said was incomprehensible to him "It was hard for me to be a single parent," she said. "Well, what can I say . . . anyway, they were your children," he said. "I know it doesn't make you feel good when I talk this way about the kids," he muttered. The woman gazed at him but said nothing.

After some time, she brought out some tea and apples. He suddenly had an enormous appetite. His uncontrollable appetite was so large that he felt as if he could eat whatever was laid in front of him. But when he took a sip of the tea, he couldn't taste anything. "What kind of tea is this," he asked. "It's quince tea . . . don't you smell its aroma," she asked. "It doesn't taste like it," he said. To him it was like drinking water boiled with a radish in it.

The woman picked up an apple and started to pare it. She was careful not to cut off the long strip of apple skin as she was paring. Looking at her, he felt as though his body was being pared, so to free himself of the feeling, he grabbed the strip of apple skin and snapped it into pieces.

The air in the room was so hot and humid that he felt he was suffocating. He started regretting his visit. "Don't you want to know how I've been," he asked. "How have you been," she asked. "I don't know," he said. The woman only spoke when she was spoken to. And he didn't want to talk much about anything. As if she couldn't talk or as if paring apples would spare her from having to speak, she picked up another apple and continued to peel it in silence. He picked up a piece of apple and took a bite. But he felt as if he had bitten into a hard rock, so he put down what was left.

"How do you think I've been," the woman asked, after peeling another apple. "I think I can guess," he said. "Then it must be as you've guessed," she said. Their conversation stopped again. He realized that he had nothing to say to the woman. He looked down at the piece of apple with his teeth marks on it. It looked rather strange on the tray. "I think I can understand about half of my thoughts, but I can't figure out any more," he mumbled. "What? Did you say something," the woman asked. "No, nothing," he said. "I wonder how this tea ended up having such an odd name, it just doesn't fit its name, quince tea," he mumbled.

At one corner of the room he leaned against a pile of comforters on the floor. Fatigue suddenly came over him, but he wasn't sleepy. He looked around the room. He soon spotted a mobile dangling from the ceiling. It was in the shape of a butterfly. And because it was partially broken, it had lost its balance and was lopsided; he kept staring at it, though, without blinking. A breeze blew in through the open window and gently shook the mobile. The shaking disturbed his gaze. He tried hard to steady it, but it was too difficult to do. As if wanting to stop the mobile from shaking, he tried to reach it with his raised hand. But unless he stood up, the mobile was suspended too high for him to reach, so he dropped his hand down.

He lowered his gaze. Skinned apple pieces were scattered about on the tray. For a while he and the woman were speechless. He couldn't think of anything suitable to say. He was about to say something at one point but stopped himself. "Did you say something," she asked. "No, nothing," he said. "I thought I heard something," she said. He dropped his head. "How have you been," she asked. "Didn't you ask that a moment ago," he said. "You're right," the woman said. Meanwhile, the neglected pieces of apple soon turned brown. He turned his head to the brown apple pieces and kept gazing at them. He wasn't sure whether he was looking at the apple pieces that were turning brown or looking at their brown color. "What are you looking at," she asked. "What does it look like I'm looking at," he said. "I don't know," she uttered. But he thought to himself that he wasn't actually looking at anything.

He closed his eyes. Right then, the previous day's clear, red sunset appeared before him. "Have you ever thought that your thoughts were all stained with blood," he asked. Without saying a word, she stared at him. He averted his gaze. "Never mind, I just wanted to tell you what I was thinking about," he said. "You look stranger than ever," she said. He didn't respond. For a while both of them remained speechless. "Don't you smell something like fish," he asked. As if trying to figure out what was going on with him, she stared intently at him. "This whole room seems to be filled with a fishy smell," he said. Looking wary, she continued to stare at him. "Do you really think I look even stranger?" he asked. "How can I put it . . . you look befuddled," she said. "I look that way to me, too," he said. Once again silence overcame them. "What are you thinking about," she asked, after a while. "I'm not thinking about anything," he said. He felt, though, that the many thoughts swirling around his mind were causing side effects.

"How would you feel if I came back to you," he asked. "I don't know, and I didn't expect you to visit me like this," she said. "I'm on parole, that is, I'm not completely free yet," he said. The woman's face appeared to stiffen a bit. He looked down again at the apple pieces. Their surfaces were now completely brown. He fixed his eyes on the changes occurring in the apples. It seemed to him that things change only on the surface. And that one recognizes things by their surface features. He felt that his thoughts were being dyed brown, the color of the apple pieces.

"What do you think of me," he asked. The woman didn't answer. "I know you have nothing good to say about me, only bad things," he said. "That's not completely true . . . ," the woman said, as her words trailed off. "Even though you think I'm all bad, it's okay," he said. He looked at her and felt that somehow she was obstructing him, so he looked away. "I went to my mother's house," he said. "You went to your mother's house?" she asked. "Yes, I did, but she isn't living there any longer," he said. "What are you talking about, your mother died long ago, even before you left me," she said. "She did?" he asked. "It seems I've been misinformed," he said. "Yeah, I think so, especially if the person I know to be your mother is in fact your mother," she said. He felt relieved that his mother had died long ago.

He surveyed the room. "There's something in this room that's nagging at me," he said. "What is it," the woman asked. "I don't know, but there's something for sure," he said. He pointed to the mobile and asked, "What do you think of taking that down?" The woman got up and was about to take the mobile down. "Well, maybe leave it alone," he said. But she took it down anyway. "Is it better now without it," she asked. "Well, maybe that wasn't what was bothering me, maybe it isn't anything in this room that's bothering me," he said. Still standing, the woman stared down at him.

"I saw an abandoned tomb near the vineyard along the river," he said, after a while. "A tomb near the vineyard, but there isn't any vineyard around here," the woman said. "But I clearly saw it," he said. "No one grows grapes here," she replied. "What do you think I saw then," he asked. "I have no idea what you saw, but I know it wasn't a vineyard," she said. "When the dam is completed, the tomb will be buried under water," he said. "And it will be the second burial for the dead person," he added. But the woman said nothing. Their gazes awkwardly connected. The woman started yawning. "Don't you smell something," he soon asked. "What smell?" the woman replied. She pretended to sniff the air. "There must be something that smells," he said again. "I smell nothing," the woman said. He sniffed around. But he couldn't smell the odor he was thinking of. With a gentle look in her eyes, the woman stared at him.

"How was it when we lived together," he asked shortly. Looking as if she didn't hear his question, the woman appeared to be thinking of something. Actually, he didn't expect an answer. He picked up the paring knife and began making knife marks on the apple pieces. With an uneasy expression on her face, she looked at him. Before long their gazes collided again, but soon they lowered their eyes, until finally they were staring at the floor. Right then, he felt a severe pain in his foot that must've become infected because of the nail he stepped on. He tried to ignore it, thinking that it wasn't a big deal.

"Where did all the people who once lived here move to," he asked. "A new town is being built a short distance away, and a new road was also constructed," she said. "I'll be moving there soon, too, since this town will be gone before long," she said. "It sounds like the new town is waiting for this town to disappear," he replied. "Well, it could be," she said. "It also seems that some people are against building the dam, since I saw some protest posters saying just that," he said. "Yes, that's true, some people don't like the idea," she said. "What do you think about it," he asked. "I don't know," she answered. "Well, I really don't care," she then immediately said, as if correcting herself. "It'll all disappear sooner or later anyway; it's just happening a little earlier rather than later," she said. "I think so, too," he said. Suddenly, he felt that he couldn't bear to be with her any longer.

Looking pained, he lifted his head and gazed around the empty room. He saw a fly darting about. Gradually, his face hardened. The woman kept her gaze on his face. When he looked at her, she finally turned away. "Your hair looks different. I mean it's so black," he said. "Oh, I dyed it," the woman replied. "I see," he said. "I'm ready for anything, except for one thing—I'm not ready to face myself," he said, as if talking to himself. The woman stared at him without saying a word. "Why are you looking at me with an angry face," he asked, while gazing at her. "Do I look angry," the woman asked. "Yes, you look angry," he said. Their eyes met again. When he lowered his eyes, he saw a dead fly on the floor. He slowly stretched out his leg and covered the fly with his foot.

"Don't you think this room is too dry," he asked. But the room was in fact rather damp. "We had rain yesterday," the woman said.

"Did we," he asked. "Oh, yes, and it rained a lot," she said. "I don't remember that it rained yesterday," he said. "Yes, it rained, I'm sure of it, since I got wet when I went out," she said. "It must've been a passing shower," he said. "No, it wasn't, it rained for quite a long time," she said. He didn't say anything more about the rain. He still felt, though, that the room was too dry. The whole room seemed thirsty.

"Please recall what I've done to you," he suddenly said, breaking his silence. The woman appeared to be deep in thought. "Well, I've already forgotten all about it," she said. "What was it," he asked. "I don't know, but it seems as if nothing really happened," she said. "And now it seems like it wasn't such a horrible thing anyway," she said. He said nothing. "It's the same with me . . . I can't remember anything," he said, after a long silence. "I now feel that anything I did wasn't actually done by me," he said. The woman was looking at him. "Don't you think it's better if I feel like that," he asked, as if talking to himself again. "What happened to you," the woman asked. "One thing I'm very clear about is that I'm not sure what happened to me," he said, slowly, as though spitting out something from his mouth. Right then, he felt that the pain in his foot was getting worse.

Silence again engulfed the two of them. "Things have changed a lot here, and it's not easy to recognize things," he said, after a while. "But some things didn't change at all," she said. But he wasn't listening to her anymore. Rather, he was gazing at an old mirror hanging on the opposite wall. The mirror's dusty surface stressed its depth of field. Things reflected in the mirror, though, were all faded, so much so that they were unable to recognize themselves. He continued looking at himself and the woman in the mirror. He felt that his mind was too hazy to even identify the woman sitting in front of him. And in the mirror the man, whose eyes were fixed on the woman, didn't look like himself, either. Feeling that the point in time he occupied was all confused, he twisted his body slightly. Like someone who was chasing away his false image, he lifted his hand and motioned himself away in the mirror, all the while glaring at himself. He again felt as though his body was contracting. As if he wanted to free himself of the feeling, he abruptly stood up. "I'd better be going," he said. "But where," the woman asked. "I don't know," he answered. But he couldn't take a step forward because of the pain in his foot. So he was forced to sit back down in a rather uncomfortable position. Soon the pain lessened a bit and he felt that he was back to normal.

Looking as though she was unable to overcome her sleepiness, the woman kept yawning. "Go to bed if you're that sleepy," he said. As though she had waited for him to say that, she immediately got up and went to the bathroom. Afterwards she came out with her face washed and then started putting on some makeup, acting as if she was all alone in the room. In the mirror he watched the woman apply her makeup. As she put on her face powder, her complexion became paler and her wrinkles disappeared. "You look like you've put on some weight," he said. "Aging, no doubt," she replied. In the mirror the woman was only looking at herself. Meanwhile, he stared at himself watching the woman in the mirror. He stared like he was trying to figure out who was who in an old photo. The woman now looked at him in the mirror. She looked like a stranger to him. The two sat there without saying anything. All the while, the woman kept yawning. She soon began to arrange her bedding, and after that she lay down. The woman was expecting him to lie next to her, but he remained sitting against the wall, with his eyes closed.

The woman soon fell asleep. "What have I done to you," he asked her, while still facing the opposite wall. The sleeping woman didn't reply. "I'd better get going," he mumbled. But he remained sitting where he was. He looked down at the woman. And he noticed that the white roots of her hair were growing and would gradually overcome the black dye. He was very tired, as if he hadn't slept for a whole day, so he rubbed his eyes with his palms. Under his closed eyelids and in the pitch-black darkness, small specks of lights flickered. The lights emerged in various shapes and then suddenly scattered, leaving their long tails of light behind. Shortly, he found himself leaning to one side. So he raised himself up. "The more I try to hold myself up, the more I slump down," he said to himself.

Afterwards, as though in a trance, he began groping around for something. In a corner of the room, he picked up the paring knife from the tray. When he grabbed the knife, his hand was shaking and felt warm. "What are you going to do with it," he asked himself, cautiously, as if he was intruding on somebody else's affairs. He then began to gouge himself slowly at his side, as if he was digging into the rotting part of an apple. And he felt that the action wasn't being performed by him, that he was somehow excluded from it. The knife was dull, so the stabbing and gouging was hard for him to do. And of course blood streamed down his side, and he watched it all in a state of intoxication. As the knife penetrated deeper into his body, more blood gushed out. The strong stench of blood rushed to his nose. "This smell must come from my imagination," he thought. As a matter of fact, he couldn't smell anything. His stabbing soon became more violent. But no expression of pain appeared on his face. No, only a tinge of satisfaction was visible. "This isn't enough for me," he mumbled to himself, trying hard to hear his fading voice.

Translated by Inrae You Vinciguerra and Louis Vinciguerra

A Most Ambiguous Sunday

"Strange . . . the vivid feelings I felt just a moment ago have vanished and now everything is so ambiguous to me. I barely feel the existence of anything. And today, which hasn't even ended yet, already feels like ancient history, like some long-forgotten day from my childhood. All the days seem like Sunday, too, as if only Sunday exists," he mumbles.

His alarm clock rings and he opens his eyes. He remains still for a moment and then, while blinking, he looks at the calendar on the wall. "It's Sunday again, a day I've never liked, a day I just can't seem to like," he grumbles. Soon he gets up from his bed. "By the way, is Sunday the beginning of the week or the end of the week? It's always been difficult for me to figure that out," he says.

After putting his clothes on, he goes to a crumbling chicken coop at one corner of the front yard and looks into it. In the grimy cage a plump hen is resting on her belly on the ground. He tries to make the hen move aside, but she doesn't budge an inch. So he pushes the hen to one side and removes the eggs that are under it. "They're still warm," he mumbles. "And thank you for laying two eggs today," he says, while looking at the hen. Well . . . this hen sure has an ugly look, but who cares, she knows how to lay eggs, just goes to show that appearance doesn't matter when it comes to laying eggs," he says. He attempts to pet the hen's head, but as if she doesn't like it, the hen dodges her head. "Since you laid two eggs today, I'll give you more food." He picks up a handful of grain and scatters it into the coop.

He walks into the house and goes to the kitchen, where he starts boiling the eggs in a transparent pot. While the eggs are being cooked, he goes to the bathroom and washes his face. He then goes back to the kitchen and sits on a chair and stares at the pot where the water is boiling with the eggs in it. "That pot looks so fragile, it might crack at any moment, but it hasn't happened yet," he mumbles. He continues watching the pot.

After a while he takes the eggs from the pot, lets them cool, strikes one of them on his head, and then begins carefully peeling the eggshell. But the eggshell doesn't peel neatly. It sticks to the egg white. "Oh my, I forgot to put the eggs in cold water after boiling them . . . it looks like a mouse nibbled on it," he says to himself. He picks the whites off the shell and eats it after sprinkling some salt on it. "Well . . . it's not bad since the yolk, my favorite part of the egg, is all intact." He tosses the half-cooked, doughy yolk into his mouth. "I don't know when it began, but I always soft boil eggs so that they're half cooked and half raw." He thinks for a moment. "I think it started after my wife died, but it has nothing to do with her death. I can still say, though, it's true that my eating habits changed after she died. I eat simply now, since I have to cook. And I've become less picky . . . well . . . I can't complain about my own cooking."

After eating the egg, he goes into his room and opens his closet and inspects his few suits, one by one. I don't see one that is suitable for this time of year when the seasons are changing," he mumbles. "They're either too thin or too thick for this weather." He chooses the thickest suit among them and wears it, but he doesn't wear a tie. "It'll be much better if I wear a heavy suit and take it off if it gets hot rather than going out with light clothing and shivering in the cold. Yes, that would be a wise choice, one that I'll be happy about."

He goes back to the kitchen and puts the other egg in his pocket along with some salt wrapped in paper and then walks out of his house. He picks up his bicycle that is lying in the front yard and walks out into an alley. Once in the alley he mounts the bike and begins pedaling, but the wheels don't move. Even though he knows the wheels aren't spinning, he continues pedaling. "Hmm, I can't help feeling that something's wrong," he mumbles. He finally gets off the bike and checks the chain. He notices that the chain has fallen off. "I see, I forgot to fix it," he says. "Is this why you've been spinning idly?" he says to his bike while kicking it. He puts it back in the yard and enters the alley again.

As if he sees nothing on the street, he walks with his back straight and his eyes staring straight ahead. "By walking like this, I can ignore things that I don't have to look at," he mumbles. Now and then he bobs his head as if reacting to somebody's greeting, but actually no one says hello to him.

His church isn't far away and he soon arrives. But at the entrance of the church he stops and stands still rather than entering. He looks at his watch. "I thought I tried to be on time, but I'm still late," he mumbles. "But compared to other Sundays I'm not that late." For a while he listens to the hymns coming from inside the church. And he pricks his ears as though they bother him. He then takes out a handkerchief from his pocket and wipes his face. He is sweating because of his heavy suit that is too thick for the season. "I should've worn a thinner one," he mumbles.

He pushes open the church door and enters. A small number of people—very small even considering the church's size—are attending the service. A young minister glances at him and greets him while preaching the gospel, but he ignores the greeting. Some people turn their heads, but they soon turn back to the front.

He sits on a bench in the back. He scans the rows of people

sitting in front of him. "I can only see the backs of people's heads," he says. "But all the heads I see are ones that I recognize. And I don't see any heads that I don't recognize. And it's better for me to face the backs of these people rather than see their faces." He sits down silently. "Strange, the inside of this church is always cool. And it's not just because the inside is darker than the outside, since it seems there must be another reason for it," he mumbles. "It's a chilling feeling rather than a cool one. Anyway, I'm glad I'm wearing heavy clothes."

As though searching for someone, he looks around. He spots an old woman with permed white hair sitting in the front row. "There she is . . . must've known I would be here," he mumbles. "That woman's wearing her hair a little high today, like a young woman. But it looks somewhat awkward to me. I should tell her about it after the service. And I'm going to ask her to take a walk with me. I know she'll like it. Yes, she's not going to say no."

Meanwhile, the minister is talking about Job and his martyrdom. He listens to the minister for a while. "This guy's never said anything moving or worth listening to," he says to himself. "He always talks about things that I can't call good stories and that always bore me to hell." Quoting The Book of Job, the minister is now asking the people to repent for their sins. He thinks for a moment. "Let me think about whether I've done anything that demands repentance, but it seems that I don't have to repent for anything," he mumbles. "If I'd known about this, I would've committed at least one trivial sin, not a bad one. Well, who knows, maybe a bigger sin will bring me greater bliss."

Just then, a fly flies over to him and rests on the back of his left hand. He shakes his hand to chase it away. But the fly, after soaring up for a second, rests on his right hand instead. He shakes his hand again and shoos it away. But the fly now rests on his forehead. So he shakes his head. The fly shoots up into the air and disappears for a second, but soon appears again and flies around him. He tilts his body so that the fly doesn't rest on him. But the fly doesn't leave and continues circling around him. "Don't you see other people here? Why only me, as though you have a special affection for me? Go away, go to other people," he grumbles loudly. People turn around and stare at him. Regardless of their looks, he just looks straight ahead in a calm and collected manner.

After the minister finishes his sermon, the choir begins singing hymns accompanied by the piano. "Following my Lord . . . ," he sings, out of tune. Soon he stops singing. "That's because the piano accompaniment isn't very good," he says. "And following the Lord isn't that easy. The more I try to get closer to him, the more I become estranged from him. And this must be the same for the Lord. Getting close to me can't be easy, either."

After the choir finishes singing and with the minister leading, people in the church begin to say the Lord's Prayer. He moves his lips, but he doesn't make any sound. "What good is all this praying," he grumbles. "I've prayed hard but nothing has worked out. Yes, prayers didn't do anything. Well . . . they worked, but I got the opposite of what I wished for. Maybe then I should pray for the Lord to nullify the prayers I've just said. But it isn't going to work anyway, since whatever I pray for won't happen." He stops talking to himself for a moment. "Hmm . . . how did I end up praying?"

After the prayer ends, a boy walks around with a contribution box and stops in front of each person, thrusting the box out and waiting for them to make a contribution. When the boy reaches him, he puts his hand in his pocket and pretends to rummage for money, then takes his empty hand out of his pocket and puts it into the box and withdraws his hand from it. As if he can't believe what he has just seen, the boy stares at him before moving on to the next person. "It should be okay, since I donated all I had," he mumbles. With the request for donations signaling the end of the service, people now begin to get up.

He rises swiftly, more swiftly than anyone else, and goes to the front yard of the church. At the entrance of the church, the minister and his wife chat with members of the congregation. He looks askance at them for a while and then turns his head away and looks at a quince tree nearby. "This tree hasn't borne any quince fruit this year," he mumbles. "Have all this year's fruits already fallen? But, as far as I can remember, I don't think I've seen any fruit on this tree this year. I wonder if this quince tree that hasn't born any quince deserves to be called a quince tree."

Soon people begin to leave the church. The minister, who has been talking with the church members, approaches him. The minister is fat and his belly is bulging. Instead of looking at the minister's face, he glances objectionably at his belly. But the minister becomes quite busy again, saying good-bye to those who have hung about and have just started to leave, as if they want to stay longer. "I can't believe that my son is a minister and I can't believe that I'm a father of a minister," he mumbles. "And what is he going to do with such a potbelly? Of course, there's no regulation that restricts a minister from having a big belly, but it still doesn't look right for a minister to have such a huge belly."

After everyone leaves, only the minister and his wife remain. "How have you been?" the minister asks. "Many things have happened, but I don't want to talk about it now in detail," he says. "And of course, I don't remember much about anything anyway." "I thought you might not attend the service today," the minister says. "Actually I didn't mean to come. It just happened," he replies. "Why don't you come to my house and have lunch with us," the minister suggests. "Did you say have lunch together at your house? Just lunch?" he asks the minister. Ashamed by his father's reply, the minister doesn't say anything further. Right then his lady friend approaches him. "How have you been?" she asks him. "Nothing really bad has happened," he answers. "I only expected bad things, but they didn't happen, though at the same time nothing good has happened, either," he says. "What are you talking about? Can't you just say that everything is fine? Why do you have to talk like that, as if you don't even know what you're talking about?" she says. "Anyway, do you have time to take a walk with me? I don't have that much time but I can still take a walk with you," he says. "But let's eat lunch at my son's house. He's just asked me to join him for lunch. Can she come with me?" he asks his son. "Of course, it'll be much better if you both can make it," his son answers.

They all walk to the minister's house, located in the backyard of the church. "What's for lunch today?" he asks. "Oh, I made some dumplings, since I know you like them," his daughter-in-law answers. "Who said I like dumplings?" he grumbles. "Of course, I eat them when I have nothing else to eat, but I don't eat them because I like them. If there's anything else to eat besides dumplings, I don't even look at them." Disheartened, his daughter-in-law lowers her head.

They soon arrive at the minister's house. There his daughter-in-law fixes lunch. Then the minister prepares to say a prayer before the meal. "Are you going to say another prayer? You've just finished praying," he says. "I don't think that your Lord will like too many prayers. It must be such a nuisance for your Lord when everyone says a prayer so often, and how can he listen to all of them anyway?" But ignoring his father, the minister begins reciting the Lord's Prayer. "Our Father, which art in heaven . . . give us this day our daily bread . . ." "Can't you make it shorter?" he asks his son. He's interrupted the prayer and his son has to begin all over again. "Our Father, which art in heaven . . . give us this day our daily bread . . ." "It's too damn long, can't you just say the last sentence?" he asks again. "Jesus, the dumplings are going to get all bloated and they'll burst," he grumbles. But brushing off his remarks, the minister continues the prayer and finally finishes it. "That's too long," he says. "One sentence would've been sufficient as a prayer for this meager meal. We're only having some dumplings for lunch and we're trying hard to be thankful for it."

They start eating. "What's in the dumplings?" he asks his daughter-in-law, after picking one up. "Vegetables and meat," she answers. He takes a bite of a dumpling. "But it doesn't seem to be filled with anything. It feels like it's empty," he says. But even while saying this, he is the one who devours the most dumplings. He finishes one helping and his daughter-in-law brings another serving and he finishes the second one. "Would you care for more?" his daughter-in-law asks. "Do you think I'm a pig?" he says. "I feel stuffed eating that many dumplings and I don't even like them at all," he mumbles.

After finishing lunch he and his lady friend leave the minister's house. "Why don't you pray to your Lord to let you lose some weight," he says, while staring at the minister's bulging belly at the door before leaving. "It's not something you attain through prayer and it's not the right thing to ask the Lord," his son replies. "Hmm, it seems that even your Lord can't do anything about your expanding waistline," he says. "Oh, my Lord reins beyond such trivial things," the minister says. "Of course, he must have many other things to take care of," he says. The minister looks at him with discontent. "Anyway, regarding your weight, it's between you and your Heavenly Father. And this father will leave now," he says. Before going into their house, his son and his wife watch him and his lady friend recede into the distance.

Leaving the downtown area, the two now enter a path along a creek. "The sky looks extremely blue today," he says. "It looks like it's scared of something. And the blue is quite dark, like the blue of a bruise, as if it's gotten beaten up by somebody." "Well, it looks fine to me," she says. "And you didn't have to be that mean to your son at lunch. It was awkward to be there," she says. "I don't think I was that bad. But if I was, I don't think he took it that way," he says. "And even though I treat him badly, it will still be okay, since he has his Heavenly Father to take care of him all the time," he says. "You . . . stop it," she says. "By the way, my son has a closer relationship with his stepfather, the Heavenly One, than me, and I like that," he says. "Where is your bicycle?" she asks. "I gave it a break today," he answers. "And, of course, because it conked out on me."

They walk for a while in silence. "The thought that I have an heir who will carry on my family lineage makes me sick," he suddenly says. "I should have dried up all my seeds." "You should be thankful to have son," she tells him. "No, I can't think that way, regardless of how much I try," he says. "How are you doing with your store?" he asks. "I rarely go to the store nowadays," she replies. "My daughter takes care of the business." "Do people buy many dolls?" he asks. "Business isn't bad," she answers. "It was good when you ran the store. I liked to go there," he says. "I would feel like I was in a different world when I was surrounded by all kinds of dolls and toys. And didn't I ask you to bring me a doll? What happened to it? Well . . . maybe not a doll, but how about a toy gun?" "What are you going to do with the toy gun?" she asks. "Well, just carry it around in my pocket," he says. "And when I get bored, I can take it out and play with it by aiming it at my temple." "Is acting your age that difficult?" she asks. "Well, not acting my age isn't easy, either," he says.

Soon they pass an abandoned water mill and enter a path on an embankment along a stream. After walking further and reaching the path's mid-point, they meet a goat that is tied to a rope and grazing on the grass. He stops and stares at it. Realizing that somebody else is there, the goat stops grazing and walks down the embankment. "I wasn't going to do anything to it, yet it avoids me," he says. The goat looks up at him suspiciously. After making sure there is no one around, he pulls the goat's stake out of the ground and pulls the rope, but the goat refuses to budge, so he rams the stake into the ground, a little distance away from its original spot. "Don't even think of pestering the goat. It must be hard enough being a goat," she says. "Well, it could be, but I don't think that it has a harder life than I do," he says.

Leaving them behind, the goat begins to walk away. "I don't know any other domestic animal that is as adaptable as a goat," he says. "Yes, goats do well wherever they are. And I think that's because they don't know where they are. And do you know that islanders graze goats on small, uninhabited islands near their home islands," she says. "Have you seen goats grazing on the tops of cliffs, all looking bold and brave while looking down from the cliffs? They could appear lonely and pathetic to spectators, of course, but the goats wouldn't know that they looked that way. And when the owner comes to take them home, they resist, as if they don't want to follow their owner and would rather be alone," he says. "Boy, you sure do know a lot about goats and I know so little about them," she says.

They stop walking and sit on the grass. At some of the stream's shallow spots women are picking spiral shellfish. For a while he gazes at them. "My wife made delicious shellfish soup," he says. "You must miss your wife while looking at those women gathering shellfish, right?" she asks. "I haven't had shellfish soup since she died," he says. "You're saying this as if the worst thing that's happened to you since her death is that you can no longer eat her soup, and if you love shellfish soup that much, why don't you cook it yourself?" she says. "But I can't cook it the way my wife did, even though I use the same ingredients . . . I just can't capture the same flavor," he says. "Yes, I remember that your wife cooked delicious shellfish soup," she says. "Just thinking that I won't ever be able to eat her soup again makes me miss my wife so much more," he says. "And there was another dish my wife excelled at—her pumpkin soup. Thanks to her, I would often eat plenty of healthy pumpkin soup." "Maybe eating shellfish and pumpkin soup are the reason you're still alive after all these years," she says. "Could be, and one time we even stole a display pumpkin from a restaurant," he says. "My wife carried the pumpkin inside her coat. I had her do that. With her bulging belly, my wife looked pregnant. The restaurant owner looked puzzled, since just a short while before she hadn't noticed that my wife was pregnant, and she asked her, 'What month are you in?' My wife said she was in the last month of her pregnancy. Actually, at that time my wife was two months pregnant."

He falls silent. "What are you thinking about," she asks. "I was thinking that if you die before me, what would I remember," he says. "What do you think you'll remember?" she asks. "I think I'll be thinking about nothing, as though you never existed," he says. "How about you? If I die first, what would you remember of me?" "I'll be thinking about your bicycle, which you took with you wherever you went," she said. "You mean that you'll be thinking about my bicycle, not me," he asks. "Well, if I think about your bicycle, it'll definitely remind me of you, since I can't think about the bicycle without thinking about you," she says. "And I'll also remember the one-piece dress you gave me one time, the only thing you ever gave me. And if I think of that dress after you die, I'll put it on. But I'll probably take it off right away because it doesn't fit me. It probably would've fit your wife, though. Wait a minute, maybe it was your wife's old dress, or your wife bought it but never wore it, so you gave it to me, am I right?" she asks. "What kind of person do you think I am?" he says. "Well, I think you're capable of doing worse than just that," she says. "What a terrible thing for you to say," he tells her.

Dragonflies dart about over their heads. As though bewitched, he watches them for a while. She also gazes at them. "Why do you think dragonflies always fly about in such a crazy way?" she asks. "They must get confused after flying about like that," he says. "And once confused, they continue flying in a confused state. And when they rest somewhere and recover from their confusion, they realize that the state they're in now isn't so good, either, so they fly about in confusion again, since they now know that recovering from confusion isn't such an attractive thing and that they don't ever want to recover from their confusion. They feel truly alive only when they're confused." "Your explanation confuses me even more," she says. "Oh, I just remembered something," he says.

He takes out an egg from his pocket. "What's that," she says. "I brought it for you," he says. "If you wanted me to have one, you should've brought another for yourself." she says. "We can share this one, and, as a matter of fact, there were two but I ate one this morning," he says. "My hen laid two eggs today. It would be good if she laid two eggs every day, but usually she only lays one, though for some reason this morning there were two." "You should be thankful for even one egg a day, and what will you do if she stops laying eggs," she asks. "Knowing you, I'm surprised that you even own a hen that lays an egg a day. And since your hen lays eggs every day, you must be feeding her on time?" "Well, I can skip my meal, but I won't skip feeding the hen," he says. "She's lucky to have a good owner like me. And feeding the hen reminds me of my own meal time, and so thanks to that I also end up eating regularly." "Sounds like you should thank the chicken for everything, including how you don't skip your meal because of her," she says. "That's not always the case though," he says. "Often I just don't have any appetite, so I eat nothing. But don't you think it's amazing that I've never forgotten to feed the hen but have forgotten to feed myself? And that it seems as if I feel hunger only through the hen's stomach, not my own." "How amazing, uh?" she says, wryly.

Meanwhile, he holds the egg firmly in his hand. "Aren't you going to peel off the eggshell?" she asks. "Oh, for a moment I forgot that I had an egg in my hand," he says. He gives the egg to her. "Why don't you peel it?" he says. "No, you do it," she replies. "Do you really think that I actually would do something myself when I can have somebody else do it for me," he asks. "Still obnoxious, I see, and it seems it's getting worse as you get along in years," she says. "Oh well, I can't really say it's lessening as I get older," he answers.

She peels off a bit of eggshell. "It's not coming off so easily," she says. "I forgot to put it in cold water right after boiling it," he says. "Recently, my forgetfulness is getting worse. One day I put an egg in a pot and forgot to turn the stove on and waited for the egg to boil." "The yolk isn't fully cooked," she says. "It's okay the way it is, as a half-cooked egg," he says. "Do you have salt," she asks. He takes out the salt wrapped in paper from his pocket. But all of the salt has spilled and nothing is left in the paper. "Oh my, the salt has all spilled into my pocket," he says. He puts his hand into his pocket and retrieves whatever salt he can. "Here's some salt," he says, as he thrusts out his palm. "I don't think I want to use that salt," she says. "Well then, you can eat the egg first then lick my palm," he says. "No, I'll dip it instead," she says. She dips the white of the egg into the salt and then begins eating. "But why do you think people eat boiled eggs with salt, why not eat them without salt," he asks. "I've never given it any thought," she says." She hands the yolk to him.

The two of them are silent while eating the egg. "This morning in the kitchen I watched the water boil my eggs," he says. "While looking at the boiling water in my glass pot, some thoughts also boiled wildly in my head, thoughts that didn't subside so easily, and I felt that my head was filled with boiling and immovable thoughts, and once they were in my head, I couldn't arrange them in any order or sort them out. And at those moments, I use to have a splitting headache, the kind of headache where you feel like all your thoughts are pouring out all at once."

Suddenly, she strikes her chest with her hand. "What is it?" he asks. "The egg . . . stuck in my throat," she manages to say. "You didn't feel like you ate an egg until you began choking, right?" he asks. "Strange, but I feel I've eaten eggs only after I'm choking on them." But she can't speak. He stares at her.

"What do you think about us living together?" she asks, after clearing her throat. "I don't think that anybody is going to call us a dirty old couple." "It sounds like it's not a bad idea," he says. "But what would I gain from living with you? Maybe we should just remain friends?" she says. "That also sounds like a good idea, but what are the disadvantages of not living with you," he asks. "So what are you trying to say?" she says. "Actually, I'm totally fine either way," he replies. She glares at him. "It's nothing new, you've always been this way—you've never taken a stand on anything," she says. "Right, that's my firm stance, that I'm fine with any situation," he says. "Yes, since I don't have any fixed position, I don't have to insist on anything and don't have to pay attention to other people's positions. I think I've been living my own way, regardless of the world out there, like a person who's already left it while still living in it." "I feel the same way, and it's becoming more so the older I get," she says." And it really doesn't matter if I live a long life or even if I die today." "You have to live longer than I do so you can witness how I lived my life and how I died, and after that you can die," he says.

The two of them fall silent. "I want to be buried right next you," she says, after a while. "But I know that it's not going to be easy, since you'll be buried beside your wife." "Even so, why not? If I can be buried between two women, that won't be such a bad thing," he says. "You're right, if the three of us can be buried together, it would be nice," she says. "But personally I don't want to be buried," he says. "Actually, I don't, either," she says.

They silently gaze at the distant mountains. "You know, goats stand prominently on hills and on top of cliffs as though they are emperors, lording over everything. And I don't know why, but to me, regardless of what they're doing, they just don't look like dignified emperors," he says. She doesn't say anything.

He again gazes vacantly at the distant mountains. "What are you looking at?" she asks, after some time has passed. "I'm looking at the fields, the creek, the mountains, and the sky. Yes, all I see are the broad fields, the creek running between the fields, fields beyond the creek, mountains behind the fields, and the sky blocked by the mountains. And to me, it looks like they're proudly revealing themselves and concealing nothing. And everything is in its place and nothing is missing," he says. She shifts her gaze from the fields to the creek and then to the mountains and sky.

"Something is happening today, everything I look at appears so vivid," he says. "And I'm clearly experiencing all my feelings, which are as vivid as the colors on a peacock's feathers, a peacock that's proudly spreading its feathers in some zoo somewhere. But I usually don't experience this, since it's very difficult for me to feel anything. And I'm pretty sure these vivid feelings aren't the last ones I'll experience, but right now I feel as if it's the last time I will." "I don't know why but I feel the same," she says. "Maybe that's because we're both getting closer to death," he says. "Today is certainly no different from any other day, but I feel that it is. It just doesn't seem to be one of my usual days." She listens quietly to him. Soon they both sink into silence.

"Why does everything look so boring," he says. "Why is it that in this country there aren't any huge lakes, endless prairies, deserts that you walk across for days, high mountain tops that you can't reach even in a day, and volcanoes boiling with lava that I can jump into?" "We have extinct volcanoes here," she says. "And I don't know why we don't even have earthquakes here," he says. "There's nothing to see, only things that bore me. Nothing impresses or inspires me. When I happen to look at them I soon ask myself why I'm even looking. So I search around, expecting to discover something different, but I fail and see the same things, again and again. Yes, what I see are mountains blocking the sky, small fields confined between mountains, and creeks barely flowing between the fields. And they're revealing themselves in such a way that says you should be satisfied with what they are. Yes, I've seen them throughout my whole life. But it's as if they're telling me that's still not enough."

They continue gazing at the things before them. "The sky, the creek, and the fields, they all remind me of a childhood incident. One time I mistakenly provoked a goat and it butted me and I fell down a rice field embankment," he says. "What did you do to the goat to deserve that?" she asks. "I got close to it and gently grabbed one of its horns in such a way that the goat didn't realize it, and I forgot that I was holding it," he says. "Suddenly, it rammed into me. Goats are usually docile, but once provoked, they do crazy things, as if they've gone insane."

"Listening to your story, I just remembered something from my childhood . . . do you remember that we used to catch locusts and eat them," she says. "That's right, we used to catch locusts, frogs, crayfish, and even snakes and eat them," he replied. "I never tried eating a snake . . . what does it taste like?" she asks. "It isn't something that you can explain to someone who hasn't actually tried it," he says. "But have you heard that if you don't luck out, snake-parasites get into your body and eat up your flesh. More horrible is when the parasites survive in your body for more than ten years and gradually travel to your head and eat up your brains," she says. "Wow, just thinking of it is horrible enough," he replies.

"And do you remember that when we were young, we must've been around six years old, we all got naked and the boys and girls paired up at the creek, and with weeping willow branches the boys tickled their partners' groins, and when a boy made his partner piss first his team would win the game," he says. "Yes, I remember, and come to think of it, it was a bawdy game, but I didn't feel that way at the time," she says. "And do you remember that we did it in the corn field?" he asks. "You seduced me, and I was innocent back then. You forced me into doing it," he says. "What are you talking about? You were the one who eyed me first," she says. "Anyway, since then we've both kind of overindulged ourselves for a while. But all our experiences have become ancient tales and are barely remembered, and now they all seem unreal, as if none of them really happened," he says. The two of them again fall silent.

"I don't think that you and I, while recalling the old days, can still go into the fields and do it," he says. "You're right, it seems impossible to me, even thinking about it, and the fields must've changed," she says. They don't say anything for a while. He moves his body around. "Don't you think that we need some stimulation, even though it might be a little late for us," he says. She sticks her tongue out provocatively and asks him, "You mean this kind of stimulation?" "No, not that kind," he says. "I mean the kind of stimulation that makes you shudder, even when you try to ignore it," he says. He closes his eyes. And without saying anything, she gazes at him.

"What are you thinking?" she asks. "I was thinking of the times we've shared together," he answers. "It was exciting when you and I met behind my wife's back, and during those times, when I merely thought about meeting you secretly, my heart would jump a bit, but not that much. And do you remember that one time when my wife was suspicious about our relationship but couldn't prove anything, even though we left her some clues?" "Maybe she knew about it but pretended not to," she says. "Maybe you're right," he says.

For a while they gaze at the fields in front of them. "This year's harvest doesn't look like a good one," she says. "But it also doesn't look like a bad one, either, and anyway I really don't care," he says. They continue to watch the golden rice fields.

Shortly, he grabs his belly. "My belly feels strange," he says. "Are you sick?" she asks. "No," he says. "It's not aching, but I feel like something is crawling inside me." "That could be maw worms," she says. "Several days ago on my birthday I took vermicide to get rid of the worms," he says. "It was my birthday, but I didn't eat anything special and only took the medicine, since I had a very uncomfortable stomach that day." "Didn't your son do something for your birthday?" she asks. "I didn't allow him to do anything for my birthday, and one reason was that it was my son, but above all, I don't like being treated special for my birthday," he says. "Yes, maybe you still have worms inside you, because even though you take vermicide, you can't get rid of all of them," she says. "And those worms are diehard . . . wait a minute, maybe you got them when you ate snakes and they're still alive inside you." "Don't even say such a horrible thing, and don't worry about me, my stomach will soon be okay," he says. "Who said I'm worrying about you," she says.

The two of them now stare at the creek. "Those people stopped picking shellfish and are beginning to leave," he says. "They could pick more but they seem to have decided to leave, as though they've already gotten plenty." "I think they'll all have shellfish soup tonight for dinner," she says. "Yes, they probably will, with all the family members sitting around eating the tasty soup," he says. "And they're going to have second helpings, too, as if they can't stop eating it." "Well, if you want to eat shellfish soup that much, I can cook some for you," she says. "But you said that a long time ago and never cooked any for me," he says. "Sorry about that. You know, nowadays I don't like doing things any more. Doing anything that I have to really think about is just too much for me," she says. They again fall silent.

"Shall we go," she asks, after a while. "Soon," he answers. "Even if we stay here a little longer, nothing will change, it'll make no difference. Well, maybe a difference will be made that really isn't any different." The two of them again gaze at the stream, now deserted after the women have left. "Isn't the stream flowing faster now?" she asks. "I really can't see the difference," he answers. "I don't know why but it sounds as if it's flowing faster to me," she says.

After a while she lifts up her head and looks up at the sky. "Look, wild geese are flying by," she says. "Where?" he asks. She points to a spot in the sky. He looks at her finger. "Don't look at my finger, look where my finger is pointing," she tells him. He docs what she says. "But I don't see anything, and it looks like nothing is flying up there," he says. "Don't you see the birds flying over there," she asks. "One, two, three, four, five, six . . . ," she counts. "How many are there?" he asks. "Wait," she says. "Seven, eight, nine, ten, it's more than ten . . . eleven, twelve . . ." "More than ten? Wow, the sky with more than ten wild geese flying across it must be quite a sight," he says. "Quiet, darn it, I lost count," she says. She again begins counting the birds. "One, two, three, no, I can't continue," she says. "Yeah, stop it, it's not worth doing," he says. "There are just too many to count at one glance," she says. "What formation are they in?" he asks. "They're flying in a *V* formation," she says. "Now they're receding into the distance and gradually fading away. And it appears as if only one bird is flying, and now I only see a dot." She drops her head. "Are you sure that wild geese really flew by?" he asks. "Do you think I'm telling you something that I didn't see, as you sometimes do to me?" she says. She again gazes up at the sky. "Now even the last bird is gone, and it's as if nothing ever flew by." "They shouldn't have shown up to begin with if they were going to fly for such a short time only . . . do you see any other wild geese in the sky?" he asks. "No," she answers. "It's as if they're saying that's all," he says. "Yes, no more birds and nothing to see. The sky is empty. It looks like it's filled with emptiness," she says.

The two of them fall silent again. "I see fish leaping into the air," she says. "One, two, three, sometimes a bunch of them leap up. I wonder why they have to leap up like that." But he's absorbed in his own thoughts and doesn't respond. "Maybe we should go back now," she says, after awhile. But the two remain sitting. He huddles up. "What are you thinking about?" she asks once again. "I'm thinking that I made a good decision when I decided to wear a heavy suit this morning, since it's getting quite chilly." Both of them say nothing for some time.

"I don't know why but I feel that next year I won't be here to see wild geese flying or listen to someone talking about them. I guess, even though I won't be able to see them, they'll still be flying in the sky, regardless of where I am, right?" he says. "Stop talking nonsense. I'm sure wild geese will be flying here again next year. And even though you don't see them, you'll still be able to hear me describe their flight. And then I'll hear the same nonsense coming from you. Well, maybe I'll hear something even worse," she says.

For a moment or two they fall silent once more. "Look, the sun's setting behind the mountain," she says. He looks at the sky. "I see the sky is turning red," he says. "By the way, do you know why the sky turns red when the sun's setting?" "I don't know," she says. "It's because the vapors in the air reflect the sun's rays," he says. "But why then is it red?" she asks. "What are you talking about, I've just explained why it's red," he says. "I want to know why it it's the color red specifically," she says. "It's beyond me," he tells her. "What I do know is that if vapors reflect the sun's rays they look red." As they gaze at the sunset, the darkness, which began rising from the earth, gradually permeates the red sky.

He watches the darkening sky. "Strange . . . the vivid feelings I had just a moment ago have vanished and now everything is so ambiguous. I barely feel the existence of anything. And today, which isn't over yet, already seems like ancient history, like some long-forgotten day from my childhood," he mumbles.

The two are again silent and motionless. "We must go now, it's getting dark," he says. But she is deep in thought. "Is it night already?" she finally asks. But now he's drifting himself. Meanwhile, the two of them continue gazing at the sky. "Everyday seems like Sunday to me, as though there's only Sunday in the week," he mumbles.

"Let's get up when the moon rises, when it gets totally dark and we can no longer recognize anything, even the person right next to us, rise as if we're surrendering to a greater power, as if there isn't any other way, as if it's finally possible for us to get up and leave," he says. "It feels strange when I look at the sky, seeing only the moon and no stars. Yes, when I look at such a sky I feel strange. At those times the moon looks as if it's being buried deep within the sky. And the sky looks like a huge grave. And if I continue looking at such a sky with that feeling, the sky really looks strange." He continues muttering odd things. "Now I can't see the leaping fish any longer," she finally mumbles, and her mumblings joined his. "Even though I no longer see them, I know they're still leaping into the air," she says

"But what am I talking about?" he says. "I think I know what I'm talking about, but I can't hear my voice. Sometimes it happens, that is, I can't hear my own voice. At those times I feel that somebody is whispering into my ear but the words can't reach me. Well, actually, right now I don't really know what I'm talking about," he says.

Not listening to him, she is preoccupied with watching the empty sky, a sky now engulfed in darkness. He lifts his gaze and also looks at the darkened sky. "Right until this very moment, I feel as if I've been living in the here and now while my mind has been elsewhere. I couldn't focus on anything. I feel like I've been living a life where I was always able to escape death just narrowly," he mumbles. He once again becomes absorbed in his own thoughts for a moment. "Why do I speak ceaselessly like this, as though I'm trying to hide myself in my mumblings?" He again briefly stops speaking. "I feel like I'm pedaling a bicycle with a loose chain and it's so useless and everything seems off track," he mumbles.

Right then, a crescent moon rises in the western sky. But the two remain seated and still, looking as if they don't have any intention of leaving. And they're no longer looking up at the sky. At that moment, another flock of wild geese flies by in the dark sky, unseen, flying as if it doesn't matter to them whether they are seen or not.

Translated by Inrae You Vinciguerra and Louis Vinciguerra

Jung Young Moon is a novelist, short story writer, translator, playwright, and teacher. He was born in Hamyang, South Korea, in 1965. He graduated from Seoul National University with a degree in psychology. He made his literary debut in 1996 with his novel *A Man Who Barely Exists*. He has also translated more than forty English books into Korean.

Jung Yewon was born in Seoul and moved to the U.S. at the age of 12. She received a BA in English from Brigham Young University, and an MA from the Graduate School of Interpretation and Translation at Hankuk University of Foreign Studies.

Inrae You Vinciguerra and Louis Vinciguerra together have translated many Korean novels and short stories into English. Inrae You Vinciguerra is a translator, teacher, and artist. She graduated from Seoul National University of Education. Louis Vinciguerra is an artist, teacher, and playwright with an MA in history from the University of California, Berkeley.

THE LIBRARY OF KOREAN LITERATURE

The Library of Korean Literature, published by Dalkey Archive Press in collaboration with the Literature Translation Institute of Korea, presents modern classics of Korean literature in translation, featuring the best Korean authors from the late modern period through to the present day. The Library aims to introduce the intellectual and aesthetic diversity of contemporary Korean writing to English-language readers. The Library of Korean Literature is unprecedented in its scope, with Dalkey Archive Press publishing 25 Korean novels and short story collections in a single year.

The series is published in cooperation with the Literature Translation Institute of Korea, a center that promotes the cultural translation and worldwide dissemination of Korean language and culture.

SELECTED DALKEY ARCHIVE TITLES

MICHAL AJVAZ, *The Golden Age.*
  The Other City.
PIERRE ALBERT-BIROT, *Grabinoulor.*
YUZ ALESHKOVSKY, *Kangaroo.*
FELIPE ALFAU, *Chromos.*
  Locos.
IVAN ÂNGELO, *The Celebration.*
  The Tower of Glass.
ANTÓNIO LOBO ANTUNES, *Knowledge of*
  Hell.
  The Splendor of Portugal.
ALAIN ARIAS-MISSON, *Theatre of Incest.*
JOHN ASHBERY AND JAMES SCHUYLER,
  A Nest of Ninnies.
ROBERT ASHLEY, *Perfect Lives.*
GABRIELA AVIGUR-ROTEM, *Heatwave*
  and Crazy Birds.
DJUNA BARNES, *Ladies Almanack.*
  Ryder.
JOHN BARTH, *LETTERS.*
  Sabbatical.
DONALD BARTHELME, *The King.*
  Paradise.
SVETISLAV BASARA, *Chinese Letter.*
MIQUEL BAUÇÀ, *The Siege in the Room.*
RENÉ BELLETTO, *Dying.*
MAREK BIEŃCZYK, *Transparency.*
ANDREI BITOV, *Pushkin House.*
ANDREJ BLATNIK, *You Do Understand.*
LOUIS PAUL BOON, *Chapel Road.*
  My Little War.
  Summer in Termuren.
ROGER BOYLAN, *Killoyle.*
IGNÁCIO DE LOYOLA BRANDÃO,
  Anonymous Celebrity.
  Zero.
BONNIE BREMSER, *Troia: Mexican Memoirs.*
CHRISTINE BROOKE-ROSE, *Amalgamemnon.*
BRIGID BROPHY, *In Transit.*
GERALD L. BRUNS, *Modern Poetry and*
  the Idea of Language.
GABRIELLE BURTON, *Heartbreak Hotel.*
MICHEL BUTOR, *Degrees.*
  Mobile.
G. CABRERA INFANTE, *Infante's Inferno.*
  Three Trapped Tigers.
JULIETA CAMPOS,
  The Fear of Losing Eurydice.
ANNE CARSON, *Eros the Bittersweet.*
ORLY CASTEL-BLOOM, *Dolly City.*
LOUIS-FERDINAND CÉLINE, *Castle to Castle.*
  Conversations with Professor Y.
  London Bridge.
  Normance.
  North.
  Rigadoon.
MARIE CHAIX, *The Laurels of Lake*
  Constance.
HUGO CHARTERIS, *The Tide Is Right.*
ERIC CHEVILLARD, *Demolishing Nisard.*

MARC CHOLODENKO, *Mordechai Schamz.*
JOSHUA COHEN, *Witz.*
EMILY HOLMES COLEMAN, *The Shutter*
  of Snow.
ROBERT COOVER, *A Night at the Movies.*
STANLEY CRAWFORD, *Log of the S.S. The*
  Mrs Unguentine.
  Some Instructions to My Wife.
RENÉ CREVEL, *Putting My Foot in It.*
RALPH CUSACK, *Cadenza.*
NICHOLAS DELBANCO, *The Count of*
  Concord.
  Sherbrookes.
NIGEL DENNIS, *Cards of Identity.*
PETER DIMOCK, *A Short Rhetoric for*
  Leaving the Family.
ARIEL DORFMAN, *Konfidenz.*
COLEMAN DOWELL,
  Island People.
  Too Much Flesh and Jabez.
ARKADII DRAGOMOSHCHENKO, *Dust.*
RIKKI DUCORNET, *The Complete*
  Butcher's Tales.
  The Fountains of Neptune.
  The Jade Cabinet.
  Phosphor in Dreamland.
WILLIAM EASTLAKE, *The Bamboo Bed.*
  Castle Keep.
  Lyric of the Circle Heart.
JEAN ECHENOZ, *Chopin's Move.*
STANLEY ELKIN, *A Bad Man.*
  Criers and Kibitzers, Kibitzers
  and Criers.
  The Dick Gibson Show.
  The Franchiser.
  The Living End.
  Mrs. Ted Bliss.
FRANÇOIS EMMANUEL, *Invitation to a*
  Voyage.
SALVADOR ESPRIU, *Ariadne in the*
  Grotesque Labyrinth.
LESLIE A. FIEDLER, *Love and Death in*
  the American Novel.
JUAN FILLOY, *Op Oloop.*
ANDY FITCH, *Pop Poetics.*
GUSTAVE FLAUBERT, *Bouvard and Pécuchet.*
KASS FLEISHER, *Talking out of School.*
FORD MADOX FORD,
  The March of Literature.
JON FOSSE, *Aliss at the Fire.*
  Melancholy.
MAX FRISCH, *I'm Not Stiller.*
  Man in the Holocene.
CARLOS FUENTES, *Christopher Unborn.*
  Distant Relations.
  Terra Nostra.
  Where the Air Is Clear.
TAKEHIKO FUKUNAGA, *Flowers of Grass.*
WILLIAM GADDIS, *J R.*
  The Recognitions.

JANICE GALLOWAY, *Foreign Parts.*
   The Trick Is to Keep Breathing.
WILLIAM H. GASS, *Cartesian Sonata*
   and Other Novellas.
   Finding a Form.
   A Temple of Texts.
   The Tunnel.
   Willie Masters' Lonesome Wife.
GÉRARD GAVARRY, *Hoppla! 1 2 3.*
ETIENNE GILSON,
   The Arts of the Beautiful.
   Forms and Substances in the Arts.
C. S. GISCOMBE, *Giscome Road.*
   Here.
DOUGLAS GLOVER, *Bad News of the Heart.*
WITOLD GOMBROWICZ,
   A Kind of Testament.
PAULO EMÍLIO SALES GOMES, *P's Three*
   Women.
GEORGI GOSPODINOV, *Natural Novel.*
JUAN GOYTISOLO, *Count Julian.*
   Juan the Landless.
   Makbara.
   Marks of Identity.
HENRY GREEN, *Back.*
   Blindness.
   Concluding.
   Doting.
   Nothing.
JACK GREEN, *Fire the Bastards!*
JIŘÍ GRUŠA, *The Questionnaire.*
MELA HARTWIG, *Am I a Redundant*
   Human Being?
JOHN HAWKES, *The Passion Artist.*
   Whistlejacket.
ELIZABETH HEIGHWAY, ED., *Contemporary*
   Georgian Fiction.
ALEKSANDAR HEMON, ED.,
   Best European Fiction.
AIDAN HIGGINS, *Balcony of Europe.*
   Blind Man's Bluff
   Bornholm Night-Ferry.
   Flotsam and Jetsam.
   Langrishe, Go Down.
   Scenes from a Receding Past.
KEIZO HINO, *Isle of Dreams.*
KAZUSHI HOSAKA, *Plainsong.*
ALDOUS HUXLEY, *Antic Hay.*
   Crome Yellow.
   Point Counter Point.
   Those Barren Leaves.
   Time Must Have a Stop.
NAOYUKI II, *The Shadow of a Blue Cat.*
GERT JONKE, *The Distant Sound.*
   Geometric Regional Novel.
   Homage to Czerny.
   The System of Vienna.
JACQUES JOUET, *Mountain R.*
   Savage.
   Upstaged.

MIEKO KANAI, *The Word Book.*
YORAM KANIUK, *Life on Sandpaper.*
HUGH KENNER, *Flaubert.*
   Joyce and Beckett: The Stoic Comedians.
   Joyce's Voices.
DANILO KIŠ, *The Attic.*
   Garden, Ashes.
   The Lute and the Scars
   Psalm 44.
   A Tomb for Boris Davidovich.
ANITA KONKKA, *A Fool's Paradise.*
GEORGE KONRÁD, *The City Builder.*
TADEUSZ KONWICKI, *A Minor Apocalypse.*
   The Polish Complex.
MENIS KOUMANDAREAS, *Koula.*
ELAINE KRAF, *The Princess of 72nd Street.*
JIM KRUSOE, *Iceland.*
AYŞE KULIN, *Farewell: A Mansion in*
   Occupied Istanbul.
EMILIO LASCANO TEGUI, *On Elegance*
   While Sleeping.
ERIC LAURRENT, *Do Not Touch.*
VIOLETTE LEDUC, *La Bâtarde.*
EDOUARD LEVÉ, *Autoportrait.*
   Suicide.
MARIO LEVI, *Istanbul Was a Fairy Tale.*
DEBORAH LEVY, *Billy and Girl.*
JOSÉ LEZAMA LIMA, *Paradiso.*
ROSA LIKSOM, *Dark Paradise.*
OSMAN LINS, *Avalovara.*
   The Queen of the Prisons of Greece.
ALF MAC LOCHLAINN,
   The Corpus in the Library.
   Out of Focus.
RON LOEWINSOHN, *Magnetic Field(s).*
MINA LOY, *Stories and Essays of Mina Loy.*
D. KEITH MANO, *Take Five.*
MICHELINE AHARONIAN MARCOM,
   The Mirror in the Well.
BEN MARCUS,
   The Age of Wire and String.
WALLACE MARKFIELD,
   Teitlebaum's Window.
   To an Early Grave.
DAVID MARKSON, *Reader's Block.*
   Wittgenstein's Mistress.
CAROLE MASO, *AVA.*
LADISLAV MATEJKA AND KRYSTYNA
   POMORSKA, EDS.,
   Readings in Russian Poetics:
     Formalist and Structuralist Views.
HARRY MATHEWS, *Cigarettes.*
   The Conversions.
   The Human Country: New and
     Collected Stories.
   The Journalist.
   My Life in CIA.
   Singular Pleasures.
   The Sinking of the Odradek
     Stadium.
   Tlooth.

ARNO SCHMIDT, *Collected Novellas.*
Collected Stories.
Nobodaddy's Children.
Two Novels.
ASAF SCHURR, *Motti.*
GAIL SCOTT, *My Paris.*
DAMION SEARLS, *What We Were Doing and Where We Were Going.*
JUNE AKERS SEESE,
Is This What Other Women Feel Too?
What Waiting Really Means.
BERNARD SHARE, *Inish.*
Transit.
VIKTOR SHKLOVSKY, *Bowstring.*
Knight's Move.
A Sentimental Journey: Memoirs 1917–1922.
Energy of Delusion: A Book on Plot.
Literature and Cinematography.
Theory of Prose.
Third Factory.
Zoo, or Letters Not about Love.
PIERRE SINIAC, *The Collaborators.*
KJERSTI A. SKOMSVOLD, *The Faster I Walk, the Smaller I Am.*
JOSEF ŠKVORECKÝ, *The Engineer of Human Souls.*
GILBERT SORRENTINO,
Aberration of Starlight.
Blue Pastoral.
Crystal Vision.
Imaginative Qualities of Actual Things.
Mulligan Stew.
Pack of Lies.
Red the Fiend.
The Sky Changes.
Something Said.
Splendide-Hôtel.
Steelwork.
Under the Shadow.
W. M. SPACKMAN, *The Complete Fiction.*
ANDRZEJ STASIUK, *Dukla.*
Fado.
GERTRUDE STEIN, *The Making of Americans.*
A Novel of Thank You.
LARS SVENDSEN, *A Philosophy of Evil.*
PIOTR SZEWC, *Annihilation.*
GONÇALO M. TAVARES, *Jerusalem.*
Joseph Walser's Machine.
Learning to Pray in the Age of Technique.
LUCIAN DAN TEODOROVICI,
Our Circus Presents . . .
NIKANOR TERATOLOGEN, *Assisted Living.*
STEFAN THEMERSON, *Hobson's Island.*
The Mystery of the Sardine.
Tom Harris.
TAEKO TOMIOKA, *Building Waves.*

JOHN TOOMEY, *Sleepwalker.*
JEAN-PHILIPPE TOUSSAINT, *The Bathroom.*
Camera.
Monsieur.
Reticence.
Running Away.
Self-Portrait Abroad.
Television.
The Truth about Marie.
DUMITRU TSEPENEAG, *Hotel Europa.*
The Necessary Marriage.
Pigeon Post.
Vain Art of the Fugue.
ESTHER TUSQUETS, *Stranded.*
DUBRAVKA UGRESIC, *Lend Me Your Character.*
Thank You for Not Reading.
TOR ULVEN, *Replacement.*
MATI UNT, *Brecht at Night.*
Diary of a Blood Donor.
Things in the Night.
ÁLVARO URIBE AND OLIVIA SEARS, EDS.,
Best of Contemporary Mexican Fiction.
ELOY URROZ, *Friction.*
The Obstacles.
LUISA VALENZUELA, *Dark Desires and the Others.*
He Who Searches.
PAUL VERHAEGHEN, *Omega Minor.*
AGLAJA VETERANYI, *Why the Child Is Cooking in the Polenta.*
BORIS VIAN, *Heartsnatcher.*
LLORENÇ VILLALONGA, *The Dolls' Room.*
TOOMAS VINT, *An Unending Landscape.*
ORNELA VORPSI, *The Country Where No One Ever Dies.*
AUSTRYN WAINHOUSE, *Hedyphagetica.*
CURTIS WHITE, *America's Magic Mountain.*
The Idea of Home.
Memories of My Father Watching TV.
Requiem.
DIANE WILLIAMS, *Excitability: Selected Stories.*
Romancer Erector.
DOUGLAS WOOLF, *Wall to Wall.*
Ya! & John-Juan.
JAY WRIGHT, *Polynomials and Pollen.*
The Presentable Art of Reading Absence.
PHILIP WYLIE, *Generation of Vipers.*
MARGUERITE YOUNG, *Angel in the Forest.*
Miss MacIntosh, My Darling.
REYOUNG, *Unbabbling.*
VLADO ŽABOT, *The Succubus.*
ZORAN ŽIVKOVIĆ, *Hidden Camera.*
LOUIS ZUKOFSKY, *Collected Fiction.*
VITOMIL ZUPAN, *Minuet for Guitar.*
SCOTT ZWIREN, *God Head.*